PRAISE FOR THE [...]

Had to Be You

"Kaye's latest ... has a solid plot, good pacing, and genuine characters.... A magnified connection and sizzling chemistry between Slater and the vulnerable Rocki keep readers turning the pages."　　　—*RT Book Reviews*

"I love this book.... This was a great romance with lots of tenderness and some suspense."　　　—Bitten by Love

"Ms. Kaye ended this series with an emotional punch.... Well done, Ms. Kaye."　　　—Under the Covers

You're the One

"Readers will ... fall for the spunky Skye, and Kaye's luscious descriptions of food and chef menus are a great touch as she continues her engaging Bad Boys of Red Hook series."　　　—*Booklist* (starred review)

"In her latest novel in the Bad Boys of Red Hook series, Kaye's humorous yet edgy storytelling shines. The distinctive characters that make up Logan's and Skye's individual families and the chemistry that sizzles between the two, set against the charm of a New York City neighborhood, will have you turning the pages with a smile. Kaye hits it out of the park again." —*RT Book Reviews*

Back to You

"Kaye throws together richly drawn love-challenged characters to launch her Bad Boys of Red Hook contemporary romance series.... A strong sense of place makes this a solid series launch." —*Publishers Weekly* (starred review)

continued ...

ALSO BY ROBIN KAYE

The Bad Boys of Red Hook
Back to You
You're the One
Had to Be You
Hometown Girl (digital novella)
Heat of the Moment (digital novella)

HOME
TO YOU

ROBIN KAYE

A SIGNET ECLIPSE BOOK

SIGNET ECLIPSE
Published by the Penguin Group
Penguin Group (USA) LLC, 375 Hudson Street,
New York, New York 10014

USA | Canada | UK | Ireland | Australia | New Zealand | India | South Africa | China
penguin.com
A Penguin Random House Company

First published by Signet Eclipse, an imprint of New American Library,
a division of Penguin Group (USA) LLC

First Printing, April 2015

ISBN 978-0-451-47284-7

Printed in the United States of America
10 9 8 7 6 5 4 3 2 1

To Claire. I doubt I'd have been able to write this without your help. You're an inspiration, a great sounding board, and an incredible support.

ACKNOWLEDGMENTS

I'd love to tell you I wrote this book all on my own. After all, part of the writer's mystique is the solitary life we live. Well, for me at least, the solitary part is a load of bunk. For me, it takes a village to make a book. Here are some of the people who have helped me:

I'm lucky to have the love and support of my incredible family. My husband, Stephen, my children, Tony, Anna, and Isabelle, who are my favorite people to hang out with. Alex Henderson and Jessye and Dylan Green, whom I love like my own kids. All of them make me laugh, amaze me with their intelligence and generosity, and make me proud every day.

My parents, Richard Williams and Ann Feiler, and my stepfather, George Feiler, who always encouraged me and continue to do so.

My wonderful critique partners, Deborah Villegas and Laura Becraft. They shortened my sentences, corrected my grammar, and put commas where they needed to be. They listened to me whine when my muse took a vacation, gave me great ideas when I was stuck, and answered that all-important question: Does this suck? They helped me plot, loved my characters almost as much as I did, and challenged me to be a better writer. They are my friends, my confidantes, and my bullshit meters.

I owe a debt of gratitude to their families, who so graciously let me borrow them during my deadline crunch. So, to Robert, Joe, Elisabeth, and Ben Becraft, and Ruben, Alexander, Donovan, and Cristian Villegas, you have my thanks and eternal gratitude.

I'd also like to thank my writing friends who are always there when I need a fresh eye or a sounding board—Grace Burrowes, Hope Ramsay, Susan Donovan, Mary Freeman, R. R. Smythe, Margie Lawson, Michael Hauge, and Christie Craig.

My dear friends, which include Laura Becraft, Deborah Villegas, Amy Greene, Anne Burger, and Ginger Francis, who have given me more love, laughter, and support than I ever knew existed. I'm so blessed.

I wrote most of this book at the Mt. Airy, Maryland, Starbucks, and I have to thank all my baristas for keeping me in laughter and coffee while I camped out in their store. I also need to thank my fellow customers who have become wonderful friends: Liz, Barbara, Mike, Teresa, Anne, Megan, and Joni.

As always, I want to thank my incredible agent, Kevan Lyon, for all she does, and my team at Penguin/New American Library—the cover artists for the beautiful job they did and my editor, Kerry Donovan, for all her insight, direction, and enthusiasm.

CHAPTER
ONE

Kendall Watkins stopped the Jeep and threw it into four-wheel drive before turning off the main road onto the sorry excuse of a trail that led up the hill to the cabin, her sanctuary. She'd gotten through a long, tough day on almost no sleep. She'd made the trip from her Boston apartment to Harmony, New Hampshire; powered through her best friend Addie's inquisition about Kendall's first heartbreak with minimal waterworks; and taken all the groceries, love, and support that she could stand.

As much as she loved Addie and appreciated the offer of her spare bedroom, right now, the last thing she needed was company. No matter how supportive, understanding, and well-intentioned Addie was, Kendall needed to be alone to lick her wounds and wallow in self-pity for as long as it took her to feel human again, or until the Rocky Road ran out—whichever came first. She had a bad feeling she'd be busy until the cupboards were bare.

Addie had told her in no uncertain terms that the grocery shopping spree was a onetime-only offer. There would be no refilling of the five basic food groups—

chocolate, wine, pasta, ice cream, and Nutella—until Kendall poked her head out of her cave and rejoined society.

From a therapist's perspective, Kendall had to admit it was a sound plan on Addie's part. Everyone knew wallowing for more than a week or two might lead down the dark road of clinical depression, but from the perspective of a woman who was just unceremoniously dumped from a twelve-year relationship with no warning and not so much as a this-isn't-working-for-me chat, a week or two didn't seem nearly long enough.

Last night, the only thing she had wanted was to escape the apartment she'd shared with David. She'd never felt at home in Boston, and she wanted to go home. Home to Harmony.

When she thought of possible escapes, a picture of the old hunting cabin immediately came to mind. She knew she could go there and no one would find her hiding place. The only person who lived within five miles of it was Jaime Rouchard, and if he caught her, she was sure he'd keep her secret and respect her privacy. As far as she knew, he and Addie were the only people in their gossip mill of a town who could.

She looked through the dwindling light of late afternoon and tried not to think of all the times she and David had gone to the cabin. She did her best to tamp down a case of sudden nerves, wiped her sweaty palms on her jeans to make sure she had a good grip on the steering wheel, and wondered if she wasn't making yet another huge mistake. When she'd come up with her plan in the wee hours of the morning, it hadn't occurred to her that the last thing she needed was to be stuck in a cabin with the Ghost of Boyfriends Past. No, she wouldn't allow David to ruin her homecoming. She refused to give him that much power.

The trail was snow-covered, and in the fading light it was difficult to discern the path at all. It was clear that whoever plowed hadn't done so recently, so she was stuck picking her way up the steep incline in low gear.

Sara Bareilles's "Gravity"—a song she'd always liked but could never relate to until today—drowned out the rumble of the engine and struck a chord so deep within her she had to blink back tears and fight for control of her emotions.

Kendall took a hand off the wheel to wipe her eyes, and the front passenger's side of the Jeep ran over something— a boulder, the edge of the trail, a snow-covered log; she wasn't sure. All she knew was she needed to get off the damn thing, since the Jeep canted awkwardly. She stopped and sent up a little prayer that she had enough clearance. After all, this was why she'd bought a four-wheel drive in the first place. It gave her the ability to go off-road, and this was definitely off-road. She eased up on the brake and tapped the gas, and the Jeep surged forward off whatever it had been on and landed with a decidedly expensive-sounding crunch of metal. "Damn." She tapped the gas again, and the Jeep grunted ahead, except this time the front passenger's side fell at an awkward angle and lurched to a stop, sitting way too low to be considered normal.

"Oh, God. This is just the icing on a total shit cake of a day. Can't anything go right?" She put the car in park— as if it would go anywhere—and banged her head against the steering wheel with a painful thud. She rubbed her forehead. The action did nothing to make her feel better. "Whoever thought that a good head bang would release tension was obviously an idiot."

Great. She was in the middle of nowhere, miles from the nearest person, in a disabled car. She took a quick look at her phone—no cell coverage. Unfortunately, in a twenty-four-hour period filled with nonstop shocks, the lack of cell coverage wasn't one of them.

Strains of Lady Antebellum's song "Love Don't Live Here" filled the car, and she considered banging her head again. "Maybe love don't live here anymore, but it did once," she mumbled, and killed the engine.

That thought pushed her over the edge of the emotional cliff she'd been skirting for the past day and a half. She stopped fighting the good fight and let loose the river of tears she'd kept dammed up with a finger, a wad of gum, duct tape, and a prayer.

She wasn't sure how long she'd sat in the cooling car, crying, when a triple rap on the driver's-side door interrupted her midmeltdown. Kendall jumped, let out a startled yelp, and blinked at the image of a hairy hulk of a man staring through the steamed-up driver's-side window. He had longish blond hair sticking out of a navy blue knit cap, a two- or three-week beard covered what looked like a square jaw, and he sported crinkles around the bluest, most intense eyes she'd ever seen. Even with tears and a foggy window clouding her vision, her gaze felt shackled to his, and, like a sleepwalker, she slowly opened the door and let out an embarrassing, hiccuping sob.

The man took what looked like a cautious step back and crouched before her, maybe to seem less threatening. "Are you hurt?" He sounded as if he didn't want to know the answer but felt awkwardly obligated to ask.

Another sob escaped. She shook her head and took what she hoped was a calming breath. "Physically, I'm fine. Emotionally, I'm a complete wreck."

He rose to his full height, rounded the front of the car, and then crouched to inspect the sunken front end. She wasn't sure if it was to look for damage or just a damn good excuse to get away from the crazy woman blubbering all over herself. He placed one large hand on the edge of the hood and pushed, rocking the car with a grunt of effort.

The next sound she heard was a manly hum of disappointment confirming her initial assessment of the situation: she was screwed.

He came to his feet in one smooth move and caught her gaze—probably to gauge her mental competency—and his expression shifted from polite but hugely uncomfortable concern to an I've-got-bad-news-for-you grimace.

Kendall wiped her cold, tearstained face. "You might as well just say whatever it is."

He looked her up and down again. "I don't want to make what is obviously a terrible day worse, but it looks as if you have a broken axle."

"A broken axle? Seriously?" She raised her gaze to the sky. "God, I know I'm strong, independent, intelligent, and resourceful, but don't you think the broken axle was just a little over the top?" She waited a beat to give God a second to strike her down, in case he was in the mood. "Okay, you win. I give up." She knew she stood beside a snowbank, but looked over her shoulder just to make sure before taking a seat. Who could blame her? After the day she'd had, she had good reason to question her own judgment. At that moment, she couldn't have cared less who the man before her was or that he, a complete stranger, would witness her tears. At times like this, self-respect was overrated. Besides, it wasn't as if he *had* to stand there and listen—he could slink off to wherever he came from.

She took a stilted breath before dropping her face into her hands and crying again in earnest. "In the past day, I've been downsized and dumped. In a month, I'll be homeless, because without my job and my fiancé, I can't afford to keep my apartment. And if that isn't enough, now you tell me I've just broken the axle on my car. I'm no crack mechanic, but even I know that's really expensive."

The snowbank gave way, and she sank another six inches. "And now I'm sitting here, in the middle of nowhere, crying in front of a total stranger, my ass is wet, and I'm stuck."

A slow, self-deprecating smile spread across his face. "I'm not much of a stranger anymore." He pulled a folded bandanna from his pocket and held it out to her. "Here, blow your nose."

She took the bandanna. "What do I look like? A five-year-old?"

"No. No one would mistake you for a child, but you've been crying with all the abandon of one."

Kendall always enjoyed arguing, but even she couldn't argue with this. After all, he was right. She shrugged, snapped the bandanna open, and blew her nose. Before she finished wiping tears from her face, he had a grip on her arm. "Come on. It's getting colder, and we're losing the light. I can deal with a lot of things, but not a frozen ass. I have a cabin just up the hill. I'll stoke the fire, and you can thaw out."

She dug in her heels. "You have a cabin?"

"Yeah, but just to warn you, it's not much."

"You're staying in the Sullivans' hunting cabin?"

"The very one."

"My father rented it to you?"

When he didn't answer, she forged ahead. "My father works for the Grand Pooh-Bah of Harmony, Jackson Finneus Sullivan III."

"Teddy Watkins—"

"Is my father. Guilty as charged." From the look of consternation on his face, she figured he must have recently been on the receiving end of her father's third degree—the same one her dad gave to anyone interested in renting one of the houses or cabins on Sullivan's Tarn. "Well, that's a relief. At least I know you're not an ax murderer. The Secret Service has nothing on my dad when it comes to looking into the backgrounds of tenants."

"Teddy's that careful, is he?"

"Oh yeah." She looked from the guy who still had a hand on her elbow to the land around them. "I'm a little surprised Jax Sullivan hasn't developed this side of the lake by now, but, then, maybe he's forgotten he owns it. I guess when you own half the town, not to mention half the banks in Chicago, you'd have better things to do than remember a falling-down cabin on a heavily forested piece of land."

The man rocked back on his heels and blew out a breath. "It sounds as if you don't like your dad's boss very much."

She shrugged and brushed the snow off her skinny jeans. "Believe me, the last thing I want to do is think about Jax Sullivan or men like him. Just because my parents think he walks on water doesn't mean I do." She shrugged. "But, then, I can't say I have feelings about him either way—"

"You could have fooled me."

"I haven't seen him since I was in grade school. By the time he started coming back to the lake, I was in college or living and working in Boston."

He didn't say anything. He just stared at her with those startling blue eyes.

"So, it's nothing personal. I don't actually dislike him, but I don't automatically like him either. He pays my parents' salary, and he must treat them well. If he didn't, I doubt they'd still think he walked on water." She shrugged. She might not know the man, but she couldn't help but lump Jax in with every other stuffed shirt with whom her fiancé forced her to socialize. She'd always wondered why David tried so hard to impress the corporate elite. Now it all made sense. "Well, enough about me. What brings you out here in the off-season?"

He stuffed his hands in his pockets. "Me? I wanted some peace and solitude. I thought this would be the perfect place to find it. I'm staying at the cabin for a few months at a cut rate and doing some handyman work."

"You can't be serious."

"Why is that so hard to believe? I'm just repairing the roof and cleaning the place up a little."

"Do you mean to tell me that the great Jax Sullivan — Harmony's own Scrooge McDuck — is so cheap, he's not even paying for your labor?"

"I think it's a fair deal."

"Right."

"You make it sound like having money is a criminal offense."

"No, but taking advantage of people should be. It's not having money that's bad; what's bad is what people usually do to keep it."

"Are you speaking from personal experience?"

She looked at her car, wondering how much money David had seen fit to leave in their—make that her— savings account. "Probably." She blew out a breath and tossed her hair over her shoulder before she shook her head. "Look, don't mind me. I just discovered that sometime in our twelve-year relationship, my ex-fiancé turned into a Jackson Sullivan wannabe. If I'd known world financial domination was what he was after, I never would have gotten involved with him in the first place."

The guy seemed to relax a little then. "We all make mistakes."

"Obviously, but in my own defense, when David and I started dating, he wanted to be a fireman—of course, we were in eighth grade at the time."

"So I take it the career switch didn't come as a complete shock?"

She shrugged. "Yes and no. In college and grad school, he majored in finance, but our plan had always been to move back to Harmony—not exactly a world financial center. I was going to open my own psychotherapy practice, and I thought he'd get a job at the bank, maybe do some financial planning, sell insurance—that kind of thing."

"He had other plans?"

"Apparently. Plans he didn't see fit to share with me. He took a promotion in San Francisco. Yesterday I got a pink slip, and then, to top off my day, I came home to find him packing. He said he didn't need a modern-day Betty Crocker with a Carl Jung fetish. His words, not mine."

"Wow, that's harsh." He leaned back against the car and tilted his head, as if looking at her from a different angle would change the picture. No such luck for either of them. "Would you have gone to San Francisco with him if he'd asked?"

She wanted to say yes, but the look in his eyes stopped her and made her really think about it. Would she have followed David to San Francisco? She'd followed him to Boston, but that was with the understanding that they'd return to Harmony. Boston was two hours away from home, not on the other side of the country. "I honestly don't know. I've never wanted to live anywhere but right here."

"I would think that if you really loved this guy, you'd follow him anywhere."

"We spent the past twelve years planning our life together, and David never even floated the idea of a move to San Francisco, or anyplace else, for that matter."

The man didn't argue; he just continued staring.

"If I used your logic, I could say that if he really loved me, he would never leave me for a job on the West Coast."

"You're right. Which begs the question: why are you wasting your time crying over a man who obviously doesn't love you? At least not anymore."

Ouch; that hurt. Tears welled in her eyes, but she blinked them away. "He might not have loved me, but I loved him." It came out on a sob, and his frown deepened.

"Not enough to follow him to San Francisco," he said softly. His eyes stared into hers, as if he were willing her to agree.

Except she wasn't feeling very agreeable at the moment. "I might have if he'd asked. Instead, he waited until I left for work to pack his things and move out of our apartment without a word about it to me. If I hadn't lost my job and come home early, I would have received nothing more than the e-mail he'd planned to send from the airport. He said he wanted to avoid the drama."

He stepped closer and crossed his arms, his gaze pinning her in place. "Look, you don't know me from Adam, but if you ask me, I think the jerk did you a favor."

"You think he did me favor?"

"Yeah. He's obviously a coward. No real man would spend over a decade with a beautiful woman like you— even with your penchant for tears—and leave you with no warning, no apology, and without so much as a good-bye. You should thank him for keeping you from wasting any more of your life on him. He probably saved you years of misery, not to mention the cost of a good divorce attorney. In his own cowardly way, he did the right thing. He set you free to be happy."

She took a deep breath and gathered her thoughts, and his words pinballed their way around her mind, hitting more bumpers than she would have thought possible. "You know, I doubt I would have ever come to that conclusion on my own, but you might be right." She stared at the tall, blond, obnoxiously gorgeous man, and wondered who in the hell he was. "If I'm lucky, maybe I'll feel that way in a few years. Right now, I'm having a difficult time working up any real gratitude."

"It won't take years, believe me."

"Who are you?" That question seemed to surprise him. She couldn't fathom why.

"Excuse me?"

"It's suddenly occurred to me that I've just spilled my guts to a total stranger and I don't even know your name."

"I'm Jack." He held out his hand in a manner so businesslike, it was odd, considering where they were and the fact that he was dressed like a construction worker.

"Jack." She tried his name on for size and found that it fit, rolling off her tongue with an unnatural ease. Jack was a no-frills, competent, strong-sounding name, and it suited him. His warm, work-roughened hand engulfed her smaller, smooth, frozen one. "It's nice to meet you, Jack. I'm Kendall."

Jackson Finneus Sullivan III wanted to curse his luck and Kendall's. It had taken him a few moments, but he'd recognized her from the pictures his caretakers and unofficial adoptive parents, Grace and Teddy, had showed him over the years. Either they were really bad photographers or Kendall wasn't nearly as photogenic as she should be, because no picture he had ever seen of Kendall came close to doing her justice.

He'd known she was a pretty girl, but the woman before him was so far beyond pretty, she wasn't even in the same time zone. She was, in a word, spectacular. Who'd have thought the quiet little mouse of a pigtailed, bucktoothed girl he remembered trailing behind Grace the summer before his parents' death would blossom into such an incredible beauty?

What man in his right mind would leave a woman like Kendall? Even with red, swollen, bloodshot eyes, a raw nose, and a bulky down coat, she was stunning enough to give any man between the ages of two and a hundred and two whiplash.

"Do you want to come up to the cabin? If I had a car here, I'd lend it to you, but I don't."

That seemed to shock her. "You don't have a car? How did you get up here?"

"I took a cab to the other side of the lake and then hiked across."

"What do you do for groceries?"

"There's a guy who lives a few miles away, Jaime Rouchard—"

"I know him."

"He's been helping me out. He keeps me well supplied with food and lumber."

"Oh, that's good." She turned a full circle. "That reminds me, I have at least a week's worth of groceries and my duffel bag in the Jeep. I know the bears are hibernating this time of year, but I feel weird just leaving it."

"No problem." When he popped open the back of the Jeep, the light spilled onto her face, highlighting her pale skin and ebony hair. Her cheeks were red from the cold or maybe her tears—he couldn't be sure—and her eyes were so dark, they looked almost black. "I'll help you get your things to the cabin, and we'll decide what to do when we get there." She had enough food to last the rest of the winter. He threw the duffel bag over his shoulder and grabbed the larger of the two boxes of groceries. "It looks as if you were planning to stay awhile."

"Yeah." She grabbed the smaller box and started up the trail.

She was tall. It was hard to tell with her boots on, but he guessed she was only three or four inches shorter than he, and most of it was leg. "Why didn't you go to your parents' place?"

"Because I don't want anyone in town to know I'm here. I didn't think anyone would find me at the cabin. I'm hiding out."

She wasn't the only one.

"My parents are on a Mediterranean cruise, and if anyone in town knew I was here, the first thing they'd do is call or e-mail my folks. If Mom and Dad knew what happened between me and David, they'd drop everything and hop the first flight home. I'd never forgive myself for ruining their dream vacation."

"I can understand that." It was the truth; for anyone other than his friend Jaime to know he was here was the last thing he needed. He'd come up to his hometown to recover from a traumatic injury, and the recovery was progressing more slowly than he'd expected. If anyone got wind of things, well, damn, he didn't even want to think about what a financial disaster that could be.

"Besides, this is something I have to deal with on my own. I love my parents. I really do. But right now, I just want to be left alone."

Well, that could be a problem. "So, no one knows you're here?"

"Only my friend Addie, and she's been sworn to secrecy. She was the one who went grocery shopping for me—and, just to be safe, she went to the store in the next town."

Good thought. He might ask Jaime to do the same thing next time.

Kendall let out a laugh. "Harmony is your typical small town—the largest thing in it is the gossip mill. Addie thought Sophie Evans over at the market would question her, since Addie did her own shopping the day before yesterday. The entire population, except Jaime and Addie, are card-carrying members of the International Brotherhood of Busybodies."

She didn't have to tell him that, but luckily, she didn't

know who he was or that he already knew everything there was to know about Harmony. Hell, his ancestors were the founding fathers. "Is your friend Addie coming here?"

"No." Kendall shook her head, and her waterfall of black hair flew around her shoulders. "She promised to leave me alone as long as I came out of my cave by the time the food ran out."

He blew out a relieved breath; if Addie showed up, he'd be outed. Not only would Addie know he was here and feel the need to inform Grace and Teddy, but Kendall would find out who he was—or who he used to be. Well, he couldn't allow that to happen.

He tucked the large box under his arm for a second to scratch the two weeks' worth of beard growth covering his face—the damn thing still itched, but it kept him warm in the wind. Besides, it was nice not to have to shave every damn day. Jax had never not shaved. When he was going for the Olympic Trials in swimming, he even waxed . . . just about everything. Since then, he'd never taken much vacation time, and in his business, beards were frowned upon. But these days, the man he used to be felt like a stranger to him. Now, with Kendall not recognizing him at all, he didn't have to pretend to be Jackson Finneus Sullivan III. Maybe that was why he didn't want anyone to know he was here. He'd spent more than a week in New York with his sister, pretending there was nothing wrong with him, pretending he was the same old Jax, and he was tired of pretending to be something he wasn't. For now at least, Jax was gone, and if he never came back, he'd deal with it.

The relief he felt was short-lived. He still didn't know what he was going to do about his unexpected visitor. If

Kendall left, his secret would be shot to hell. She'd probably run right to Addie and tell her why she couldn't stay
at the cabin. It didn't take a mathematical genius to
know that Addie would add up the clues and cook his
goose. And Kendall finding out who he really was
wouldn't do him any good either. For whatever reason,
she didn't have a very high opinion of the Grand Pooh-
Bah. He'd have to ask Jaime when he acquired that mon-
iker. She might have said it was nothing personal, but it
sounded very personal to him.

He didn't know why he cared what Kendall thought of
him. Okay, so that was a lie. He knew why he cared. What
straight man in his right—albeit slightly damaged—mind
wouldn't want a chance with a woman like Kendall Watkins?

But any kind of relationship with Kendall would be
full of complications. Even if he could count, he wouldn't
be able to number them all. No, he needed to keep it
strictly platonic, because when it came down to it, he
needed to keep her here at the cabin to protect both
their secrets. "You know, there are two bedrooms in the
cabin and I'm only using one. You're more than welcome
to the spare."

She looked over her shoulder and smiled. "I couldn't."

Sure she could. And if he didn't want her hightailing it
back to town, he'd better talk faster, because the cabin
was in sight. "If you're serious about hiding out, it sounds
as if your options are rather limited."

"I am serious."

"Look, if you want to be alone, I'll leave you alone.
I'm not the best company right now anyway."

"Really? Why's that?"

And she thought the townspeople were nosy. Hello,

Pot. Meet Kettle. Shit, if she was going to be staying at the cabin, she'd figure it out eventually. His head ached in earnest now—it had gone from the normal, constant, after-a-concussion dull ache to an almost blinding pain. It was nothing unusual. Ever since his accident, he'd had bouts of nightmare headaches, the frequency of which were decreasing. Unfortunately, the headache fairies had chosen now to make an appearance. "I was in an accident recently and had a head injury. I'm still not quite myself." He held his breath, waiting to hear about how the Grand Pooh-Bah of Harmony hit a tree while skiing, but she said nothing. By now, he knew her well enough to know that if she'd heard about the accident, she'd tell him all about it. She wasn't one to hold back.

"Wow, I'm sorry to hear that. But after all I've dumped on you, and considering that you've seen me at my worst, you're not telling me very much here. What happened?"

"They tell me I skied into a tree. I don't have any memory of the accident—actually, I can't remember anything that happened that day. I just remember waking up in the hospital a few days later with a headache like you read about. I'd been in a medically induced coma, and they had to operate to reduce the pressure on my brain."

One of her dark brows rose. "And that turned you into someone not quite yourself?"

He'd turned into someone completely different, or at least he felt as if he had. "I've changed. I can't do some of the things I used to do. It's been about a month, and supposedly my brain is still healing. There's no way to know if the difficulties I've encountered are permanent."

She blew out a visible breath. The temperature had plummeted with the sun. "It sounds as if you're lucky to be alive."

"That's true enough."

"The accident obviously hasn't affected your speech."

"Actually, it has a little bit. Sometimes I can't remember the exact word I'm thinking of. It's as if it's right there, but I can't reach it. I don't think it's noticeable to anyone but me."

"What else?"

"There's no such thing as personal boundaries with you, is there?"

She stopped, turned toward him, and shot him a smile. "I'm a psychotherapist. I'm trained to be nosy."

"Right. So this is purely professional interest."

"Would it make you feel better if I said yes?"

"I don't know if anything would make me feel better right now. Well, maybe those wicked strong painkillers they gave me at the hospital. That is, if you think completely out of it equals better." He didn't, but if his headache didn't subside, he might have to rethink his position.

"Oh." She gave him the same clinical nod he'd seen doctors use before giving him a diagnosis. "You're grieving the loss of whatever it is you may have lost. That's completely normal."

"Thanks, I think."

She started up the slope again. "I'm just trying to get all the information I need to decide whether or not I'm crazy to even consider staying at a cabin with a perfect stranger. You know a heck of a lot more about me than I know about you."

"True. Okay, here's the deal. I can't make sense of anything having to do with numbers. I couldn't dial a phone if you gave me the phone number. I can't add. I can't count money. I can't even tell time. I used to be a math whiz, and now I look at a receipt for groceries and get confused."

"Can you still read?"

"Yes."

"That's odd, isn't it? You would think that if you can't read numbers, you wouldn't be able to read words."

"I didn't say I can't read them—I just can't . . . I don't know . . . work with them, I guess. It doesn't make sense. But from what the doctors say, brain injuries rarely make sense."

"What's the prognosis?"

He shrugged. "I'm told that the brain can form new connections somehow, so there's a chance I'll regain what I lost. But then there's a chance I won't. I'm supposed to go back in a few weeks for another MRI."

She quickened her pace and ran across the small front yard to the porch and set the groceries on the table he'd made out of two sawhorses. Her breath came out in plumes of white from the exertion. "If you're supposed to be recovering from a head injury, why are you working on the cabin?"

"What else am I supposed to do to keep from going completely crazy?"

"Aren't you supposed to rest?"

"I did for the first couple of weeks, and the doctors said I could go back to a normal level of activity."

She paced the porch, as if she were afraid to go inside. "Rebuilding a roof isn't exactly normal activity, is it?"

"Well, it's hardly an extreme sport."

CHAPTER
TWO

The moment Kendall stepped into the cabin, she felt as if she'd stepped back in time—except for the incredibly gorgeous stranger following her. The furniture was the same; the place even smelled the same—well, if you added the acrid scent of burnt meat to the mix. "Did you leave something cooking on the stove?" She headed right for the kitchen.

"Not for a few days. I'm still trying to get the smell of petrified roast out of the air. Luckily, the smell came through the roof before I managed to burn down the cabin. I have no idea how long I'd left it in the oven."

"Too long, obviously." The pan still lay unwashed in the sink. "It might help if you did the dishes." She turned on the tap to scalding, put the stopper in the drain, and threw in a healthy splash of dish soap. The pan needed to soak.

Jack set the box of groceries on the counter. "I was going to get around to that, but I was trying to get a section of the roof cabin dried in before I lost the light."

"Did you?" She looked at him then and got caught in his gaze again.

"No." He took off his hat, and his hair stood straight

up with static electricity. He smoothed it down with one big hand. "I got sidetracked by an unexpected visitor with car trouble."

"Oh." She looked inside the box to cover her embarrassment, but felt heat fill her cheeks. She really shouldn't stay. Not with him. God, she couldn't believe she was actually considering taking him up on his generous offer. It was crazy.

"Don't feel bad. I probably didn't have a prayer of getting the tar paper on the roof anyway. I guess now we can both pray we don't get snow tonight, because if we do and it warms up, we might both end up getting wet."

She watched him to see if he was just being polite or telling the truth. His color seemed to have faded, or maybe it was just the florescent overhead light. He squinted, as if the light hurt his eyes.

"Are you okay?"

"Yeah, just a headache."

"Do you need to take something?"

"No. I don't like feeling out of it. I have painkillers, but I'm trying to keep it to nothing stronger than Tylenol."

"And the last thing you need is an unexpected houseguest." She turned off the water and shook her head. "I'm sorry. I shouldn't be here."

"I really don't mind the company." He put his hands in his pockets and leaned against the counter. "I'm not lying about that, which is just as much a surprise to me as it seems to be to you."

She really needed to put on the clinical mask she wore when treating patients. She didn't like being an open book.

He pushed himself away from the counter and rocked back on his heels. "Look, if you decide to stay, I promise to give you all the space you need. I'll be up at first light. I need to catch Jaime before he leaves for work to tell him about your Jeep. As soon as I return, I'll get to work on the roof. Don't expect to sleep in, but rest assured that you'll have the cabin to yourself for most of the day."

She bit her lip and watched him. He'd thrown off his coat and his sweater when he came inside and was wearing a tight, long-sleeved T-shirt that fit him like a second skin. She thought David had been a fitness freak—he went to the gym all the time—but when it came to being ripped, Jack had David beat. Not that she was comparing them or anything.

Jack shuffled his feet under her scrutiny, and she realized she'd been staring at his six-pack. Jeez, she was pathetic.

He cleared his throat. "I'll talk to Jaime and ask if he can help you out with your car. He owns the garage in town, but I know he has a lift at home."

She wavered.

"Sleep on it. If you want to leave, you can call your friend in the morning on my sat phone. Besides, you don't want to drag her out this time of night. It's almost full dark. Her car might end up in the same condition yours did."

"Fine." She grabbed a few containers of Ben & Jerry's and stuffed them into the freezer. "Since it looks as if I'm staying the night, I'll make dinner. It's the least I can do. Besides, I'm hungry." That surprised her. She hadn't felt like eating since David dumped her. Maybe there was something good that came from spilling her guts. She just prayed she'd overcome the residual embarrassment.

When she turned back around, Jack had his eyes closed, his neck was bent so he was chin to chest, and he'd pressed two fingers against the bridge of his nose. He stepped out of the light into the darkening hallway, blinking as if the light made his headache worse. "I really hope your ex wasn't kidding about the Betty Crocker thing. I've learned that microwaveable and canned meals leave a lot to be desired."

"You're in luck, then. I happen to be a phenomenal cook. Why don't you take some Tylenol and go lie down? I'll get the other box of food off the porch, take an inventory, and figure out what to make for dinner."

"You'll holler if you need help?"

"Jack, if there's one thing I'm sure I can do on my own, it's cook. Go ahead and lie down—you really don't look so good." His color was worse than it had been when they'd first met. She didn't know what he normally looked like, but even with his face pale and lines of strain around his eyes, he was still gorgeous. She'd never really thought about other men before—she'd never really looked at anyone other than David—not sexually at least.

If Jack usually looked better than he did today and people knew he was in town, the female population of Harmony would be stopping by with food for the hot single guy.

Jack nodded, groaned, and then, still holding his head, disappeared down the short hallway, leaving her blessedly alone.

Maybe cooking would keep her mind off her problems. There would be time enough to wallow in self-pity and decide what to do about the immediate future after she did something constructive.

She looked through the groceries at hand and found Jack to be a typical man: he had meat, potatoes, vegetables, and assorted frozen and canned dinners. All that processed food would kill him. It was no wonder he hadn't been able to kick the headaches; this stuff had enough additives and preservatives to last a decade.

Shepherd's pie came to mind—it was fast and easy, she had all the ingredients, and, above all, it was comfort food. Jack looked like he could use a little comfort, and, Lord knew, it wouldn't hurt anything but her waistline. Shepherd's pie sounded even better than eating a ton of pasta and putting herself into a high-carb coma. It wasn't gourmet, but, then, David was the one who wanted her to cook more sophisticated meals, and turned up his nose at casseroles, calling them peasant food. He bought her a subscription to *Bon Appétit* magazine for her birthday to encourage her transformation from Betty Crocker to Julia Child. She shook her head at the memory and wondered why she'd never noticed that he tried to turn her into someone she wasn't.

She reached into the cabinet and pulled out the cutting board; it was right where she'd left it the last time she'd been there.

This wasn't the first time she'd escaped.

The hunting cabin was one of the private, family-only houses on the estate, like the lake house. She'd never known her dad to rent out either before.

She peeled and cut half a dozen potatoes and looked around. The place did need a lot of work. Maybe her father only rented it in exchange for doing the heavy work he could no longer handle on his own. That would make sense. Her dad was still in good shape, but way too old to be scrambling around on roofs, especially midwinter. She laughed at his cheapness, knowing if she mentioned it, he'd blame it on his Scots-Irish upbringing. She set the potatoes to boil, gathered all the ingredients she needed, and then got down to the business of cooking.

An hour and a half later, the cabin smelled like heaven, and Kendall felt more in control. Cooking always soothed her. She'd made a simple salad, the entrée was ready to come out of the oven, and the table was set. All she needed was for Jack to join her.

She hadn't heard a sound from him since he'd headed down the hall, and didn't know if she should just let him be or wake him for dinner.

She could leave a plate for him. He certainly didn't need to feel obligated to entertain her, and vice versa. Still, she did feel obligated. This was his cabin, for as long as the lease lasted, and she had no business being here.

Kendall tiptoed down the hall to use the bathroom, and was surprised to see he'd set her duffel bag on the queen bed in the master bedroom. She peeked in and found Jack asleep on a twin bed in the smaller room. His shoulders were so broad, he seemed to overflow the mattress, and his feet hung off the end.

At first she thought he'd just given her the larger of the rooms to be gentlemanly, but it looked as if he'd been using the smaller room all along. Odd, that. His bags were tossed on the floor, clothes hung from the chair in the corner. The dresser was littered with papers, a laptop computer lay closed on the small writing desk, and what looked like a pile of laundry had been kicked into the corner.

The shepherd's pie needed to rest for twenty minutes before they could eat it, so she tiptoed back into the main room and stoked the fire. The cold night air added a chill to the cabin, and while the bedrooms and bathroom had small radiators, most of the heat came from the woodstove.

She refilled the long-dry iron kettle kept on top of the stove to add some much-needed humidity to the air and prayed she'd remembered to pack her lotion. She could feel the moisture being sucked from her already dry skin.

She checked her watch: it was half past six. Jack had been asleep for almost two hours, and dinner was definitely ready. From the contents of his refrigerator and the cans of soup, chili, and stew she saw in the trash, he had to be hungry for a home-cooked meal.

"Jack?"

She turned on the hall light and stood in his doorway, trying to decide if she should wake him.

———

Jax squinted against the light shining in his eyes. An angel stood silhouetted against the glow, her dark hair shining, but her face wasn't clear. He really wished he could see her face.

"Jack, dinner's ready. Did you want to get up to eat?"

No one ever called him Jack. The scent of something amazing brought him closer to consciousness, and his stomach growled. It was food, but nothing like the stuff he'd been eating lately.

His head cleared enough for him to realize that the headache had receded to its normal, dull, postconcussion throb.

The woman moved closer. "Jack, are you awake?"

Kendall. Okay, he hadn't died and gone to a cabin in heaven. That was good, or at least he thought it was. If you had asked him before he lay down, he probably would have had another answer. "Yeah, I'm awake." He rolled to a sitting position and waited for the vestiges of sleep to dissipate. "Something smells wonderful. Thanks for cooking." He got to his feet and remembered what he was wearing—or wasn't: namely pants and a shirt.

Kendall's shocked intake of breath told him she'd noticed his state of undress before he did. And if she kept staring at him like that, his boxer briefs weren't going to be able to hide his natural reaction. His head might not be in top working order, but the same couldn't be said for his body. Oh yeah, his body's reactions were completely normal, if not a bit embarrassing. He turned his back to her and reached for his jeans, looking over his shoulder.

She stared wide-eyed.

"Just let me get dressed. I'll be out in a minute."

That got her moving. She backed up until she hit the wall on the other side of the hallway. "Right. I'm sorry. Take your time. I'll . . . I'll just wait outside."

He turned his head before he smiled. Well, he supposed it was nice that Kendall seemed to like what she saw. He couldn't remember the last time a woman looked at him like that, but, then, he wondered if he'd simply stopped noticing.

Dating had always been complicated for him. No matter how nice the woman seemed, he couldn't help but wonder if it was him she was interested in or his bank balance and social stature. He'd been unpleasantly surprised so many times, it hardly seemed worth the time and effort to start a relationship. He'd never been at a loss for a date to whatever function he'd needed to attend, but he knew how much time it took to make a relationship work, and time had been the one thing of which he didn't have an unlimited supply. Until now. Now he had nothing but time.

Jax dragged on a sweatshirt, buttoned his jeans, and ran a hand through his hair. He supposed he was as presentable as he'd get. He found Kendall serving up a steaming casserole. "That looks and smells amazing."

Kendall's eyes shifted to him, her cheeks pink, either from the steam coming off the casserole or embarrassment at the compliment. "It's just shepherd's pie—nothing gourmet."

"Give me good home cooking over gourmet any day. I haven't eaten anything that smells this good in a very long time." Probably since her mother had cooked for him before the accident. It seemed like a lifetime ago.

He scooped up a forkful and groaned as the combination of flavors hit his taste buds. Onions, carrots, peas, corn, and beef in a savory gravy spiced with rosemary and thyme. He smiled, because it was something he could do with his mouth full.

"There's wine, if you can have it. I wasn't sure if you're on any medication. . . ." She let that thought trail off.

He looked up at her, then chewed and swallowed. "Wine is good. Would you like me to open a bottle?"

"No, I've had one breathing—I used a little in the shepherd's pie, knowing the alcohol would cook out. I just wasn't sure—"

He took a last, longing look at his plate and pushed away from the table. "I'll get it. I don't know if there are wineglasses—"

"In the cabinet to the right of the sink. Top shelf."

He strode into the kitchen, surprised to find it not only clean, but sparkling—something it hadn't been before he conked out. If he'd been the one cooking, the place would have looked like a bomb had exploded in it. Here, everything she'd used was already washed, dried, and put away. The wine bottle sat, breathing, on the counter. A good wine—he recognized the name. He tried to read the numbers, knowing they would tell him the vintage, but failed to make sense of them.

Failing was getting easier to handle since he'd long since given up waiting for divine intervention. He comforted himself with the sure knowledge that the accident could have been much worse; he could have died or ended up a paraplegic. There were a lot worse things than not being able to deal with numbers.

The glasses were right where Kendall said they'd be, so he grabbed the bottle and glasses and headed back toward the table. The fire in the Franklin stove lit Kendall's face, and he stopped in his tracks, his bare feet silent on the worn wood floors. God, she did look like an angel—an angel who could cook and pick out a decent bottle of wine. Not a bad combination at that.

He forced himself to get on with it. "Here you go." He filled the glasses and handed one to Kendall before taking his seat. "Here's to new friends."

"To friends." She raised the glass and looked at him, the fire reflecting in her dark eyes. And not for the first time, he questioned the intelligence of the man willing to give her up.

Jax tucked into his meal, and after a few minutes of stuffing food in his face, he remembered his manners. He forced himself to slow down and take the time to wipe his mouth on a napkin made from a folded paper towel. "This is really good. I hope you made enough for leftovers."

She looked up from her still-full plate to his, which contained only a bite or two more. "There won't be if you keep eating at that speed."

"Oh, sorry." He stilled his fork. "It's just that I haven't had any decent food since I got here."

She laughed, and the smile that lingered on her face was enough to take his breath away. "Go ahead and eat."

Kendall nodded toward what was left of the casserole. She unwound her hair from her makeshift bun and the strands fell to frame her face. She should have looked a mess, but Kendall's classically beautiful features were sexy enough to make a desert dweller drool.

Her gaze went back to her almost untouched plate and she bit her lip. "I'm done, and there's plenty more— feel free to finish it up. I'm happy to have an excuse to cook. It's therapeutic, especially cooking for someone who appreciates it as much as you do."

He refilled his plate, forcing himself to take a few scoops of green salad just for show. If he'd been alone, he would have eaten right out of the casserole dish and wouldn't have wasted stomach space on salad. "Since I fully support your quest for inner peace and clarity, feel free to do as much therapeutic cooking as you can stand. I'll even pay for the ingredients. I know it's selfless of me, so don't embarrass me with your gratitude. Really, it's the least I can do."

Her laugh rang out clear and strong, and for the moment, at least, he felt whole. The dull throb of his headache and the fact that the vintage of the wine was still a mystery to him didn't seem to matter so much. Kendall's laugh somehow filled that empty space within him he hadn't even known existed.

———

Jax left the cabin at first light and hightailed it to Jaime's place. He was pounding on the door with a heavy hand before the sun cleared the ridge.

Jaime answered the door, wearing a pair of jeans and

nothing else. He sniffed the air, scratched his bare chest, and then looked in the direction from which Jax had come. "Did you finally burn down the cabin?"

"No, it's worse."

Apparently the lack of smoke satisfied his curiosity about the cabin, because he nodded and stepped back, wordlessly inviting Jax to enter. "How can it be worse than turning the cabin into a bonfire?" Jaime headed toward the kitchen—hopefully to make coffee.

Jax followed, tugged off his coat, and threw it over the back of a barstool before sitting. "Kendall showed up yesterday evening just before dark."

Jaime looked up from counting out scoops of coffee. "Kendall Watkins?"

"Do you know any other Kendalls?"

"No. Now that you mention it, I don't think I do. But, shit, man, I haven't had my first cup of coffee yet, so give a guy a break, would you?"

"Sorry." Jax could relate. He hadn't successfully made coffee since his accident. Between the unfamiliar coffee-maker and his inability to count, he'd been eyeballing everything and still hadn't hit the correct ratio of coffee grounds to water. The coffee, if you could call it that, either tasted weak as dishwater or resembled the sludge you found in the bottom of an oil pan after not changing said oil for thirty-thousand-plus miles.

Jaime pressed the button to brew and turned back to him. The scent of fresh ground beans—Jaime was a coffee snob, thank God—wafted over to Jax, and he took a slow, appreciative sniff. God, he'd missed good coffee.

"So, I guess your secret is out now." It wasn't a question.

"What secret?"

"You have more than one?"

He did—at least from Jaime. Shit.

"Kendall and Addie are best friends, so as soon as she tells Addie who's staying at the cabin, everyone in town will know where you're holed up."

"Oh, that. No, it turns out Kendall's in hiding mode too. I've offered her the second bedroom in the hopes that her need for privacy will ensure mine."

"And what does her asshole of a fiancé think about the two of you shacking up together?"

"David, right? Well, I doubt he cares. He dumped Kendall the day before yesterday. I've never met the man, but he sounds like a dickhead."

Jaime nodded. "That's an apt description. His folks bought the Browns' old place after you went away to school. You know, the one on the ridge overlooking the lake."

"From what I could make out through her tears, Kendall said he took a job in San Francisco without telling her, and started packing after she left for work. If she hadn't lost her job, she'd have come home to an empty apartment and a Dear Jane e-mail. The cowardly bastard."

"She lost her job?"

"Yeah, downsized due to budget cuts."

Jaime's eyebrows rose. "Sounds like she had the mother of all bad days."

"You're not kidding, and the future isn't looking too bright either. She said she's going to lose her apartment in a month. She can't make the rent without Dickhead and a job."

"Most people can't. I guess you're seeing layoffs from the other side of the desk now, aren't you?"

This was an old argument. Jaime didn't always approve of Jax's business dealings, but, then, Jaime didn't have stockholders and a board of directors to answer to either. And now neither did Jax, which, surprisingly, came as a relief. But he didn't have the time or inclination to jump on the well-worn path of their usual heated discussions. "Look, I didn't come here to debate corporate policy. The reason I hiked all the way out here was to ask for a favor."

Jaime's brows rose in apparent suspicion and he poured them coffee, handing over a big mug. "What kind of favor? And why do I get the feeling that I'm going to end up on the wrong side of either Kendall or her father—maybe both?"

Jax didn't bother hiding his smile. He and Jaime had been covering each other's asses since they were in Pull-Ups. "Because you're exceptionally perceptive?"

He took a sip of coffee and stared at Jax over the edge of his mug. "Well, get on with it."

"Fine. Kendall didn't recognize me. She thinks I rented the cabin at a reduced rate in exchange for fixing up the place."

Jaime's eyebrows rose higher. "And just who does Kendall think you are?"

"I introduced myself as Jack."

He laughed. "Well, that certainly was a stretch. And you think she's not going to figure it out on her own? Jack, Jackson . . ."

"She hasn't yet."

"So, what do you want from me?"

"I want you to back up my story."

"I see."

"If you don't, then she'll tell Addie—"

"And your cover will be blown."

"Exactly."

"Remind me again why you're in hiding?"

"I don't want to get into it right now. I promise I'll explain later." Telling Kendall about his—what the hell was it anyway? A disability? Maybe. God, that certainly wasn't a comforting thought. . . . Still, telling her, a stranger for all intents and purposes, was one thing; telling a man he'd known all his life, a man who knew the old him better than anyone else, was a whole different animal. Kendall hadn't known him; she'd known of him, which reminded him . . . "How come you never told me that people call me the Grand Pooh-Bah of Harmony?"

Jaime choked on his coffee. After catching his breath, Jaime turned his wry grin on Jax. "Kendall mentioned that, did she?"

"Answer the question."

"What good would my telling you have done?"

"It would have kept me from being blindsided by it."

Jaime shrugged. "You'd have been blindsided regardless, and let's face it, Jax, no one would have the guts to say it to your face. Jealousy is an ugly thing, and that's why people call you the Grand Pooh-Bah in the first place."

"Kendall wasn't jealous, but she's not one of my biggest fans—although I think it has more to do with the similarity between her perception of my career and the career goals of her ex than anything else."

"And if she doesn't know who you are, she can't hold her preconceived notions against you."

"Exactly." Kendall just needed a little time to get to know him and learn that he wasn't the uptight asshole she thought he was. It was as if she'd confused him with one of his uncles. Yeah, he just needed a little time—that was all. He smiled at the simplicity of his plan.

"Uh-huh, that's what I thought."

Jax was all about preventing Jaime from thinking anything further about his reasons for keeping his identity, such that it was, under wraps and searched for a change of subject. It took him a second, but then he remembered. "Kendall broke the axle on her Jeep on the trail to the cabin, so she's pretty much stuck. I was thinking maybe you could tow it here and fix it for her. I'll pay for everything, and, well, if you could take your time with the repairs. You know, tell her you're having trouble getting your hands on the parts or something."

"Oh, man. You'd better not be thinking what I think you're thinking."

So much for his attempt to change the subject. "I'm not thinking anything of the sort. I'm just trying to protect my privacy—"

"And the fact that Kendall is the hottest thing to come out of Harmony in the past fifty years never crossed your recently concussed mind?"

"I took a blow to the head, Jaim, I'm not brain-dead or blind."

"Shit, Jax. She and David the Douche Bag have been dating since she was in a training bra. I remember. They were about twelve. And in case you haven't noticed, Kendall's not fling material. She's on the rebound, and the youngest daughter of Grace and Teddy. They might not appreciate you messin' with their little girl."

"I'm not planning to mess with anyone, especially not Kendall. Now is not a good time for me to get involved. And, like you said, she's not fling material." She was fantasy material, centerfold material, marriage material, but definitely not fling material. "And for your information, I don't mess with women. Every woman I've ever dated knew the score."

"They might know the score, but there isn't a woman alive who doesn't think she can turn the game around and come out the victor."

"That's true enough, but, like you said, Kendall isn't the type." She was nothing like the worldly women he dated—not that she wasn't worldly, per se, just not jaded and greedy. "Besides, Teddy would kill me."

Jaime seemed to contemplate that. "Maybe not. Teddy and Grace love you like a son. But if you and Kendall did start"—he made a lewd hand gesture that had Jax contemplating using Jaime's head as a doorstop—"they'd expect you to marry her."

"Who said anything about marriage? Are you nuts? Teddy and Grace might be like parents to me, but that goes only so far. I have a feeling that in Teddy's eyes, no man would ever be good enough for his little girl—not even me. Besides, I don't take advantage of women. Kendall's far from over her shit of an ex. Hell, I found her sitting in her broken-down Jeep, crying her eyes out."

"And you didn't run in the other direction? Brave man."

"I thought about it, and, believe me, it was tempting, but I had to make sure she wasn't hurt."

"And you're sure she wasn't crying over the car? A broken axle is tear-worthy, much more so than David Slane. In my opinion, he's no great loss."

"I'm sure you're right, but she doesn't see it that way. She spelled it all out for me, and the busted axle was the last in a long list of woes."

He gave a what'cha-gonna-do shrug and dismissed it. "Right, then. Back to your dilemma. You said you need to keep Kendall in the dark to protect your privacy. Tell me: how does being stuck in an eight-hundred-square-foot cabin with Kendall Watkins accomplish this?"

"Kendall's here to wallow in self-pity, and she brought enough ice cream to fill the freezer to support her claim. I'll be on the roof, working during the daylight hours, giving her plenty of time to wallow to her broken heart's content. She also mentioned that she finds cooking therapeutic. I need to eat."

"She cooks like her mama?"

Jax couldn't help but smile when he remembered the masterpiece that was Kendall's shepherd's pie. "Maybe better."

Jaime's eyes widened at that. "Hell, maybe I'll marry her myself."

Jax opened his mouth to tell Jaime to leave Kendall the hell alone, but stopped before he'd formed the words. No matter how much he disliked the thought of Kendall and Jaime together—shit, he hated the thought of Kendall with any man, actually—he had no right and, without question, no reason to feel that way.

Jaime didn't bother hiding his irritating grin. "Yeah, that's what I thought you'd say."

"I didn't say anything." At least he thought he hadn't. Had his injury messed him up more than he realized?

"You didn't speak the words, but, brother, you didn't need to. The death glare you gave me made words unnecessary."

"I didn't—"

Jaime waved away his rebuttal. "Now that I know how you feel, I'll keep your little secret, and I'll fix Kendall's Jeep. Slowly. I just have to remember to call you Jack. I think even I can handle that."

"Thanks." Jax didn't bother arguing over what Jaime saw as interest in Kendall. He wasn't interested in her at all, but that didn't mean he wanted anyone else to be either. He took the last swig of his coffee and stood. "I'd better get back before Kendall wakes up."

CHAPTER
THREE

Kendall awoke with the morning sun shining in her eyes. She rolled over to wrap around David's bigger, warmer, and usually welcoming body, only to encounter a cold sheet. That second, it all came back. She remembered everything that had happened in the past two days, and her swollen eyes burned with fresh, industrial-strength tears. The echo of residual pain from a battered and badly bruised heart made itself known. It was like whiplash; the seriousness of the injury didn't reach its peak for a few days.

All she wanted was to draw the shades, pull the covers over her head, and allow sleep to envelop her like anesthesia overtaking a surgical patient. Oh, to be happily oblivious, to float painlessly on the calm, warm sea of dreamless sleep. But instead of sleeping, her mind spun like a whirling dervish.

She remembered the expression on her boss's puffy, pale face when he'd broken the bad news. The man had looked over her left shoulder the entire time, never once meeting her gaze. He'd known they'd done the same job, but that she'd done the job far better than he ever had.

He'd also known that the only reason he hadn't lost his position and bloated salary was because of his seniority.

Returning home to find David packing all of his belongings had hit her like a hard punch to an existing bruise. She remembered so clearly the second David's words broke through the fog of utter disbelief.

"I've been transferred to the San Francisco office. I'm moving," he'd said in his oh-so-superior tone. David hadn't even bothered to turn to look her in the eye. She'd never noticed it before but now had to admit that David was a coward. Jack had been right about that.

"You're moving?" Her fight-or-flight response had been effectively triggered, and she was a fighter. "I suppose the fact that you never mentioned it to me answers any other question I might have." Except maybe what happened in their relationship that brought them to that point, and how she, a psychotherapist, could have been so blind.

Things had been strained between them for the past few months, but she'd attributed that to David's stress at work, their inability to reach the monetary goal he'd set before they would marry and return to Harmony to begin the life they'd planned, and the ebb and flow of any long-term relationship.

She'd taken a deep breath, cemented her resolve, and raised her chin before confronting him. "Since you failed to mention the transfer, I gather you don't want me to go with you." It wasn't a question.

David had turned away from his side of the closet, and his look of derision knocked the wind out of her. Even in memory, it brought a fine sweat to her chilled brow. "As if you would. I'm a smart man, Kendall. I attained a perfect score on my SATs, remember?"

As if he hadn't reminded her at every opportunity. For the first time, she hadn't hidden her eye roll.

He'd stabbed a finger in her direction. "You are so dead set on going back to our backwater hometown, you refuse to see any other way." His voice had risen. Pent-up vitriol spewed from his mouth, contorting his features. She almost didn't recognize him.

She'd curled against herself and wondered what she'd done wrong, but the cloak of timidity had not rested easy on her shoulders. It had scratched like a rough wool sweater on bare skin. The fact that he'd made her feel timid, even for a second, only increased her anger. How was this her fault? "You never asked me to even consider a move. How dare you assume anything—not to mention be angry for something I've never said or done."

"I didn't need to ask. I know you better than you know yourself. San Francisco does not fit into your plan of a fairy-tale life."

Some Prince Charming he'd turned out to be. She lay in the cabin in the woods, remembering, and laughed through her tears.

She wished she'd laughed in his face. At least she'd have stood up for herself. The scene came into focus like a movie on the big screen of her mind. "First of all, I never wanted the fairy tale—I wanted something real, whole, loving, and meaningful. And it was never my plan— it was ours. I didn't make it alone, David. We shared dreams, goals, expectations."

"I've outgrown you. I've outgrown this . . ." He'd held out his hands to encompass their home, their relationship, their shared life. "The rent's paid through the end of next month. I've already had my name removed from the lease. I've taken half our savings, most of which I put in. You can keep the furniture and everything we bought together—I don't want it. I thought that was only fair."

"Fair? You think this is fair? And just when were you going to tell me you were leaving?"

"I've made up my mind on the matter. Discussing it is a waste of time, and you know how I hate wasting time. I planned to e-mail you."

She remembered feeling as if she'd been kicked in the stomach. The wind had been knocked out of her. She hadn't known until that day that words could cause physical pain. "We've been together twelve years, and all you were going to give me was a Dear Jane letter?" Her words had come across as breathless, and now she hated herself for sounding so damn weak.

"No, it was a Dear Kendall e-mail. And this is exactly what I was trying to avoid. This drama. It's as if you can't get enough in your own small life, so you have to delve into everyone else's to get your fill. I suppose being a therapist pays better than watching soap operas, although when you consider what you made at the hospital, it doesn't beat it by much, does it?"

She'd been too dumbfounded to respond. She clenched the sheet in her fists in the hopes it would anchor her in the present. Through the sheet, her manicured nails bit into the tender flesh of her palms. But even that didn't stop the memories from bombarding her.

David had stood before her, hands on hips, in what she always thought of as his he-man pose. "That's why you went into psychotherapy, isn't it? To feed your desperate need to dissect every word, movement, emotion, and trauma?"

"I wanted to help people." She cringed again at the

memory; she wished she'd sounded forceful and sure of herself, but she hadn't.

"Yes, it helps feed your need to be selfless, doesn't it?"

"Excuse me?"

"Kendall, you'll bend over backward to help any poor sot. It makes you feel superior."

"Superior? You actually believe that?" Even in the midst of the traumatic event, a little voice in the back of her mind had pointed out that this was a classic example of projection on David's part.

"Of course I do, or I wouldn't say it."

She couldn't catch her breath. The sobs were coming so fast, she felt lightheaded. Thank God she hadn't cried in front of David. No, she'd waited until she could fall apart in front of a total stranger.

She remembered the look on Jack's face when he'd encountered her midmeltdown. He'd looked as if he'd wanted to be anywhere but there to witness her breakdown, but not willing to force anyone, even a stranger, to cry like that alone.

But not David. No, if it had been up to him, he'd have left her to discover him missing, to have no closure, save whatever he'd have written in the damn e-mail. He'd never been a good writer.

"David, we made love just yesterday. You had this all planned. You knew, and you still . . ."

He'd actually had the balls to look smug. "You're a beautiful woman. No man in his right mind would turn you away. I just need more than a modern-day Betty Crocker with a Carl Jung fetish."

Pain bloomed in her chest, filling every empty space, and she gasped for air. She felt violated. She wanted to stop reliving the awful scene, but the vision of his smug face stayed clear in her mind.

"I need someone who can be a partner in my life, someone who can hold her own at cocktail parties and entertain clients, not just point out their personality disorders. I need someone who is my equal—or as close as I can find. Unfortunately, that's not you." His voice had taken on a decidedly oily tone that made her skin crawl even in memory. She'd wondered where the boy she'd fallen in love with had gone, and mourned his loss.

Even in the midst of those painful words, she'd taken a deep breath and willed her rational, clinical side to take control. Heat had flooded her face, prickles had risen along her skin, and her fingers had clenched harder into tight fists. She'd taken a slow inventory of her emotions, categorizing them. Fear had vied for first place over hurt and anger, but it was a tight race.

She'd felt removed from the situation and wanted to know a few things. "How long have you felt like this?"

He'd shrugged, as if every word hadn't crushed the small pieces of what was left of her heart. "I don't know. I suppose it's been coming into focus since after grad school."

"For three years you've been lying to me?" The roar of the ocean had filled the space between her ears and swamped her with a sense of unreality. She'd felt as if someone else's life was falling apart, not hers. But it had been her life. She'd known it then, and she had to face it now.

With David, Kendall had shared her hopes, her dreams, and her body—the whole time she'd shared a lie.

She'd realized it then, but right now, lying here crying in the cabin, the truth of it hit her like a wave of ice water.

She should have seen it coming. She was a psychothera-pist, and none of her training had prepared her for this eventuality, this moment in time, this kind of utter devas-tation. Just like when David had first dropped his bomb-shell news on her, she felt completely, irretrievably lost.

Jax heard the sobbing from outside the cabin. He broke into a run and crashed through the door of Kendall's bedroom seconds later.

She let out a sob-filled, startled yelp.

He found her curled around a pillow. Except for a tearstained, blotchy, and slightly swollen countenance, she looked unharmed, but he still did a quick scan of the room to make sure there were no intruders. She was alone; the only threat to her health were painful-sounding, con-vulsive gasps.

Jax had heard people say before that they felt as if they had their heart in their throats, but he'd never expe-rienced that particular sensation—until now. He released the breath he'd held in a whoosh, willed his heart rate to return to normal, sank onto the bed beside her, and ran a shaking hand through his hair. "You scared the shit out of me. What's the matter?"

She hiccuped, shook her head, and tried to dry her eyes on the bedsheet.

"Are you sick?" He asked the question even though she looked as if she'd just woken from the mother of all nightmares.

She shook her head again, still sobbing but trying to hold it back, and was unable to speak through the tears.

"Just upset, then? Okay, I can handle that." He was a pro at soothing sobbing women. He had more experience with it than he'd ever wanted. Her racking sobs still made his hair stand at attention and his chest feel as if it were stuck in an ever-tightening vise, but he ignored it. For years, his sister, Rocki, would wake sobbing. The accident that took both their parents had haunted her dreams. "Come here." He scooped Kendall out of bed like he would a child, sat her across his lap, and rested her head on his shoulder.

Kendall curled her shaking body against his, rested her head against his chest, and buried her wet face in his neck.

He rubbed her back, kneading the tense muscles. "Kendall, I'm right here. I'm not going to let anything or anyone hurt you."

It took her a while—he wasn't sure how long—but eventually her sobs quieted to an occasional sniffle and her breathing evened out, the tremors lessened, and she slowly slumped against him, spent, deflated, her muscles relaxing either because of his ministrations or from sheer exhaustion.

"Shhh. Just breathe. I've got you. You're gonna be okay. I promise." That was something he could do. He wasn't sure how, but he'd make sure that no matter what, she'd be taken care of.

After what felt like days, Kendall raised her head and met his gaze with bloodshot, swollen eyes. "I'm sorry." Her voice sounded raw and brittle. "I'm not usually like this. Honest." She took a breath and blinked back more tears, obviously trying to rein in her emotions. "It's just that I woke up and everything hit me at once. One second I was reaching for David, and the next I was watching a horror flick of Godzilla stomping over my whole life."

"It's not your whole life—this is a temporary setback.

In fifty years you'll look back and see this as a lucky break, and thank God for it."

"I know that—intellectually. But I—"

"Needed another good cry. I understand. It's not a big deal, really." Her hair smelled like jasmine and warm, sleepy woman, and felt silky when it brushed against his hand as he massaged her neck and the base of her scalp. "I hiked over to Jaime's this morning. I needed to tell him I'm ready for more building materials, and we talked about your Jeep. He's agreed to work on it at his place and keep mum."

"But I don't know how much—"

"We're going to work it out in trade. He needs a hand, and I've offered to lend it." He didn't feel the necessity to expound upon what exactly Jaime required a hand with—namely filling his bank account with the cost of parts and labor.

"I do have money—I just don't know how much."

He couldn't help but laugh. "It looks as if we have that in common." He might not have his old knack for numbers anymore, but he'd spent years ensuring that his sister had more than enough to live comfortably for the rest of her life, without worry. He'd done the same for himself.

The look on her face told him he'd missed the old solidarity target. "We really do have an amazing amount in common. Both of us recently turned corners in our lives. Neither of us are the people we were before we came here."

She shrugged but didn't pull away.

"And we both have the gift of time—"

"Aka unemployment."

"If you want to mince words, be my guest. Still, we

have time to take stock of our new situations, figure out who we are, and envision what we'd like our futures to hold."

She didn't say anything. He wasn't sure if that was good or not. "Kendall, most people spend their lives walking down the same road. Every day, they drag themselves through the same rut. After a while, that rut gets so deep, you can't see anything but the ditch you've made. If either of us was in a rut, we've been blasted out of it now. And we have the opportunity to investigate all the new and different paths available to us."

"I never saw my life without David, not once. He's been a part of me for so long, I'm not sure who I am without him. It's . . . I don't know . . . scary."

"All new things are scary. Scary and exciting. That's how we know we're alive. We've survived, we've changed, but we're strong enough to get back up after being knocked down, or, in my case, knocked out. This is a new beginning for both of us."

"Are you sure you weren't a therapist in a past life?"

"Definitely." Although he'd seen his fair share of therapists after his parents' death. "I just turned my corner earlier than you did. I've been at this longer. I've reached the point where the shock and memories, or lack of memories, have worn off. You'll get here—probably a lot faster than I have."

She twisted in his arms, hers coming around him, and pulled him in for a hard hug and held on. "Thank you." She whispered in his ear and then pulled back, looking embarrassed, as a flush rose from the plunging neckline of her nightgown he hadn't noticed until that moment.

Holy hell. He wished to God he hadn't noticed, or at least not while she sat on his lap. He swallowed convulsively. The warmth of her skin heated the silken material, burning his hands splayed across her back.

"When I came here yesterday, all I'd wanted was to be alone, but now I'm so thankful I'm not. I'm glad you're here."

"Me too." His voice rasped through his throat, sounding like a metal canoe dragged across a pebbled beach. He slid her off his lap and onto the bed. The skirt of her nightgown pulled taught around her thighs, and he bit back a groan.

"Jack? Are you feeling okay?"

He stood and avoided looking at her. "I'm fine." But his voice sounded foreign, gravelly, and strained.

"You're flushed. Do you have another headache?"

The answer depended on which head she was talking about. The one on his shoulders was doing just fine; the one in his pants was definitely aching. "No—" He felt as if he should say more, but what? "I'll be outside if you need anything. I have work to do."

"Oh, okay." Her voice wavered uncertainly as he closed Kendall's door behind him.

———

It was a difficult task to work up a sweat outside in the mountains of New Hampshire in January, but Jax accomplished it. He was unloading lumber from Jaime's Tundra pickup, and the last thing he wanted was to slow down. If he did, he would have to talk, and talking wasn't something Jax was interested in—not even to his friend Jaime, and definitely not about himself.

There were so many unknowns in his life right now, talking about them made his head ache worse than it already did.

Jaime came around the tailgate and leaned against the side of the truck, his gloved hands stuffed in the pockets of his Carhartt jacket. "Where's Kendall?"

"She went for a hike up to the ridge."

Jaime nodded and looked in that direction, spotting Kendall's tracks in the snow.

"How long ago did she leave?" Jaime probably had a better notion of that than Jax. Jaime was a good tracker, and Jax knew damn well that he could tell from her footprints how long ago she'd taken off.

"I don't remember." His sense of time was so severely skewed, he couldn't even go there. It could have been a few minutes or a hell of a lot longer—he didn't know, and it was driving him insane.

He followed Jaime's gaze and stared at Kendall's footprints and the path she'd taken toward the ridge. A second later, the image of her in her negligee eclipsed everything else. He wished the vision of her hadn't been branded on his brain, but he couldn't unsee it. He'd tried. He'd been trying for a week. It hadn't worked yet.

"I managed to get just about everything on your list and avoided Ernie's questions over at the hardware store. Where do you want me to put the receipts?"

Jax slid the sheets of plywood onto the frozen, snow-covered ground. He grabbed the stack, rested it on his steel-toed boot, and walked them over to lean against the wall under what was left of the porch roof. "Just total what you spent on the lumber and groceries you brought over. My wallet's inside on the dresser in my room. Take whatever I owe you; there's plenty of cash." If he was wrong, Jaime would tell him and he'd figure out how to get more. There was a lot more where that came from— or at least he thought there was. For a man who'd never had to worry about money, he had spent an inordinate amount of his life doing just that. He had a lot of money but no real life. Looking back now, he saw what a waste of time it had been.

When he'd come to, alone in the hospital after the accident, he hadn't ached to see his bank account balance or how the market closed that day. No, he ached to see the people he loved—his sister, Rocki, and Kendall's parents, Grace and Teddy, who had unofficially adopted them after their parents' deaths. He remembered searching his mind, wondering if he'd forgotten someone. A woman, perhaps? But when he'd closed his eyes, the only female's image that had come to mind that day had been the face of his late mother—so clear, so real, as if she'd come to him in his dreams. The shock of it sent him bolting upright into a sitting position. The blare of medical equipment and the movement had split his screaming head in two, and then the nurses were there, holding him down.

"But—" Jaime tore off his gloves and ran a hand through his too-long sandy brown hair and lifted an aristocratic brow, his looks at odds with his demeanor.

But what? What had they been talking about? Money. Right. "Leave the paperwork on the dresser. I'll look at it later." Not that it would make a bit of sense to him. Still, that didn't stop him from trying. Who knew? Maybe his mathematical talent would return just as quickly as it had disappeared. He waited until Jaime kicked the snow off his boots and stepped into the dilapidated cabin before releasing a relieved breath. He rubbed the indentation in his skull where, a few weeks ago, doctors had drilled the hole to relieve the pressure on his brain.

Jax stared through the branches of pine trees toward

the ridge where Kendall hiked, and then above it into the crisp, bright blue winter sky. The one time he took a ski vacation, he'd inadvertently ended up playing chicken with a tree and lost. One doesn't realize what a big part numbers play in daily life, and the loss would suck for anyone. For him, a fund manager, a man who built his life on numbers, it achieved cosmic-joke status.

Breathing in the crisp, pine-scented air, Jax concentrated on the cold seeping through the soles of his work boots when he heard the cabin door slam behind him, followed by the sound of footsteps stomping through snow. He didn't look at Jaime. He knew he'd been found out—not that he'd tried overly hard to hide it. And why was that? From the look on Jaime's face, it was obviously something better contemplated at a later time.

"What the hell is going on with you?" Anger, urgency, and the live wire of frustration rolled off Jaime and slammed into Jax's central nervous system with all the subtlety of a no-holds-barred electroshock therapy treatment rendered by Dr. Frankenstein.

He'd known sooner or later he'd have to tell Jaime the painful truth—all of it. And he supposed, if Jaime had entered the cabin sooner, he'd have known a lot earlier. As it was, in the back of his mind, Jax had expected Jaime to confront him. After all, Jaime was smart and definitely not like one of the guys he'd worked with who would pretend to be your best friend but not really give a shit about you or your life. Still, he hadn't been prepared for the ferocity of Jaime's reaction.

Jax blinked, slowly moved his aching head, and focused on Jaime. Wow, he didn't have to have a master's degree in the study of body language to know that this was not going to be pretty. Jaime bounced on the balls of his feet in a fighter's stance—hell, even his hands were fisted—and the look of concern mixed with anger and hurt eclipsed everything else. Shit.

He lifted a brow, hoping the subtle challenge would remind Jaime of the live-and-let-live attitude to which he usually subscribed.

"Come on, Jax. That King of the Lake House superior smirk is not going to work with me. I've known you since we were, what—four or five?" He lowered his shoulders and crossed his brawny arms.

Grace had shown him a picture once of his fourth birthday party, and, as always, Jaime had been there, right by his side.

"Something's way off with you, and I want to know what it is."

How does one say he's lost his mind—or at least an important part of it—without sounding like a fucking basket case or a loon?

"What's with the stack of cash in your wallet?"

"Where else do you keep cash?"

Jaime got in his face. "It's not in order." Each word was punctuated. He stepped back and dragged his hand through his hair. "Even when we were kids, you kept your change in different pockets because you hated when the coins were mixed. Hell, you still sort your cash by denomination and have all the faces pointing the right direction. That wallet you have in there"—he shook an accusing finger at the cabin—"is one step above wadded bills stuffed in a paper sack. Unsorted currency is normally enough to make your ass twitch. A wallet in that condition would send you completely over the edge."

Jax opened his mouth to say something—anything—to shut Jaime up, but he was like a snowball bounding downhill, picking up girth and speed and rolling over everything in its path—even Jax's attempts to change the subject.

"And since when do you leave that much money just lying around? Shit, Jax, you have enough there for me to live comfortably for a good six months. Put it in a coffee can or somethin'."

"Jaim—"

"And just why is the clock facing the wall? You can't read the time if you can't see the face. Did that blow to the head knock a screw loose?"

Jaime's form took on that eerie stillness he always got before he lost his temper. Jax had never had that look pointed at him and couldn't afford another blow to the head. Not now—possibly not ever.

Jax held up his hands in surrender. "I can't read the time, okay?"

Jaime stopped. "So turn it around."

Jax tore off his gloves and scrubbed his cold hands over his face. "You don't understand. Ever since my accident, numbers don't mean anything to me. I can't make sense of them."

Jaime stepped back and sat hard on the tailgate. "You're a freakin' human calculator."

"Not anymore, I'm not. I seem to have fried that particular memory chip. If you gave me a calculator, I wouldn't know what to do with it."

Jaime gave him a who's-punking-whom look.

"I mean, I know what it's for. I just can't . . ." He pulled off his hat and ran his frozen fingers through his hair, tugging on it as if that would change anything. "I have a stack of cash, but I can't count it, and even if I could, I wouldn't know how much anything is worth." He blew out a breath that didn't begin to release the frustration he felt during every waking moment. "It's like that part of my brain just disappeared."

Jaime rubbed his hands on his thighs and leaned forward. His eyes squinted almost shut, as if he were trying to read two-point type. "No shit?" He rubbed his chin. "So I could have swiped all the big bills, and you wouldn't have known?"

"Pretty much." He let out a rusty bark of laughter that sounded strange to his ears. He hadn't had much to laugh about lately. Shit, his life, even before the accident, was no night at the Laugh Factory. He couldn't remember the last time he'd had more than a polite chuckle, unless he counted the time he spent in Red Hook with his sister and her new family. There was a lot of laughter there, even though they were dealing with serious issues. Unlike him, they'd never forgotten how to laugh.

Unfortunately, the loss of laughter wasn't as noticeable as losing his ability to do anything with numbers, but it had been lost just the same. At least laughter, once rediscovered, no longer evaded him.

A staring contest ensued between him and Jaime. Jax watched the wheels of Jaime's mind spin as he judged the ramifications with his usual lightning speed. His expression grew more and more serious. He started at shocked, made a quick right into contemplative, and parked in the handicapped spot by the front door of stunned. His eyes widened until he finally blinked and let out a long stream of air, as if he were blowing up an invisible balloon. "Wow, it sucks to be you."

Jax laughed again. This time it didn't feel so foreign. "Tell me about it."

"So, are you stuck this way forever?"

"I don't know, but, then, no one does." He shrugged as nonchalantly as he could manage without the aid of acting lessons. "I'm supposed to go back for another MRI. I have the date written down—not that it means anything to me. I'm hoping they'll call to confirm the appointment." He rolled his shoulders, trying to dispel the sudden tightness. He hated even thinking about this stuff. "The doctors tell me the brain heals, forms new connections or something, so it might come back. It might not."

"And you're hiding out here because you don't want anyone to know?"

"I'm not hiding."

Jaime's brow rose again, almost hitting his hairline. "The hell you aren't. You could be staying in the lake house—a freakin' palace compared to this place."

"It's too big and too empty."

"It wouldn't be empty if you weren't hiding. What's with the secrecy? You're not going to be able to hide it for long."

"I just needed some space. If Addie saw me, she'd know something was up, and she wouldn't hesitate to call in the cavalry. Grace and Teddy would ditch the rest of their once-in-a-lifetime Mediterranean cruise and run home. Rocki would drop everything and leave her new family, and I'd become her newest pet project. That's not happening. There's nothing anyone can do but wait and see if my brain heals, so why worry them?"

"And if Addie knew you were in town, it would kill your chances with Kendall."

"This has nothing to do with Kendall, and you know it. I had no idea she'd show up here. Besides, there's nothing between Kendall and me. Who the hell would want someone who can't even count spare change?"

Jaime ran a hand over his face. "That's just fucked up. I never thought about it before, but numbers are everywhere."

"I never thought about it either—until recently, and now it's the one thing I'm trying not to think about. That's why I'm here." He looked at the sagging, leaking roof. "Here there's something I can do—I can fix the roof, clean the place up. I can accomplish something between now and the date of the MRI."

"And how are you going to do that without measuring things?"

Jax pulled a pencil from behind his ear. "I can pull out the rotted pieces and put new ones in their place. I can measure—I just mark where I have to make the cut and cut it. I can do this. I'm going to do this.

"I have to do this, or I'll go crazy thinking of everything I can't do."

CHAPTER
FOUR

Kendall climbed, breathing deep and steady as she traversed the steep trail. Her thigh and calf muscles screamed from exertion, but she kept up the punishing pace, trying to outrun her demons, wishing the part of her mind that saw and heard them had an on/off switch. If it had, she hadn't discovered it. She'd thought getting away from the cabin, where the memories had assaulted her for the past week, would do the job. It failed miserably.

Maybe she needed to take Jack's advice. She had turned a corner, and the view from her new vantage point was unfamiliar. There were so many trails branching off from where she stood, but not one would allow her to return to what had been. Even if she'd wanted to, it was as if a fire had destroyed all remnants of her past with David. The life she'd lived no longer existed in anything other than memory. It hurt like hell—the physical pain between her breasts was still sharp and clear and ever present—but she'd get past it. At least she wasn't coming out of this period of her life empty-handed. She had her master's degree. She'd learned a lot and she'd keep her credentials, her three years of work experience in her field, and all the knowledge she'd gained, and nothing—not David or anyone else, for that matter—could take that away from her, save a blow to the head like Jack had suffered.

She tried and failed to push that thought from her mind. Talk about demons. She wouldn't trade hers for Jack's if given the choice. No, at least now she had a real sense of control, something Jack didn't have.

She took a deep breath and tried to clear her mind. She needed to look toward the future—a future she'd never imagined but one she would choose for herself, not one given to her or one for which she'd have to settle. She wished she could help Jack as much as he'd helped her, but, unfortunately, there was nothing either of them could do. Her only option was to wait and help him deal with whatever came. Maybe he could be her first patient in Harmony. The thought brought a smile to her face, and then she rejected it—she was already too personally involved with him to be clinical. But she could be his friend, and that might be the best thing for both of them.

Jack had been a good enough friend to point her in the right direction, probably wishing he had the same options she had. The least she could do was to continue. No matter how difficult the path before her was, she'd get through it, for both their sakes. He might be farther down the trail than she was, but she'd catch up quickly, and maybe they could discover their individual paths together.

It was as if she stood at the edge of a cold mountain pool, where the water sparkled like diamonds in the clear morning sun. Fear clawed at her; her lungs seized with the knowledge that if she jumped, the water would engulf her, stealing the heat from her body. She wasn't sure how to prepare for the cold, harsh reality of how to move forward with her life. Still, it was time to take the plunge.

"My future." She said the words aloud and hated the quaver in her voice. Not good enough. She was going to attack her future with courage and she needed to believe that. "My future." There She was loud and clear and sounded strong. She took a deep breath and mentally jumped. Envisioning a picture of her perfect life. A chill traveled the length of her spine. For as long as she could remember, every vision of her future had included David.

She wished for mental scissors so she could cut David out of every picture she'd imagined. Her wedding day—she ripped off the figure of David standing beside her and had no image with which to replace him. No stand-in. No idea of what kind of man she'd look for or even if she'd ever consider marriage again.

She wanted a family, of that she was certain. And when she thought of the word *family*, she pictured a traditional one. So, yes, she'd like to marry eventually, but she moved that picture far into the future. In order to marry, she'd have to date. God, she'd have to start all over, and she hadn't dated since spin the bottle was in vogue. How did one even date now?

She'd seen her single friends struggle in the dating pool and had always felt lucky, smug even, certain in the knowledge that she'd never have their problems. After all, she and David had been the perfect couple—or so she'd thought. They'd never even fought. She wondered if that had been a good thing. Had she just gone along with what he wanted in order to get along? Always looking at her future as part of a team instead of going after what she'd wanted for herself.

Had she abdicated her goals for what she thought

were their shared goals, only to discover she was the only one doing the abdicating? She had. She'd done everything for the greater good, which, she now realized, translated into David's good.

She sat on a rock, the cold seeping through the seat of her jeans. Great. These lightbulb moments just wouldn't stop. They were coming so fast, it felt as if she were in a dark room with a strobe light flashing on a picture long enough to highlight a relationship problem and reveal her lack of a backbone and her apparent malleability. She shook her head to clear the image. She'd have to think about past mistakes later. Right now, she would look to her future.

The first thing she needed was a job. She could look for available office space in town to start her therapy practice. She was free of the constraints of David's list of things they must achieve before returning to Harmony. That was a positive. She could do what she'd always wanted to do; she just needed to be able to make enough money to live on while she got the practice up and running. She should look into the feasibility of taking out a small-business loan. She didn't know anything about the Small Business Administration and the loans available to small businesses, contracting with insurance carriers, advertising, or anything of the sort, but she was smart and she could learn. She'd never taken any business courses because she thought David would handle that side of the practice. That wasn't her brightest move, but she would figure it out.

She hoped to avoid moving back in with her parents, if at all possible. She was independent and wanted to continue to be. An SBA loan might give her enough if she lived frugally, and there was always the possibility she could do work with the local hospice, and maybe even take a part-time job at the hospital doing social work. There were definitely options.

She had a plan and, right now, she liked the look of it. So she rose from her perch on the rock and rubbed her frozen backside. She was going to hike up the ridge—it had been her goal—and then she'd go back to the cabin and make a hearty dinner and tell Jack all about her revelations.

Jax had his mouth full of nails and was doing his best not to swallow them while he furiously hammered an eight-foot piece of plywood onto the newly rebuilt and repaired roof trusses.

A few days ago, he'd checked the weather forecast when he'd stopped at Jaime's home. At the time, the meteorologists forecasted no snow all week. He hoped more than believed the forecasters here were better at predicting snowfall than they were in Chicago, where he'd lived and worked until his accident.

That thought brought him up short. He supposed technically he still lived in Chicago. After all, he owned a penthouse on the Magnificent Mile with an amazing view of Lake Michigan. He'd thought the view would be great for resale—not that he ever got to enjoy it. His work hours were such that he'd leave before the sun rose and return long after the sun had set. He should have gotten the place with the city view instead. Live and learn.

Whether or not he still had a job was the one question for which he didn't have an answer. He'd taken a leave of absence and didn't want to contemplate what he'd do if he didn't recover sufficiently to resume his position.

He set his mind back to the job at hand: hammering sheets of plywood onto the replaced, repaired, or sistered trusses. The repairs had proved to be slow work, because he'd spent most of his time running up and down the ladder. Up to measure, down to cut, up to install, back down if the cut wasn't perfect—which was more often than not. It had been so long since he'd done any work with his hands that didn't involve a computer, and longer still since he'd had to eyeball the length of something without the aid of a measuring tape, so a perfect cut was a rare thing.

His leg and ass muscles would take a while to recover from all the climbing. If he could have counted the steps, he was sure they'd be enough to have climbed to the top of the Sears Tower.

He pulled another nail from between his lips and hammered it home. At least at this stage of the job, there wasn't a lot of cutting to be done.

The sun dipped below the edge of the mountains, and the temperature dropped with its departure. He sent up a prayer that the wall of clouds growing closer by the minute would dump the snow they contained on the mountains and not on the lake. He wasn't ready. He needed to hurry the hell up and get the rolls of tar paper, which silently mocked him from their resting place on the porch, nailed onto the roof so the cabin would, once again, be dried in.

"Jack, I'm back." Kendall's voice startled him, and he almost swallowed a nail.

He spat the rest of the nails into the box, wiped his hands on his grungy jeans, and decided to shut down for the day. There was no way he'd get the rest of the tar paper on before dark.

Sliding onto the porch roof, he grabbed hold of the tree limb and swung down, landing neatly. Unfortunately, the jarring didn't do anything to help his ever-present headache.

Kendall's cheeks were pink with exertion, her eyes so dark and bright, they looked like sparkly onyx jewels in a field of white. She wore a bulky cream-colored fisherman's sweater, a navy blue down vest, jeans, and worn hiking boots.

"Did you have a good hike?"

Her forehead wrinkled as if she were deciding how to respond. "Are you familiar with that quote, 'Wherever you go, there you are'?"

He tugged off his hat and rubbed his throbbing temples. "Buddha, right? So you realized that you can't outrun, or, in this case, outhike your problems. Yeah, I'm intimately familiar with the concept. Why do you think I'm here?"

One of her dark, highly arched brows rose, and his fingers itched to trace the curve. "Are you trying to outrun your problems?"

He scrubbed the back of his neck to keep from reaching for her and didn't meet her eyes. The woman didn't beat around the bush. "Maybe I was at first, but we both know how well that works. Now I'm just ... I don't know ... dealing with it in my own time, in my own way. Or at least that's what I tell myself."

A smile played around her full, reddened lips. "And do you believe it?"

He didn't know what the hell to say to that. Since he saw no reason to stand outside in the cold when they could do this inside by the fire, he headed for the door.

Kendall followed him inside and just watched and waited, like the therapist she was. Damn it. Being under the constant scrutiny of a trained therapist was getting to be a drag.

Jax pulled off his coat, tossed it on the hook in the mudroom, and ran his hands through his hair, hoping to erase the hat head he was sure he sported. He'd love to lie to Kendall, but he couldn't—not to her, not about who he was now. "For the most part, I do believe it." He went to the kitchen and leaned into the refrigerator, reaching into the back for the stash of beer Jaime had brought over one night. He held a bottle out to her. "Want one?"

She shook her head and wrinkled her nose.

"Wine?" He didn't wait for an answer, just grabbed a glass and wondered if she was really interested in his answer or merely in the habit of asking probing questions. Either way, he felt no irritation. It didn't matter why Kendall asked. Not really. She might be terribly hurt and upset about losing David and her job, but that didn't stop her from being who she was: an incredibly compassionate person.

When she'd told him she'd become a therapist because she wanted to help people, he knew it to be a calling, not an occupation. Kendall might ask questions out of habit, but she cared about the answers and was an active listener. He reminded himself that she was like this with everyone—he wasn't special.

Jax passed her the wine, carried his beer into the main room, and took a seat on the old leather club chair—giving himself the space and distance to study her.

She watched him, obviously waiting for him to explain himself further. Dammit. "A lot of what I'm dealing with is a waiting game, and I'm not the most patient of men. I hate not being in control of my recovery. And, yes, that's just another one of my faults that has come back to bite me in the ass."

She hadn't followed him out of the kitchen, not that he'd expected her to. The place was so small, they could carry on a conversation from different rooms. It didn't much matter. Kendall turned to the refrigerator without saying anything. But, really, what was there to say?

He set his beer down and threw a fresh log into the stove, kicking up a bunch of sparks. It caught almost instantly.

Kendall pulled her head out of the refrigerator, holding an armful of food against her chest. "I understand your frustration over the lack of control." She bumped the refrigerator door closed with her hip before dumping her load on the counter. "I get it. You can't control the healing process, and I can't seem to control much of anything either." She blew out a frustrated breath and began chopping vegetables with gusto. She slid the knife through a green pepper from base to cap without cutting through, wrenched the two sides apart, and then, making quick work of it, sliced them into thin strips.

Something in her tone had him taking a healthy swig of beer and crossing the room to the kitchen area.

"You know, while I was hiking, it occurred to me that I might have been able to solve the problems David and I had, but I was too dense to see that they even existed."

Her back was to him, her posture straight and tense. He stood close to her and took the knife-wielding hand by the wrist.

She dropped the knife on the cutting board, obviously

stunned. Good—she needed to hear him. God, if he could do one thing, he'd find this David asshole and beat him to a bloody pulp for hurting Kendall the way he had.

She turned around so they were chest to chest, thigh to thigh, and as she looked up at him, anger shot from her dark charcoal gray, sometimes black, eyes. But this anger looked as if it was aimed at herself. "I ignored the problems; I allowed them to fester. I knew better than to do that. I'm a freakin' marriage and family therapist, for cripes' sake. What does that say about me?"

"Only that you need to work on your mind-reading skills."

She shot him a quelling look tinged with the possibility of physical retaliation, but he ignored it.

"Hey, I'm a guy. I know how hard it is to talk about relationship problems when the conversation is forced on you. It's harder still to initiate it. Kendall, I can almost guarantee you that the problems that existed were David's. From what little I know of the man, he doesn't strike me as the least bit courageous." And that was being kind. "If you'd been aware of the problems, I'm sure you would have dealt with them immediately. I might not know you well, but I can tell you're not one to let things lie."

Her brows arched at that.

"Am I wrong?"

"No." She let out a defeated breath and returned to chopping. "But I knew something wasn't right—"

"And now you're kicking yourself for not forcing it out of him?"

"Something like that."

"I see." And he did. He was sure trying to get the dickhead to fess up to whatever was wrong wouldn't have done her any good. But with Kendall, it was the lack of effort that bothered her. "Can I help?"

Without a word, she handed him a few carrots and a peeler. He started on the peeling—one of the very few things he knew how to do in a kitchen. He stopped mid-swipe. "You know, I'm willing to bet if you had forced the issue, Dave would have acted like the coward he is and avoided all confrontation. He doesn't like drama, right?"

She nodded.

"Kendall, a man isn't offered a transfer across country and expected to leave the next day. It takes a few months, at the very least, which means Dave made his decision a long time ago. He was biding his time. He wasn't about to bring up the fact that he was unhappy or had problems with the relationship because he'd never planned to fix it. If you had known that or figured out his plan, you would have ended the relationship." He resumed peeling. "Ending the relationship before his transfer came through would have been terribly inconvenient for good ole Dave. By not saying a word, he was able to choose the end date. He could run away and entirely avoid the messiness that comes with ending a long-term relationship. It would have worked too, if you hadn't had the bad luck to lose your job. Like I said, the man is a coward."

Kendall blew out a frustrated breath and slammed another onion on the cutting board before cutting the end off with one swift slash of the knife. "I know he's a coward. I get it. But, Jack, there were two people in that relationship. . . . It's never only one person's fault. I have to accept at least some of the blame. I want to make sure I know what I did wrong so I won't repeat my mistakes."

He reached into the overhead cabinet and took out a couple of plates and then rooted around in the silverware drawer to get the utensils. He figured he might as well set the table, since she was doing all the heavy lifting cooking-wise. "Okay, I can see that. I'll give you leave to take the blame for not recognizing a narcissist when you saw one." He looked up from the plates he put on the table. "You were a kid when you and David got together. What did you know about narcissistic tendencies then?"

"Nothing, but I know all about them now, and all the psychology courses I aced didn't help me recognize it in David. Some therapist I am."

He took the three quick strides back to the kitchen and stood too close to Kendall, to make sure he had her attention. "Do you know that saying 'A lawyer who represents himself has a fool for a client'?"

"Yes." She rummaged through the pantry and pulled down a box of chicken broth and one of rice, measured both, and set the broth to boil.

"I would imagine it's the same for doctors and therapists. You can't treat yourself or people you love because of your lack of distance—you can't be dispassionate and see things without emotion. So, no, this has nothing to do with your profession. It doesn't make you any less of a therapist."

"Really?"

"Do you have more carrots?"

"Sure." She passed him the bag.

He took a bite of one he'd already peeled and then offered it to her in turn.

She bit off a piece and chewed thoughtfully, as if she were deciding whether or not to say more.

"I'm just beginning to realize how much of my identity I gave up being part of a couple. I think it was a gradual thing. But, then, I don't know—I can't remember a time I didn't think of what was best for us and put that above what I might have thought was best for me."

"There's a fine line between compromise and giving in, isn't there?" He watched as she tossed salt and butter into the boiling broth and added the rice.

"Now that I'm looking at it with a critical eye, I see that what was best for us was synonymous with what was best for David. I was trying to be a team player and ended up being a doormat without ever realizing it. I had no idea. How could I be that blind?"

Kendall turned her attention to a thin steak she pulled out of the refrigerator. She rubbed something on it and sliced it and a weird-looking root. In a measuring cup she mixed together soy sauce and a few other things he didn't recognize; then she left the meat and all the vegetables in their own bowls.

She gave the rice a stir and looked at the timer she'd set. "You know, I've always seen myself as so strong and independent, and now I'm wondering if I haven't been lying to myself all along." She turned and lit the stove beneath a huge cast-iron skillet and, wrinkling her nose, slid him a sidelong glance. "My wok is better, but this will do in a pinch."

Jax watched her for a moment and then leaned against the counter. "Kendall, there's something to be said for reflecting on failures and successes. But, then, nothing good can come of it if you're too busy beating yourself up to see the good in what you've accomplished."

"I suppose you're right." She left the pan on the heat and turned, giving him her full attention. "And, for your information, I didn't beat myself up—I just had a hard time envisioning a future without David. I don't think I've ever done that before—well, not since before I packed away my Barbie and Ken dolls, anyway. But even on that front I've made some headway—it just didn't come easily."

"The best things don't."

Kendall poured oil into the hot pan. He watched the oil spread and shimmer in the overhead light. "I've been waiting for three years to do what I really wanted to do: move home. You see, David had this list of goals we had to achieve before we married and returned to Harmony."

Jax took a sip of his beer to keep from calling the guy a controlling prick.

Kendall threw the onions, peppers, and carrots into the pan and tossed them around. "Today on my hike I realized that I'm free to do what I want to do. I don't have to follow David's list anymore. I don't have to live in Boston. I can move back to Harmony just as soon as I give my landlord notice and pack my apartment." Her eyes sparkled, her face glowed, and she wore a natural smile. It looked good on her. Really good. "I can make my own decisions. I no longer have to live up to David's conditions. I have options. I can find a new job, try to get a small-business loan to open my own counseling center, or both. I'm a hard worker."

"Sounds as if you accomplished a lot on your hike."

She shrugged and grabbed the strips of beef she'd sliced, and what she told him was fresh ginger and garlic, and added them to the pan, tossing the contents wildly but with surprising accuracy. Nothing landed outside the pan—amazing. The place smelled like heaven. The next thing he knew, she poured a soy-sauce mixture into the pan. She stirred a good shot of sherry into a cup, mixing in the same white powder she'd rubbed into the steak, and then poured the cloudy mixture into the pan. Within a few minutes, the sauce had thickened and the food she put on the serving plate looked like it could have come out of his favorite Chinese restaurant, the one his sister lived above on Mott Street in the center of New York's Chinatown.

Kendall carried the rice and the stir-fry to the table, sat, and reached for his plate. She piled the food onto both dishes without even asking.

"Thanks. This looks delicious."

"You're welcome." She shrugged as she took a bite and looked like one of those food judges on the cooking channel. "You watched me throw it together. It's not difficult."

"Not for you. For me, it would be almost impossible." He took a bite and almost groaned.

She held up her fork. "I guess I could stay with Addie or my parents until I find a place of my own."

"You could stay here for as long as you want. You know, cooking in lieu of rent. I don't know about you, but this is definitely working for me."

He could tell from the look she shot him and the fake laugh that she didn't believe him. "I'm serious. But if it's not something you'd consider—"

"I think my parents would have a hard time with my moving from David's place to yours—even if we're only friends. They're a little old-fashioned. No one would believe a woman and a man could live together as platonic roommates unless one of them was gay—which I'm pretty sure is not the case here. And this is a very small town."

He was well aware of that and he was definitely not gay, but he saw her point. It didn't mean he liked it. Even he had to admit that if she were rooming with Jaime, Jax wouldn't believe they weren't sleeping together. Just the thought of it made his head ache.

What straight guy wouldn't want to have Kendall in his bed? Well, except for him. Not that he didn't want Kendall in every way humanly possible, and he spent a hell of a long time imagining all the ways he'd take her. Yeah, wanting her was never the issue; deserving her was.

Kendall deserved way better than a man like David, the narcissistic prick, and she deserved better than a man like Jax. She deserved a man with all his cylinders firing. He might not deserve her, but he could help her, couldn't he? "Doesn't the guy who owns this place have about a half dozen other cabins he rents out? I would think he'd give you a screamin' deal on a rental."

She took a sip of her wine and looked at him over the rim shaking her head. "Oh no. There's no way I'd ever ask a favor of Jackson Sullivan. No, I'm going to do this on my own."

Jax refilled her wineglass and wondered what the hell he'd done to make her dislike him so damn much. "You know, Kendall, no matter what you say, I hardly think he'd be doing you a favor. How many of those cottages does he have rented out all year?"

"None. They rent in the summer, and the same families come year in and year out."

"Well, it's a long time until summer. And if you were to rent one, it would give you a landing pad for a few months until you knew exactly what you were doing, and it would give him more income. It's a win-win."

He barely kept himself from shaking his head. What the hell was he doing? If Kendall knew who he was, he'd be lucky if she'd even talk to him again. And once Grace and Teddy came home, he'd be outed. At least they were on a long cruise—he remembered giving them the longest option available when he had his assistant book it, since there wasn't much for them to do around here this time of the year. Plus, as much as they denied it, the cold got to them, and who wouldn't want to get away from the harsh New Hampshire winters?

He just wasn't sure how much longer he had before they were due to return.

———

Jaime stood examining the Range Rover in the first bay of his heated garage on Main Street. He took a deep breath, and where he should have smelled only grease, motor oil, and quickly melting slush—something that smelled all kinds of gross even this far away from Boston—he smelled freakin' green apple shampoo.

Hell, he hadn't thought his day could get any worse, and now this. Now not only did he have to replace the whole hydraulic system in a twenty-year-old Range Rover—fuckin' Brits; every single one of their cars was a nightmare to fix, and getting parts was a royal pain in the ass—but he had to deal with her too. "What do you want, Addie?"

"How do you always do that?"

He didn't need to look to know that her lips were pursed as if she'd just eaten a particularly sour lemon, or that she probably wore all beige, unless this was one of her gray sweatshirt days. Both colors made her look like she was three weeks past her expiration date, not that she cared.

Addie Lane dressed in shapeless, colorless clothes.

She had all the style sense of a body pillow, and that was just fine with him. She might fool the rest of Harmony's male population, but he knew how she looked when Kendall dressed her up—he'd seen her at a bar in Boston, and it had taken half a night of drooling over her for him to realize it was Addie. Now he knew what kind of body was hiding under all those layers of ugly, oversize clothes, and he wasn't about to tell her that the last time he snaked her shower drain, he'd sniffed every bottle of crap she had in there to discover the culprit—she smelled like her green apple shampoo. "I've got eyes in the back of my head. Happy now? What the heck do you want?" He heard her blow her bangs out of her eyes in exasperation. Fine. The sooner she told him off, the sooner she'd leave.

"You have to promise not to say anything to anyone."

"Why?"

"Because I promised, and I swear, if you tell, I'll cut your balls off with a rusty nail clipper, Jaime Rouchard."

He winced at the thought—knowing Addie, she'd figure out a way to do it. "Then don't tell me. Far be it from me to force you to divulge a secret. I'm not that interested." Besides, he already knew what she was going to say.

"I need to. I need help."

"Now, that's interesting. What kind of help, and why me?"

"It's a logistics thing. Besides, as much as I dislike you, you're the only one in town I can trust."

"Damn, Addie, you certainly have a way of sweet-talking me into doing your bidding."

"Look, if you help me out, I'll owe you one. Okay?"

"And just what do you think I need from you? You're a kindergarten teacher. I already know my numbers and letters, thanks."

"I can help in the office."

"Not interested."

"I can clean the place up a little."

"Next."

"What do you want?"

Yeah, he wasn't even going there. It wouldn't be at all gentlemanly, and there was no way she'd ever agree to it.

"Come on, Jaime. It's for your own good. Aren't you still best buds with Jax?"

"Yeah. What does he have to do with anything?"

"I can't tell you unless you promise me."

"Fine. I don't have time for this, Addie. Just tell me what it is and what you need."

"You promise not to breathe a word to a soul?"

"What the hell do you want, Addie—a blood oath?"

She mumbled something under her breath about all men being bastards. "David dumped Kendall, ran off to San Francisco, and left her flat on the same day she lost her job. So she came home, but she doesn't want anyone in town to know, so she's been hiding out at the Sullivans' hunting cabin for the past week."

"And you're telling me because?"

"Because your place is close by. You can check on her and make sure she's not doing something stupid."

"Like what?"

"OD'ing on Ben and Jerry's, crying into her wineglass— I don't know what she's going to do. She's never had her heart broken before."

"Sure she has. Don't you remember what she was like when she was—what?" He thought back. "Twelve years old, when Jax and Rocki were sent away? She moped for months."

"She missed Rocki."

"Oh no, she missed Jax. She followed him like stink on a skunked dog. I should know—Jax and I spent half the summer trying to lose her."

"That's horrible."

"What the hell do you expect? We were sixteen. What teenage boys would want a twelve-year-old following them around, ratting them out about every last thing they did?"

"Kendall doesn't want her folks to find out because she knows if they did, they'd run home and ruin their cruise."

"So, you want me to spy on her?"

"Not in a creepy, Peeping Tom kind of way. You can just stop by, say you saw the smoke from the chimney."

"Fine. And you think she's going to invite me in and tell me what's going on in her life?"

"I don't know. Still, at least you'll know if she's alive. Her cell doesn't work, and neither does the landline, since they never rent the place out."

"If I promise to stop by and make sure she's alive, will you leave me in peace?"

"It would be my pleasure."

He heard her stomping across the cement floor toward the door. "Oh, and, Addie, don't forget that you owe me one." A big one. "I'll be collecting someday soon."

She let out a rumble worthy of the new Dodge Charger SRT Hellcat. And, despite his best intentions, he just wondered how she purred when she was happy.

CHAPTER
FIVE

K endall woke up from a dream to a banging noise, and realized that she was breathing heavy and Jack's face was the last thing she saw before . . . Oh, God, she'd never had a dream like that before. She rolled over in bed, almost surprised to find herself alone—it had seemed so real. Sinking farther into the mattress, she tried to get her breathing under control. Her heart raced, her skin felt three sizes too small for her body, and no amount of deep breathing stopped the ache. Every bang brought back the dream vision of Jack over her. She pulled the pillow over her head and moaned, "Stop the banging."

If the earsplitting, body-shaking volume was any indication, the hammering was coming from the roof directly over her bed. The pillow was not only an exceptional noise blocker, but it also brought to mind those *NCIS* episodes where Ducky talked about what good weapons pillows make for suffocation.

Between the lack of air, the noise, and the dream that had brought her to the brink of orgasm, any prayer of sleep and wallowing in peace was summarily dashed.

She sat slowly, her head throbbing in time with the incessant hammering. Too much wine and not enough dinner had not only fed her erotic imagination, but it had also led to the morning's cotton-mouthed, whopping, mother of all hangovers. She was an exceptional candidate for the next Excedrin Extra Strength commercial or a session with a battery-operated boyfriend—maybe both. God, she needed the hair of the dog or, at the very least, a toothbrush.

Jack obviously didn't have the same problem, since he was the one on the roof, making that ungodly racket. He'd eaten so much the night before, he probably could have topped it off with a fifth of whiskey and still have passed a sobriety test.

When it came to drinking, Kendall had always been a lightweight. David used to say she could get drunk toasting at a wedding.

David. She'd really thought he had been her other half, her partner in life, her soul mate—she'd been so clueless. She'd never seen that sometime between her eighth-grade homecoming dance and now, all the dreams he'd espoused had turned into lies.

How many years had he been using her, just waiting for a convenient time to move on?

Another sound broke through the constant banging, and she swore it was coming from Jack's room—which was odd, because she was pretty sure he was up on the roof causing the racket. She rolled out of bed and heard it again on her way to investigate.

When Kendall stepped through the door, a hunk of plaster the size of a half-dollar fell and hit the floor before crumbling further. Damn, spiderweb cracks were spreading across the ceiling at an alarming rate. She hightailed it out, holding her aching head. If she didn't stop Jack soon, his bedroom ceiling would end up on the floor, and, last she checked, the floor wasn't where ceilings belonged.

She ran through the cabin, groaning with each step, and threw open the front door. "Jack, stop!"

The cold stabbed her bare feet. The sound of something—or make that someone—sliding down the roof toward her, preceded by a shower of snow, had her instinctively reeling back against the rough-hewn siding of the cabin. The cold seeped through her thin satin nightgown. She'd been plenty warm with the woodstove, heaters, and four quilts and blankets—not to mention the dream. Standing outside without so much as a robe was a different story.

A head popped down from the porch roof sporting the same smile she'd seen in her dream. "Good morning, Sleeping Beauty."

"It might have been, except for the banging, the wine hangover, and the little problem of plaster raining down in your room."

"What?"

His head disappeared from the edge of the roof. He must have stood, because she heard a step, and then his body flew into her line of vision, hanging from a branch of a nearby tree. And then, with the grace of a gymnast, he dropped to the ground.

"My, that was impressive." She looked around the porch and wondered where his ladder was.

Jack wiped his gloved hands on the thighs of his jeans and took a step toward her. "Did you just say what I think you said?"

"Did your accident affect your hearing?"

"No, not that I've noticed."

"Then I'm guessing you heard me correctly. The ceiling above your bed is falling down." Falling down, falling down. The ceiling above your bed is falling down, my fair lady . . . God, she really was losing it.

"Shit." He ripped off his gloves and hat and then raked his fingers through his too-long blond hair. "That's really not good."

"I take it replastering the ceiling was not part of the scope of the job."

"It is now, or your father will kill me." He looked at her again and turned away. "You'd better get back inside—you're freezing." It wasn't a question.

She looked down and saw that the goose bumps on her arms weren't the only noticeable reaction to the cold. She wrapped her arms over her breasts, turned, and retreated to the cabin, trying to remember the color panties she wore—they were probably clearly visible through the thin, champagne-colored fabric of her nightgown. God, she hoped she wore panties. She'd had so much wine, she didn't remember getting dressed for bed last night.

Jack was right behind her; she could feel the cold radiating off his coat. She stepped into the hallway just as something crashed; then a plume of dust flew through the open door of his bedroom. She stopped short.

Jack ran into her from behind and wrapped his arms around her to keep them both from falling. "Fuck. Um . . . sorry."

"Are you apologizing for your language, running into me, or causing the ceiling to cave in?"

"Both the language and for running into you. The cave-in is in my room, so no apology necessary there."

"Oh, really? Do you think you're the only one the cave-in is going to affect?"

His hand, big and warm and callused, spread over her

stomach, where it snagged on the delicate fabric of her gown. The tip of his thumb slid beneath her breast, but the pressure of his hand dragging her from the doorway took away any question of an intentional boob graze. He wasn't copping a feel; he was going all he-man and protective. She didn't know which would have made her angrier—probably the he-man thing. She let out a derisive growl.

He poked his head into her room. "Let's just hope it stops at the bearing wall, shall we?"

Seriously? "You think the ceiling in my room could cave in too?"

"Anything's possible. I don't know how long that roof was leaking, but it certainly compromised the integrity of the plaster in my room. Water has a way of traveling."

"It does?"

"So it seems. The major leak was over the mudroom, so I suggest you hurry up and grab some clothes while I check it out, unless you don't mind meeting Jaime Rouchard in your nightgown." The frown on his face told her he didn't like that scenario at all.

"Jaime's coming here?"

"Eventually. How else am I going to get my hands on drywall, tape, and mud? I might ask him to go to the Home Depot in Concord, just to be safe."

"You think Ernie at the hardware store is going to rat you out to my dad?"

"Don't you?"

"Probably, unless Jaime can come up with a damn good story as to why he needs drywall."

Jack blew out a breath and rocked back on the heels of his work boots. "I'm going to hike down to Jaime's and tell him what I need, just as soon as I take a few measurements—or you take a few measurements. If you wouldn't mind, that is . . . I think all I need are the room dimensions, and Jaime can probably take it from there."

"Jaime's very nice to drive all the way to Concord to avoid Ernie's questions."

"True, but I pay well. Or at least I think I do."

She didn't bother hiding her laugh. "You do realize that Dad's going to take one look at the cabin and know you've replaced the ceiling." When she looked back, she found him staring at her, and the expression she glimpsed on his face the nanosecond before it disappeared brought to mind what she was wearing, which wasn't much. But at least it seemed as if he liked what he saw.

Jack looked away quickly, and his face turned the beet red that only redheads or true blonds suffered. "Yes, but, really, with the water damage, the ceiling needed to be replaced long before my hammering caused it to crumble." His voice sounded strained—a dark grumble that raked against her every nerve ending, the way the rough skin of his hands had snagged on her nightgown. His hands were fisted at his sides, his cheekbones looked as if they were chiseled out of granite, and his golden stubble shone in the morning light pouring through the window.

Kendall might have been with only one man in her entire life, but she knew what it felt like to be wanted in a purely sexual way. It was simple biology, really, or maybe chemistry. Pheromones or hormones—she wasn't sure what exactly caused it, but she knew physical attraction when she saw it. It didn't seem to matter that she knew it was a natural human instinct to ensure the survival of the species. There was nothing more to it than that. Jack was a healthy male adult, and as much as they say humans are not animals, when it comes to sex . . . well, the lines definitely blurred—something she would be smart to remember. Sexual attraction did not a relationship make—not that she was looking for a relationship. She needed time to figure out where she went wrong with the last one before she contemplated even dating again.

Dating. Just the thought of it sent a spear of dread through her. She'd never really dated, and wasn't looking forward to starting to do it now. She rummaged through the dresser she'd stashed her clothes in, grabbed a few things, and took a deep breath before facing him once again. She didn't look at him, though—she wasn't a coward, but she wasn't that courageous either. "I'll just get dressed, and if you could find a tape measure, I'll get those room dimensions written down for Jaime." She waited until she heard his footsteps retreating, and hesitated a moment longer before softly closing her door with a click.

⸺

Jax waited until he heard the snick of Kendall's door down the hall before he sat on his plaster-strewn bed, held his head in his hands, and groaned. The woman was a menace to the entire celibate male population.

Celibacy was not his natural state—well, at least not until the accident. It hadn't bothered him before, but having Kendall here for the past week was definitely making his monklike status a real trial.

He reminded himself that celibacy was his choice, after all—he had the phone numbers of several of the nurses he'd met at the hospital stuffed into his wallet to prove it. Hell, they'd even offered to drive, since they knew he wouldn't be cleared to handle heavy machinery until after his next MRI. It wasn't as if he could call them—at least not without help—and the last thing he wanted to do was have Jaime or, God forbid, Kendall dial the phone for what he knew would be nothing more than a booty call. He didn't know what he wanted, but dinner and a game of mattress tag wasn't it.

Jax was far from a saint, but even he had a moral compass. He'd never had sex with one woman when he was jonesing for another, and he'd never imagined being with anyone other than the woman he was with at the time. He'd spent the past week considering it but couldn't talk himself into being with someone when the only woman he wanted was Kendall, which left him in his current predicament: waking up from erotic dreams of her, hard and hot and breathing heavy.

He scrubbed his hands over the rough stubble of his face. It was too bad he couldn't control his subconscious as well as he could his conscious mind. Sitting there with the ceiling falling down around his head and Kendall's scent still wafting over the musty aromas of dust and wet plaster, he wondered if he truly had control of either.

The feel of Kendall's body tight against his was indelibly imprinted on his psyche. For a brief moment during their conversation, it had been all he could do not to wrap his arms around her and pull her to him. Face-to-face. Breasts to chest. Mouth to mouth. For a brief moment, he let himself imagine what it would be like to kiss her, to take her mouth, to taste her and lose himself in Kendall. Then he allowed his imagination to go well beyond a kiss, straight to the animalistic urge to possess her, to make love to her in every way humanly possible, and then keep her close and protect her. For a brief moment, he wanted to know her in a way more intimate than he'd ever known any other: mind, body, and soul. He'd never had the urge to take care of anyone before— not in any way except sexually. It wasn't as if the thought of sex with Kendall wasn't blinking like a huge, flashing fluorescent neon light in the forefront of his mind, but what he felt for Kendall was so much more complicated, so much stronger, and a great deal more confusing than anything he'd felt for a woman before. He was trapped right in the middle of dangerous territory, but no matter how many times he told himself not to go there, he couldn't stop himself from doing just that.

Another piece of plaster fell from the ceiling and landed next to him on the bed. He tried to focus on it, but all he saw was Kendall in that sinfully sexy nightgown, looking like the Venus de Milo probably did to the ancient Greeks when she still had all her parts.

The memory of Kendall in that sexy, classy, amazing negligee gave him a more powerful physical reaction than he'd had from seeing any woman before. He scrubbed his hands over his eyes. Shit, he wished for the second time that he had the ability to unsee Kendall the same way he'd unlearned everything he knew about numbers. Unfortunately, with Kendall, he was blessed, or perhaps cursed, with total recall.

He knew her scent, the feel of her skin, the strength of her body against his, the softness of her hair, and, thanks to the bright sunlight shining through the bare window, that she slept commando beneath that wisp of silky fabric.

He hadn't known women actually slept in getups like hers. Lord knew if she were going to bed with him, the damn thing would be off within seconds. That's what he'd always assumed lingerie like that was for—a prelude to foreplay, a sign that the woman wearing it wanted to do anything but sleep. No, a woman who wore that kind of lingerie wanted multiple orgasms, she wanted to lose her voice screaming her lover's name, she wanted to go more than three rounds. Wearing lingerie like that was a serious, I-hope-you-ate-your-Wheaties-this-morning warning. And to think that for the first night in his erotic dreams, Kendall had worn baggy T-shirts and flannel sleep pants. Even in those, she'd been enough to drive him crazy. Every night since had been worse, but now, knowing what he knew, seeing what he'd seen, wanting her the way he did, he might never again be able to sleep under the same roof. He dropped his head in his hands, closed his eyes, trying to erase Kendall's image, and groaned again.

"Jack, are you okay? Is it another headache? Do you want me to get you your medicine? Water?" Hands squeezed his knees and slid up his outer thighs.

His eyes shot open, and there was the real Kendall, kneeling before him on the plaster-littered floor, wearing a pair of faded denim jeans and a worn Boston College sweatshirt with the collar of a faded blue-plaid-flannel shirt poking out beneath the open neck. Concern created a gully between her dark brows—brows he'd wanted to trace more times than he could count, if he could count—which served as punctuation marks for her every expression.

He swallowed hard, and she leaned in closer, sliding between his splayed legs. His heart rear-ended his rib cage, and every muscle in his body vibrated with the need to touch her, but he knew that if he did, if he gave in, he'd be lost.

"Jack, what's wrong?"

Her eyes met his. He couldn't look away, no matter how hard he tried. It was like being caught in a riptide, and he was dragged underwater, powerless to fight it, his only option to go along for the ride and hope that when he was tossed back on the jagged shore, he would still be in one piece.

Kendall's eyes widened, darkened, if that was possible, and her expression, with only the movement of her brows, morphed from one of concern to inquiry, and then slid into a knowing, powerful, self-assured. A damn sexy expression he'd never before seen grace her face.

Her breath caught, and she held it as she slid her hands to his waist and trailed her fingers over his abs. The shock of her hands on him through his shirt was enough to have his stomach muscles tighten so violently, they all but kicked the air from his lungs. She continued her exploration, pausing on his chest, where he was sure she could feel the gallop of his heart beneath her fingers.

"In all my life, I've only really kissed one man. I've only wanted to kiss one man. Until now. Now I only want to kiss you."

"Kendall—" It had been his intention to stop her, but when her fingers wove through the hair at the back of his neck and her lips touched his, all the myriad reasons why this was a very bad idea floated away like smoke from a chimney.

Her kiss was so soft, if not for the warmth of her lips, he could have believed he'd imagined it—until he breathed, dragging in the tantalizing scent of her. It wasn't perfume; maybe it was her soap or shampoo, but her scent was just like her—light and fun with an unexpected hit of seduction that sneaks up on a guy and grabs him by the throat. Her next kiss was less tentative, but no less innocent. God, she was sweet.

His arms wrapped around her, dragging her up and over him as he lay back on the bed. When her hand fisted in his hair, he growled, and when he felt the weight of her body cover his, her breasts pillowed against his chest and her long legs straddling his hips, he lost his tenuous hold on the last frayed thread of his control. Jax took possession of her mouth like he'd dreamt about since she'd come crashing into his life. He cupped her head, changing the angle, and returned the kiss, which went from innocent to incendiary with one deep, hard stroke of his tongue. She tasted of coffee and toothpaste and desire.

He slid a hand along her back, beneath the flannel shirt, amazed by the heat and softness of her skin. Had he ever paid attention to the feel of a woman's skin before? If he had, he couldn't recall. His hand explored each bump of her spine, the dip of her waist, and the dimples right below the loose waistband of her jeans. He wished he could trace the same path with his mouth.

She slid higher, ground her pelvis into his, and damned if his dick didn't jump for joy. It didn't seem to matter that he might very well end up with a permanent zipper tattoo. All that mattered was the sweet sound she made and the way her eyes shot open in surprise and what looked like amazement. Her breathing came in gasps as he kissed her neck, tugging down the collar of her sweatshirt and surging against her heat, swallowing back a groan of his own. God, he didn't think he'd ever been this hard with clothes on. He cursed the layers and layers of clothing separating them. All he wanted to do was touch, kiss, and lick her bare skin. Okay, that wasn't all he wanted. He wanted all of her. He wanted her now. And he wanted her with a fierce, mindless urgency that rattled him and left him panting and shaking.

Kendall rose above him, and, with one swift move, pulled both her shirt and sweatshirt off.

For the second time in one day, all the air burst from his lungs. He stared and realized he'd never seen a woman as intrinsically beautiful as the one offering herself to him now. "God, you're breathtaking." And she was. Dark, almost black, hair fell over her beautifully shaped pale shoulders, teasing her collarbones. The baby-pink lace bra was incongruous with the outfit—but, then, he wasn't sure if there were bras that would reflect denim and flannel. Her skin was opalescent, so pale; he could see the faint blue veins on the inside of her arms. Although he knew it was a mistake, he couldn't stop himself from touching her just once more. But he knew all the same that if they went any further, she'd regret it, and he couldn't stand the thought of her regretting a second of their time together.

"Jack?"

It was all he could do not to cringe. He felt more like Jack than he did Jax or Jackson Finneus Sullivan, but he doubted she'd understand the subtle difference. If she knew the truth, she'd see him as a man just like her ex. Maybe she'd have been right before the accident, but that's not who he was now. "Kendall." He took a deep breath and sat, taking her hips in his hands and sliding her toward his knees and away from his straining erection.

Kendall stared at him a moment and then practically vaulted from his lap, grabbed the inside-out ball of her wadded shirts off the floor, and hugged them against her chest. "I'm sorry. I . . . I thought that you wanted . . ."

"I did. I mean, I do. It's just that you're on the rebound—as cliché as that sounds, that's where you are right now. And me, I don't even know where I am. The thing I do know is that I don't want to be your rebound guy. I don't want to do anything that you'll end up regretting. If we're nothing else to each other, I hope we'll always be friends, and, as a friend, I can't . . ."

A look of horror crossed her face. "You want to be friends?"

"We are friends. As for what I want—" He shook his head, trying to gather his thoughts, trying to figure out how to explain the jumble of feelings ping-ponging around his brain. "Kendall, we're in two different places, you and I." He stood and pulled the tightly held bundle of knotted shirts from her—she didn't let it go easily, and then she hugged herself, covering her breasts with her crossed arms.

Hurt and confusion radiated from her, her eyes wide and glassy.

He took both her forearms in his hands, forcing her to bare herself to him once again before tugging her against him and placing a gentle kiss on her swollen lips. "You have to believe me when I say I want you. I think that's more than obvious." He ran his hands down her back to her waist and pulled her closer so there was no way she could miss his raging erection. "But this can't be just about sex—at least not for me. I want you to want me, not just because I'm here and we're attracted to each other. Not just because you're curious about what it would be like to be with someone other than David. I want you to be with me for the same reasons I want to be with you—because there's no one on earth with whom I'd rather make love."

"But I—"

He cut her words off with another kiss. "Believe me, this is not over. You need time, and I guess I do too. Let's just hope what they say is true."

She held him close and buried her face in his neck.

She fit against him like they'd been molded to each other's specifications—the perfect height; their arms were the perfect length for hand holding; and, he knew, if they were to walk with their arms around each other, hip to hip, their steps would match too.

She burrowed closer—was that wetness he felt against his neck? Had he made her cry? He couldn't tell.

"What is it they say that you hope is true?"

"Time heals all wounds. We're both wounded, just differently." But then when he thought about it, maybe they weren't so different after all. They'd both had the foundation of their lives rocked with the force of a catastrophic earthquake. They were both trying to envision a life completely different from the one they'd led before. They were trying to find their balance on a swiftly shifting landscape. For better or worse, they had only each other to lean against and hold on to.

"I don't want you to be my rebound guy, Jack. I want you because of who you are."

"Have you ever been on the rebound before?"

She pulled away slightly, and he saw fire in her eyes. "You know I haven't."

"Then you don't really know that, do you?"

"I know what I feel. I don't want to be with you because I need to prove I can. I don't want to be with you because I'm not complete without a man in my life. I want to be with you because I care about you, and, well, when I'm with you, I feel this overwhelming, urgent, almost uncontrollable need to rip your clothes off and have my way with you. I've never felt that way before—not even with David. Nothing even close. I never thought I could feel like this."

"Yeah, well, the feeling is definitely mutual." He was all for sexual honesty, but damn, he wished just this once she'd have kept that beautiful mouth of hers shut. He stepped back, turned away, and raked both hands through his hair. It was either that or dragging the rest of her clothes off and taking her up against the wall. "Christ, Kendall, I'm trying to be a gentleman here, and you're not helping."

"I don't want you to be a gentleman."

"Yeah, I got that. But do me a favor and put your shirt on anyway."

CHAPTER
SIX

Jack stood in his room with his back to her, shaking, so charged with frustrated sexual energy, he vibrated with it.

Kendall wanted to slide in behind him, pull his tightly tucked T-shirt out of his pants, and run her hands over the bare skin of his stomach and chest just to see his reaction. Still, the pleading in his voice had her following his stupid instructions.

"Fine." She pulled the two shirts apart and fumbled with the buttons on the flannel shirt. Her hands shook, and she felt like a chastised child. She finally got the damn buttons unfastened and shoved her arms through the sleeves, holding the button band together in a tightly fisted hand, and stomped out of Jack's room.

What had she been thinking, throwing herself at him like that? And why, of all the men in the world, did Jack have to be the one man who, no matter how badly he wanted her, put honor above all else? She'd usually find that quality really attractive—just not now.

She grabbed her jacket by the front door, stuffed it under the same arm that held her wadded sweatshirt, and stomped out to the porch, slamming the cabin door. Cold air sliced through her, stealing her breath, which wasn't surprising, considering she'd yet to button the damn shirt.

"Running away?"

She hadn't heard Jack follow her. Every muscle in her back coiled into knots. "No. I just needed some air." Which was the truth, but she also wanted to get away from him—not that it worked.

"If you were going for air, it looks as if you got more than you bargained for." He stepped forward and pulled the two sides of her shirt together and buttoned the third button, making quick work of the rest, while she stared dumbly up at him. She wondered if that was a dimple she spied peeking through his beard. He took the sweatshirt and coat from her, turned the sweatshirt right side out, and then pulled it over her head, as if she were a four-year-old.

"I can dress myself."

"Then let's see you do it before you freeze to death."

She punched her hands through the sleeves and tugged the sweatshirt down. "Happy now?"

"Not by a long shot."

"Welcome to the club."

He held her coat for her to shrug into, which she grudgingly did. She zipped it right up to her chin, stuffing her hands into the pockets to keep them from shaking or from possibly reaching up to either to kiss him or strangle him. Either would have been a mistake. But, then, she imagined, even mistakes could be enjoyable.

Jack blew out a long and tortured breath and ran his hands through his hair—again. "Kendall, I didn't put the brakes on to hurt you."

All the steam she'd built up cooled and left her feeling like a deflated balloon hovering a foot off the ground. "I know you didn't. It's just that I'm—"

"Frustrated?"

"Yes."

"Horny?"

"Incredibly."

He smiled at that. "Welcome to the club. I'd kiss you now, but I'm afraid it would be like adding gasoline to an already raging fire."

"But you said you just wanted to be friends."

"No, I said we *are* friends. There's a difference."

"If there is a difference, it's lost on me."

"I never said *just*. I said we are friends. But I'm not saying that's all we'll be. I'm not putting any boundaries on our relationship."

"What's that mean—friends with benefits?"

Blue eyes squinted in the sun, revealing tiny lines at the corners. "It means we're friends now, and there's no telling what we'll be in the future. It's a starting point—who knows where we'll end up? After all, we never really know what the future holds, do we?"

"I guess not." She turned it over in her mind, not that it helped. This was just great; she was dealing with a closet Confucius. She was more confused than ever. "So, we're friends without boundaries."

He moved closer and looked down at her with one of those self-deprecating, totally disarming smiles that made her want to reach up and feel if the dimple she spied in his cheek was real or just a play of light on his beard. "So, does that mean you'll take the measurements of the room for me?"

"Sure, why not? What are friends for?"

Jack's smile rounded into a pearly white grin, and he opened the door. "After you."

He followed her into the cabin, and she made sure to swish her hips—just a little. Boundaries. Bah.

Kendall saw Jack's sat phone on his desk while she was taking the measurements and decided, while he was on his quest for drywall, he wouldn't mind if she called her friend, Erin. Besides, who else could she bitch to— Jaime? She didn't think so. And there was no way in hell she could call Addie. But Erin would be there for her, and, on the plus side, she was all the way in Boston, living with the new loves of her life, her fiancé, Cameron, and his little girl, Janie.

Kendall gave herself a pat on the back for fixing them up. She had known the three of them would be perfect for each other, and, in that respect at least, she'd been right. Too bad she didn't have that same psychic karma when it came to her own life.

She handed the measurements to Jack and followed him back to the door, admiring how his jeans molded to his ass. Damn, was he playing tit for tat?

He turned back just before he stepped off the porch and gave her a quick kiss on the cheek, then jumped off the porch and strode down the path toward Jaime's place.

Boundaries, my ass. Kendall closed the door and headed straight for the sat phone. She dialed Erin's number from memory, curled up on the couch that was never quite big enough, and pulled a quilt over her.

"Hello?"

"Erin, it's Kendall."

"Kendall, I've been so worried about you. Where the hell have you been? Jodi called and told me what happened at work. I'm so sorry. I've been calling your cell and the apartment nonstop for a week."

"I'm sorry. I should have thought to call you. It's just that so much has happened, and I've been . . . overwhelmed, I guess. I had to get out of the apartment. There were just too many memories there, you know?"

"Too many memories at the apartment? You're not making sense, Kendall. Are you all right?"

"Yeah, I'm fine now." And she was. Even after the fiasco with Jack, she was still much better than she'd been before she'd met him.

"Is David with you? Because no matter what time I called your place, no one answered."

"Um . . . that's the thing. After I was laid off, I went home early and caught David packing. It turns out he was offered a job promotion in San Francisco and decided to take it."

"You're moving to San Francisco?"

"No, you don't understand. I caught David packing to move out. He'd planned to slither away without even telling me he was leaving."

"What were you supposed to do—figure it out on your own?"

"No, he said he wanted to avoid the drama of an in-person breakup and planned to e-mail me a Dear Jane letter from the airport."

"That . . . that . . . that—"

"Asshole? Dickhead? Coward?" Kendall found herself smiling. Erin was never one to curse, so Kendall helped whenever she could.

"Yes, any or all of the above will do. Do you want to come over? Cam and Janie went over to his dad's for the day. We can hang out here or do some retail therapy."

"No, but thanks. I'm in Harmony. I couldn't stand to

be in the apartment, and, well, I needed to disappear for a while and get my head together."

"Are you okay, sweetie? I know you might not think this now, but maybe it's for the best." Erin sounded angry at David and concerned about her, yet not surprised by the turn of events.

"Not you too."

"What are you talking about?"

"Don't tell me you couldn't stand David either." There was silence on the other end of the phone.

"Why didn't you ever say anything?"

"Because what did I know? The two of you have been together since—what? Puberty? And, really, Cam is the first man I dated seriously. I was hardly in a position to be giving you or anyone else relationship advice. Besides, every time I asked how things were going between you and David, you said you were happy. I honestly couldn't understand it. I thought he must be different in private, because every time I met him, I thought he was kind of a . . . well, you know."

"A prick?"

"Yeah, that'll work."

"I thought we were happy, but you know what they say about hindsight being twenty-twenty. Well, let's just say the view from here hasn't been pretty, and, believe me, I got an eyeful. It's making me question my sanity and my occupation. How can I be a therapist and not have seen the signs? Am I blind?"

"Kendall, you didn't see the signs because you're not your own therapist. You of all people know how important distance is, and when it comes to your own life, there is no distance. This has nothing to do with your ability as a therapist. David was the only man you've ever dated, and you'd been together forever. I'm sure the relationship was comfortable, and it was all you've ever known. You had no other personal experience with which to compare."

She certainly did now—at least when it came to kissing—although she couldn't really consider what she and Jack had done a mere kiss. It was so much more. It was explosive; it was like nothing she'd ever experienced before—not even when she and David were hot and heavy for each other. It made her question every sexual experience she'd ever had with David. Comparing her sex life with David to the kiss with Jack was like comparing a firecracker to a nuclear bomb. She'd never known she could feel like that—so wild, so out of control. It scared her, but, then, a part of her wanted to experience it again.

"I could come up there, if you want—just give me directions. I'll let Cam know, and we can have a sleepover. I don't want you to be alone."

"I'm not."

"I thought your parents were still in Europe on their cruise."

"They are."

"Are you staying with Addie, then?"

"No, I came up to the hunting cabin. I thought I could come up here and no one in town would know. I wanted to be alone and reassess my life, and, more importantly, no one would e-mail or call my parents and tell them what happened. I don't want to ruin their vacation."

"Okay, I can understand that."

Erin might understand, but she couldn't keep the sound of hurt and disappointment out of her voice.

"I turned up the trail to the cabin and broke the axle

on my Jeep. So there I was, sitting in my broken-down car, crying my eyes out, and the next thing I know, there's a guy knocking on my window."

"But you said the cabin was miles from anywhere."

"It is. It turns out Dad rented the cabin to someone at a reduced rate in exchange for fixing the place up. I was stuck—the Jeep wasn't going anywhere, so he invited me to stay. It was too late to go hiking to the closest house, so now I'm here with Jack."

"Are you nuts? You're staying with a complete stranger who is serving as your parents' handyman? What do you know about this guy? Give me the address, and I'll come get you."

"You don't have to. Jack is great, really. I told you about how my dad checks out everyone who rents any of the houses on Sullivan's Tarn, so I know he's not an ax murderer. It turns out we have a lot in common. He's up here for the same reasons I am—"

"He lost his job and his fiancé left him too?"

"No, at least I don't think so. I never asked him if he was involved with someone else. He doesn't wear a wedding ring."

"Someone else? You make it sound as if the two of you are involved. What's going on? And just because he doesn't wear a ring doesn't necessarily mean he's not married. Most men who work with their hands don't wear rings—it's a hazard. I went on a couple of dates with a carpenter who lost his ring finger because his wedding ring got caught on a nail while he was falling off a roof. He survived the fall—his finger, however, didn't, and neither did his marriage, apparently."

Kendall's face tightened. Could that be why Jack put the brakes on their, for lack of a better word, kiss? Could he be in a relationship with someone else? God, and she'd practically thrown herself at him. Of course, she'd planned to only kiss him, but that Robert Burns poem was as true now as the day he wrote it: *The best-laid schemes o' mice an' men/Gang aft agley.* Or, in her case, incendiary. And what was the poor guy supposed to do? She knew he was attracted her; that wasn't the problem.

"Kendall, are you still there?"

"Yeah, I'm here. I was just thinking."

"So, on a scale of one to ten, how hot is this guy Jack?"

"Off-the-charts hot—maybe even hotter. I think there are dimples hiding behind his vacation beard. It's hard to tell, though."

"Uh-huh."

"And he could use a haircut, but I kind of like the just-curling-over-the-collar, a-little-on-the-scruffy-side look."

"You do? David was always so . . . I don't know, perfectly groomed."

"Not Jack—no, he and David are nothing alike. And what can I say? The man looks great in a tool belt. The whole slightly scruffy, he-man thing really works for him."

"Is it working for him or for you?"

"For him. Jack and I are friends."

"I see." The way Erin said that had all the hair on Kendall's arms standing at attention. "Kendall, there are all kinds of friends. What kind of friends are you and Jack?"

"He says we're friends with no boundaries, and I'm trying to figure out what that means, so I called you. I'm completely out of my depth. I've never done this before, remember?"

"Yes, you have."

"Not since I was prepubescent. It's different as an adult."

"What happened?"

"I kissed him, all right? He was sitting on his bed, with his head in his hands, groaning. I thought he had a head-ache—he gets wicked bad headaches since he went headfirst into a tree—and, well, I'd just finished getting dressed—"

"He's seen you naked?"

"No. But he's seen me in my nightgown. By mistake. Twice."

"How does one see you in your nightgown by mistake, twice?"

"The first time, I woke up reaching for David, and then I remembered everything that happened. I was ly-ing in bed, reliving every word. It was ugly—you can't imagine. Anyway, I'm lying there sobbing uncontrollably, and the next thing I know Jack runs in the room like he's ready to fight an attacker or something. He takes one look at me in all my snotty, midmeltdown glory, picks me up as if I were a child, sits me on his lap, and lets me con-tinue to cry all over him. It was a little awkward once I calmed down and he realized what I'd worn to bed."

"Why? What do you wear to bed?"

"Well, you know how David was. He had a fit when we moved in together and he realized I slept in T-shirts and shorts in the summer and sweatshirts and sleep pants in the winter. He insisted I wear the kind of slinky, sexy nightgowns you see in magazines."

"You wear those kinds of nightgowns with your body, and they actually stayed on you for more than a min-ute?"

"Unfortunately, with David, yes."

"Seriously? And you put up with that?"

"Yeah, I did. I always chalked it up to picking my battles. I think I did that a lot."

"So, what happened when Jack got an eyeful of you in all your snotty sexiness?"

"He was a gentleman and avoided looking at me, and his voice got all deep and gravelly, and, well, he looked, I don't know, overheated."

"I'll just bet he did."

"Then he made an excuse and hightailed it out of my room."

"Okay, so that was Sex Sighting Number One. What happened the second time?"

"That was this morning. He was up on the roof working, making an unholy racket, and I heard a strange sound coming from his bedroom. I knew he was on the roof, so I went to look, and the ceiling was falling down."

"What?"

"You heard me. The plaster ceiling was cracking and falling, so I ran out to tell him to stop banging on the roof."

"In your nightgown."

"Well, I hardly had time to get dressed, now, did I? Anyway, I told him about the ceiling, and we both ran inside, and the next thing I know, he goes all he-man and pulls me to him, like I needed protection from the plaster."

"Uh-huh."

"Don't give me that. It was entirely innocent. Anyway, he got all grumbly again and told me to go get dressed."

"You're kidding!"

"No, I'm not. So I went to get dressed, and when I was finished, I heard him groan, like he was in pain."

"I'm sure he was. I hear a case of blue balls is terribly uncomfortable."

"Erin, I thought he had another one of his bad headaches. When I went to his room, he was sitting on his bed with his head in his hands, so I knelt down in front of him to make sure he was okay. And, well, the look in his eyes was not from pain—even I have enough experience with men to know that look."

"Oh, really? So what did he do?"

"Nothing. I . . . well, I kissed him."

"And?"

"God, Erin, David was the only man I ever kissed besides my dad, and he doesn't count. I didn't know it could be like that. It never was with David—not even close. Not even on the same spectrum. I mean, I felt a little tingly and all, but with Jack, it was—"

"Mind-blowing? Earthshaking? An out-of-body experience?"

"Yeah, that."

"Oh, my. So, what went wrong? I know something did, because you don't sound like you've just had the best sex of your life. You wouldn't be calling me if you had."

"We didn't. Not for lack of trying on my part. I was on top of him, and, well, I knew I wasn't the only one into it. But when I ripped off my shirt, he sat up and told me we needed to stop. He said I was on the rebound, and he didn't want to be my rebound guy, and that he was being a gentleman. He said he wanted to be friends."

"Friends? Really? He actually said that?" Erin gave her a highly articulate, all-men-are-bastards growl.

"God, Erin, I wanted to die. How pathetic am I? I practically jumped an injured man who probably has a wife or girlfriend waiting for him at home."

"First of all, give yourself a break. He can't be that injured if he's up working on the roof in January, for God's sake. And you don't know that there's anyone in his life. Although if Jack's as hot as you say he is, then there's a distinct possibility. But look at Cam—he's the hottest man I've ever known, and he hadn't had a relationship in more than two years."

"Only because Janie was in and out of the hospital. Having a seven-year-old with a brain tumor would tend to make dating difficult."

"Or maybe he was just waiting for me."

"Maybe he was waiting for me to fix you up with him. You're welcome, by the way." She could almost hear Erin rolling her eyes. "I knew you'd be perfect for both Cam and Janie, and I was right."

"Oh no, Kendall. We're not discussing me. This is your therapy session, remember?"

"Isn't *that* convenient?"

"Oh yeah, for me it is. It's not too comfortable lying on the therapist's couch, is it? Now you know how I feel."

"Thanks."

"So, how did you leave it with Jack?"

"He told me to put my shirt back on."

———

Jax hiked to Jaime's house, kicking himself the whole way there. God, how could he have been so stupid? Friends without boundaries—what the hell? He didn't even know where he came up with that brilliant idea. No wonder she'd looked at him like he'd gone nuts. And that was right before her face froze in horror.

He'd never forget Kendall's look of shock and humiliation when he pushed her away. She'd been primed and ready and more than willing, and like an idiot he had gone and turned into a fucking Boy Scout. "I did the right thing." If he kept repeating that, maybe he'd start to believe it.

It wouldn't have been fair to Kendall to take advantage of her in a time of weakness. But no matter how many times he told himself that, the other part of his mind was calling him everything from a coward to a fool. Hadn't he told Rocki that it takes a brave person to allow someone to get close, and risk losing them in the end? Looks like he could give advice but he couldn't take it.

It hadn't helped that he'd relived every second of their encounter over and over and over again. The way she tasted, the softness of her skin, the scent of her all hot and bothered, and the sounds she made. God, those sounds would haunt him until the day he died.

He did his best to readjust himself. He didn't think his dick would ever forgive him, which explained his constant erection. A long hike in the bitter cold should have solved his not so little problem. Unfortunately, it only served to make the hike to Jaime's house that much more uncomfortable. He stepped wide, hoping to help things settle in his pants. God, he must look ridiculous.

When he reached Jaime's cabin he stopped on the porch, took a few deep breaths, and willed his hard-on to disappear. He wasn't sure how long he stood there in the cold, but none of the old standby erection crushers of his youth were working. Not even picturing his ninth-grade Spanish teacher, Mrs. Parker's, wrinkly prune face did the trick. He might have had half a chance if the sight of Kendall straddling him, wearing only a pair of jeans and a baby-pink bra, would stop flashing through his brain.

There was no solution for it. As it was, his nose was frozen, and he couldn't feel his toes. He couldn't stand there freezing any longer; he'd just have to go inside and keep his jacket on. No problem.

The cabin door opened before he'd even knocked and revealed Jaime wearing his typical shit-eating grin. "Are you coming in, or are you going to stand there freezing your balls off for another ten minutes?"

Ten minutes? That sounded like a long time. Jax tugged his jacket down and smiled, doing his best to make it look natural. "I have a problem." A big, big problem. Her name was Kendall. But that wasn't why he came.

"Just one? Come on in, take off your coat, grab a cup, and tell me about it while I finish my breakfast."

Jax followed Jaime inside. "It's wicked cold this morning." He tried for a convincing shiver and unbuttoned his jacket but kept it on. "Coffee sounds good. Thanks." He made tracks to the kitchen and kept his back to Jaime while he filled a mug.

Jaime sat at the breakfast bar and ate with one eye on him. "I saw you stomping around outside, like a bull separated from the cows but within scenting distance, so you might as well come clean. What's up?"

He almost groaned. "I need some drywall. It turns out the roof leak was worse than I thought, and now the ceiling in my bedroom is falling down."

"Uh-huh, but that's not why you stood out on the porch in the freezing cold for ten minutes, nor is it why you're still wearing a coat when it's seventy-four degrees in here."

This time he didn't bother stifling his groan. He took a sip of really good coffee and leaned against the counter. "Kendall came running outside straight from bed to tell me the ceiling in my room was caving in, wearing a night-gown right out of *Maxim*—not only was it hot as hell, it was classy. I never knew women actually wore things like that to bed—not to sleep anyway." He shook his head, trying once again to erase the image of her.

"What the hell was she doing in your room?" Anger followed confusion. "You went there, didn't you? And if she was in your room, why weren't you there with her? What the hell is wrong with you? Are you nuts?"

Jax was just about to tell Jaime that it wasn't any of his business what he did or didn't do.

"You did. You so went there. Damn, what's it been—a week?"

He wasn't sure how long he'd known Kendall. All he knew was that it felt as if he'd known her for a long, long time—long enough for him to imagine doing any number of things with and to her. Time was relative, especially to him.

"Damn, and I thought I'd gone fast with my last girl-friend. It took me a good two weeks before I found out what she wore to bed, and, believe me, what I found out would never be shown in any magazine, and it definitely wasn't classy."

"Kendall wasn't staying in my room, and, no, I didn't go there." But, God, he'd wanted to. "Nothing happened." Nothing he wanted to discuss with Jaime. But something had happened. Something he was sure would change his life. The question was, Would it change in a good way or a very, very bad way? He figured right now, the odds were not in his favor.

"Oh, right, nothing happened. I believe that. If nothing happened, then why are you walking around like you have a tent pole in your pants? Something happened.

And you'd better hope to hell that her daddy doesn't find out you've been sampling the goods, or you'll wish that tree you hit had finished you off."

"She kissed me—that's all. And I put a stop to it as soon as I could."

Jaime just raised an imperious brow. "She must be one hell of a kisser, then."

Jaime had no idea, and if Jax had anything to say about it, he never would. "What the hell am I going to do? I put a stop to it this time, but, Christ, Jaime, I'm no saint. And Kendall, well, she's—"

"The hottest thing to come out of Harmony in the past fifty years?"

"I was going to say she's special. But nothing happened, and nothing can happen until she figures out where her head is and I figure out what's going on with mine. She's on the rebound, and I'm . . . damaged."

"Maybe your big head is, but your little head has a mind of its own. Besides, you said yourself there's no telling how your brain will heal. Are you planning to be a monk for the rest of your life? Just because you can't count doesn't mean you can't have a relationship. And it doesn't sound like your little disability makes a damn bit of difference to Kendall Watkins." He stopped and then raised an eyebrow. "She knows about it, right?"

"You said it yourself: we've been sharing a small cabin for more than a week. Of course she knows. And, believe me, there's a definite attraction. I just don't want to be Kendall's one regret."

Jaime laughed at that and stood, collecting his plate and coffee cup, and then headed to the sink. "Oh, don't worry about that. I'm sure the past twelve years with David is number one on the list of Kendall's regrets."

"Shit, Jaime, it's not only that. She's . . . innocent. She's never dated anyone but that jerk. It's a lot of pressure when a woman tells you she's only ever kissed one other man."

"She said that? Wow, I guess that sucks for her, because David didn't let the fact that he was dating Kendall ever stop him from sampling the goods from half the girls in school when he lived here. He was always a bit of a horn dog. Lord only knows what he did in college. Kendall went to Boston College, and he went to Harvard, so it would have been easy to for him to double dip, if you get my drift. Hell, if I remember correctly, Kendall even caught him feeling up Suzie Charles once. You know Suzie—she had a rack that you could shelve a six-pack on and still have enough room to play. I was surprised Kendall didn't dump his sorry ass then."

"If I have anything to say about it, David will be the last man to take advantage of her. I'm not going to. So, for now at least, we're friends, and that's all. Now." He pulled the room measurements from his jacket pocket. "I need some drywall, mud, and tape. Do you think you could make a run to the Home Depot in Concord for me?"

Jaime snapped the dishwasher door closed and wiped his hands on a towel. "Sure, but not for a few days. I'm in the weeds. I'm replacing the hydraulics on a Range Rover and rebuilding a transmission. But if you want, you and Kendall can take my truck and go yourselves. The keys are in the ignition. It will be good for the both of you to get out of the cabin." He turned and shot Jax a smile. "That should keep you safe for a few hours, at least."

"Safe?"

"Hell, yeah. If you're serious about wanting to be a good guy and not take advantage of Kendall, you're going to need protection. Face it, man: if she's half as hot and bothered as you are right now, you're going to be in a world of hurt when she gets you alone again. You, my friend, might just have the world's most sexually frustrated female on your hands."

"Why do you say that?"

Jaime cracked a smile and shrugged. "You know how rumors are. You can't believe everything you hear, but over the years I've learned that there's always at least one kernel of truth in all of them. And if Kendall is as inexperienced as she claims, she has no one with which to compare Dave."

"Of course she doesn't. But what does that have to do with anything?"

"Let's just say that I've heard from more than one reliable source that David was a real dud in the sack. He couldn't measure up, if you get my meaning."

"Women talk about things like that with you?"

"No, of course not. But it's amazing what a man can learn sitting next to a bunch of women on Ladies' Night. After a few drinks, the lot of them invariably start talking about their best and worst sexual experiences. David's name is always mentioned. And I doubt his nickname, *Little Napoleon*, was meant to be a badge of honor."

CHAPTER
SEVEN

B y the time Kendall got off the phone with Erin, she had a plan in place. If Jack wanted to be friends, that's exactly what they would be.

She might have been placed firmly in the friend zone, but she'd be damned if she was going to make it comfortable for him. She had a lot of male friends. Unfortunately, she'd never before had the urge to kiss any of them and rip their clothes off. So, just because the ball was in Jack's court didn't mean she wasn't going to play by her own rules. It could be fun.

Kendall took out all her sexual frustration by cleaning up the mess in Jack's room. She started sweeping, only to give up and use the broom handle to knock the loose pieces of plaster off the ceiling. It had to come down anyway, and it felt really good to demolish something. Who knew?

By the time she got the worst of the plaster off, her hair, her clothes, and every piece of furniture in the room was covered with an inch of dust and chunks of plaster. After most of the cleaning was done, she rearranged the furniture so it was piled along the side where the ceiling was more or less intact, stripped the bed, and tossed the sheets on the pile of Jack's dirty laundry. Then she dragged everything to the mudroom and started a wash, stripped down to her bra and panties and tossed her own clothes in with the rest, and headed toward the shower.

As Kendall rinsed the dust and grime out of her hair, she thought she heard something.

"Kendall?" There was a knock on the door. "Are you in there?"

"Yes, come on in." The shower had a frosted-glass enclosure so Jack would be able to see her silhouette and she'd be able to see his, but neither of them would be able to see the particulars, which worked for her.

He stepped into the bathroom, and she wished she could see the look on his face. "You're in the shower."

"You didn't hear the water?"

"I thought it was the washer."

"I have that going too. I'm multitasking." He didn't move, so she finished washing her hair, arching her back a little more than normal while she rinsed. The water ran over her breasts, and the cold air that rushed in from the open door flirted with her nipples.

She'd never known what a turn-on teasing a man could be. She'd tried with David, but nothing she'd ever done had made much of an impression on him. But, then, everything was different with Jack. No matter what she did, when they were in the same room, she had his full attention and she basked in it, soaking it up like a cat in a sun-filled window. She took the bar of soap and ran it around her breasts and belly, working up a lather.

Jack stood like a statue.

"Did you need something?" She put her foot on the bench and lathered up her leg, sliding her hands from her thigh and down her calf to her foot. She thought she heard him groan, and didn't bother hiding her smile—it wasn't as if he could see it.

She soaped her other leg and then turned to rinse, running her hands all over her body before squirting conditioner in her hair and working it in.

Jack still hadn't answered her question. He stood, seemingly transfixed, his feet shoulder width apart, rooted to the floor.

She'd never understood what women who danced naked for men got out of it—well, other than pretty good money. She had a friend in college who stripped for tuition. Now she was beginning to understand the rush of power she must have felt at having a man watch her every move, knowing how she was affecting him. Knowing Jack watched her, wanted her, and seemed incapable of taking his eyes off her was a complete turn-on. Warmth pooled low in her belly—all it would take was one touch in the right place and she'd explode. She wasn't sure which of them would end up more frustrated—her or Jack.

Kendall finished rinsing the conditioner out of her hair and turned off the water. All she could hear was heavy breathing—hers or his, she wasn't sure. She opened the door a crack and stuck her hand through. "Jack, could you hand me a towel?"

After a moment, when he still hadn't moved, she snapped her fingers. "Jack?"

That startled him. "What did you say?"

She squeezed water out of her hair. "I asked if you'd hand me a towel." She stuck her hand out again, and it came in contact with terry cloth. "Thanks." She took her time drying her face, then ran the towel over her hair before wrapping it around her body and tucking the corner between her breasts.

Jack still hadn't moved.

She took a deep breath to make sure the towel was secure. It was one thing to face him through frosted glass; it was another to step out of the shower with nothing between them but a towel. Still, she went for it. It wasn't as if she had much choice – it didn't look as if he was going anywhere.

She had to look up at Jack since he was still in his boots, which added a good inch to his already impressive height. It was as if the small bathroom had shrunk with him in it, stealing all the air and replacing it with his scent—a combination of wood smoke and pine, with a hint of man. He didn't look happy. His lips formed a tight line, the vein by his temple throbbed, and the scar beneath the part in his hair turned a darker shade of red.

Kendall reached up and touched that spot and felt a divot beneath the smooth, hot skin at his hairline. "What's this?"

"That's where they drilled the hole through my skull. They said the bone will heal in time."

She trailed her finger down the side of his face, over his rough beard, and felt another larger indentation in his cheek—she'd suspected his beard hid a set of killer dimples. This was more of a crease than a divot, but, then, he definitely wasn't smiling now. No, his expression defied description—the closest she could come was a cross between a grimace and a frown. She supposed he could be gritting his teeth too. "Did you want something?"

His eyes flashed with a degree of unmitigated, raw hunger that surprised even her. Maybe she'd pushed him too far?

Jack blinked, and the muscle in his jaw jumped. He took a deep breath and looked like if he could count to ten, he'd be on his third or fourth round. "Jaime—" It came out in a croak. He cleared his throat, swallowed hard, and tried again. "Jaime isn't going to be able to make a run to Concord for a few days, but he offered to let us use his truck, if you're okay driving it."

"Sure, I guess. I mean, how hard can it be?" The way his eyes flared again told her that was a bad choice of words, but it didn't keep her from smiling. She never knew that being bad could be so much fun. She could only hope all this teasing was having at least as much of an effect on him as it was having on her.

She sneaked a peek at his fly—unfortunately, he had both fisted hands stuffed in the front pockets of his jeans, making it impossible to gauge her progress. The lack of knowledge in that respect was not unusual for her; she wasn't sure if she was just blind to it or if David had superhuman control, because she'd never once seen him tent his pants the way they talked about in the romance novels she loved to read. But, then, she had to take those with a grain of salt—they were fiction after all, and she knew this because almost every hero she'd ever read about sounded as if his erection reached porn-star proportions. Unfortunately, she'd never seen a pornographic film. Still, she didn't imagine men could be that different size-wise. Could they? She wasn't sure, but was definitely interested in finding out. Maybe she'd talk to Erin about renting one when she returned to Boston.

"Are you done in here?" Jack's voice sounded pained.

"Me? Um, sure. I still have to do my hair and makeup, but I can do that after I get dressed." She didn't wait for a reply; she slid past him and out the door, feeling his eyes on her all the way down the hall to her room. Score one for the novice.

Kendall looked through the clothes she'd brought. She hadn't packed to impress—that was for sure. Her only plan was to veg alone in a mountain cabin, but, then, she told herself, sexy was all in the attitude, anyway. She slid into her prettiest bra-and-panty set, because even if he never knew what she wore beneath her clothes, she'd know. She took her time smoothing on shea butter lotion with a hint of frankincense and myrrh, her favorite scents, and then pulled on a plain white tank, her moss-colored mock-wrap sweater with a shawl collar that dipped low on top and had an asymmetrical hem, gray stonewashed jeans, and her favorite cowboy boots with tassels hanging from the top that swung with every step. They might not be very practical, but when it came to shoes and boots, practicality was way overrated.

"Kendall, when will you be ready to leave?"

She stepped out of her room and almost ran into Jack. "Five minutes. Why? What's the rush?"

"I was thinking we could have lunch out—I'm hungry. It'll be my treat."

She headed back to the bathroom to do her makeup, shaking her head all the way. "Oh no, we'll go dutch. We're friends, remember? You taking me out to lunch would be too much like a date, and friends don't date, do they?"

"Sure they do. How do you think you go beyond friendship?"

She turned toward him and stopped just inside the bathroom. "I figured having sex would do the trick. But if you think friends date, then I guess we wouldn't be breaking your rules." She went to the sink and pulled out her makeup case.

"Rules?" He hovered in the doorway to the john,

looking like the dictionary definition of the word *indignant*. "I don't have rules."

"Oh, come on. Of course you do—you're a man. You probably have a whole list of things that have to happen to prove to you that I'm not on the rebound." Just like David with his list of things that they had to accomplish before they could set a wedding date. Just the thought of being caught in the same kind of situation made her angry. She bit her lip to keep from saying so, then changed her mind. To hell with keeping her mouth shut and going along to get along. She was starting down a new path, and she'd say what she thought. Holding back had never done her any favors. "You know"—she turned to him, eyeliner in hand—"just because you have rules doesn't mean I have to follow them. I never agreed to play that game. I can do whatever I want."

"I'm not playing a game. I have no rules. I just think it's too soon for you to jump into something like—"

"Sex? And who gave you the power to decide what I am or am not ready for? Maybe it's you who's not ready, and, if that's the case, that's fine. That's your choice. But don't think for a moment that you can decide anything for me. I'm done with abdicating my decision making. From now on, my life, my sexuality, and my future are in no one's hands but my own. Got it?"

"Oh, I got it, all right." His voice went down a few octaves along with his volume, but the words seemed to echo in her very bones. He was pissed, that much was obvious, but not frighteningly so. His anger was hot as hell but held in check, like the controlled burn of a rocket launcher. "But you need to understand something too. I'm not David. I don't take advantage of people, and I don't play games—not with you, not with anyone. And just so we're on the same page, there's one more thing you need to know."

"Oh, really? And what's that?"

He stepped closer, close enough for her to see the silver in his blue eyes and feel his coffee-scented breath on her cheek. "The next time you invite me into the bathroom when you're showering, you'd better be willing to share a whole lot more than just the hot water, sweetheart. Are we clear on that?"

She grabbed the edge of the porcelain sink and held on. Oh, my. It made her want to strip back down to nothing and turn on a lot more than just the water. "Crystal."

Jax held his breath while Kendall made her way across the cabin to the door. He'd never seen her wear makeup before. The first time they'd met, most of the makeup she'd worn was running down her face. She didn't need it, but even he had to admit that whatever she'd done looked natural but accentuated her already stunning facial features. And then there was what she'd done to her eyes, all smoky and sexy. That alone took her from stunning to stellar, and she'd accomplished it all in what she said was five minutes flat.

He remembered his last girlfriend used to take two hours to get ready to leave the house, and a two-hour wait seemed like a dog's age compared to Kendall's five minutes.

The high heels of her boots tapped out a rhythm across the worn wood floor. She knew the path to Jaime's place as well as he did, so there was no reason to point out the ridiculousness of her choice of footwear. If Kendall was anything like his sister, she wouldn't care, but, then, Rocki would run a track meet in stilettos, and, knowing her, she'd probably medal. He might have to hold Kendall up by her belt loops the entire way down the hill to Jaime's, but he figured there were worse things than holding Kendall close for a long hike.

Jax helped Kendall with her coat and watched as she pulled on a cute knit, billed cap before wrapping a matching scarf around her neck and mouth. All he could see of her were those amazing dark eyes and her perfectly shaped nose. That alone was enough to make walking a chore.

"Do you have the measurements I took?

He patted his pocket. "Right here. Jaime was nice enough to figure out the number of sheets of drywall to buy, and I made a list of the tools I'll need to get the job done. We'll pick those up too."

"That's not necessary. We can sneak into my parent's garage and get everything on the list. You shouldn't have to spend a bundle on tools that Dad already has. He'd blow a gasket if he knew you were buying duplicate tools. He has a thing about that."

Jax shook his head. "No, it's not worth taking a chance on you being spotted. Besides, it's not a big deal. Come on, I'm starved."

Kendall slid the whole way to Jaime's place, and he was right: there were worse things than keeping Kendall from killing herself on the way down. And right now, any excuse to touch her worked for him, since he'd only allow himself platonic touches for the foreseeable future. And wasn't that just the berries?

He helped Kendall into the cab of the truck, which, without a running board, required the use of upper body strength, and then did some deep breathing exercises on his way around the back of the truck before he slid in beside her.

He didn't know if she was wearing perfume or what the hell it was, but she smelled so good, it made him want to permanently attach his nose to her body. "If you just go down here"—he pointed to the end of Jaime's drive—"there's a trail that will bring you to the highway so we can avoid driving through town entirely."

"I know that, but how do you?"

"Jaime told me about the shortcut this morning."

"Oh." She started the truck and put it in four-wheel drive before shifting into drive. "That was nice of him."

No, that was a quick save. He had to remember to mind his p's and q's.

"It will take about forty-five minutes to get to Concord."

He buckled his seat belt. "Is there a particular reason you're telling me that?" He realized that she'd been telling him the timing of things a lot.

She looked at him and then back to the sorry excuse for a road. "I thought it was about time you started re-learning the things you lost. When a person has a brain injury, and he loses the ability to walk, he goes to physical therapy to learn how to walk again."

"And you think if you tell me how long things take, my brain will heal?"

She shrugged. "I don't know if it will heal, but you'll start to relearn things. You'll have the information to put time and numbers together, and you'll do it. It will just take time."

He did not want Kendall teaching him how to count like a freakin' kindergartener, and he didn't want to be anyone's little pet project.

"Oh, now you're angry."

"I am not."

"Oh yes you are. I've seen you angry, remember?"

"No, you haven't."

"Liar." But she said it with a smile on her face. "In the bathroom, about an hour ago. Don't tell me you weren't angry when you issued your little warning."

"That wasn't a warning, Kendall. It was a promise."

"If you were trying to scare me, it backfired."

"Scaring you was never my intention."

She raised an eyebrow at that. "It would have served you right if I had done the first thing that came to mind."

As tempting as it was to ask, he knew he'd be walking straight into dangerous territory. He had been angry, but he'd been more turned on than anything else. Still, at least they'd gotten off the subject of fixing him.

"You're not curious?"

Oh, he was curious, all right—the way a person who has a fear of heights is curious about skydiving. "I suppose I am, in a purely theoretical way."

"That's easy for you to say now that we're miles away from the closest shower."

He watched and waited. He'd learned a long time ago that the less you say, the more information you obtain. Dealing with a therapist was a challenge, but even Kendall wasn't immune to the power of silence.

"No, I don't think I'm going to tell you. I'll just keep it in my arsenal for possible later use. So, back to your little anger issue."

"I have no anger issue."

She ignored his response and continued without even sparing him a glance. "It's not as if a person comes out of the womb, telling time and judging distance. It's something people learn from the time they're babies."

Silence was his only weapon, although he could think of much more pleasant ways to shut her up. Unfortunately, he didn't think it was safe to kiss her while she was driving. The last thing he needed was another head injury.

"I just thought if you were given the information, you'd see the difference between the five minutes it takes me to put makeup on and a forty-five minute drive."

"Why do I get the feeling this will be the longest forty-five minutes of my life?"

"It's a male-ego thing. Jack, you're strong and smart and kissable. And this problem of yours isn't permanent, so do yourself a favor and get over it already. Let me help."

"Do I have any choice?"

"No."

"Fine."

Kendall blathered on about time and distance and he tuned out, well, as much as he could sitting next to her. He might not have listened closely, but she had his full attention in every other way. He watched the expressions cross her face and picked up on her little habits, like the way she bit her lower lip when she was trying to remember something, the way her face lit up when she talked about her friend Erin and some little kid named Janie, and the cloud that settled over her when she talked about losing her job.

Jack went around the truck and helped Kendall out—as much as she'd allow. Still, she didn't snatch her hand away when they walked to the restaurant. He'd been right: she was the perfect hand-holding partner—her hand slipped right into his without a lot of jostling for a comfortable position. It was as easy and as natural as their kiss had been. Maybe *comfortable* was the wrong word, because their kiss had been anything but comfortable. Still, even with all its heat, they had no problem coming together without any teeth gnashing or nose bending. In his experience, if a couple had to work on holding hands and kissing, the sex would suck. He had a frighteningly strong feeling that if or when he and Kendall finally made love, he'd be down for the count, if he wasn't already.

He might be mentally challenged, but he had enough of his faculties intact to know that Kendall Watkins was a rare gem. He might not be able to tell time, but he knew that a woman who could shower, dress, and be ready to hit the town in less time than it took him to get antsy was a keeper. And to be able to do that and look good enough to stop traffic, which she accomplished twice between the truck and the front door of the restaurant, was a real feat.

By the time they made it to the table and ordered drinks, he was rethinking his brilliant idea about taking Kendall out in public. She might not notice all the male attention she garnered, but he sure as hell didn't miss it, and, for the first time, he didn't appreciate the knowledge that his date would be the object of several fantasies that weren't his.

"You're still mad?"

"I'm not mad."

"Then why are you making your mad face?" She held up her phone, pulled up an app that turned the damn thing into a mirror, and turned it at him. "See? That's your mad face."

He pushed her hand down until the phone lay flat on the table, but he didn't move his hand off hers. Fine, so he was mad—just not at her.

She didn't pull her hand away; she only smiled at him like she would a recalcitrant child. "Low blood sugar? I didn't fix you breakfast this morning."

"Kendall, you don't have to fix me breakfast, but I'd appreciate it if you'd order lunch."

The server was the one multitasking now. He stared at Kendall's cleavage, pen poised, waiting for her order.

"Oh, right." She shot the guy an indulgent smile. "I'll have the lobster BLT with a salad and the house dressing on the side."

Jax cleared his throat to get the server's attention. "I'll take the Hangover Burger, medium rare, with fries." He stared at the guy until he backed away.

"Yup, that's definitely a mad face."

Time to change the subject. "Kendall?"

She smiled sweetly. "Yes?"

"In the truck you said that you worked as a social worker at the Boston Children's Hospital."

"I did. I'm surprised you remember. You were so distant, I thought you might be having an out-of-body experience."

He ignored the gibe. "But you're a licensed marriage and family therapist, correct? Doesn't that make you overqualified for a hospital social-worker position?"

"I don't know if *overqualified* is the right word. I have my master's in social work, and I'm a licensed marriage and family therapist. One of the reasons I took the position at the hospital was because it gave me the opportunity to clock my clinical hours and have the supervision necessary to be licensed. After I had my hours, I took the exam, but I didn't want to start a practice in Boston, only to have to leave it in a year or two. I'd planned to go out on my own when I moved to Harmony."

"What were you waiting for?"

"David. You see, he had a list of things we needed to accomplish before we could set a wedding date and move home."

She tried to pull her hand away, but he held on and leaned forward. "So, those were the rules you threw in my face this morning?"

She stared at their joined hands and shrugged. "Maybe." It took a while before she finally looked at him, but her defeatist expression took away any sense of victory he thought he'd feel after winning the waiting game. "Six years ago David asked me to marry him, and I said yes. When we started talking about a wedding date, he said he wanted us to finish college first. That sounded reasonable, so I agreed, but then in our senior year, David thought we should wait until after grad school."

"And what did you want?"

"I wanted to get married, but, again, waiting until we finished our education didn't sound unreasonable, so I didn't argue. Then, after grad school, he wanted to wait until we saved enough money for a down payment on a house. When I told him I didn't want to wait, he said he was only thinking of me, that he wanted to be a good provider, blah, blah, blah. Personally, I didn't care if we lived in a shoe box."

"But he did."

"That's what he said, and I believed him at the time, but now I know better." She made a face he couldn't catalog. All he knew was it wasn't good. "The only reason I agreed to move in with David was because we were engaged. I couldn't afford to live alone in Boston on my salary. Besides, living together was the only way we'd be able to save money. It would have been impossible if we had to pay rent for two places on top of my student loans. I had two choices: move in with David or move home. As you can imagine, my parents were less than thrilled with my decision to live in sin." She shrugged as if it were no big deal, but he knew her parents; he knew what it felt like to let Grace and Teddy down. "It didn't seem as if I had much of a choice, so I took the job at the hospital, where I could get my clinical hours and supervision for my license."

"Which is a huge accomplishment."

She shrugged it off as if it were nothing. "Now I see all David's rules and conditions for what they were. He was stringing me along for six years, and I don't understand why I didn't see it then. Six years is a long time."

"Do you miss him?"

She looked at their joined hands and shook her head. "No, not in the way I thought I would. I guess I miss the idea of him. Now I see that what David thought was best for us translated to what was best for him. Lesson learned. I'll never make that mistake again."

"Right. You're finished abdicating your decision making. Your life, your sexuality, and your future are in no one's hands but your own." He squeezed her hand. "I remember."

"Sorry." She bit her bottom lip so hard, he was worried she'd draw blood. "I guess I was painting you with the same brush, and that wasn't fair, but . . ."

"But nothing. You need to decide what you want. I'm not making the rules, Kendall. I learned a long time ago that the only things I can control are myself and my actions. Contrary to popular belief, I have no great urge to control anyone's life but my own. Now, that's not to say, hypothetically at least, that I have no interest in being part of someone else's life. But being part of someone's life is more about sharing than control, isn't it?"

"In theory, yes. In practice? I'm not so sure."

"You wouldn't use only one test subject if you were doing a study, would you?"

"No."

"Yet that's essentially what you're doing, isn't it?"

She didn't disagree, but she didn't agree either. She just tucked into the meal the server set in front of her. She took one bite of her sandwich and let out an appreciative groan—the same sound she'd made the second she'd straddled him earlier.

He shifted in his seat and stared at his burger, but the only thing he wanted to bite into was sitting on the opposite side of the table.

CHAPTER
EIGHT

K endall let Jack help her back into the truck, not because she needed help, but because he'd taken her hand as they exited the restaurant and she was loath to let it go. His hands were now firmly on her waist, and she leaned back against him, craning her neck to see his face. "You're not going to answer my question, are you?"

At the restaurant, when Jack had handed her a stack of cash with which to pay the bill, she'd found four slips of paper stuffed into the billfold, each containing women's names and phone numbers. Before he ripped them from her grasp, she'd read the offer of a sponge bath — aloud. It was clear that he'd taken them and stuffed them in his wallet. It was clear that he'd known exactly what they were. And it was also clear that he hadn't had enough interest to even look at them. His face had turned so red, it was laughable as well as charming.

"Look, when I left the hospital, all the nurses knew I wasn't allowed to drive until after my next MRI, so a few of them offered me a ride to the hospital."

"From what I saw, that wasn't the only kind of ride Rita was offering."

He lifted her right off her feet and sat her in the truck like he would a child and closed the door.

Kendall was still laughing when he climbed in beside her. "Where to, Romeo?"

"Home Depot." He didn't look happy.

Jack obviously wasn't one who appreciated being teased—at least not about women's telephone numbers, which only made teasing him all the more fun. He huffed and grumbled like a bear while she started the ignition and turned toward the strip mall.

Kendall followed a still-grumbling Jack into the Home Depot. He grabbed an orange cart and looked like a man relieved to be back in his element. He whistled his way through the store, collecting materials. Sheets of drywall stood on end between the cart's upright bars, which were obviously designed to hold the stuff. A tub of mud sat on the other side, along with a pile of tools. He set a box of drywall tape on the cart and turned to her. "Why don't you go get the paint while I finish up here? We'll need a gallon of primer and a gallon of paint."

She tilted her head. "How do you know how much we need?" She didn't even know that.

"Jaime told me. I'll meet you there once I finish up here."

"Okay," she turned and walked toward the front of the store, feeling the heat of his eyes on her the whole way down the long aisle. "Paint?" She didn't know where the damn paint aisle was. She stopped, looking for signs.

"Can I help you?" The man who had helped Jack load the drywall smiled down at her. "If you're looking for your husband, you might try the lumber aisle." He pointed behind her. "He said there was damage to the lathe, so he's going to have to rip it down and add furring strips to the ceiling joists, since they're in bad shape."

She must have had a quizzical look on her face.

"They give you something to screw or nail the drywall to."

"No, I know what furring strips are—it's not that. It's just that Jack's not . . . never mind." She didn't need to tell the man Jack was not her husband. "Thanks, but, actually, I was looking for the paint aisle."

"Oh, you're one of those divide-and-conquer couples. Right this way." He headed in the opposite direction, so she followed. "The couples who can shop separately are my favorites. I bet you even get your hands dirty."

She smiled at that. "How did you know?"

"No rings, and your manicure looks like it's taken a real beating."

It had. "I was pulling down plaster first thing this morning."

"You know, they say a couple who can go through a remodel together can get through anything."

"I hadn't heard that. But I suppose it makes sense."

"It sure does. It takes teamwork and good communication—especially when you're trying to drywall a ceiling. You two will do fine."

He stopped in front of the paint desk. "I'll just go on back and make sure your husband has everything he needs. He said you came all the way from Harmony. I'd hate for you to forget something and have to make a trip back."

"That would be great. Thanks for all your help." She shook her head, wondering what made the man think she and Jack were married. But, then, she'd never come to a home-improvement store with a friend before. Actually, she'd never come to a home-improvement store with anyone but her father. David couldn't even manage to hang a picture. She'd always handled everything like that. She'd even painted the entire apartment — alone. He was supposed to help but remembered that he had to work that weekend. She'd always thought that had been a convenient excuse.

"Can I help you find something?"

She blinked and found the paint guy staring at her while she'd been woolgathering. "I need a gallon of paint and primer."

He motioned to the wall of color chips. "Color?"

"White."

"Flat, satin, or gloss?"

"Flat ceiling paint." There, that was easy. She grabbed a couple of rollers, covers, brushes, and a paint tray while the guy shook the daylights out of the can. She thought about buying a tarp, but figured an old sheet would work just as well.

"Ready to go?"

Jack's voice made her jump. He stood so close, his breath warmed her cheek.

The damn man was always sneaking up on her. "Just about." She reached for a roll of painter's tape and tossed it on the pile.

"Here, let me take that." Jack took the tray and put it on the cart while the guy came around to add the paint to their pile. "I think we're done, unless there's something else you want to look at."

"You know, actually, there is. Go on ahead and check out. I'll be there in a minute."

He gave her a quizzical look but nodded, and she headed toward the aisle where she'd seen the tile. Plain terra-cotta tile was cheap, so she didn't think twice. She visualized the inside of the oven and kicked herself for not having the idea before she'd left; she would have measured the damn thing. But, then, she'd had other things on her mind, and the last thing she was thinking about was dinner. She grabbed the tiles she thought she needed and carried them back to the checkout line.

Jack did a double take.

"They're for dinner. Let's stop at the grocery store on the way home. I need to pick up a few things." Actually, she needed to stock the pantry with more food than she'd ever purchased at one time before. She'd thought the food Addie had sent would hold them over longer, but she'd never seen anyone eat as much as Jack. Then she'd heard about the nor'easter headed their way, and that always meant making sure she had a three or four days' supply of food and water on hand—and with Jack, she'd have to double the usual amount. On the bright side, at least she'd have plenty of time to cook, because after their discussion over lunch, she needed to do some serious therapy.

Jax lied like a rug and sent Kendall into the grocery store alone, claiming he wanted to make sure nothing was stolen from the back of the truck. He hated lying, but the last thing he wanted to do was tell her he was going to the pharmacy next door to buy a box of condoms.

He watched her disappear through the sliding doors, took the keys from the ignition, and then ran to the pharmacy.

He didn't want Kendall to know sex was even a remote possibility—because it wasn't. Or at least it shouldn't be.

But he was only human and didn't think he'd survive another of Kendall's shower scenes or seeing her in one of her every-man's-fantasy nightgowns. Or, God forbid, if she kissed him again. Jaime was right: he needed protection in more ways than one.

He came to a screeching halt in front of the checkout counter, where two teenage clerks stood chatting. "Condoms?"

The guy at the desk sporting a sorry excuse for a mustache shot him a you-lucky-dog grin. "Aisle nine."

Shit, more numbers. "Show me."

The girl came around the counter and walked a few aisles over. "They're just down here, sir"—she pointed—"on your right."

Great. Now he had a teenage girl watching him buy condoms. He felt like a complete perv. "Thanks." He waited until she'd turned back to look for his normal brand. His gaze landed on a bright blue box he'd never seen before and he did a double take. Vegan condoms? Damn, only in New Hampshire. He shook his head, grabbed a small box of large-size Trojans, and ran to the front, where he threw the box and his Amex card on the counter. He was back in the truck in no time and sat for what seemed like forever, waiting in the cold for Kendall, with the box of condoms burning a hole in his pocket.

Jax watched Kendall push an overloaded grocery cart to the truck. It looked like he'd be eating damn well.

The first thing she handed him when he got close enough was his billfold. "It's probably a good thing you can't count, because I just did a lot of damage."

He stuffed his wallet into his back pocket and grabbed the economy-size toilet paper threatening to slide off the top. "I don't know if I should be excited about the prospect of more good food or worried about your need for therapeutic cooking."

Kendall didn't say anything; she just bit her lip and helped him stash the groceries in silence. He went to return the cart and found her waiting impatiently behind the wheel with the engine running.

He didn't say anything for miles. He did his best to count mile markers, trying to remember the order of numbers he saw swimming in his head when he closed his eyes. He did his best to hold the familiar feeling of panic at bay; he'd rather deal with that than deal with Kendall's lip-chewing shutout. She drove in silence for a long uncomfortable while. Finally, he couldn't take it anymore. "You're being unusually quiet. No pointing out mile markers? No telling me how fast you're going?"

"You hate when I do that."

It was the truth, but anything would be better than watching her abuse that poor bottom lip. "What's the matter?"

"Maybe nothing's the matter. Maybe I'm just PMSing."

"Are you?"

She looked at him and laughed. "Usually when a woman brings up PMS or cramps, men shut up and leave them alone."

"Not if you're related to my sister, you don't. You can't. She'd chase me down and tell me every gory detail. She's even made me go out in the middle of the night to buy her tampons and chocolate, and one time she forced me to pick up her birth-control pills. There are some things big brothers are not supposed to know—his sister's choice of contraceptives is one of them—but nothing is sacred with her."

He knew his face was flaming, but at least it got Kendall laughing again and, for a moment, chased the shadows out of her eyes. "You're under no obligation to talk about whatever it is that's bothering you, but if you want to, I'm here."

"I just want to go home."

So did he. *Home.* He let the word roll around his mind and tried to remember what it felt like to walk into his place in Chicago. *Cold* and *impersonal* were the first two words that came to mind when he pictured stepping into his apartment after a long day at work. It held all the warmth one would expect from walking into a hotel room.

The cabin might not be his legal residence, but, for now at least, it felt like what he thought home was supposed to feel like. It was full of memories of spending boys-only weekends with his dad, doing guy stuff—like drinking his first beer. It's where his dad taught him to shave, told him about women and sex and love and the responsibility that comes along with all three. He remembered the day he and his dad picked out that horrible couch for the hunting cabin. He'd wanted the bigger one, but his dad refused to buy it. He didn't agree then but now had to admit his father's reasoning had been sound. When he'd asked his dad why, his old man told him that he'd known Jax would end up sneaking girls up to the cabin, and, in his experience, it was a lot easier to get a girl in trouble on an innocent-looking couch than it was to talk her into bed. His dad bought the small, uncomfortable couch so Jax couldn't get in too much trouble with the girls on it. Turns out the old man was right. Jax never did get lucky in the cabin. But then his parents had been killed, and he and Rocki had been sent away to different boarding schools. Ancient history.

Now he was a grown man, and the cabin was old and

run down, but with Kendall there, it felt different than it had before. And while that feeling made him want to pack his bags and run, at the same time, he dreaded leaving. Being with Kendall felt too good. Unfortunately, in his experience, nothing that good survived. And when that feeling died, all that he would be left to deal with were the scars. He didn't need any more scars, but, then, it was probably already too late to come out unscathed. Shit, his head hurt.

"I bought a pack of cards."

He groaned. "Why?"

"To play strip poker. Why else do you buy cards?"

"Gee, let me think. . . . How about to teach a brain-damaged guy numbers?"

She slid a sideways glance. "Think of it as multitasking."

"You just want to get me naked."

"Maybe." She shot him a smile, and just like that his dick danced in his pants.

"What caused the sudden mood change?"

She shrugged and pulled off the highway onto the track to the cabin, and stopped to put the truck back in four-wheel drive. "I just thought of something that made me feel better about life in general."

"I'm afraid to ask what that could be."

"Chicken."

"Maybe, but whatever it is, I'm hoping it has something to do with all that food you bought."

Kendall hauled in the groceries while Jack brought in the building supplies. Every time he stepped off the porch, his gaze swept the clouds gathering in the distance and heading their way. "Looks like it's going to be a doozy of a nor'easter."

"Sounds like it too. It was the talk of the grocery store. But don't worry—I bought plenty of milk, bread, and toilet paper."

"I knew I could count on you to think of the necessities of life. But if you knew about the storm, why didn't you mention it to me?"

She shrugged. "I knew as soon as you heard, you'd be anxious to get home and finish working on the roof. Your worrying wouldn't get us home any sooner."

He pulled a few sheets of drywall out of the bed of the truck, set them on the top of his booted foot, and shook his head.

"Problem?"

"No. I find it funny that you think you've got me all figured out."

He didn't mean *funny* as in *ha-ha*; he meant *funny* as in *weird*. "Don't I?" She grabbed four more grocery bags. "I am a professional. Or at least I have a license that says I am." She looked him up and down, trying to imagine him naked. "It's not that difficult."

He took a step closer, drywall and all. "And what exactly have you learned?" His deep voice sounded loud in the sudden stillness around them. It was as if the earth were holding its breath, waiting for the storm to hit.

She didn't think this was the time or place to mention that he could turn her on just by breathing, or that she'd somehow acquired an insatiable lust for him—one she'd never felt for anyone before. He'd figure that out all by himself in due time. "I've learned a lot of things about you, but mostly that you're a ridiculously good guy with a very strong moral code."

He let out a breath he seemed to be holding and looked equal parts relieved and disappointed.

"Lucky for me"—she put on what she thought was a sexy smile—"I'm a code breaker."

Kendall didn't wait to see his reaction. She didn't need to; the choking behind her said she'd hit her target. She took the last of the groceries into the house and dug through the bag of personal items containing the three boxes of condoms she'd bought. It was the first time she'd ever purchased condoms—David had always handled that when they were younger. Kendall hadn't known what size to get, so she bought a selection—choosing the largest box she could find of medium, large, and extra large, since she couldn't imagine a guy as big as Jack needing a small. She ran to her room and stashed them in the bedside table before Jack returned.

The clerk's eyes had just about bugged out of her head as she rang up the condoms. She probably thought Kendall was opening a brothel. "Gag gift," Kendall had explained, and smiled innocently. The whole innocent look was way too easy to pull off for her peace of mind. Her lack of experience had never bothered her before; after all, she and David had been each other's firsts. He'd never complained, and she'd never felt as if she'd missed out on anything, until she met Jack. Kissing Jack had been an experience like no other—just the thought of it was enough to leave her squirming in her seat. She'd never before experienced that much heat and intensity. Now she wondered what else she'd missed.

"Earth to Kendall."

She turned to find the object of her erotic musings talking to her. "What?"

"Are you okay?" He came closer and felt her fore-head. "You look a little flushed."

No doubt. "I'm fine."

Jack trailed a finger down the side of her face and lifted her chin, forcing her to look at him. "Are you sure?"

She dragged her gaze from his and cleared her throat. "Positive."

"If you don't need help putting away the groceries, I'll get to work on the roof. I need to get it dried in before the storm hits, so we don't lose another ceiling."

"I know. Go ahead. I'll square away everything in the kitchen and then make dinner."

She put away all the food, reorganized the now-overflowing pantry, and then scrubbed the unpolished terra-cotta tiles with kosher salt, hoping her idea would work, because she'd had a killer craving for pizza. Since her pizza stones were gathering dust in her kitchen in Boston, she knew she'd have to improvise. She laid the tiles tight against each other, lining both oven racks. They overhung the rack just a hair, but if the door closed, it might actually work better than the too-small pizza stones she'd always used. The tiles certainly increased the surface area. Visions of bread making flew through her mind and made her mouth water. More space meant larger pizzas, and when you were feeding a guy who ate as much as Jack did, that was a good thing. She held her breath and closed the oven door. It worked.

Kendall did a little happy dance and measured out enough flour to make two large pies. She loved baking bread and making dough; all the stirring and kneading were great outlets for stress and frustration. And that was something that had been building since she'd opened her eyes that morning. The banging coming from the roof did nothing but remind her of the dream she'd woken to, the kiss that left her hot and needy and humiliated, the condoms in her drawer, and the man on the roof. She blew out a breath and took out all of her sexual frustration on the dough. At the rate she was going, she'd need to make a hundred crusts to center herself.

Two hours of cooking, cleaning, and laundry later, she pulled on a coat and stepped outside, picking her way around the cabin, following the trail of packed snow until she saw Jack standing on the roof. She didn't bother asking him how he was doing; she could tell from the set of his shoulders all was right in his world. Lucky man. "Question."

"Shoot."

"How do you feel about anchovies?"

"Love them. You?"

"Same."

"Anything else?"

The first flurries were already falling; the roof would be slick in no time. "How's it coming?"

"Almost done."

"Be careful you don't fall off."

She ran back inside and started on a Caesar salad. If Jack loved anchovies, he'd probably like that too.

———

Jaime sat in his office with his back to the door. He entered the part number into the computer and then added the time for labor. He'd found out years ago that if he wanted to concentrate on anything—especially stuff he hated, namely paperwork—he had to have his back to the action.

The hair on his neck stood on end, and when he took a breath, he knew why. He cringed and didn't even bother to turn around. "Addie, what the hell are you doing here?"

"Nice to see you too."

"That's not an answer to my question." He turned to look at her—it was a Mud Brown Day. Man, that was worse than Sweatshirt Gray. She wore a long, shapeless skirt; those ugly faux UGGs she favored when the weather went bad; and an oversize, shit-brown hoodie. Her hair was long, and if she'd done something with it, it could have been pretty. Today it looked like a bunch of five-year-olds had used it as a paintbrush. "What the hell happened to your hair?"

She shrugged as if she didn't care that she looked more ridiculous than usual. "Today we were finger painting." She held up her hands to display that every color of the rainbow was stuck under her short nails. "If you think that's bad, you should see my smock."

"There's some decent soap in the shop—go scrub your hands with it. It'll get anything out from under your nails. Your hair is above my pay grade."

"I didn't come here to wash up."

"I know that. What I don't know is why you're here."

She came in and frumped her way to the seat opposite his desk. "I'm worried about Kendall. There's a storm coming, and I'm not sure she has enough food."

Food was the least of her worries. "I let her use my truck to go to Concord today. She wanted to pick up a few things at the grocery store, and I needed a part—it was a twofer."

"But she's all alone in that cabin."

"There's propane heat, a gas oven, a woodstove, and

oil lamps. If the electricity goes out, she can always melt snow to flush the toilet. She'll be fine."

"But she's alone."

"She knows where I am, and I told her to just leave the truck by the cabin in case she needs anything else. Hell, I'm not going to need it."

"Is she okay?"

He shrugged. Kendall was way better than he was at the moment. Hell, she was probably having great sex to boot. Unlike him. He hadn't been with a woman since setting eyes on the walking, talking wet dream he'd been about to hit on, until he'd realized it was Addie. He hadn't been able to get her out of his mind. It had been three months. Three long, sexless, frustrating-as-hell months, and it was all her fault. "Kendall seems fine."

Addie didn't look like she believed him. She had that men-are-clueless-Neanderthals look about her. She didn't know the half of it. She would never suspect that all it took was a whiff of her damn shampoo to give him a stiffy and that he'd spent more than a few nights doing nothing but picturing her naked.

"I think maybe I should go check on her."

"Not a good idea. Kendall wants to be left alone, Addie. She did everything she could to get rid of me when I stopped by."

"Well, that's understandable. After all, what's a man know about a broken heart?"

"What do you know about it?" He saw a flash of pain in her eyes, but it was gone so fast, he thought he'd imagined it.

"None of your business."

He needed to get closer to her. And, yes, in the past three months he'd not only embraced celibacy, but he'd also discovered he was a fucking masochist. He rose, stood in front of her, and leaned back against his desk, looking down at her. "What if I want to make it my business?"

"You what?" Addie looked dumbstruck and pissed. She waited until she got totally torqued before she rose and was nose to chest with him. She was the perfect height for him to catch the scent of green apple in her hair. She couldn't step back because the chair was right behind her, so she tipped her head up and glared.

"You heard me." Man, she had the most kissable mouth. He hadn't noticed it until she'd walked into that Boston bar with it painted hooker red. But looking at her lips now, even slightly chapped, made him want to kiss her. He couldn't fight it anymore. He gave up.

"And what do you think you know, Einstein?"

"I know what you're hiding under those clothes. I saw you that night in Boston with Kendall. And, like it or not, I can see you now too. I wanted you then, and I still want you." He expected her to be angry at the admission; he'd been trying to avoid her for months. When that didn't work, he'd hoped to hell she'd be interested.

She laughed in his face. Not just a chuckle either—a full-throated laugh that sounded sexy as hell, even if it felt awful. Yeah, he hadn't expected that.

She fell back into her chair and hugged herself, as if she were laughing so hard, her stomach hurt.

"Oh, that's a good one, Jaime. I don't know what you think you saw, but it wasn't me."

"It was too." He put his hands on the armrests of her chair and leaned into her, and her scent surrounded him. "You can deny it all you want, but you and I both know I'm right."

"You're crazy."

"Apparently." He might be crazy for wanting her. Little Miss Virgin Kindergarten Teacher. Hell, she even taught Sunday school. But he'd tried to forget about her for three months, and he was done. "Go out with me."

"Right. So everyone in town will know? I don't think so."

And what was wrong with that? He was hardly a leper. "We don't have to go anywhere in town. We can go to Concord or to Boston."

"Why?"

"Because I want to get to know you."

"You've known me all my life. You're going to have to come up with a better one than that. Besides, I don't need to be the laughingstock of Harmony. Just cut the crap, Jaime, and tell me if the lane up to the hunting cabin is plowed."

"No, it's not. And it's snowing already. Did you get new tires yet? Last time I looked, your tread was low."

Addie rolled her eyes and pushed him away from her and the chair, forcing him back against his desk. "My tread and everything else about me is my business, not yours. Besides, you're the only one in town who sells tires, so you know I didn't."

"I thought you might have gone to Concord. Why don't I order some for you? I'll put them on right after the storm. You need to stay off the lake road until I get a chance to plow it. With the storm coming, I doubt I'll get to it until after the weekend."

"What do you have against me going to visit Kendall?"

"Nothing. Why would I care either way?"

"I don't know, but I know something is up." She crossed

her arms over the chest he'd been dreaming about for three months, the same one he hadn't known she'd kept hidden all these years. "Do me a favor and have Kendall call me, please."

"She doesn't have a phone that works."

"Let her use yours. If I don't hear from her in the next two days, I don't care if I have to hike across the lake, I'm going to see her and make sure she's okay."

"Since when did I become your errand boy?"

"About the same time you asked me out. What can I say? The world's gone mad."

CHAPTER
NINE

Jax laid the last row of tar paper, with one eye on the sky. He just hoped it would survive the nor'easter. He wasn't too worried, though. After all, he'd spaced the nails a hell of a lot closer than he'd been taught to the summer he'd worked as a roofer. The memory brought a smile to his lips. It was the first time he told his uncles to pound rock salt. They controlled his trust fund until he turned twenty-five, and they thought threatening to cut off the money would make him dance to their tune. They'd never made that mistake again. Jax got a job at a roofing company the next day and spent the summer humpin' seventy-five-pound packs of shingles up two and three stories in the Chicago suburbs during one of the hottest summers on record. He'd loved it.

The scent of something cooking came right through the roof and made his stomach grumble. It smelled like pizza, but he couldn't imagine Kendall ever pulling a frozen pizza out of the box and tossing it in the oven. He doubted she'd ever eat anything out of a box—that just wasn't her. No, Kendall was all about sensuality; no matter which of the five senses she was using, she went all in. Everything she cooked smelled, tasted, and looked too good to eat. Everything she wore was soft to the touch but had style. And the way she danced around the kitchen, to music better suited to the bedroom, when she thought he wasn't looking told him everything he'd imagined she'd be like in bed was probably dead-on. It was in the way she did everything, from walking across a room to kissing. Damn. He sat back on his heels and then checked the sky again. They'd be shut in the cabin, riding out the storm with no TV, no Internet, not even many books. He was in serious trouble.

He checked one more time to make sure he hadn't missed anything, cleaned up his tools, and threw the rest of the tar-paper roll on his shoulder to haul down the ladder.

The stove and heaters were propane, so no problem there. If the electric went out, they had a generator, or they could just do things the old-fashioned way and take all the food in the refrigerator and stick it out on the enclosed back porch. For light, there were oil lamps in every room. Jax had spent his first week at the cabin doing nothing but chopping wood, so there was plenty of firewood for the season, much less for a nasty nor'easter.

He picked up an armful and stacked it on the front porch. In blizzard conditions, it was a bitch to trek to the woodpile and back. Plus, it was the best excuse he could come up with to release his pent-up frustration and avoid going back in the cabin with Kendall—the root cause of it all. He was in no rush to face her.

The thought of being stuck in the cabin for days alone with Kendall was enough to make him sweat, even with the temperature dropping. Maybe he should have bought the economy-size box of condoms, because he had a feeling that if he were to slip, it would be a very, very, very long fall from grace.

He stripped out of his coat, and a few minutes later his sweater, in his quest for physical exhaustion. The wood-pile on the porch was waist high by the time Kendall stepped outside and plucked his coat and sweater off the porch rail. "I'll take these inside."

"Thanks."

"Dinner will be ready in about fifteen minutes, if you want to get a shower."

All it took was the word *shower*, and he was right back where he started that morning—dry-mouthed, breathing heavy and hard. Damn, he was seriously screwed. There was nothing between him and Kendall but his quickly dissolving moral code and a small box of condoms.

Jax tossed the armful of firewood onto the stack and followed Kendall inside, watching the hypnotic sway of her hips all the way to the kitchen.

He was going to have a shower, all right—a very cold shower.

Kendall stopped and turned to him as if she'd just re-membered something. "Jack." She rested a hand on his sweat-soaked shirt and then licked her lips—lips he couldn't seem to stop staring at. "Let me know if you need me to wash your back or anything else."

"If I did, we'd be in there a hell of a lot longer than fifteen minutes, sweetheart. I wouldn't want to spoil the dinner you've worked so hard to prepare."

Her eyes widened and she sucked in a breath. "I thought you had no concept of time."

"I don't, but I do have a memory." His hands went to her waist, slid beneath the sweater and the tank, and stroked the warm, smooth skin just above her low-riding jeans.

She curled the fingers on his chest into a fist, shirt and all.

He pushed her hair behind her ear and then leaned in to whisper, "And I remember that when I'm truly inspired, I can go for hours." He nipped her earlobe and then sucked it into his mouth to soothe it, until he heard that sound she'd made when she'd taken her first bite of her lobster BLT at lunch. "And you inspire the hell out of me."

He tried to back away, but she had his shirt in her fist. He grabbed ahold of the back of his shirt and pulled it off. "I'll just go toss this into the mudroom."

Kendall released the shirt, and the way her gaze roamed his chest and abs made him thankful he'd never given up competitive swimming. He'd gone from his high school team to his college team, and then right into Masters swimming. The 2,500 meters he swam every morning before work not only kept him sane, but also kept him in insanely good shape.

———

Kendall watched Jack walk shirtless to the bathroom, and had to remind herself to breathe. He looked almost as good going as he did coming. She'd always had a thing for men's backs—broad shoulders tapering down to a narrow waist, and, God, no love handles. Even David— the guy who spent two hours a day at the gym—had love handles. She'd known Jack would look good without a shirt on, but she'd never seen anyone look that good, except maybe David Beckham, but it wasn't as if she'd seen him in the flesh. She turned around, poured herself a glass of wine, and downed it.

She had to concentrate on dinner, not washboard abs

and back muscles that flexed as he walked. And she wasn't going to get started thinking about how good he looked in a tool belt. No, she was going to concentrate on food.

Kendall slid the pizzas she'd placed on a sheet of tinfoil off the cookie sheets and onto the heated terra-cotta tiles, and set the timer. She looked around and did a mental checklist. The table was set, the salad was chilling, and she'd already made a dent in the nice, big bottle of Chianti she'd chosen. She refilled her wine, tried to erase the picture of a naked Jack in the shower, with water cascading over his well-defined abs, until the timer went off. It hadn't worked. When the buzzer went off, she pulled the tinfoil out from beneath the pizzas and spun them around the best she could. Normally she'd flip them too, put the top one on the bottom and vice versa, but she was already on her third glass of wine and really didn't trust herself not to take a header into the oven.

"Kendall?"

"Yes?" She followed his voice and found Jack in his room, wearing nothing but a towel.

"Where's my dresser?"

"I slid it into my room." She stared at the slash of muscle that ran from his hip bone toward his pelvis on both sides and disappeared beneath the white terry cloth.

"Why?"

"Why what?" He didn't have much chest hair, but maybe she just couldn't see it because he was blond and the lighting was bad. "Do you wax your chest?"

"No, not anymore. I used to when I was on the swim team in college—less drag." He ran a hand across his chest. "Why is my dresser in your room?"

Her mouth had gone dry. She tried to swallow. "Because it's too dusty in yours, and with the plaster raining down the way it was, I deemed the room uninhabitable."

"You deemed my room uninhabitable?"

She nodded and took a step closer. "You didn't want your dresser and clothes ruined, did you?"

"No, but it's my room. My bed."

"Your bed was trashed, but don't worry. I pulled off all the bedding, grabbed your dirty clothes, and threw them in the wash. They're all folded and put away. And I don't think there's much hope for your mattress—it's drenched."

"But ..."

"At first I tried just sweeping up the plaster, but it just kept falling, so I whacked it with the broom handle and dislodged what I could—it all has to come down eventually."

"Yes, but my bed—"

"That's when I slid your dresser into my room. It's not a problem—there's plenty of space for your things. I grabbed the computer off your desk and then moved the rest of the furniture out of the way of the remaining plaster. With you banging up there on the roof, well, you just never know, do you?"

The way Jack turned a full circle, if he struck a pose and put on a thoughtful expression, he could be an underwear model—that is, if he put on underwear.

"Even after I swept, the dust was horrible. Just come out of there and close the door so it doesn't get into the rest of the cabin again. As it is, I already had to dust the whole place, and, unfortunately for you, I don't find cleaning therapeutic, thank you very much."

"Kendall, I never asked you to clean. Cleaning is not the problem."

She wished she'd brought her wine, because for some

reason, this conversation was very confusing. "Okay, so what's the problem?"

"The problem is that we're both tall and the couch is short."

She didn't understand, but that could have something to do with the towel slipping down his hips as he stalked back and forth over the dusty floor. "What does the couch have to do with anything?" She jumped just a little when the timer went off. "Are you planning to eat in your towel? Or maybe naked? If you are, you won't hear any complaints from me, but if you want to dress for the occasion, now would be a good time. Dinner's ready."

Jack stomped the three steps to her bedroom and slammed the door. She thought she heard him cursing again.

"Jeez, I try to help a guy out, break my back knocking down a freakin' ceiling, sweep and dust, do his laundry, and cook dinner, and do I get so much as a thank-you? No. All I get is an angry man stomping around in a towel."

But then when she thought about it, that wasn't such a bad trade after all.

———

Jax cursed a blue streak as he threw the towel against the wall and rummaged through his drawers for clothes—clothes that Kendall had washed and folded and put away. He'd gone up to work on the roof, and when he'd come down, he'd found out that Kendall had demolished the remaining ceiling in his bedroom and moved him into hers without so much as a word.

He didn't bother with underwear—something about knowing she had her hands all over his shorts was a turn-on—which in and of itself made him worry about his mental capacity, not to mention his ability to button his damn fly. Unfortunately, both problems seemed minor compared to his reaction to the thought of sharing the bed with Kendall. His body screamed, "Hell, yeah!" but his brain told him to run while he still could.

By the time he'd gotten both problems under some semblance of control, he went out to the kitchen and found Kendall with her head practically stuffed in the oven.

She wore blue pot-holder mittens on her hands. "God, I really miss my pizza paddle." She closed the oven door, turned, and almost ran into him.

"And here I thought you'd never buy frozen pizza."

"Frozen pizza?" The look she gave him was enough to make him want to sleep with the light on, a knife under the pillow, and one eye open.

"Don't get me wrong—I'm not complaining. It looks amazing." He scanned the counters to make sure there were no weapons close at hand.

"You think I bought this?"

Of course he did. He'd never seen pizza that looked that good in any New York or even Chicago restaurant, for that matter, and definitely not in Harmony. "Are you trying to pull one over on me? Come on. No one could make a pizza at home that professional-looking without a brick oven and a pizza chef."

She slammed the pizza wheel he'd never seen before into the first pie with such force, the sound made him jump.

He watched while she sliced the pie in perfectly even pieces, making short work of it, like it was second nature. She'd done it without ever taking her pissed-off glare away from him.

"Think again. And as for the brick oven, I improvised and made my own."

And to think he'd just spent the past few minutes wondering about his sanity, when all the while maybe he should have questioned hers. "You made a brick oven? How did you manage that one?"

She walked over to the oven and opened it up before doing a really good impression of Vanna White. "What do you think the terra-cotta tile I picked up at the Home Depot was for, Einstein? Oh, and thanks for the professional comment. It's good to know that the four years I spent cooking at Pizza King downtown weren't wasted. Mine's better, since I perfected my recipes for the crust and sauce—I'm not a fan of sweet pizza. Tomatoes are sweet enough on their own, don't you think?"

She was still obviously pissed over his frozen pizza comment, if the way she attacked the second pizza was anything to go by. While he was busy trying to scrape his jaw off the floor, she'd gathered both pizzas and left him standing in the kitchen.

Jax grabbed her forgotten, half-filled wineglass and the bottle of Chianti and hit the table, prepared to grovel. He set her wineglass in front of her and took a seat, to find she'd already put three big pieces on his plate. His mouth watered, but he waited to eat. He'd be damned if he'd ruin the dinner she'd slaved over.

Shit, he hated groveling even more than apologizing, because in order to really grovel, you had to apologize too—something else his father had taught him. Unfortunately, he didn't listen when his dad told him never to comment on a woman's cooking, except to say it was wonderful. What the hell had he been thinking? Hadn't he told himself she wasn't the type to buy prepared food?

Jax cleared his throat. "Kendall." He waited until she looked at him; it took a second. "I'm sorry. I didn't mean to offend you. I just didn't think anyone, even you, could throw together a homemade pizza in the time it took me to finish the roof. Actually, except for you, I've never seen anyone make one worth eating. Thanks for cooking." He held his breath as she watched him, as if she were trying to decide if she should let him live.

She must have ruled in his favor, because she shot him a smile and picked up her first piece. "It's okay. I might be a little oversensitive about my pizza." She looked away, but he couldn't seem to stop staring at her. Why would anyone who cooked as well as she did be sensitive about it? He and every other man he knew would give their right arms to have food like this on a daily basis.

Kendall tipped her head back and closed her eyes as she slid a slice between her lips. She bit down and let out a groan that sounded as if it should come from the bedroom, not the dining room—that is, unless they were both naked. Her eyes flew open and met his. Embarrassment flooded her cheeks.

Jax took a sip of his wine. Kendall looked and sounded as if he'd caught her in the throes of an orgasm. Without breaking eye contact, she took a napkin and swiped off a string of cheese hanging from her chin. "Sorry, but I've forgotten how incredible my pizza is. I haven't made it in ages."

"Why the hell not?" He reached for a piece, and she watched as he took a bite. And oh, God, he couldn't blame her—this pizza was definitely groan-worthy.

"David didn't appreciate eating with his hands, or the calorie count. He ate pizza with a fork and a knife, if you can believe that." She was lost in thought for a moment and then shuddered. "God, I almost married a Ken doll."

He shot her a quizzical look but didn't bother asking. After all, his mouth was full.

"You know, Barbie and Ken? He was an overly orange tool who looked pretty but had no sense of humor. No wonder Barbie dumped him for G.I. Joe."

He couldn't help but grin and hold up his wineglass in her honor. "Well, that's certainly good to hear. See? I told you it wouldn't take that long before you realized he did you a favor."

"I guess you're right." Since he'd made room on his plate, Kendall, who, he realized, had a thing about making sure he ate vegetables, put a huge scoop of salad on it. He was relieved when she laughed at the look he shot her that told her in no uncertain terms that he had no intention of eating salad when there was perfectly good pizza within reach.

"If you think the pizza is good, just wait until you get a load of my Caesar salad."

He didn't say anything; he just kept eating, and tried to figure out what the hell to do about the fact that there was only one bed fit to sleep on. His mattress obviously had taken the brunt of the leak, as it was soaked through and weighed a ton. There was no way in hell anyone was going to sleep on that.

"Do you want to tell me what's bothering you?"

"No."

"Do it anyway."

He put down his half-eaten slice and leaned forward. "This two-bedroom cabin just turned into a one-bedroom, and the couch is too small for either of us to sleep on."

"Well, then, it's a good thing that queen bed sleeps two."

He let out an exasperated breath. "Kendall, I can't share a bed with you."

She swatted the thought away as if it were of no more annoyance than a housefly. "Sure you can. There's plenty of room."

"There's not a big enough bed on the planet for the two of us to sleep in—not if you want to get any rest."

Her mouth formed a surprised O—but that surprise quickly turned to disappointment. "That wouldn't be a problem for me, but you obviously don't feel the same." She thought a moment, and then her face brightened. "I know—I'll go stay with Jaime. He has plenty of room, and I'm pretty sure he won't mind."

"Like hell you will." He stood up so fast his damn chair tipped back and hit the floor. He planted his hands on the table and leaned in so close, their noses almost touched.

"You know, you're wearing the same expression you wore when you warned me about inviting you into the shower, and your voice has that same dark, deep tone that brings to mind things I've only read about in *Fifty Shades*." She swallowed and licked her lips. "I never found dominance sexy until now. But it doesn't mean I want to call you sir or anything."

"Shit, Kendall, are you trying to kill me?" He'd never gotten into bondage before, but the vision of Kendall tied to his bed, wearing nothing but a satin gown, shot his blood pressure through the roof and his sent his dick searching his jeans for an escape route.

"If I wanted to kill you, you'd know it. No, I'm trying to be the rational adult here. I'll be kind just this once and ignore the fact that you seem to think you have any right to tell me where and with whom I should sleep."

He picked up his chair and sat, wondering if he'd survive the rest of the conversation with that damn image of Kendall tied to his bed rattling around his brain.

"You don't want to sleep with me—"

He held up his hand interrupting her. "I never said that." He was going straight to hell; he was sure of it. "The problem is that I do want to sleep with you."

She didn't say anything; she just raised a disbelieving brow.

"Okay, that's not entirely accurate. If I shared a bed with you, I could pretty much guarantee that neither of us would sleep for a long, long, long time. Maybe days."

She sucked in a breath, her skin turned an incredible shade of pink, and her eyes darkened. "Let me see if I have this right." He was surprised her voice was so calm and level; still, it was different, deeper and raspier, and it seemed to send a message to his body that bypassed his brain. "You want to have sex with me, and I want to have sex with you, but because of some manly code of honor or perhaps a lack of trust in my ability to run my own life, you won't allow it." She looked at him for confirmation or denial, but got neither. She'd rendered him speechless—a first. "And yet you don't want me to sleep at Jaime's for fear of what—that I'll jump the first man I see?"

If she was going for the shock factor, she was succeeding spectacularly. He cleared his throat to make sure his voice would work. "No, of course not." He got up and paced the length of the room and turned back. "Kendall, I can't imagine any straight man not wanting to be with you. I don't trust myself around you, so why in the hell would I trust Jaime?"

She stepped closer. "You're exasperating."

"And you're not?"

"You don't suffer from brain damage; you suffer from sheer, unadulterated stubbornness. Now listen and listen good. I don't want Jaime. I want you. I like you, when you're not being a chauvinist pig. I think you're sexy as all get-out, with and without a tool belt, and you're sweet and kind and smart. Do you think that if I can't have you, I'll hop into bed with the first man I see because of some deep-seated fear of being alone?"

"You're not afraid of being alone, Kendall. I'm just not sure you know what you want in a man or a relationship so soon after ending one that lasted almost half your life."

She looked like she was either going to throttle him or kiss him, and, frankly, he'd prefer being choked.

"I've always known what I wanted—that hasn't changed. I just wasn't smart enough to see that the man I was with lied to me about wanting the same thing."

Okay, he'd give her that. "Fine. But, sweetheart, that doesn't change the fact that I'm not a good bet." He took her hand. "Come on over here and sit down."

He was surprised she complied. He sat her on the couch and held her hands in his as he turned the coffee table into a chair. "I don't know what I'm able to give to a relationship now. If we were to get together that way, it could end badly. I care about you, and I really don't want to hurt you."

"I'm not asking you to marry me, Jack. I like you. I want to spend time with you. I want to feel the way I did when I kissed you. I've never felt that way before. What in the hell are you so afraid of?"

Jax's breath froze in his lungs, and his adrenaline spiked, sending his heart drumming like the Energizer Bunny on crack. He didn't look at her; instead he stared at their joined hands. "I'm afraid my brain is stuck like this, and I'm afraid of you—what I feel for you. I don't know what it is, I don't know how to control it, and not being in control scares the shit out of me." He snuck a glance, and she didn't look at all put off. "Kendall, I've changed. I'm not the same person I was before the accident. I knew where I was going then. I had a plan—a plan that just exploded in my face. I don't know what my life will look like a week, a month, or a year from now."

"So? I'm not the same person I was before David dumped me either. I know the person you are now, and I really like you. You know me, and you really like me too. Can't that be enough?"

"What if it's not?"

She leaned back and studied him in a way that made all the hair on his arms stand on end. "I don't know who hurt you, and I'm not going to ask, but I'm sorry."

Heart-pounding, sweat-soaking, jaw-breaking fear raced through him, the kind of fear you feel when you can't breathe, when you're trapped and can't get out, when you have to escape or you'll blow. He took one breath and let it out slowly, ruthlessly ignoring the urge to run. "No one hurt me."

She didn't buy it. "Maybe not intentionally, but you've lost someone you loved a lot. Opening yourself up to someone new can be terrifying."

"Are you charging by the hour?"

"No, it's what I've told myself every day since David walked out. Just because one man hurt me doesn't mean they all will."

He looked at her then and leaned forward, dropping

her hand but resting his on her thighs. "Kendall, I never want to hurt you."

"And I don't want to hurt you. But I'm willing to take a chance on getting my heart stomped on to feel like this one more time." She leaned into him and kissed him.

Kendall might have initiated their kiss, but he'd be damned if this time he wasn't going to take at least half the credit for it. This time, he wasn't too stunned to react. This time, he was the one on top.

Then he picked her up and carried her into the bedroom, because the couch wasn't nearly big enough for what he had in mind.

CHAPTER
TEN

K endall knew a lot of strong people. Her years working with kids who had cancer made sure of that.
She'd seen her share of patients with trauma—she
knew all the signs—and for a moment there, Jack had
exhibited all the symptoms of a man on the edge.

She'd held her breath and watched him pull himself
out of the deep, dark hole of desolation she'd unknow-
ingly ushered him into. He was terrified, he was wounded,
and yet he stayed and overcame it.

People rarely surprised her, but Jack had. She'd never
seen anyone with the control he had to compartmental-
ize whatever trauma he'd suffered—and it was trauma,
of that she was sure—and move on as if nothing had
happened. If she hadn't spent an inordinate amount of
time studying him, if she hadn't been trained to see the
signs, she might have missed it. She was sure he'd fooled
a lot of people before her—even professionals. He was
just that good, but she was better. She saw the pain, the
terror, the fear, and she'd heard the denial as he slammed
the steel door down on that part of himself.

She didn't know who or what had hurt him, but something had, and he had gaping open wounds that he ig-

nored. He had learned to navigate life normally, but that
didn't change the fact that they existed. And she'd bet her
degree that trauma was the reason he'd avoided a physical relationship with her. It was also the reason that, except for the accident, she knew so little about him.

Then she kissed him, or maybe he kissed her—she
wasn't sure. In the kiss all those feelings he'd held in
check, all the terror and the fear, the pain and loss were
exposed. It was in the dampness at his hairline, the tremor
of his lips when they brushed hers, the tension radiating
off him, and the hammering of his heart. She felt it all,
and when he pulled away, breathless, and looked into her
eyes, she saw the moment of surrender.

The kiss that followed held none of the desperation,
none of the urgency. It was like going from a raging ty-
phoon into a calm, clear, sheltered lagoon. Gentle waves
of pleasure surrounded her, warmed her, lifted her, and
when she opened her eyes, she saw that she hadn't imagined it. Jack held her in his arms like a movie star and
carried her down the short hall to their room. He stopped
at the threshold, and she found herself staring into his
clear blue eyes.

"Kendall, you're sure about this? About me?"

"Totally and completely sure." So sure it scared her.
She'd never felt such certainty at a time where there was
absolutely no proof, no validity, no reason to feel so confi-
dent. Kendall heard her mother's voice in her head saying
the same thing she'd said a million times: "Remember,
Kendall, to always follow your heart." And that, she realized, was what she'd been doing since the second she'd
seen Jack standing beside her car. She might end up with
it broken, but, then, what was the good in having a heart if
you never gave it a workout?

She had gotten lost in his eyes again, something she did on a regular basis, and didn't realize they'd moved until she felt the bed beneath her. She wasn't sure how he managed that—she wasn't a small woman. There was no groaning, no jerking, just solid strength and fluid movement and stillness. Then the bed dipped beside her, and she saw nothing but Jack.

He lifted the hem of her sweater and slid his finger along the gap between her tank and jeans.

She reached to rip off her sweater and shirt in one fell swoop, but he stilled her. "Slowly. We have days and days. There's no rush."

Her heart hammered in her chest, but the look in his eyes, the banked passion she saw there, made her still, made her breathe, made her anticipate.

Jack was obviously in the driver's seat on this little voyage, so she lay back, determined to enjoy the ride. He slid her sweater up and over her head.

The cool air hit her bare arms and breasts through the light fabric of her tank and lace bra, but then his eyes roamed over the same area, warming and tantalizing her skin like a touch.

He laid her back against the pillow and slid his work-roughened finger down the inside of her arm to her hand. Lifting it to his lips, he kissed her palm before raking his teeth over the spot and then soothing it with his tongue. With his every touch sparks flew up her arm and scattered through her breasts and to her core.

He kissed the tip of her index finger and then slid his tongue up to the fleshy spot between her fingers and sucked.

She didn't bother holding in her moan; she'd never known that her hand was so sensitive.

He teased her fingers, kissing, nipping, licking until she squirmed.

Heat pooled in her core, and her breathing grew shallow. When he drew her finger into his mouth and sucked, she nearly came off the bed. "Jack."

His eyes met hers, and what she saw there—the want, the hunger, the need—would have brought her to her knees if she'd been standing. "Slow." He murmured against her wrist and proceeded to kiss and lick and nip his way up her arm, igniting every nerve on the way to her shoulder, and then bypassed her neck entirely. "I love the way you taste, your scent, your heat."

He lifted her other hand and made love to it with his mouth, his teeth, his lips, hell, even his beard. He turned her into a moaning, quivering mess.

She ached for him, arching against him as he made his way to her shoulder and then down between her breasts, drawing her tank down to expose bare skin but not touching them. Leaving them aching.

She was burning up, and he'd hardly touched her.

He slid her tank higher so it rested just under her breasts. "Look at you. So beautiful." He straddled her legs, caressing her waist, never stopping, spreading heat wherever he touched. He kissed and licked her stomach, and the rasp of his beard sent tremors through her, leaving her muscles trembling under his lips.

She arched her back, reaching for more contact, moaning, pleading, panting. And just when she didn't think she could take any more, he slid his tongue into her navel, and, like a finger pulling a trigger, heat seared through her straight to her core, and she came, screaming his name.

She was not a screamer, but, then, she'd never been

teased like that before. She'd never been loved like that
before. She'd never been controlled like that before.

She didn't know what to do when, even after an orgasm, she shook with a need to touch him, to curl her
body into his, to melt against him and feel his weight.
"Jack, kiss me."

His eyes met hers, and his lips curved into a conceited
grin. "Oh, I have been."

She reached down, grabbed ahold of his hair, and
tugged him up higher. His lips met hers in the same in-
stant her legs wrapped around his waist. She swallowed
his groan and arched her back, and when his fly hit hers,
she echoed the noise.

Jack dragged his mouth away from hers, and his breath
fanned her face. "I wanted to make love to you slowly."
His voice was rough, but he wore a smile. "I knew I
should have tied you up."

She tugged up his T-shirt. "Next time."

He grabbed it from behind and, kneeling over her,
pulled it off.

He had the most incredible chest she'd ever seen.
"God, you're beautiful." She ran her hands over him,
making his muscles spasm under her touch.

Jack was all tanned skin and sinewy muscle, with the
well-defined pecs of a swimmer, not a bodybuilder. He
had flat brown nipples just screaming for attention and
a stomach she could do laundry on. She tugged the first
button of his threadbare jeans and they all popped open,
freeing his erection. "Oh, my." She sucked in a breath
and stared. It was huge. Not that she had much to compare it to. Either David was really lacking, or Jack could
double as a porn star. She'd definitely pay money to see
a movie with Jack in it.

Under her gaze, his erection seemed to grow before her eyes, and it moved and pulsed. A drop of liquid appeared on the slit, and she couldn't help it: she licked her lips.

"Kendall." It was that warning tone all over again. His face looked as if it had been chiseled from granite, and the muscles in his neck stood out.

The word *yes* came out on a moan. She reached out with her index finger, the same finger he'd sucked on a lifetime ago, and smoothed the liquid over the head.

Every muscle in his body tensed, and a breath hissed between his teeth. "It's not too late, you know."

"For what?"

"To tie you up."

She wrapped her fingers around his girth and felt smooth skin move over hot steel before giving it an experimental squeeze and earning a groan for her effort.

He mumbled something she thought might have been a prayer, or quite possibly a curse. It was hard to tell.

Strong hands grabbed both her wrists and pulled them up over her head. One hand held them in place, and the other tugged her bra and tank up under her chin. Jack dipped his head, and a talented tongue slid over a peaked nipple, drawing it deep into his mouth, while his free hand drew lazy circles around the opposite breast. With every tug of his mouth, she grew more restless, fighting his grip on her wrists, arching her back, and praying he'd do something to relieve the ache building within her. Praying he'd take her shirt off.

She was just about to curse his very name when he pulled her tank and bra over her head and then tugged on the button of her jeans. The zipper slid down, seemingly of its own accord. She raised her hips, thanking God she'd chosen her loosest pair.

He rubbed his cheek against the distended nipple of one breast—he was such a tease. "Now, if I let go of your wrists, do you promise to be good and keep them there? You're going to need to hold on to the headboard."

"Only if you promise to make it worth my while."

He slid his mouth to her ear. "No worries there, sweetheart." Jack freed her wrists and waited until she grabbed the headboard before giving her a kiss that ended too soon. He shot her his warning look that promised retribution if she misbehaved, which did nothing but tempt her. But a moment later, her pants and panties were tugged off, and she got lost in his eyes again.

Jack sat back on his heels, and his gaze slid over her with such intensity and heat it felt like a touch.

Any thoughts of misbehaving flew right out the window. If he kept looking at her like that, she'd do just about anything he asked.

"Damned if you're not the most beautiful thing I've ever seen." He kissed her long and slow and thoroughly, a kiss so full of promise, it brought tears to her closed eyes.

The overhead light shone on his blond hair and caught the blue of his eyes as he nudged her thighs apart and kissed his way down the column of her neck, between her breasts, and lower. His warm breath washed over her mound. She'd never had anyone look at her the way Jack did, like she was a delicacy and he a starving man. She thought she'd feel embarrassment, but if it was there, the excitement she felt overshadowed it. He kissed the insides of her thighs and licked her, separating her swollen and aching center. The tip of his tongue pressed against the tight bundle of nerves, and she sucked in a breath, feeling the pressure of something growing, heating, building. Then he slid a finger into her, filling her, twisting, stretching, sliding deep, and then retreating. His tongue never stopped licking and teasing, thrumming against her. So many sensations that she was drowning in feeling, reaching and climbing so high, she wasn't sure there was enough oxygen. A second finger slid in; it was too tight, but then he sucked, drawing her into his mouth and curling his fingers, hitting that perfect spot from the inside that sent her flying.

Waves of pleasure rolled over, crashed around her, and stole her breath. It was too much, but he released the suction and soothed it with the flat of his tongue, all the while filling her with his fingers, going deeper with every pass, harder, faster, filling her until she burned. So deep she swore he'd touched her womb. But even the little bit of pain increased her pleasure, adding layer upon layer of feeling as one orgasm rolled into something so much more.

———

Jax had never been so nervous in his life. Not even his first time. But, then, his first time hadn't been with an inexperienced girl. Avery hadn't been that much older than him, but she was no girl; she was a woman, and she was a connoisseur of sex. She had turned out to be an excellent teacher, and he had been a most willing student. She'd taught him almost everything he knew about pleasuring a woman's body, and he knew a lot. He had that part down; it was just the emotional connection he had problems with.

Kendall was so small and tight that even after three orgasms, he wasn't sure he wouldn't hurt her. And he didn't know how, after holding back for days, if he'd be able to cling to his control.

He kept her balanced on the edge of orgasm, drawing her higher and higher. Each one stronger than the last. She'd opened her body to him, her heart, her mind. Good thing he'd perfected the one-handed condom application, because if he stopped, if he lost contact, she'd fall away, and he didn't want to lose her, lose this.

"Kendall, look at me."

Her eyes slid open and focused on his—dark and dreamy and so unguarded, so trusting, so sweet.

He kissed her, making love to her mouth as he slipped his fingers from within her. Tilting her hips and blowing out a breath, he slid the head of his erection inside her. He groaned and forced himself to stop when all he wanted to do was thrust into her, to claim her, to possess her, to pleasure her. Shit, she brought his inner caveman to the surface. His jaw clenched, his temple throbbed, and damned if his vision didn't blur.

"Jack?" her breathy voice had his balls drawing up. "Jack, I need you." Then her hands came around him, drawing him closer. Her legs wrapped around his waist, and she bucked against him, pulling him in, and when he retreated, her ankles tightened, stopping his withdrawal.

He pressed in closer, moving slowly, hanging on to the last threads of his control.

"Jack, please. I need—"

"What do you need, sweetheart?"

Her dark eyes opened and her stare drilled into him, her nails dug into his shoulders, and her legs tightened like a vise around his hips. "I need you. I need all of you."

His control snapped and he thrust into her. He heard her cry out, but couldn't stop. Every stroke drew him closer, deeper, and farther toward the edge, and she met him thrust for thrust. She was demanding, dragging his mouth to hers, sucking on his tongue and raking her teeth over it.

Kendall went wild in his arms, completely open, completely uninhibited, completely his. Her body spasmed around him, dragging him into the abyss, guiding him as he flew and catching him when he landed.

Jax concentrated on breathing, the sound of Kendall's heart racing beneath his ear, and the caress of her hand sliding hypnotically over his shoulders and down his back in soft, fluid patterns. He knew he should roll over—he was probably crushing her—but he was loath to break the connection; once he did, it would disappear like it had never existed. He'd lose the feeling of wonder and wholeness. He'd never felt whole before. But in this moment, he was complete, stable, happy. Oh, fuck, he was happy.

———

So that's what she'd been missing. Kendall had half a mind to send David a nasty text—or her condolences. She wondered what else was different with Jack. Other than the obvious: the man could ring her bell without even taking off her panties. David couldn't ring it if she'd held it out for him and showed him where to put the mallet.

She lay beneath Jack, loving the weight of his big, hard body covering hers, and the fact he was still inside her and seemingly content to stay right there. He wasn't rolling out of bed to shower or wash up, as if trying to erase any evidence of her on him.

Her hands slid over his shoulders and down his back, exploring, learning, caressing. She'd wondered if he was asleep. And then every muscle in his entire body seized. "Jack, what's wrong?"

"Nothing." He pushed himself up, taking his weight on his forearms, and slid deeper inside her. Her inner muscles tightened around him, and heat surged through her.

Jack closed his eyes and kissed her like he was searching for something, desperately demanding a response to an unasked question. Her mind knew something was wrong, but her body didn't get the memo. Neither, it seemed, did his. He reached down, raising her thigh to his hip, changed the angle of penetration, and slid deeper. His pelvic bone hit that perfect spot, and she bucked against him.

He wasn't kidding when he said he could go for hours. This time, though, he didn't make eye contact. It felt as if he were intentionally avoiding it. The distance scared her. "Jack."

A sheen of sweat rose on his chest and back, and he drove her on but didn't answer.

"Jack, please. Look at me."

His eyes met hers and she saw a flash of panic; then he blinked and it was gone. He held her gaze and thrust into her to the hilt and stilled. His erection pulsed, sending little sparks cascading through her. "What do you want, sweetheart?"

"You. I want all of you." Even the parts of him he hid from the world—she wanted them. She never wanted him to hide from her.

"That's a damn good thing, because, Kendall, you already have me. The good, the bad, and the damaged." He brushed the hair off her forehead and kissed each eyelid, then her nose and the corners of her mouth before tracing the seam of her lips with his tongue.

He loved her slowly, holding her gaze as if he were

afraid to blink. He drove her up with a swivel of his hips and unerring aim and held her there, riding the edge of the wave until he sent her flying higher yet, and then buried his face in her neck and let go.

She lay in his arms and listened to his heart slow.

"Be right back." He gave her a quick kiss and rolled out of bed and walked naked to the bathroom to take care of the condom. She enjoyed the show, because she'd never seen a more beautiful man.

He slid back in beside her, wearing nothing but a smirk. "Like what you see?"

"Yes."

Jack pulled her closer so they lay on their sides facing each other.

Her mind raced as his hand slid soothingly up and down from her shoulder to her hip. Mesmerizing. Everything she thought she'd known about sex had been wrong. Questions flew through her mind. Was it that David was horrible lover, or was it just that Jack was amazing? Could it be both? Was there something about Jack — a chemical reaction — that made her hot, or was it just David that shot her into the subzero range?

"You're awfully quiet. It's not a natural state for you. Having second thoughts?"

After just having the best, most intense, most intimate sex of her life? Hardly. "Second thoughts about you and me? No, absolutely not." She pushed him onto his back and pulled herself up on his chest so she could see his face.

"But you're upset about something." He shoved his arm under his head, and she wanted to trace the line of muscle with her tongue. He ran the pad of a thumb across her bottom lip, and she wondered if he had somehow rewired her body so his every touch sent shock waves directly to her core. "You always bite your lip when you're trying to figure something out or you're upset. Oh, and that death glare you have is pretty scary too."

She raised a doubting brow. "I don't have a death glare."

"Next time I see it I'll take a picture. But I'll do it from a distance. So, tell me why you're biting your lip."

She'd turned into a walking cliché. She was having her first was-it-good-for-you talk. But not. "Is it always like this?"

He pushed a pillow against the headboard and sat up in bed. "Is what always like this?"

Her face flamed hot enough to make s'mores. She didn't know what to call what they had just done. Sex? Making love? Sleeping together? Bumping uglies?

"You're pretty adorable when you're embarrassed."

When he laughed at her, Kendall hit him with a pillow.

Jack shot her a grin. "Thanks," he said, and then shoved the pillow behind his back.

"You stole my pillow."

"I didn't steal it—I just kept it. You're the one who gave it to me—no take backs. Now come here and get comfortable." He pulled her between his open legs and leaned her back against his chest. "There, that's better. This way we can talk, and I still have fun stuff to play with."

"Fun stuff?"

"Every guy's dream toys." He slipped a hand beneath each breast and rubbed his thumbs over the nipples—nipples that stood at attention the second he touched them. "See? It's like magic. You have beautiful breasts."

"They're not very big." And they looked even smaller than usual in his big hands.

"They're perfectly proportioned for your body." He traced a figure eight around them with one hand. Over and over. His other hand toyed with her belly button. "So, back to your question. You need to be more specific."

She was having a really hard time concentrating with Jack running his hands all over her body. "I don't know what to label it. Sex? Making love? Whatever it is that we just did. Is it always like that?"

"For me? No, it's never been like this."

She let out a breath, and the tension bubbled away. Then she realized he hadn't said it was good or bad, just different. And she'd sooner die than ask, *Was it good for you?* "How is it different?"

He was quiet—too quiet. Maybe he was trying to figure out a nice way to tell her she was a really bad lay. She couldn't take it anymore, so she hummed the theme to *Jeopardy!* I'll take difficult sexual conversations for a thousand, Alex.

Jack gave her boobs a squeeze and made a buzzer sound. "What is the difference between competing in the hundred-meter fly at a club meet and winning the gold at the Olympics?" He drew her closer, his lips brushing her ear and his beard rubbing against her shoulder. "All swim meets are alike—when you're swimming the hundred fly in any meet, you're doing the same stroke, the same distance—it's the same thing. So, basically, there's no difference when it comes to the act, but competing in the Olympics means so much more. It's something you train for your whole life, something you dream about from your first swim meet, and not just to compete, but to win the gold—it's life-changing. Kendall, you're my gold medal."

And just like that, she tumbled head over heels, in deep with Jack. "Wow. That's probably the nicest thing anyone's ever said to me."

"So, what about you?" The tip of a callused finger circled her belly, and she remembered what happened earlier when he played with her navel. Her breathing sped up, and she had to fight both her embarrassment and her arousal. She had half a mind to carry on a conversation while playing with his dream toys and see how coherent his answers were.

She took a deep breath and pressed his hand to her belly, stilling it. "It's never been like this for me either. But I can't even say that it's basically the same thing. It was so different, it would be like comparing curling to professional ice hockey. But I guess that only works if you're like me and don't understand curling at all. I mean, who would want to participate in a sport that combines shoving rocks around and cleaning?"

She felt the rumble of a chuckle through his chest into hers. "God, I spent the past seven years having appallingly bad sex, and I never even knew it. I just thought it was always forgettable and boring—either that, or I was frigid."

He choked and coughed, then laughed and resumed his playtime activities. "Frigid? You? That's hilarious."

"Comparing sex with you to what I've known would be like comparing a Stanley Cup win to receiving a participation ribbon because you're on the last-place team in the Pee-Wee Curling League."

He blew out a breath that washed over her ear. "Wow,

that's harsh." The hand beneath hers slid south, close—so close all her stomach muscles tensed—but not touching.

She put more pressure on his hand to keep it from roaming. "How could I not have known? And now I'm wondering what else I'm completely clueless about. I'm questioning everything."

"I'm sorry, but if it makes you feel better, I question everything too."

"You do?"

"Yeah, like right now, I'm questioning what you'd do if I did this." He slid his fingers down between her lips. Her hand pressed his harder against her body, at first to stop him and then to guide him. He sucked her earlobe into his mouth, and the other hand strummed her nipple in time with his fingers. She would have answered him if she could speak: What is, Having my sixth orgasm, Alex?

CHAPTER
ELEVEN

Jax watched Kendall sleep and thought of all the ways he'd completely and royally fucked up. He should have told her who the hell he was the second he'd met her. But he knew if he'd done that, she'd never have given him the chance to redeem himself in her eyes—which had been his grand plan. Well, that and keep her with him so she didn't let anyone know he was here.

As it was, he still didn't know what he'd done that made her despise him, but whatever it was, he didn't think it would be easily overcome. Kendall was one of the most stubborn women on the planet. She'd obviously gotten that particular personality trait from her father.

Oh, man, *Teddy*. Jax's normal headache expanded to fill his skull with pain—the kind of pain that made him want to sit alone in a dark room in the fetal position. He couldn't even think about what Grace and Teddy would do to him if they found out he'd just had the time of his life debauching their youngest daughter, and couldn't wait to do it again.

He knew he should have confessed all to Kendall before they'd made love. But if he had, she would have wanted to kill him. He'd seen her reaction when he inferred she'd bought prepared food, and he couldn't imagine what she'd do to him when she found out she'd been making love to the Grand Pooh-Bah himself. Whether or not he'd survive the experience really didn't matter; in the end he'd still lose Kendall.

Jax knew what it was to lose almost everything you loved. Hell, fourteen years ago, he'd lost both his parents, his coach, his swim team, and his shot at the Olympic Trials, and had come way too close to losing his sister.

Oh yeah, he knew what loss felt like, what it tasted like, what it smelled like, and he knew how it could eat you from the inside out. He was on intimate terms with it, and he'd spent the past fourteen years avoiding ever having to meet the fucker again.

Somehow Kendall had changed things, and now history would repeat itself and he'd lose everything again. His career, his future, and his dream—Kendall. The fact he was going to lose her was pretty much a given; his only uncertainty was when.

In his rational mind, he knew nothing this perfect could last. Better to not even go there, avoid it at all cost. He'd spent the past fourteen years keeping his distance. He'd made a kind of art of it. He hadn't met one person who tempted him enough to even consider bending the rules—until he'd looked into the red-rimmed, puffy eyes of Kendall Watkins.

He'd known that Kendall was different from the first second he'd spotted her crying in her car. Now he knew he should have sent her down to Jaime's and let him deal with the fallout. Hell, he should have run to Jaime's as soon as he'd seen the car and stayed the hell out of it. After all, he'd been in hiding. What the hell had he been thinking?

His gaze traced the outline of Kendall's face relaxed

in sleep—she was so beautiful, seriously gorgeous on a purely physical level. But when he'd looked into those deep, dark, mysterious eyes, he hadn't been strong enough to send her away. He'd wanted to protect her and keep her with him. He hadn't planned to take advantage of her, but he'd be damned if he'd let anyone else have the opportunity. He saw how well that worked.

Kendall slid closer, and the sheet fell below her breasts. She had the look of someone who had been thoroughly loved and completely satisfied—lulled into a post-multiorgasmic stupor, and then she'd fallen into an exhausted sleep. Her hair was a tangled mess, her cheeks were red from beard burn, her lips were swollen from his kisses, and her pale skin glowed pink in the light coming from the hall.

His time was running out. As much as he'd like to, Jax couldn't keep Kendall in the cabin for the rest of their natural lives—if he could manage it, he would. But Kendall would find out the truth eventually—either when Grace and Teddy returned or as a result of Addie's innate curiosity. He didn't know when or how, but he knew the end result: Kendall would hate him.

She'd hate him for lying to her, hate him for who he was, and hate him for doing the same thing to her that her ex had, and he wouldn't even blame her.

He was completely responsible, and when all was said and done, he'd do the one thing he'd never wanted to do to Kendall: he'd hurt her.

Since there was no way in hell he'd be able to sleep with a headache, he might as well go clean up the mess from dinner. His stomach growled, reminding him that mind-blowing sex always made him hungry. Maybe if he ate something, the headache would recede. It was worth a try.

He took one more look at Kendall, knowing that all too soon she'd be gone, then slid out of bed, threw on his jeans, and tiptoed out, closing the door behind him.

Cleaning up the dishes and kitchen was a breeze. All he had to do was finish eating the pizza and salad, which, he had to admit, was pretty good for something green and slightly wilted, and then put the dishes in the dishwasher. No fuss, no muss, and, in his eyes, a miracle.

He'd never seen anyone cook without the kitchen ending up looking like ground zero. His sister, Rocki, could make a mess just boiling water—he'd witnessed it. He didn't know how Slater, Rocki's fiancé, could stand it. Maybe he put a big Do Not Enter sign in the doorway of the kitchen. But if Slater felt about Rocki anywhere near what Jax felt for Kendall, he figured the fact that Rocki was the Terminator of kitchens and bars was just one of the things Slater loved about her.

Jax sat on the couch in the dark living room. He leaned back, closed his eyes, and had the urge to call his sister. They were close—closer than any other brother and sister he knew. She'd been the only person in the world that mattered to him—well, except for Grace and Teddy. That was, until he'd met Kendall. Kendall mattered. She mattered a whole lot. She mattered so much, it scared him.

He didn't know what time it was; he didn't even know what day of the week it was. He'd lost track. Rocki didn't work Sundays and Mondays, and the rest of the week she and her band played from ten at night to two in the morning—that he remembered, he just didn't know when that was. Maybe if he looked at the clock and just didn't pay attention to the numbers, he'd figure it out. He stared at his watch and concentrated until his vision blurred.

He needed to call Rocki. He needed to hear her voice. He needed to figure out what the hell to do about Kendall and the mess he'd made of his life.

Kendall touched his shoulder, and he jumped—he hadn't even heard her. "Why are you sitting here in the dark?"

"Headache."

"I'm sorry. Do you want me to get you anything? Aspirin? Motrin? One of your pain pills?"

"No, but thanks. It's probably just tension. It doesn't make sense, but whenever I get frustrated, I end up with a wicked bad headache."

She slid up behind him and rubbed his shoulders, "I've always heard that sex is an amazing tension reliever. What's got you so keyed up?"

He didn't think telling the truth—that he was terrified of losing her—would help anything. "I couldn't sleep and started thinking. That's never a good thing. I wanted to call my sister, but I don't know what day it is—I've lost track. I don't know what time it is. I'm just frustrated as hell."

"It's—let me think . . ." Firm hands kneaded his shoulder muscles. "It's Sunday at about eleven o'clock, which is a little late to call. Whenever anyone calls after ten, I have a little heart attack, wondering who died. But you know your sister, so if she's not the kind to mind, I'd be happy to dial her number for you."

"No, that's okay. Jaime programmed the numbers I need into the phone. You know, the hospital, nine-one-one, his number, my sister's."

Her thumb dug into the muscle where his shoulder connected to his neck. It hurt like hell, but in a good way. He groaned. "Hold on a minute. I need some lotion. Your shoulders and neck are in knots."

"Lotion?"

"Yeah, it reduces friction."

He dropped his chin to his chest and felt the strain. A second later, warm, slick hands slid over his shoulder, and the scent he always associated with Kendall surrounded him.

"There. Isn't that better?"

Great, now he was not only frustrated and worried; he was horny. "Sweetheart, are you trying to kill me?"

"No, I'm trying to relax you."

"That lotion smells like you. And I can't be in the same room with you and not want you. There's one part of my anatomy that's anything but relaxed."

"Because of my lotion?"

"No, it's the scent of you mixed with the lotion that kills me. I love rubbing against you and getting your scent all over me. This way isn't as much fun."

"It's not supposed to be fun; it's supposed to be relaxing. I'll buy unscented next time I get out to a store, or maybe I'll spring for real massage oil."

A picture of Kendall covered with massage oil filled his mind, as he pictured his hand slipping over her breasts, her belly, her thighs, and making love to her, all wet and slippery and hot.

"Did I hurt you?"

"Huh?" Her hands on him felt fantastic. She had strong extremely talented hands—when she'd squeezed his cock earlier, he'd nearly come.

"You groaned like you were in pain."

"No, not pain exactly. It's more like a cross between heaven and hell. Ecstasy and misery."

"I like the heaven and the ecstasy part—it's the hell and misery we need to work on."

"I was just imagining making love to you with you all

covered in massage oil, our bodies sliding against each other, so hot, so slick, so hard."

She pressed something rigid against the knot on his shoulder and let out a groan of her own, whether from excitement or effort. He also didn't know what the hell she was jabbing him with. Her elbow? She leaned forward and put her weight on it. Her breasts pillowed the back of his head. It hurt like hell, but after a second the muscle seemed to relax. "There you go." She massaged the spot lightly with her fingertips, removing any residual tension, and then repeated the process on his other shoulder.

He sucked in air through his teeth and waited out the pain. "Where'd you learn to do this?"

"One of the physical therapists I know at the hospital teaches massage part-time. Therapeutic massage, sensual massage for couples—she even teaches animal massage."

"What kind did you learn?" He leaned forward, and she ran a slick thumb between his shoulder blade and spine. It felt so good, it should be illegal. So good it earned another groan from him that had nothing to do with the problem he was having in his pants.

"Therapeutic and sensual. I don't have pets. She taught me, and then we'd take turns giving each other massages—you need someone to practice on."

"You practiced sensual massage on a woman?" He pictured Kendall rubbing her hands all over a woman's naked body. He'd always thought it would be a turn-on, but with Kendall it wasn't. He didn't want her hands on any body but his.

"Couples are supposed to practice on each other, but David wasn't into it. So Joni taught me the sensual massage class more in theory and description than in practice."

That was a relief. "Were you naked?"

"I practiced therapeutic massage on Joni, and she practiced on me—not that she needed the practice, but fair is fair. And, no, while receiving a massage, you're not naked. You're on a table under a sheet." Kendall put more lotion in the palms of her hand and rubbed them together and started working the muscles of his upper back in earnest.

He leaned forward a bit more and hoped she'd never stop. "But you're naked under the sheet, right?"

"Yes, but you're covered."

"It doesn't matter—you're still naked."

"So? The person giving the massage is dressed."

"Not in my imagination, you're not."

"You have a very dirty mind." Her voice got that raspy-breathy tone he remembered very well, and he figured she had a very dirty mind too.

"That doesn't sound like a complaint."

"It's not."

He reached around, grabbed her wrist, and pulled her in front of him. She wore nothing but his T-shirt, the one he'd tossed into the great unknown in his haste to get naked. Damned if she didn't look better in it than she did in one of those silky gowns. He splayed his legs and pulled her closer. His face was right at boob level, and his hands grabbed a firm handful of her incredible ass. He'd hardly had time to explore her—he figured it could take days or weeks to learn all her curves. He slid hands from the thigh to waist and back, teasing the crack. "How are you feeling?" He nuzzled her breasts.

She rubbed his neck and pulled his face to her breasts more firmly.

"Shouldn't I be asking you that question?"

"I'm good. Thanks to you, my headache is just about

gone. What about you? Are you sore?" Even in the dim light he could see that she blushed to the roots of her hair. God, she was sweet. "Here?" He slipped his hand between her thighs and sucked in a breath. "You're so wet, you're dripping."

She dropped her head to his shoulder.

"What's got you so hot?"

"Touching you."

He slipped a finger inside her, and her muscles tightened around it. "Are you sore?"

"No, but I ache." She spoke into his shoulder

"You're sure? I don't want to hurt you." His thumb slid over her, and her body gripped his finger like a fist. "So responsive."

He reached into the pocket of his jeans while he slid another finger into her. "Take the shirt off. I want to see you."

Jax ripped the condom wrapper with his teeth, tossed it on the floor, popped the buttons on his jeans, and pushed them down below his knees.

Kendall stood in front of him naked, watching him roll down the condom. "Climb up here, sweetheart, straddle me, and let's christen this couch."

"But . . ."

"I don't want to hurt you. This way, you're in total control. You can take me any way you want. You can make yourself come any way you want." He slid down the seat a little more and helped her, until she was kneeling over him. "Have you ever made love like this?"

"No."

"Just hold on to my shoulders and lower yourself on me. I have a feeling you're going to love it."

"But what about you?"

"I love being with you, in you."

He watched as her body joined with his—it was so hot. He clenched his teeth, held his breath, and prayed for control. The look of ecstasy that crossed her face almost sent him over. She took him in slowly, going deeper with each movement, experimenting with the angle of her body. He knew the second she found her G-spot. Her eyes shot open and glowed in the dim light, she made that sound deep in her throat that made him crazy, and her nails dug into his shoulders.

He gripped her hips, helping her, following her lead, lifting her on the retreat, until she took all of him. Her hand pressed against her stomach as she rocked forward, pressing her pelvis into his, and then she went wild in his arms.

As she rode him, eyes closed, back arched, her hair flowing around her in midnight waves, one hand went to her breast and the other around his neck, drawing him closer.

He sucked her breast into his mouth. He was so afraid he'd finish before she did, he took emergency precautions, sucking in time with the swirl of his thumb over the taut, swollen flesh where they were joined.

"Jack," Kendall's eyes met his, and he watched her soar.

He took over, keeping her rhythm and drawing out her climax, thrusting, lifting, grinding. And when she came again, he followed her over.

She lay, boneless, draped over his shoulder like a rag doll. "Wow. I didn't know . . . I mean, that was so . . ."

It seemed as if the only muscles he could move were his lips, so he smiled against her breast. "That was all you, sweetheart." He'd never forget the look on her face when she took charge of her own pleasure. "So beautiful."

"I guess all those squats I did in the gym actually were good for something."

He kicked off his pants, stood, and carried her back to bed.

———

Jax brought in an armful of wood and threw it in the copper holder. "There's probably two feet of snow out there, and it's still falling."

He leaned against the wall and watched Kendall working in the kitchen. Just watching Kendall move was quickly becoming his second-favorite pastime. The first was making her scream.

Kendall reached for something on a high shelf and her ass cheeks peeked out from under his shirt, and he nearly groaned. He'd tried to talk her into cooking naked, but she didn't fall for it. She said frying bacon could be hazardous. "The good news is, the roof isn't leaking."

"Dad will be happy."

"Not when he finds out about us, he won't." He'd seen Teddy unhappy, disappointed, and even angry. He wasn't looking forward to seeing Teddy after he found out he and Kendall had been occupying the same cabin.

She shot him an over-the-shoulder smile. "How do you know? I think my parents are going to love you."

"If I were your father, I'd break both my legs." Lord knew, if he ever had a daughter who looked like Kendall, he'd follow her around with a shotgun.

"Daddy's just a big, old teddy bear."

Wow, she really didn't have a clue. The Teddy he knew was so far from a Teddy bear, it was laughable. Not that he wasn't a great guy; Jax loved him like a father, but, shit, he'd heard about what Slater had gone through when he started seeing Rocki, and Rocki wasn't even Teddy's baby girl.

"You have nothing to worry about when it comes to Daddy. It's my mother who can be scary. She looks like the world's sweetest woman—and she usually is—but she has a way of breaking people. She's a master of psychological torture and guilt."

"Good to know." Or should he say thanks for the reminder? He'd been on the wrong side of Grace a time or two, and Kendall was right about the psychological warfare and well-targeted bombing strikes using the oldest weapon out there: guilt.

Kendall jumped when he came up behind her and kissed her neck. "That's not going to help me get breakfast on the table."

"I'm good with Wheaties if there's something else you'd rather do than cook."

"I don't eat food out of cardboard boxes, and someone ate all the leftover pizza."

He slid his finger round and round her navel, because he knew it drove her wild. "I had to keep up my strength. And you should be happy I ate the leftover salad too. You were right—it was good." He nipped her ear. "Can I do anything to help?"

She groaned and wiggled her bottom against his fly. "Leave me to make breakfast."

That wasn't what he wanted to hear. He was eyeing the counter and wondering how she felt about kitchen sex. "Tired of me already?"

"No, it's just that you're too distracting."

"You think I'm distracting? You're the one strolling around in nothing but my shirt. Who's distracting who here?" When he spun her around, she looked entirely too pleased to know she was driving him crazy. He loved that little hitch in her breath right before he kissed her.

Jax took her face in his hands and kissed her, softly, slowly, and thoroughly. Memorizing the feel of her cheeks against his palms, the sounds she made in the back of her throat, the taste of her. There was something about her that drew him in — an overarching sweetness that brought him to his knees. All it took was one kiss, and he was lost. One kiss, and he knew if he slid his lips down her neck, he'd feel her pulse race against his lips. One kiss, and she'd melt against him. One kiss, and she was his for the taking.

When he raised his mouth, her eyes were dark and unfocused. "Damn, but you're addictive."

She wrapped her arms around his neck and pulled him down for another kiss.

"Kendall?"

"Uh-huh."

"Sweetheart, something's burning."

Her eyes opened so wide, it was almost comical — that is, until she pushed him away. The scent of burnt butter filled the space between them. "Get out!" She grabbed the pan with a pot holder and headed toward the sink. "See? I told you you're too distracting. Get out."

"Where do you want me to go? We're in the middle of a nor'easter."

"I didn't mean *go* out. I meant get out of the kitchen. Go . . . go build something."

"Fine." He went back to the bedroom and grabbed another T-shirt, put on his work boots, and went to figure out what to do with the first bedroom. The ceiling wasn't going to replace itself.

CHAPTER
TWELVE

Kendall shoved the kitchen window open to let in air. She couldn't believe she'd let Jack distract her enough to burn the butter.

While Jack might be fine with a bowl of Wheaties, she wasn't. She stifled a shiver.

Kendall had awakened in an empty bed last night, starving—unfortunately, before she could get anything to eat, Jack had distracted her—again. She hadn't eaten a thing since their early dinner, and Lord knew she'd burned enough calories. She wasn't sure how many, but she imagined that sex with Jack would burn quite a few.

When it came to sex, Jack was a man who demanded participation—something she really appreciated. Especially last night.

Kendall had never made love like that. She'd never been in charge of her own pleasure or her partner's. Even though she had no idea what she was doing, Jack hadn't made her feel like she was lacking. He just led her through the steps of a new dance until she found her own rhythm and let her take over, never trying to direct her. Letting her discover the secrets and pleasures of control. He never made her feel foolish or embarrassed.

Just the opposite: he supported her and gave her the time to experiment, and when she figured it out, she'd never felt so free, so uninhibited, so powerful. It took a while, but Kendall had slowly taken all Jack had to give, and when they were so close she didn't know where she stopped and he began, she looked into his eyes and saw everything— the wonder, the fear, the excitement, the need, the lust, the sense of connection. She saw every feeling she felt for him reflected back at her. She didn't know what to label what it was between them, but she knew it was strong, it was freeing, it was fun, and it was something she wanted to keep close to her heart forever.

Kendall went back to cooking, and after a few minutes, she heard the high-pitched squeal of a saw. She concentrated on turning the bacon and sausage while she put together her favorite breakfast comfort food: almond French toast. Twenty minutes later, she had breakfast on the table and called out, "Jack, food's on."

He came out of the spare bedroom, brushing off a layer of sawdust that stuck to his arms and chest. He was dressed in his work jeans, boots, and an old T-shirt that was practically see-through, and he blinked at the food on the table. "Sweetheart, it's not as if I don't appreciate you cooking like this—I mean, it's great—but I don't want you to feel as if you have to."

"Oh, I don't. I just like cooking, and it helps me think."

He waited until she took a seat and then joined her. "Should I be worried?"

She thought he'd meant it as a joke, but when she went to pass him the almond-sliver-covered French toast, she saw he was honestly worried about something. "Why would you think that?"

He shrugged and filled his plate. "It just occurred to me that we haven't really talked about stuff."

"Stuff?"

"Relationship stuff." Jack had filled his plate, but he wasn't attacking the food, and that alone was unusual.

Kendall watched him roll his sausage to the side of his plate, trying to avoid the syrup.

"Do you want another plate?"

"Huh?"

"You have a thing about your syrup getting on your bacon and sausage."

"I don't have a thing."

She raised an eyebrow and hid a smile. "You totally have a thing."

"How did you know that?"

"I noticed it when I made pancakes that first morning. It's kind of cute."

"I'm not cute."

"I never said you were. I said the fact you don't like your breakfast meat to touch the syrup is cute. *Cute* like *quirky*, not puppies-and-kittens cute."

He didn't seem at all appeased. Actually, he looked a little nervous.

"What kind of relationship stuff do you want to talk about?"

For someone who brought it up himself, he didn't look like he wanted to talk about it at all. No, he looked more like a kid who was forced to do something he found very distasteful, like eat vegetables. "I haven't been in many relationships, but I've heard enough contemporaries complain about the relationship talk. Although it sounded as if most of the talks were initiated by women."

"You haven't had many relationships?"

He took a bite of his French toast and shook his head before his eyes shot open. He probably didn't notice the slivered almonds in his haste to protect his bacon and sausage from the offending syrup. "This is . . ."

"Way better than Wheaties?"

He nodded and took another bite.

"Why?"

He looked up, confused. He finished chewing, swallowed, and took a sip of coffee. "Why what? Why is it better than Wheaties?"

"No. Why haven't you had many relationships? I mean, you're in your thirties, right?"

"I just haven't had time. I graduated from high school early, started college as a sophomore, and was in a five-year BA/MBA program, but I got out in three and a half. I've been working since just before I turned twenty."

"What are you, some kind of genius or something?"

He shrugged, "I never paid much attention to labels. It was just easier to blow through college—I was younger than everyone else, and I couldn't drink—at least not legally. And with my . . . my family, I couldn't afford to get into any trouble. Besides, I had responsibilities."

"Still, you've been out of school for a while."

"That's true. And until the accident, I've been working crazy hours. No time for relationships."

"Weren't you lonely?"

He shrugged again. "I was too busy to think much about it. Besides, it was no different from my life in school. I took an insane amount of credits to get out as soon as I could. I wanted to be settled so that when my sister graduated from high school, she could come live with me. Our family is a bit of a nightmare."

"A lot of families are. So, did your sister move in with you?"

"No, she's kind of a free spirit. She wanted to study music, so she ended up following her own dream and going away to school."

"That must have been hard for you. But, then, I don't know of many older brothers who would really want their little sister living with them and cramping their style."

"Not much of a style to cramp. If anything, it would be the other way around. My sister is forever telling me to get a life. Now, it seems, I have no choice. I guess when you come close to losing your life, you realize time is not something you should waste, even if you can't really account for it."

"It's a little after eight in the morning."

"That's not what I was getting at."

"I know." She didn't really know what to say. For some reason, she felt like a consolation prize. Lose your ability to add and get a girl. She took a bite of her French toast and then ran a piece of sausage through her syrup before she ate it. When she looked back at Jack, he was watching her and cringing a little. "It's good."

"We'll have to agree to disagree. Years of eating cafeteria food makes you either not care if the food-service worker piles everything on, not bothering to separate it, or it makes you care. A lot."

"I take it you're the latter."

He nodded.

"Okay, I get why you're weirded out about syrup on your breakfast meat, but I still don't understand why you're initiating the relationship talk when you look as if it's the last thing you want to do."

"I was kind of hoping you'd do the honors. You're the one with all the relationship experience, not to mention a master's degree in the damn things."

She laughed at that. "Being able to see the problems in other people's relationships and psyches in no way makes me an expert on my own relationships—obviously. You know enough about my disaster of a past relationship to glean that. What makes you think I'm in a hurry to figure out or put a label on whatever it is we're doing here?"

"Maybe I was hoping you'd want to."

"Jack, it's not that I have an aversion to it; I just don't know what to call this. I don't know how much this attraction has to do with our close proximity. I mean, if you put two straight people of the opposite sex on a deserted island, don't you think they'd eventually get together?"

"We're not on *Gilligan's Island*, for goodness' sake. Hell, if either of us wasn't interested in the other, I would hope we would be strong enough to say thanks, but no. Or, at the very worst, one of us could have left."

God, she felt her face flame like a Bunsen burner. "You did say no, remember?"

"I was trying to be a fuckin' gentleman, Kendall. Do you have any idea how badly I wanted to rip your clothes off? I could barely control myself. I was afraid I'd lose it completely and take you up against the wall like a freakin' animal."

She swallowed hard. "Against a wall?"

He nodded. "Against the wall, in the shower, over the counter, on the table. Damn, I don't think there's a spot in the cabin I haven't pictured—" He stopped speaking and looked away.

"Pictured what?"

He shook his head as if to erase the images he saw flash through his mind. "It doesn't matter."

"Of course it matters! What the hell are you trying to say, Jack?"

"I care about you, okay? And I've never cared about someone the way I care for you and still wanted to . . ."

"You wanted to what? Remember, I've only been with one other person. Sexually, there's no comparison — hell, on every level there's no comparison. So you're going to have to spell it out for me."

"I never wanted to have a relationship outside of bed with anyone but you."

"Really?"

He scrubbed his hands over his face. "Really. I like you. I respect you. I want more than just sex."

"Uh-huh."

"Kendall, I want to make love to you."

"That's what I thought we've been doing. So we're good there, right?"

"Oh yeah, we're real good there."

"So, what's the problem?"

"Nothing. Never mind." He stuffed his last piece of bacon into his mouth and picked up his plate. "Thanks for breakfast. It was great." He looked at her plate. "Are you finished?"

"Hell, no."

"Well, I'm just going to get back to work. Call me when you're done, and I'll help with the dishes."

"So, that's it? You're just going to run away?"

He walked backward, slowly. "I'm not running away, I'm going into another room to rip the shit out of the ceiling."

"Okay, if that helps you sleep at night."

"What do you mean?"

"Just what I said. You're running away—not far, mind you—but away."

She let him go. She'd watched *House of Cards*; she'd seen people have sex up against the wall. And while Kevin Spacey didn't do it for her, Jack did, and the thought that he could be so desperate for her that he couldn't make it to the bed had her rubbing her thighs together. So if he wanted her and she wanted him, what the hell was the problem? There wasn't a whole lot to do in the cabin except fix the ceiling, cook, eat, and make love. And, really, it's not as if the ceiling was going anywhere.

The door was closed, but she still heard the muffled sound of male grunting, the splintering of wood, the crunch of plaster beneath behemoth boots. The man really did have big feet.

She got up from the table and went to the bedroom, grabbed Jack's phone, and dialed Erin. "Erin, it's me."

"Hi, me. How's it going?"

"I don't know. I just had the strangest conversation with Jack. I just don't get it."

"Okay, explain."

Kendall recapped the conversation.

All Erin did was laugh. It took a while for her to stop. "Kendall, so when you were with David, how was your sex life?"

"Boring compared to what I've been doing with Jack."

"And what, exactly, have you been doing with Jack?"

"Nothing boring, I assure you."

"Different positions?"

"We've only been together that way for less than twenty-four hours."

"And did he make you crazy?"

"Yes. What are you getting at, Erin?"

"Just that when guys get crazy, it tends to get a little kinkier, a little dirtier, more intense, more physical, more urgent, and sometimes the control—or lack thereof—scares them. It's the difference between making love to you and, well, for want of a better term, fucking your brains out."

"Erin!"

"Now, just hear me out. There's nothing wrong with letting a loving relationship get a little crazy. Don't you ever want to feel out of control?"

"I feel out of control every time Jack touches me—heck, even sometimes when he looks at me."

"Oh, my."

"Yeah, and he's turned me into—"

"A nymphomaniac?"

"How did you know?"

"I thought the same thing when Cameron and I first got together."

"Does it calm down?"

"God, I hope not. Of course we have Janie, so there's no kitchen-table sex until after bedtime. But Cam is horrible; he starts teasing me as soon as he gets home. It's like hours of foreplay. By the time Janie's asleep, we're so hot and bothered, we rarely make it to the bedroom for round one. Thank God Janie's a heavy sleeper."

"So, this is normal?"

"I don't know about normal, but with Cam and me, it's always been this way. But, then, maybe I'm just easy."

"I know that's not the case. How many men did I fix you up with?"

"Way too many. What did you expect? They were all

carbon copies of David, and not to stereotype or anything, but firefighters are hot, whereas financial analysts
. . . not so much. And before you break your arm patting
yourself on the back, you never fixed me up with Cam."

"It was a fix-up. You two just didn't know it. When I
recommended you for the home–health care position, I
had a feeling you'd be perfect for Cam and Janie in more
ways than just caregiving."

"No, it was worse. I seduced my boss, or maybe he
seduced me. But, then, it could have been Henry."

"Henry?"

"Henry the Eighth. We started watching *The Tudors*.
Who knew history was such a turn-on?"

"Erin, I feel as if I'm missing stuff."

"Explain."

"Well, David wasn't very—"

"Good?"

"No, not good. Not very interested. He was mechani-
cal at best."

"And that's all you know?"

"Well, except for what Jack and I . . . and what I've
read. But I didn't think it was real. Not until now. I just
thought, it was . . . you know . . . fiction."

"It's not. Kendall, we read the same books, and I can
attest to the fact that it's all very real. The only things
that might be exaggerated are the length and girth of the
hero's erection, and his staying power, but I do like to try
to make Cam lose control."

"How do you learn to do that?"

"You experiment. Believe me, he'll enjoy it. Good
luck, and call me later and tell me how it goes."

"Wait . . . I don't know if I can do that."

"Kendall, you're such a lady. Jack's not going to see

you as anything else unless you take matters into your own hands and show him."

"But what if he doesn't want that?"

"Believe me, Kendall, all men want that."

"David didn't."

"It's like that famous Jerry Hall quote: 'My mother said it was simple to keep a man, you must be a maid in the living room, a cook in the kitchen, and a whore in the bedroom.' You just need to show him you're not always such a lady."

Jax ripped the rest of the plaster and lath off the ceiling and, with Kendall's help measuring, together they cut and installed the furring strips perpendicular to the ceiling joists.

He thought Kendall would take off as soon as the measuring was done, but she stuck around, and she stuck tight. She even helped him hold up the large sheets of drywall as he hammered them onto the furring strips.

He had to hand it to her: the woman had some serious upper-body strength, and he already knew she had strong legs. Visions of her riding him had left him hot and distracted all day.

Kendall wasn't averse to getting her hands dirty either. She was great with a pencil and a drywall saw, and she had a blast helping him mud and tape the joints. By the time they finished up for the day, they had the drywall installed, the first coat of mud was drying, and they were covered with dirt and dust.

He folded the ladder and rested it against the wall and turned to her. "Thanks for your help. I think it would have taken me three times as long to get it done alone."

"You're getting better, you know."

He wasn't sure what she meant, and it must have showed on his face.

"You just said it would have taken you three times as long to do this alone."

He shrugged. He used to be the king of hiding his thoughts, but either he'd lost the ability, or Kendall just got really good at reading him.

"I spent the day asking how many of whatever it was you needed, and you told me. And except for a mistake or two—which I think is completely normal—you were able to calculate small numbers pretty well."

"I hadn't noticed."

She obviously had, and the look of pride on her face made him want to kiss her, so he did. She tasted like drywall dust and Kendall—he never thought he'd find dirty, dusty, and sweaty sexy, but she rocked it.

Even after a hell of a kiss, she still beamed at him. Damn, he hadn't had anyone look at him like that since his mother watched him make the Olympic Trials. "When was the last time you tried to do anything math-related?"

"Before you came here. I got so frustrated looking at things and not being able to make sense out of them, I stopped."

She pulled the damp T-shirt clinging to her chest and abs away from her skin in a vain attempt to cool off. "I think after we get showered and fed, we should pull out the cards. I also bought a few books when I was at the store. They had a pretty good selection of grade-school math primers."

Shit, looking at children's math books was the last thing he wanted to do—except maybe have that discussion he had been trying to have during breakfast. He'd never had to have a Where Is This Relationship Going? talk, and his first try failed miserably. Still, he didn't have to know how to do algebra to know his window of opportunity was closing at an alarming rate. And, for the first time, he wasn't looking for a relationship escape hatch. He was looking for just the opposite, although since he'd never wanted a relationship to work before, he didn't hold out much hope. Still, he had to try, didn't he?

He couldn't take his eyes off Kendall—she was a mess. She had a big dollop of drywall mud on her shirt right above her left breast, and her hair was covered with so much dust, she looked like she wore a powdered wig. He reached over and peeled the clump of mud off her shirt. "Close your eyes."

Kendall closed her eyes and raised her face to his, her mouth tipped into a secret smile.

"Keep them closed, okay?"

The smile got bigger, and he stepped closer, her body warm against his. She smelled like drywall dust, clean sweat, and wildflowers. He couldn't help but kiss her again while he ran his hands through her hair, trying to dislodge most of the dust. When the kiss turned deeper, he wrapped her long hair around his hand and tugged her head back to get better access to her mouth and swallowed her moan. All thoughts of cleaning her up were replaced with thoughts of stripping her out of her clothes.

"I'm getting in the shower." She slid out of his arms and stripped off her T-shirt on her way out the door and looked over her shoulder. "Are you coming?"

No, but he planned on coming right after their shower.

She had her jeans slipping down over her hips before she made it out of the room, and kicked them off in the hall on the way to the bathroom. The bra came next, and then she shimmied out of her panties.

Jax followed her lead, wondering where this side of Kendall had come from. Sure, the first time they'd kissed, she'd taken off her top—he'd just about lost it when she had—but he also remembered the uncertainty and doubt he saw in her eyes even before he pushed her away. It didn't help her confidence any when he told her to put her shirt back on. Yeah, he probably could have handled that better, but, damn, he'd just wanted to get her covered up before he started listening to his little head instead of his big one. The way he'd wanted her scared the crap out of him; he'd never felt the urge to possess someone before. He'd always liked sex—who didn't?—but what he'd felt for Kendall went way beyond lust. It was animalistic. He'd wanted to rip the rest of her clothes off and grab her by the hair and take her. He had to get a grip. Right now, he figured all the blood in his body was racing south, and there wasn't enough blood in his head to even think.

Kendall started the water, stepped into the shower, and pulled him in behind her. He'd been dreaming of Kendall in the shower ever since she put on that little show of hers that had him hard for hours. Now she stood under the spray, washing her hair, eyes closed, her face turned up, her back arched, her breasts with nipples pebbled in the cool air, and rivers of soap sluicing down her body in interesting streams.

"You are so damn beautiful."

"I'm a mess, but thanks. This water feels so good." She pulled him under the spray with her. "Your turn."

He turned into the spray and let the water wash over his hair and face and shampooed the dust out of his hair.

He was in the middle of rinsing when Kendall slipped

her arms around his waist, her front to his back, and soaped him up—everywhere.

He blew a stream of air through his teeth. "Kendall?"

"Jack." One soapy hand slid up and down his erection while the other slid lower and cupped his balls, gently rolling them in her hand.

It felt way too good. He groaned and knew he needed to put a stop to it before she had him shooting all over the tile wall. He grabbed her wrist and turned around to face her, taking control of the soap. He had fun washing her breasts and the rest of her body—paying special attention to every nook and cranny.

She bit her lip and spread her legs a little more.

Jax let the water rinse over all the places he washed before his fingers teased the sensitive flesh at the apex of her thighs, where she was hot and wet. He slid a finger deep inside and swirled his thumb lightly against her.

Kendall bit her lip. "This isn't going according to plan."

"You had a plan?"

She tried to hold back a moan, but he coaxed it out of her.

"Are you disappointed?"

She grabbed onto his shoulders and rested her head against his chest as she ground against his hand. "No. Not . . . Oh, God. Yes. Just like that. Oh, Jack."

He loved watching her come, feeling her muscles convulse around his fingers, or, better yet, his dick. "Sweetheart, we need to move this to the bedroom."

"Why?" The question came out on a moan, and his dick jerked like he'd been hit with a live wire.

"Because I didn't bring a condom."

"You don't need one."

Jax's face froze in the steam, and he stepped back.

"Um, sweetheart?" He wasn't sure how to proceed. He could almost hear his sister Rocki's voice in his head saying, *Awkward!* "Are you on birth control?"

Kendall sat on the shower bench, and her face turned cherry red. "Yes, but that's not what I meant. I don't want ..."

Jax frowned. "You don't want what?"

"I mean, I want ... You see, David never wanted ... so I've never tried to do it ..." She stared at his dick, shot him a quick glance, and then ping-ponged her gaze off the three shower walls she could see.

He pushed back his irritation at hearing her ex's name. "David never wanted what?"

"He never wanted me to ... you know. So I've never ... And I was thinking—I mean, if you want me to. Umm."

Jax felt dizzy and grabbed the shower stall door. "Are you trying to tell me you've never performed oral sex on a guy?"

She nodded her head, her face still flaming.

"You wanted to and he said no? Was he gay?"

She looked at him as if she'd just wondered the same thing. "No. No. No. He couldn't be." She was doing some serious talking herself out of the idea.

Maybe the guy was just asexual. "He's probably not gay, because from what I hear, gay guys like blow jobs just fine."

"Do you?"

He couldn't help but smile. "Is that a trick question?"

"No. I was just wondering, because, well, David never ... and you never asked ..."

"It's not something that's easy to ask for, especially since not everyone feels comfortable doing it or even wants to. Besides, when it comes to pleasure, it's definitely one-sided."

"But so is what you do to me."

"I love making you come with my mouth. I love the taste of you. It also serves to relieve the pressure of the Ladies Should Always Come First rule. But with a guy, it's different. A woman can have multiple orgasms—men can't."

"You have." She wore a very self-satisfied grin.

"That was an anomaly, believe me. That's never happened to me before. So, there's the recovery time—not that it has to go that far. It's one thing to start, and a totally different thing to finish." He'd always had stellar control, and he'd had only one lover who liked taking him all the way in her mouth. He'd never worried about being able hold back before, but everything was different with Kendall. He didn't seem to have much control over his reaction to her. He wondered if he'd be able to keep himself in check when just the thought of her mouth on him had his balls drawing up.

"I didn't think you wanted me to."

"I thought if you wanted to, you'd do it. Believe me, sweetheart, I wouldn't stop you—ever."

She reached for him, sliding her hand from base to tip, dragging up a groan from the soles of his feet. She licked her lips, "I want to . . ."

The sound of her voice made the base of his spine tingle. "Sweetheart, if you keep talking about it, I'm gonna be the one needing to sit down."

The water was growing cold, so Jax turned the taps off.

"Come on, let's go to bed." He pulled her up against him and kissed her. She was still so red in the face, it was almost comical. "Next time we'll do it in the shower. This time, though, let's start off somewhere more comfortable and closer to condoms."

"But we don't need—"

He tugged her out of the shower, tied a towel around his waist, and wrapped her up in another. "Believe me, sweetheart, the thought of your mouth on me makes me so hot, I don't trust myself to behave. I can just about guarantee we're going to need several."

She grabbed another towel and ran it over her hair and walked out of the bathroom. "I guess it's a good thing I bought some then, huh?"

He did a double take. "You bought condoms?"

"When I was in the grocery store." She went to the bed-side table, opened the drawer, and took out three large boxes. "I didn't know what size, so I bought a variety."

"Well aren't you just the good little Girl Scout? And you look so innocent." Jax couldn't help it—he laughed so hard, his eyes watered.

"It was pretty embarrassing. The look on the clerk's face was priceless. I told her it was for a gag gift."

That got him laughing even harder. He grabbed the box of large and, in case they ran out, tossed the others back in the drawer.

"I was trying to be responsible."

"Me too. I ran over to the pharmacy while you were in the grocery store. Where do you think I got my stash?"

"I thought you traveled with them."

"No, I hadn't planned on you, and I didn't think I would end up needing them in a cabin alone in the woods. I didn't bring any with me." He dried her off and pulled down the covers on the bed. "Get in before you get cold. I'll keep you warm."

Kendall slid between the sheets, and he tossed his towel and followed. First he pulled her against him and rolled her under him, kissing her. Exploring her mouth, playing tag with her tongue. She pushed him away, hands on his shoulders. "What if I don't do it right?"

"Sweetheart, it's not rocket science. Just, you know, watch the teeth."

"Do you want it?"

"I want whatever you want. Whatever you're willing to give me, and nothing that makes you feel uncomfortable. All you have to do is tell me what you want, sweetheart, and it's yours."

"You mean it?"

"Every word." He took a deep breath and let it out slowly. Grabbed her hand and wrapped it around his dick.

Her hand tightened around him, and he gritted his teeth as she slid her hands over him, stopping to cup his balls, raking her short nails over them lightly, making him hiss out a breath.

"Did I hurt you?"

He shook his head.

She slid a finger over the head, spreading around the precum already leaking. It was all he could do not to pump into her hand.

He put his hand around hers and squeezed harder, just like he liked it, and groaned when she got the perfect grip. He looked at the ceiling and started thinking about drywall and mud, rotting plaster—anything to avoid watching her little hand jack him off.

A second later, wet heat slid over the head and a tongue lapped around the sensitive ridge. His stomach muscles clenched so tightly, it made it hard to breathe. "Damn, girl, that feels amazing." He looked at her, her head over his erection, her mouth full, her still-wet hair ticking his stomach and thighs, and her dark eyes on his.

Kendall's mouth followed her hand as she took him deeper with each pass. When she hollowed out her cheeks and sucked, it was all he could do not to raise his hips.

He ran his hand through her hair, holding her head, leading without pushing. He needed to be able to pull her off him before he got too close. But it felt too good. His heels dug into the mattress, his thighs shook, and he forgot to breathe. When his balls drew up, the tingling at the base of his spine told him it was time to pull out. "Kendall, stop, or I'm going to come." He tugged on her hair to pull her up, but she didn't heed his warning—just the opposite.

She slid her hand farther between his legs, pressed hard against his perineum, and, like she'd hit a fire-the-torpedoes button, he lost it with a roar.

He groaned, saw stars, and came like he'd never come before, his entire body vibrating. She didn't let up; she kept sucking and working it until he felt like one huge exposed nerve.

Every muscle in his body twitched, his stomach muscles ached from the strain, and his mind splintered into a million pieces. It took him a minute or two before he could think straight and get his breathing under control. "Damn, sweetheart, where in the hell did you learn to do that?"

She smiled and licked her lips, looking like a cat who'd just knocked over a gallon of cream. "I put a few things together between what I learned reading and that sensual massage course."

He pulled her up to him and kissed her senseless. "What else did you learn at that sensual massage course?"

"I guess you'll have to wait and find out, won't you?"

CHAPTER THIRTEEN

Kendall watched Jack sleep and didn't bother hiding her satisfied smile. Oh yeah, things were going really well, and, thanks to her talk with Erin, Jack had finally stopped treating her like a china doll. She might be walking funny for a few days, but she'd succeeded in making him lose control three times in the past few hours and had loved every minute of it. She felt powerful, in charge, in control, and that was something she'd never experienced before. Everything about her sexuality, her life, her future had been dictated by David, and she'd just gone along with it. Now she was in charge, and although it was scary, it was exciting, new, and empowering.

Kendall slid out of bed and pulled on a sweatshirt, a pair of leggings, and thick wool socks, and headed to the kitchen to figure out what to make for dinner. As far as she could see, the only bad thing about being in a secluded mountain cabin during a nor'easter was that there was no available takeout.

She stared into the refrigerator, thoughts tumbling through her mind like dice on a craps table. The snow had stopped, and her parents would be back in town any day now, so, really, there was no reason to continue hiding out at the cabin. She could go to town and see if there was space available—either a storefront or a house close to downtown that would serve as an office and living space. She needed to find out about SBA loans and check out the want ads for a job. She might be able to get a part-time job and start a practice—heck, even if she got a full-time job, there was no reason she couldn't start seeing patients on weekends and in the evenings.

Her fingers itched to make a to-do list. She'd always been a huge list maker, and she realized she hadn't made a list since she met Jack.

Jack. Where did he fit into this new life of hers? How many of the changes, realizations, and plans she'd made had he been at least partly responsible for? If she hadn't met Jack, would she still be lying around wallowing in her sorrow and eating Ben & Jerry's? She would still be under the assumption that sexually there was something wrong with her. Now she was pretty damn sure there was absolutely nothing wrong with her at all. Unfortunately, she couldn't say the same thing about David. But, then, David was no longer her problem. Thank God.

She'd been staring into the fridge like it was some kind of crystal ball, and she still didn't have a clue what to make. She needed something quick and hearty with lots of protein, because she had a few other things to check off her sexual bucket list, and she wanted to make sure Jack had the energy he needed. She pulled out the eggs, cheese, leftover veggies, and meat—when all else failed, a good frittata was fast, easy, and yummy.

"I didn't say you could leave the bed, young lady." She'd just smiled at the sound of his voice, but then she felt teeth on the back of the neck, strong arms wrapping around her waist, and her feet leaving the floor.

"Jack, if I don't cook, you don't eat. We haven't even had lunch, and I don't know about you, but I've worked up quite an appetite."

"The only appetite I have is for you."

Jack set her back on her feet, and she turned in his arms. God, she could get used to this. "I'm not buying it. I've watched you eat almost nonstop since I got here and tossed some food down in front of you—of course, I had to watch my fingers when I fed you."

He backed her up against the counter and kissed her neck, nipping her earlobe, sending tingles to all her girl parts. "You do bring out the animal in me."

"I know. Isn't it great?"

He gave her one of his crooked smiles. "I'm just glad you think so. I was having a hard time keeping the tiger caged around you. But then you did everything to pick the damn lock."

"You just bring out my adventurous side. I feel like I've been living kind of a half-life. I didn't know it could be any different. But now I know, and I'm really glad I'm not there anymore."

"Are you happy you're here?"

She looked at him and saw a flash of uncertainty. At least she thought she had. She remembered her suspicions about his loss. Not that she knew what it was—he never mentioned it—but it was there between them, and it was a real, living, breathing elephant in the room. "I am happy. I thought that was pretty evident."

"Do you want to stay here? With me?"

"Are we talking physically or metaphorically?"

"Definitely metaphorically."

"Jack, where are you from?"

"Chicago."

"And don't you have a life there to get back to?"

"If my brain heals, I have a job, but a life? No, no life."

She didn't have much of a life either. But she was going to start living one. "You know, as a therapist, I have to tell you that after a traumatic event, you shouldn't jump into anything serious for a year or make any major life changes."

"What's your definition of a traumatic event?"

"A death of a loved one, divorce, and I would say a traumatic brain injury would qualify."

"So, what are you supposed to do for this year while you're not jumping into anything serious or making major life changes?"

"That's a good question."

"Sweetheart, I have a feeling you don't choose serious—it just kind of creeps up on you. And, no, I didn't have a life in Chicago, but after the accident, I wished I'd had one. Once you come close to dying, you have a real aversion to wasting any of the time you have left." He stood there looking much younger than she'd ever thought he could. "I couldn't remember anything about the day of the accident—I still can't. I'm told I was skiing and caught an edge and went headfirst into a big tree." He said it like it was nothing, but he touched that spot by his scalp. "I looked like I'd gotten run over by a truck."

She laughed because he'd wanted her to, but she didn't think it was at all funny. She could imagine him all battered and bruised, and the thought of him injured made her heart hurt.

"I'd been in a drug-induced coma for a few days, and when I woke up, I was alone in the ICU. I didn't know where I was, and whether or not those drugged-out dreams or nightmares I had were real or imagined. I remember wanting to see my sister and some family friends, and wondering if there was a woman out there I loved and who loved me. I didn't remember anyone, and I thought, Shit, what if I have amnesia or something? That's when I freaked out, and all the nurses came running. I still had the drain in my head, and when I got up, the amount of fluid draining increased. They were not happy with me."

"I imagine you weren't the easiest patient."

"That's an understatement."

"It must have been terrifying."

"The nurses were quick to tell me that my sister and our friends had been there the whole time, and that, no, I wasn't married and didn't have a girlfriend—at least one who cared enough to show up."

"I'm sure they did. Were those the same nurses who gave you their phone numbers?"

He did one of his one-shoulder shrugs. "Yeah, actually, they were. But, Kendall, they didn't mean anything to me. No one did. That was my problem. Once I woke up, I realized I'd spent most of my life either going to school or doing my job, and I didn't know why. I mean, I was good at it, and, sure, I guess I got some enjoyment from it, but I didn't choose it. I was groomed. It's a family business, and I'm all the family that's left."

"Your parents?"

"They're gone. I have some uncles, and when I graduated, I was supposed to take my rightful place in the family business."

"What did you want to do?"

"I don't think I ever thought about it. It's kind of like being born a prince. You don't choose to become a king— you just do. I didn't think there were options. I loved swimming, but . . ." He shook his head. "My folks died right before the Olympic Trials, and I was transferred to an all-boys boarding school. I lost my home, my team, my coaches."

"And your sister?"

"All-girls school."

"You lost everyone you loved and your dreams on the same day?"

"It felt like it at the time."

She felt tears welling in her eyes, and she realized that with Jack, she'd lost all the ability to see him and his situation clinically. "I'm so sorry."

"Shit, sweetheart, don't cry. Please. I can't stand to see you cry." As he pulled her to him, her face found that spot in the crook of his neck. He smelled so good, like soap and laundry detergent and something intrinsically him.

She sniffed. "I'm not crying."

"Right, your eyes are just leaking."

"You know how women are when they're PMSing— we just dissolve into tears for no reason."

He wiped the tears with his thumbs and shook his head. "You slay me, Kendall. You're the first woman I've ever cared about. I can't help but think that means something. Whatever this is, for me, at least, it's serious. I guess you need more time."

"Jack, it's not like that—"

He cut her off with a kiss. The kind of kiss that speaks volumes but leaves you wondering if you're translating it correctly. "I'm going to go sand some drywall and put on another coat of mud."

She'd suddenly lost her appetite, but she knew she had to cook something just to get her thoughts in order.

And then she had to make a list.

Jax stepped out to the porch and squinted at the bright morning sun. He needed to grab another load of firewood and cool off. Kendall was in the cabin cooking breakfast half-naked. He turned to find Jaime striding through the snow, looking like he needed a stiff drink or a cup of coffee at the least, which meant he needed to warn Kendall.

As Jaime drew closer, Jax grew more concerned. Not only did Jaime not look happy—the guy usually walked around with a smile on his face—but he also looked more than a little pissed off. "What's wrong?"

Jaime came up on the porch and stomped the snow off his boots. "Well, good fuckin' morning to you too."

The last time Jax had seen Jaime this pissed, both of them had ended up bruised. "It was going great until you got here."

"Oh, I can imagine how great. You're enjoying the hell out of yourself, and you're leaving me to clean up after you."

"Excuse me?"

"Addie stopped by the shop just before the storm hit, worried about Kendall being up here all alone during the storm."

"And?"

"She was afraid Kendall was running out of food, so I told her that Kendall was fine and that I lent her the truck to go Concord to do some shopping and to pick up a part for me."

"Good. That's good. So we have no problems then, right?"

"No problems? Are you serious? Jax, if you haven't told Kendall who the hell you are yet, you've got more problems than you can count."

"Funny. Very funny."

"I'm deadly serious. There are some things men shouldn't do—having sex with a woman under false pretenses is one of them."

"Kendall knows exactly how I feel about her."

"And who does she think has all these feelings for her? Jackson Finneus Sullivan the Third, the Grand Pooh-Bah of Harmony, or some carpenter named Jack who got knocked upside the head by a tree?"

"Jaime."

"Yet you'll let her think she's sleeping with someone you're not. Isn't that the same thing?"

"I care about her."

"Yeah, and which one of you is that—Jax or Jack?"

"Jack. I don't know if Jax will ever come back, or even if I want him to."

Jaime shook his head. "There was nothing wrong with my friend Jax that a realignment in priorities couldn't fix. All work and no play . . ."

"No life."

Jaime leaned against the porch rail. "Yeah, pretty much. Look, word in town is that Grace and Teddy are expected back any day. The nor'easter might have slowed them down a little, but, dude, you'd better come clean with Kendall, and soon. If not, I don't see this ending well for either of us."

"Us? What are you worried about?"

"What am I worried about? I'm up to my eyeballs in your lie. It was one thing covering for each other when we were kids. I could even deal with slowing down the axle repair—Kendall doesn't have a clue how long car repairs take. But as for the rest, if Kendall gets hurt and Addie finds out I had anything to do with it, she'll turn me into a eunuch. Painfully and slowly."

Jax had known Addie all his life—sure, he hadn't see her often, but people didn't change that much. "She's a kindergarten and Sunday-school teacher. How scary could she be? Face it: Addie's a pussycat."

"Oh no, she's not. She's a small mountain lion who has already tasted blood. You don't know. She's very protective of her friends. And what's going to happen when Teddy and Grace get wind of it? And they will, because I seriously doubt you and Kendall are just playing tiddly-winks in there."

"Shit, Jaim." He sat on the porch and put his elbows on his knees. "What the hell am I going to do? I've tried talking to her about us, the future, but she's skittish as hell."

"Can you blame her?"

"No, but I can't help but think that when she finds out the truth, she's going to think I'm just as bad as that dirt-bag David."

"She might, but you still need to tell her the truth and beg for forgiveness. Oh, and don't you dare tell her I knew anything about your alter ego."

"She's going to hate me. She's been hurt by her ex, and she's going to think I did the same thing."

"Then you have to prove to her that you're not usually a dirtbag. Look, I've known Kendall for a long time. She's reasonable, and if she's sleeping with you, she cares about you."

"I need more time."

"No, you're all out of time. If you wait any longer, you're just being a selfish prick."

Kendall hollered out the door, "Jack, breakfast is ready."

"Sweetheart, we've got company. You might want to get dressed."

Shit. She knew cooking almost naked was a mistake. She ran to the bedroom and threw on clothes, and hoped to hell she wasn't still blushing when she stuck her head back out to find Jack and Jaime in what looked like a Mexican standoff. As soon as they saw her, the two of them went from looking like they were about to beat the crap out of each other to best buds. "Everything okay?"

"Hey, Kenny."

"Jaime, what are you doing here?"

Jaime grabbed her and wrapped her in a bear hug, lifting her right off her feet, and gave her a kiss on the cheek before setting her gently back on the floor. "I just dropped by to check on you. How's it going, beautiful?"

She looked from Jaime to Jack and back again. There was definitely something going on between them she wasn't privy to, and it didn't look anything like a bromance. "I'm doing well. Breakfast is ready and I made a ton of food, so why don't you come join us?"

"Don't mind if I do. Thanks." He shot Jack a smug grin and sauntered in, pulling off his hat and coat.

Kendall didn't have time to figure out what was going on between them, so she ran back to the kitchen to get another place setting and more coffee.

She set Jaime a place and told the guys to dig in while she went to hunt down her coffee. She needed a cup with an alarm that went off when she moved more than three feet away from it, because she was forever losing her coffee. When she returned, the guys had their heads together, and they were fighting under their breath. "Okay, what's going on? I know something's wrong, because neither of you have touched the food."

Jaime looked up from his cup and shrugged. "Addie came by the shop the other day asking me to check on you. She said you were up here all alone, and, with the storm coming, she was worried you'd run out of food."

"I'll give her a call later." She turned to Jack. "Addie's a bit of a worrywart. She wasn't happy I came up here on my own. I'm surprised she hasn't stopped by before now."

She served them both the buckwheat pancakes she'd made, which looked so good, she'd even taken a picture to post on Pinterest when she got home.

Jaime took the syrup Kendall passed to him and drowned his sausages.

Kendall risked a quick side glance at Jack. He looked almost ill for a nanosecond.

Jaime took a bite, groaned, and speared another sausage. "If Addie says anything, you tell her I lent you my truck to go shopping in Concord, okay? Oh, and you picked up a part for me. It was the only way I could keep her from coming out here and finding you and Romeo."

"Okay. But I'm not too worried about it. I'm sure if I call and tell her about Jack, she won't freak out too badly." She reached over and gave Jack's thigh a squeeze. "She's a little overprotective. Besides, it's about time Jack met some people. It's not as if he's been hiding back here — he just hasn't had a car."

Jaime looked up from his plate and shot Jack another look.

She cleared her throat. "And speaking of cars, how's the Jeep coming along?"

"It's finished. You can pick it up today, if you want. It's in the garage at the house, and I plowed the lane."

"How much is it going to cost? I forgot to pack my checkbook, so I need to stop by the bank and get cash. I wish I'd thought of it when we were in Concord."

"Don't worry about it. Jack paid for the parts, and I just worked on it in my free time. It was no big deal."

Jack glared at Jaime, and Jaime glared right back between bites of food.

"What's going on between you two?"

Both men shoved pancakes in their mouths and the groan fest began. She was used to people praising her food, but, right now, it only annoyed her. She sat back, sipped her now-cold coffee, and watched them. "You might want to slow down. This isn't a competition."

"The faster we eat, the sooner Jaime will leave."

"And miss a third cup of coffee?"

"You've only had one."

"I know. The first is to warm me up, the second is to enjoy after we eat, and the third to savor on the walk back."

"Then I'd better put on another pot." She hightailed it into the kitchen and reheated her cup in the microwave while she made fresh coffee. She really missed her Keurig—well, David's Keurig. But, then again, there was something about listening to the gurgle and perk that reminded her of home and family.

She popped her head around the corner. Both men were going at it again in angry whispers and pointing their forks at each other. She was glad she hadn't bothered to set out knives. She took a deep breath and grabbed the fresh pot. "You guys doing okay?"

They sat ramrod straight when she rounded the corner, as if they had been caught lighting matches behind a barn.

"We're fine, gorgeous." Jaime's smile looked tight and drawn. "I may have to steal you away from Jack." The name Jack came out on a hard consonant, with a whisper of an -ass at the end.

"Try it, and you won't ever eat again."

"Why's that?"

"You'll be dead."

Jaime guffawed. "You're the one on borrowed time. All I have to do is sit back and wait."

"What are you two talking about?"

"How much will it cost me to get you to leave right now?"

Jaime picked up his plate. "It's only fair that I do the dishes after such an amazing breakfast. I should walk up here for lunch and dinner. I'll get to eat great food and make my hands Palmolive soft."

Jack took the plate out of Jaime's hand. "That won't be necessary. I'm sure you have other things to do."

"Not at the moment. Hey, Kendall, aren't your parents due back tomorrow?"

Jack gripped the plates so hard, his knuckles turned white.

"Umm, I'm not sure. What day is it?" She was glad she hadn't eaten much. The thought of leaving Jack turned the coffee in her stomach sour.

"Tuesday. The airport opened back up this morning, and most of the roads are cleared."

"No, they're coming home on Thursday, if I remember correctly. But, then, I left their itinerary in Boston."

She watched Jack visibly relax.

Jaime raised an eyebrow. "You're not picking them up at the airport?"

"No, the Grand Pooh-Bah gave them the trip. I'm sure he arranged for a limo."

Jack looked like a guy with a bad case of colitis. "You saw that on their itinerary?"

"No, but my parents didn't ask me to pick them up, and since they thought I'd be in Boston, I'm sure they would have. Besides, the Grand Pooh-Bah had a limo take them to the airport. I'm sure even he would realize they'd need a ride back."

"Come on. This guy can't as bad as you make him sound."

She couldn't help but laugh at the look on Jack's face; it was as if he were insulted for the poor little rich boy. "Ask Jaime—he was best friends with him growing up."

Jaime just smiled. "Oh, he's worse. Jax and I have been friends all our lives, and you know he's never once invited me to visit him in Chicago."

"Chicago? Hey, Jack's from Chicago too."

Jaime shook his head. "What a co-winki-dink. Well, I'd better hit the trail."

She got up. "I thought you wanted another cup of coffee."

Jaime tugged on his coat. "I just remembered I have something to do. I'll take a rain check. Your Jeep is out of the garage, and I left the keys in it for you, so whenever you want to drop by to get it is fine."

"Are you sure I can't pay you for labor?"

"I'd rather trade in food. When you get tired of Jack, you just come down to my place. I have an extra bedroom, and I'll give you carte blanche at the grocery store."

Jack stood, pushing his chair back so hard, Kendall was surprised it didn't hit the wall. "I'll walk you out."

Kendall rose and followed him to the door "Thanks for coming by, Jaime, and for all your help with the Jeep. I really appreciate it." She gave him a hug.

"You know where I am if you need anything, Kenny. Anything at all."

"Thanks, but I'm fine." She pulled away, and the look he gave her made her feel like someone had walked across her grave.

Jack gave her a worried look and then followed Jaime out. It was a wonder she wasn't overcome with testosterone poisoning with those two. She picked up the dishes and tried to figure out what the hell just happened.

CHAPTER
FOURTEEN

J ax wanted to kill Jaime. He gave Kendall a kiss before he followed his ex–best friend out, thinking he'd have to wait to get far enough away so Kendall didn't hear Jaime's screams.

Jaime stepped off the porch and knocked his shoulder. "Sorry, man. I went too far. But in my own defense, I didn't know you told her you were from Chicago."

Jax stuffed his hands in his pockets and trudged down the lane. "I don't lie to Kendall."

Jaime shot him a what-the-fuck? look.

"I just didn't tell her my full name. I've never lied to her about anything. She asked me where I was from, and I told her."

"Right, Jack. You're absolved of all sin. Feel better now?"

He looked around, noticing how the snow-covered trees cut the bright blue sky. He felt like shit.

"She talked about you—the Grand Pooh-Bah—and you didn't tell her. You had the perfect opportunity."

"With you right there?"

"At least you'd have some protection."

"Jesus, Jaime. I'm going through hell here, and you're roasting marshmallows and enjoying the show."

"You're not the only one in deep shit, Jax. Kendall's never going to forgive me for going along with your plan. You'd better tell Kendall I advised against your dastardly little plan. But, then, by the time I found out about it, it was already a done deal, wasn't it? The only choice I had was to go along with it or blow it for you. And God help me if Addie gets wind of it. Fuck, you have no idea the shit storm you just rained down on me."

"Did you try to talk me out of it?"

"Hell, I don't remember. All I know is that for the first time in years, I looked at you and you looked like my best friend again. I don't know what the hell it is about Kendall, or maybe it was the knock on the head, but it was like the prick you've been since you went away to that hoity-toity boarding school disappeared. I was just happy to have the real you back, man."

"All these years you thought I was a prick?"

"Well, yeah. Whenever we got together, all you would do was talk about work. If you weren't on the phone, you were on the damn computer."

"I had responsibilities."

"Right. And no one but you could handle that stuff when you were on vacation."

"Exactly." Jax took a deep breath of crisp air and felt it in his stomach muscles. He couldn't keep the smile off his face. Kendall had just about worn him out last night. He couldn't believe she was the same woman he found sobbing in a car a few weeks ago.

"So, tell me: who the hell is running the show now, Mr. Irreplaceable?"

He thought about it and shook his head; he had no idea. He hadn't even thought to ask, and he hadn't missed his work or the people he worked with. "I don't know."

"Well, they must have found someone because the world hasn't come to a screeching halt, and I'm still getting my statements. My money is still being managed. Maybe you're not so irreplaceable after all."

"For both our sakes, I hope you're right. I didn't mean to be a prick, though."

"You know, Jax, I'm starting to think this bump on the head was the best thing that ever happened to you. You always looked so miserable and stressed, and, well ... I don't know. Isolated. Since you came back from spending Christmas in New York with Rocki, you've been different—in a good way."

"Thanks. Um, look. I can't remember if I had my assistant schedule a limo for Grace and Teddy. I need to call her and make sure."

"So call her."

"Yeah, well, that's the thing. You didn't program my office number into the phone, and I don't know it."

"I have your office number at home. I'll call Anne."

"Who the hell is Anne?"

"Anne Pivens, your secretary."

"Oh, Mrs. Pivens."

"You didn't even know her first name?"

"Of course I know her first name—I just don't think of her by her first name. She's been Mrs. Pivens since I got there."

"Well, Anne and I have become friendly over the years— I call, you put me off, she feels bad and tells me how you're doing. I'll make sure she knows to take care of the limo."

"Thanks. Oh, and Jaime?"

"Yeah?"

"If you ever make a play for Kendall again, even in jest, I'll break both your legs."

"I hear ya. I love Kendall like a sister. Believe me, she's not my type. You have nothing to worry about there, bro."

"So, what's your type?"

"You wouldn't believe me if I told you."

———

Kendall did the dishes and thought about how to handle her parents. She wasn't looking forward to telling them about her breakup, and then there was the whole issue with Jack. How was she going to explain that?

Jack must have walked all the way to Jaime's, because he'd been gone a long time.

The kitchen was clean, the bed was made, and a crazy sexual bucket list had been written. And then she started sanding the last coat of mud. They'd be able to paint soon, and the room would be done.

Maybe she and Jack could take off to Boston for a few days and have some more time together without having to explain their relationship to her parents. She didn't want to go back to the apartment, but when she pictured herself there with Jack, it didn't seem too terrible at all. And if David ever caught wind of it, he would definitely be put out, and that worked for her too.

"Kendall?"

"In here." She'd closed the door to keep the dust inside the bedroom—not that it really worked. Dust was like ghosts; it seemed to walk right through walls, no matter how careful you were.

Jack pulled his overshirt off as he came through the door, leaving him in a T-shirt. "You don't have to do this. It's messy and dusty."

"It gives me an excuse for another shower."

He climbed the ladder behind her. "You're looking forward to our next shower?" His lips skimmed her jawline, and she leaned back into him, turning a little for a kiss.

"Oh yeah. Sex in the shower is on my sexual bucket list."

"You have a list?"

"I do now."

"Really? Wow, this I gotta see."

"Oh no, you don't. My list is private."

"Not if I'm expected to perform these sexual feats, it's not."

She felt his erection against her bottom and she pressed farther into him. "Mmmm. If you keep that up, we're never going to get this room done."

"So?"

"So, I was wondering if you wanted to go to Boston with me for a little while. I have to pack my apartment and give my landlord notice. I thought since no one knows I've been here, except Jaime and Addie, it would also give us a little more time together without having to tell my parents."

"You and me in Boston? Sounds good. When do you want to leave?"

"Before my parents get back. I'm really not looking forward to having to tell them about David in person. And then there's the whole situation with us."

"Situation?" His hand wrapped around her waist tightened, and tension shimmered around them.

"Come on, Jack, they're my parents. They're not going to be happy when they find out we're together so soon after David dumped me. I'd like time to ease them into it."

"Oh, okay. We can take as much time as you need."

"You don't mind?"

"No. Why would I? If we can get the room sanded, we can put a coat of primer on this afternoon, and this evening we can paint it and put the furniture back."

Kendall smiled and felt all gooey on the inside.

"What?"

"I like the *we* part."

Jack kissed her quickly. "You don't happen to have spanking on your list, do you?"

Spanking? No. Not that she couldn't add it, and it definitely expanded the possibilities. She'd read *Fifty Shades*, mostly for kicks during her monthly book club—not that they actually ever read full books, but after a glass or two of wine, the ladies really got into reading excerpts. "Do you want to spank me?"

"That depends. Are you a naughty girl or a nice girl?" His voice got all deep and gravelly, and just the sound of it was enough to make her hot.

"Nice is so overrated. I'm really getting into the whole naughty thing."

He slid his hand over her rear, and she had to squeeze her thighs together.

"You have the greatest ass I've ever seen. Half the time I don't know if I want to kiss it or spank it. Right now, I want both."

"Jack, what else is on your sexual bucket list?"

"With you?"

"Well, I'm not interested in what you want to do with someone else."

"Sweetheart, there's no one else I want to do."

"Good answer."

He ran his hand around to her front and slipped it into

the waistband of her pants and under her panties. "After our first kiss, it was all I could do not to rip off your jeans and take you up against the wall like an animal."

"Oooh."

"Yeah, oooh. And seeing you on your knees between my legs—well, you know damn well what I was thinking then. But you already checked that one off your list, didn't you?"

"I really liked it."

"I gotta tell you, for someone who'd never tried it before, you're a natural. That was the best I've ever had. If you get any better at it, I might not survive." He slid his hand lower and sucked in a breath. "Kendall, damn, you're so hot and wet."

She couldn't believe what he could do to her with just his voice. She held on to the ladder and ground into his hand. "I'm thinking we need a break. Either that or we're going to end up making love on the ladder."

"Sounds interesting."

"Really?"

"But dangerous. And, right now, it might just be combustible. I'd be in hot water if we burned down the cabin."

"So, no chutes and ladders?"

"Not unless it's an adult version of the board game."

"Then I guess you'll have to get your ants out of my pants."

"We could play Operation later."

She bumped her bottom against him. "Or Monopoly. You still can't count. I would win."

"You would cheat."

"Yes, but you wouldn't know."

Jack's palm landed on her backside with a decisive thwack and a sting that left her throbbing. "Get back to work, and I promise to haul you over my knee later."

"Oh, my."

———

The next morning Kendall woke up to moaning. And not the good kind. "Jack, what's wrong?"

He rolled over, and she got her first look at him. He was pale, a little on the green side, and sweating profusely.

She pushed the hair off his forehead, which was clammy. "Headache?"

"Like you read about."

"Why didn't you wake me?"

"I thought it would go away."

Men could be such babies. "It looks like you were wrong. Didn't any of your nurse girlfriends tell you that you need to stay ahead of the pain? That means Motrin as soon as you feel one coming on. Have you taken anything?"

"No."

"What do you need?"

"A bullet."

"Very funny. Motrin and Tylenol, or are you ready for the hard stuff?

"The hard stuff."

"Okay." She swung her legs over the edge of the bed. "Where is it?"

"Medicine cabinet." Jack groaned again and covered his eyes with his arm.

She got out of bed, and a shiver ran through her—she

wasn't sure if it was from the cold or concern for Jack. His color was off, plus the pain she saw in his eyes and the strain in his body—everything about this scared her. Should she take him to the hospital?

She shaded her own eyes as she turned on the obnoxious overhead light and opened the medicine cabinet. She pulled down a prescription bottle, but it was prescribed for Jackson Sullivan. "I don't see it. Are you sure you put it in the cabinet?"

"It's on the second shelf."

There was only one prescription bottle in there—right next to the Motrin and Tylenol. TAKE TWO EVERY FOUR HOURS AS NEEDED FOR PAIN. But the prescription was for Jackson Sullivan. Jax never came to the cabin. He hadn't been there in years. Why would he have a prescription here?

"Jack, Jackson." She heard blood rushing through her ears. "Oh, God. No. He can't be."

She looked at the date of the prescription. Last month. December. She remembered her mother saying that Jax was coming before Christmas for a ski vacation. Her face tingled like a million bees were stinging her, their buzzing filled her ears, and her vision grayed. Her hand shook so badly, the medicine sounded like a maraca.

Jack—her Jack—was Jax. She closed her eyes, and her hand clamped onto the edge of the porcelain sink. She couldn't deal with it now. No, she'd medicate him, and once he got better, she'd kill him.

Kendall blinked her eyes, trying to clear the gray fog closing in on her and realized she was holding her breath. Not good. She took a deep breath and blew it out slowly, then another. She was fine. She was in control. She was strong. She was also an idiot. Jack—Jackson. Wow, how could she have fallen for that? He'd even told her his parents had died—she'd never put the two together.

She remembered Jax's parents and their funeral. The whole town showed up to pay their respects. Everyone loved Jack and Marie Sullivan. She remembered Jax that winter day, wearing a black suit and overcoat. He looked nothing like the boy she'd followed around the summer before—no, he looked like a man. A stranger—his expression blank, his eyes dead. He looked as if he were made of wax, like one of the statues she'd seen at Madame Tussauds the time her parents took her to New York.

Jax might have stood beside both his uncles, but even at twelve years old, she'd known he was alone. His sister, Rocki, had survived the accident that killed their parents and was still in the hospital.

That had been the last time Kendall saw Jax. When she'd tried to speak to him, he'd looked right through her, as if she didn't exist, didn't matter, didn't count. He'd been in shock. She knew that now. Back then, though, all she knew was that it hurt.

That was fourteen years ago.

Kendall could almost forgive herself for falling for David; she'd been a child then. She didn't have that excuse now. She'd fallen head over heels in love with Jax Sullivan, the Grand Pooh-Bah of Harmony—a money-hungry, narcissistic, megalomaniac just like David.

But the Jack she knew, the Jack she'd made love to, the Jack she saw in her dreams was sweet and honest and loyal. Jack was an illusion.

She moved mechanically to the kitchen, grabbed a

water glass, and filled it. When she returned, he was lying in the same position. "I have your meds, Jax. Can you sit up?"

His eyes shot open, and he looked at her—she couldn't tell if the pain she saw was because of his headache or because she'd caught on. In the end, it didn't matter. Nothing mattered. "Your name is on the prescription bottle." She struggled with the childproof top and coaxed two pills into her shaking hand.

"Sweetheart, I can explain."

"Not interested." She handed him the water and the pills. "Just take your medicine and give me your phone."

"Why?"

"Why the phone, or why am I not interested?"

He downed the pills and groaned.

"I'm not interested because, if you remember correctly, I'm pretty good at getting lied to. I've heard all the excuses before. And I need your phone because if the headache hasn't subsided, you're going to have to take more medicine in four hours, and last I heard, you can't tell time—unless that was a lie too."

"I never lied to you."

"I'm going to set an alarm—I wouldn't want you to accidentally OD on this stuff."

He reached for her, but she snatched her hand away.

"Kendall, please listen to me. Sweetheart, I love you."

"Yeah, I've heard that line before too. I shouldn't have believed it then, and I'm certainly not falling for it now." She set the prescription on the bedside table along with his water, picked up the clothes she'd laid out the night before, and went into the bathroom to change. She'd be damned if he'd ever see her naked again.

She'd tossed most of her stuff in the car last night.

Jack—make that Jax—had put his leather duffel by the door. How could she not have noticed it was Gucci? She took a quick scan of the cabin, making sure she hadn't left anything.

There was a rap on the door, right before it was pushed open and her father walked in.

"Daddy?" She reached up and gave him a kiss. "I didn't think you were getting back until Thursday."

"No, we were supposed to be back on Tuesday, but our plane was delayed coming out of New York. We just got home, and I saw the smoke, so I came to check it out. What are you doing here, Kendall?"

"I just came up to see Addie for a few days."

"Is David with you?"

"No, he's in San Francisco. I thought I'd check on Jax before I left. He's not feeling well."

"Jax is here? What's wrong with him?"

"Headache, I think. But, then, he's a little green, so I guess it could be the flu or a virus. He doesn't have a fever, so I just gave him his pain pills. I'm going to head home. I have a busy day, and I'm already running late."

"You're going to stop to see your mother, young lady, aren't you?"

"Sure, Daddy."

He wrapped his arms around her and kissed her forehead.

"I'm glad you're home."

"Me too, baby girl." He didn't say anything else, but he didn't need to. It was written all over his face.

She was so busted. "Bye, Jax," she called out over her shoulder.

"Kendall, wait. Don't go." She heard Jax's footfalls coming behind her. She grabbed her bag and coat on the way out, but didn't bother putting it on. She stepped out of the cabin and slammed the door on her past, and took the first step into her future.

The bright sunlight shone off the snow, temporarily blinding her. She didn't register the cold cutting into her. She couldn't feel anything; she was numb.

———

Jax heard Kendall stomping around the cabin as he tried to feel for his pants. His heart raced, shooting blinding pain through his skull with every beat. He stuffed his legs into the pants, stood, and swallowed back bile. He had to stop her. He had to.

"Bye, Jax."

"Kendall, wait. Don't go." He ran down the hall, right into Teddy.

"Jax, what the hell is going on?"

He reached for the door and stepped out, and then blinding light hit him. Pain shot through his eyes and head like bullets, his knees buckled, and he went down hard, right before he puked his guts out.

Teddy laid a hand on his back as he heaved. "She's gone, son. She's gone."

He was cold, cold like he could remember being only once before—the day he buried his parents.

"Come on, let's get you inside." Teddy helped him up, tossed Jax's arm around his shoulder, and walked him back to the bedroom. The half-empty, economy-size box of condoms lay right next to his painkillers, and the glass of water on the bedside table. Both sides of the bed were messed up, the indentation of Kendall's head still clear on her pillow. "Put a shirt on. I'm taking you home."

"I am home."

"Dammit, Jackson, I can't leave you like this, and I can't kill you. Grace would have my head if I did either. Now get dressed. We're going to the lake house."

"I can't. I have to find her."

"Son, in the shape you're in, you couldn't find your way out of a wet paper bag."

A sweatshirt hit Jax in the chest.

"Put it on. What the hell were you thinking, coming up here like that? And just how did you and Kendall—" He held up his hand. "Never mind. I really don't want to know."

"I love her, Teddy."

"You had better, since it looks to me like you're already sleeping with her." A pair of socks flew at him. "Can you get those on yourself, or are you gonna start ralphing again?"

He braved the glare to stare at Teddy.

"It's not as if I haven't dressed you before, son. Hell, I even diapered your ass a time or two. Whipped it too."

Jax winced as he remembered the time when he was thirteen and Teddy caught him and Jaime taking a joyride in his parents' car. "I couldn't sit down for days. Neither could Jaime." It was never mentioned again. Jax always wondered if it was to cover his own ass. Still, Teddy never left the keys in the ignition after that.

"You're lucky you didn't kill yourselves. I suspect Jaime had his hand in this too?"

"No, sir."

Teddy gave him his I'm-not-buying-your-bullshit stare.

"He was an accomplice after the fact. I didn't give him much of a choice—he either had to back me or rat me out."

"That's not a good position to put a friend in, and you know it."

"I was desperate."

"I hope you can live with whatever it was you did. I hope it was worth it. And I hope, for your sake, you can make this right, because if I ever see that look in my little girl's eyes again and know you put it there . . ." He shook his head. "Get up, and let's go. Grace is waiting on me, and damned if I know what to tell her."

The problem was, neither did he.

"And you might want to hide the evidence before we leave, son, because knowing Grace, she and Addie will be up here to clean. There are some things a parent just doesn't want to know."

Jax tossed the box of condoms into the drawer with the others and groaned at the expression on Teddy's face. He'd seen all three boxes. What could he say? Telling Teddy that his daughter bought them and was unsure of the size smacked of throwing Kendall under the pro-verbial bus, but he didn't want Teddy to think he was a total horn dog either. "It's not what it looks like—"

Teddy held up his hand. "I do not want to know."

Boots hit Jax in the chest none too gently. He didn't bother saying anything; he just stuffed his feet in them. "I'm going to brush my teeth."

"Fine. I'll get some soapy water and go wash down the porch."

"Teddy, can you please just leave me here? I can't tell you anything until Kendall does. . . . I can't break her confidence."

"No, son. I couldn't even if I wanted to. I refuse to keep anything from Grace."

"You never told her about the joyride."

"Let's just say you and Jaime weren't the only ones who learned a hard lesson that day. Lies of omission are still lies. And that's a slippery slope."

"Yeah, I figured that one out on my own."

CHAPTER
FIFTEEN

Kendall threw her Jeep in four-wheel drive and took off, stopping in front of Jaime's place. She knew he was home; both his trucks were out front. She didn't bother knocking, and just walked in. "Jaime, where are you?"

"Kendall?" He stepped out of the kitchen, holding a dishtowel. "Hey, gorgeous. What's up?"

"I came to collect something." She stepped close and leaned in like she was going to kiss his cheek or whisper in his ear—right before she grabbed his shoulders and kneed him in the balls, knocking the air right out of him. "You son of a bitch. I know Jax put you up to it, but, shit, Jaime, we're not children anymore. I thought you were my friend. What kind of friend would knowingly allow another friend to make a fool of me?"

He croaked something that sounded like an apology.

"I guess friends don't usually knee each other in the balls either, so now we're even."

"Kenny," he limped over to her and grabbed her arm. "Listen to me, dammit. I don't know what went down between you and Jax, and I don't want to know. I really, really don't." He shook his head, his face looked pasty, and his voice sounded off. "But, Kenny, you're the best thing that's ever happened to Jax, and he knows it. He made one mistake. Don't let one stupid move ruin what you two have together."

"Whatever we had—past tense—was based on a lie. Jax Sullivan is no different from David. Hell, he's worse. He knew what happened, and he still lied to me."

"Bullshit. I know David the Dickhead. The only person David ever loved was himself. It's different with Jax. Until Jax met you, he'd been in an emotional deep freeze. He hasn't had a thaw that I know of since his folks died. When they died, it was like he turned into a different person. These past two weeks have been the first time I've seen my best friend in more than fourteen years. Kendall, he loves you, and I can't help but think you had more to do with bringing my best friend back to the world of the living than that knock upside the head did. That was just a wake-up call. You sparked a fire in him I haven't seen for far too long."

She couldn't talk about this anymore. If she did, she'd fall apart like Humpty Dumpty. All the king's horses and all the king's men couldn't put Kendall together again. "I have to get out of here."

"Okay, but you shouldn't be driving when you're this upset. Remember what happened last time?"

She remembered, all right, and that meltdown was nothing compared to what she knew was coming. "I'll be fine."

"Kendall, promise me you'll think about what I said. The two of you are like siblings to me. I don't want to lose either of you."

She just nodded and then ran. She couldn't breathe; she might never breathe again. God, her whole body ached from holding herself together. But Jaime was right about one thing: she shouldn't be driving to Boston. Not now.

Ten minutes later, she pulled up to Addie's house and banged on the door.

As soon as she saw Addie in her Pepto-Bismol pink footie pajamas, it was as if the floodgates shot open.

"What the H-E-double-toothpicks is wrong? Are you hurt?" Addie's arms came around her and dragged her inside and into her cozy kitchen. "Sweetie, David's not worth all this. It's been two weeks—I knew leaving you alone was a mistake."

"It . . . it's not David. It's J-J-Jax."

"Jackson Sullivan?" Addie filled the teakettle and turned to face her. "What does he have to do with anything?"

"I didn't recognize him. He lied to me, even after I told him about David." Humiliation washed over her like the spray of muddy water from a passing bus after a big thaw. She hiccuped. "And oh, God, I threw myself at him."

"You did?"

Kendall closed her eyes and nodded. "I slept with him—a lot."

"You had sex with Jax Sullivan?"

"Oh yeah."

"Good sex?"

"Better than the best sex you've read about. He did things to my body I didn't even know were possible. Oh, God, I may never have sex that good again."

"He's not the only man on the planet with a dick, believe me. They're all just dicks with two legs and a little, itty-bitty brain."

"I trusted him. Addie, I fell in love with him. But he's no different from David."

"Whoa, slow down. Where was Jax?"

"At the cabin."

"He was at the cabin all this time? You've been together for two weeks, and you didn't bother to tell me you were ripping up the sheets with the Grand Pooh-Bah?" Addie pulled a half dozen tissues out of the box and handed over the wad.

Kendall started shredding them. "I didn't know. That's the whole point. He lied to me. He said he was a tenant fixing the roof for a reduced rental rate. He said his name was Jack. I didn't recognize him—he has a beard, his hair was longish, he was dressed like a construction worker, he even had callused hands. The Jax Sullivan I know of never did a day of manual labor in his life. What would he be doing reroofing the hunting cabin? I never put the two together in my mind."

"So, you thought you were going home with a total stranger named Jack?"

"No, I knew my dad would have checked him out. Besides, it was late, and I didn't want to call you to come get me, so I stayed in the spare room." She nodded while she blew her nose. "He lied."

"No, not technically he didn't. His name is Jack."

"He's always gone by Jax or Jackson. He's never ever been called Jack before. Jack was his father."

"How do you know? You haven't seen this man for fourteen years. He lives and works in Chicago. Maybe everyone in Chicago calls him Jack."

"Well, then, why did he say he was renting his own cabin?"

"You tell me. Why would he say that? And why was

he staying there instead of the lake house? If I knew he was home, I'd have covered for Grace and kept him fed and the pantry stocked, at least."

She didn't know how much to tell Addie. She could just imagine what people in town would say, not to mention the impact on his career, if they found out that Jax didn't come out of the hospital with all his faculties. Maybe Jack went to the cabin to hide; if no one knew he was in town, no one would discover his brain injury. He'd told her, but maybe he didn't want anyone else to know. It wasn't her story to tell. "He might have had his reasons for not wanting anyone to know he was in town. Maybe. Possibly. It's not inconceivable."

"Reasons you can't share with me?"

Kendall nodded.

"Were they valid?"

"Maybe."

"What would have happened if you'd known who he was?"

"I would have called you to come and get me."

"And I would have known he was in town."

"You wouldn't have told anyone."

"You know that and I know that, but would Jax know that?"

"Maybe—maybe not. You tell me."

"Jax is an enigma. It's like he walks around in his own little bubble. You see him sometimes when he comes out—which is rarely. He always comes alone, unless Rocki meets him. And when he's here, he might go to town, but it's as if no one ever touches him. It's—"

"Like he's in an emotional deep freeze?"

"Exactly."

"That's what Jaime said. He seems to think I thawed him out or something."

"Jaime might be a complete ass, but he's also pretty perceptive. If anyone would know, it would be Jaime. They've been best friends since they were little kids."

"And now my parents know." She covered her face with her hands. "God, they probably think . . . hell, I can't even imagine what they think. Dad caught us, and before I left, he told me to go see my mother. I can't, Addie. I don't even know what I'd say. 'Oh, David broke my heart, and I jumped into bed with the first man I saw—literally'?"

Addie put the tea tray together and started making breakfast. "Well, you'd better think about it, because I'll bet you all my poker money that your mother will be here within the hour."

Kendall dropped her head to the table and gave it a few bangs. Damn, it didn't help this time either.

CHAPTER
SIXTEEN

———

Jaime checked the clock and headed toward the sink to wash off the grease. It was time he took the bull by the horns, or maybe the wildcat by the whiskers. Whatever. He tossed the bag of frozen peas he'd been using as an ice bag back in the shop freezer, and wished he had a steel cup. He had a feeling he was going to need one. At least Addie was small; he could probably deflect her kicks, and it's not as if he were unprepared. Besides, how much trouble could he get into in a kindergarten classroom?

He drove down to the elementary school and spotted Addie's car in the lot. He knew the kindergarten had its own play area, since he was the one who bought and installed the little kids' play equipment. He went around the school, let himself into the gated area, and slipped inside the classroom.

He'd never been in Addie's classroom before. It contained tables surrounded by the world's smallest chairs, and all the bulletin boards were covered with colorful pictures. The room was empty of people but neat and tidy. He knew she was still in school, and the lights were still on. He heard humming and followed the sound. The door to a storeroom was open just a little. He found her standing with her back to him, refilling paint containers and humming a familiar tune—something his great-grandma used to listen to, something from the 1930s or '40s. Then she broke out into song, and he realized she must have been humming the intro.

Her voice shocked him. He was amazed that something that big could come from someone so small. He didn't know much about music, but he knew greatness when he heard it. Addie wore a green corduroy jumper with a putty-colored turtleneck, matching putty-colored kneesocks, and butt-ugly brown penny loafers. She danced to music only she could hear, belting out the lyrics with such feeling, he felt like a voyeur. The song was about running into an ex-lover for the first time, knowing that he'd moved on when she obviously hadn't. She sounded hurt and wistful and so damn sad.

Just the thought of her wanting some guy that didn't deserve her had an unfamiliar feeling crashing over him and his hand tightened on the doorjamb. He waited until she finished the song with "I still love you so." She held that last note for at least two bars, but he had a feeling she could hold it longer if she wanted to—her voice was just that strong. When the sound of her voice faded, he gave her a standing ovation.

Addie jumped, spilling red paint all over her hand and the table. She spun around, and it looked like her face had paled, but it was hard to tell with that hideous putty-colored turtleneck. She looked almost ghostly, which made the dark circles under her eyes more pronounced.

"Sorry, Addie. I didn't mean to scare you."

"Right. That's why you failed to go to the office to be announced or even to knock. How long have you been standing there?" Her cheeks were turning pink, which beat the whole White Lady Ghost look she'd been rockin'.

"You were humming the intro and I followed the sound. You're the most amazing singer I've ever heard."

Her glare was filled with so much fire, he was amazed the school was still standing around him. She swallowed hard and wiped her paint-covered hand on her ugly jumper. "What are you doing here?"

So her voice was off-limits too? Shit, you'd think she'd at least thank him for the compliment. Instead, she looked steamed that her little secret wasn't so secret anymore. Too bad. "I wanted to see you . . . to explain about the whole Jax-and-Kendall mess. I know you're probably angry."

She raised an eyebrow.

"Furious?"

She crossed her arms.

"Irate?"

"All of the above. But you don't owe me an apology— you owe one to Kendall."

"I already did that, right after she did her best to make sure I would never be able to reproduce."

That got a smile out of her. It would.

"My hands were tied. There are reasons I can't go into, but, well, I thought I was doing the right thing for everyone involved. Including you."

"Me?"

He walked over to the sink and wet a half dozen sheets of paper towel and did his best to clean the spilled paint. "Yeah, you. I didn't want you put in as uncomfortable a position as I was. I really hated keeping secrets from Kendall."

He took her by the hand, stood her in front of him,

pulled up both sleeves, and helped her wash her hands like only a grease monkey could. It didn't hurt that he got to put his arms around her and pull her up against his chest, her ass tucked tight against his fly. Okay, tight was probably a bad idea. He stepped back while he scrubbed red paint off her. "But if you'd seen Jax, though, Addison, you'd have gone along with the ruse too. It's like he's back. The old Jax. Do you remember what he was like, Addie?"

She nodded. "Kendall's hurt and upset, but when she told me what happened, it was as if things started to add up. She didn't share it with me, but it sounded as if she realized he might have had a good reason for his actions."

"Several." He turned off the taps and handed her a few towels.

"And you?"

"Me?" He thought her dress should be put in the closest burn pile. "I didn't have much to do with it, other than to tell him to come clean with her. I don't know how she found out, but, man, she was pissed."

"Have you heard from Jax? Is he okay?" Of course she'd be more concerned about Jax than him. Talk about takin' one for the team; he'd gotten kneed in the balls and didn't get an ounce of sympathy.

"Nah, you know how guys are. They tend to lick their wounds in private."

"Unfortunately for Jax, that wasn't an option. He was supposedly sicker than a first-year teacher during a flu epidemic. Teddy took him back to the lake house."

"Teddy was there? At the cabin?"

"Oh yeah. He walked in just before Kendall left, and after she found out she'd fallen into bed and in love with the Grand Pooh-Bah of Harmony. Teddy knows. I don't know how he knows, but Kendall knew she was busted big-time. And believe me, Kendall knows her daddy."

"So does Jax. Hell, so do I." He'd been on the wrong side of Teddy's hand once, and he'd never forgotten it. "Maybe Jax being sick wasn't such a bad thing. Grace won't let Teddy kill him until he's better, at least."

"We have to do something."

"What in the hell can we do?"

"You can go and see Jax, make sure he knows that Kendall has feelings for him and make sure he's okay, and report back to me."

"And what's your role in this little mission?"

"I'll work on Kendall. Maybe I'll go help her pack up her place this weekend. She's moving home to Harmony. If you tell me what's going on with Jax, I can let a few things slip ... accidentally ... on purpose."

"Just make sure I don't have to do anything that's going to put Kendall on the attack again."

That got a smile out of her. Damn, but she had a great smile. "You should do that more often."

"What?"

"Smile. You have a beautiful smile, and you should sing. You would win *American Idol* if you showed up."

"I don't sing."

"I have to disagree, since I stood here listening to you for about three minutes."

"I don't sing in public—ever."

"Not even karaoke?"

She shook her head.

"Why?" He stepped closer, and as he caught her scent, he was almost happy to find out Kendall didn't do any permanent damage. But he didn't think he would ever smell green apple or tempera paint again without getting a woody. Shit.

She just shook her head.

"So, now I know two of your secrets. I know how gorgeous you are when you don't dress like a bag lady, in clothes ten times too big, and I know your voice could make angels weep."

"Jaime . . . please—"

He put a finger on her lips to stop her. "Addie, I'd never do anything to make you feel uncomfortable. If you choose not to share your talent with anyone but me, that's your choice. But, baby, it's a real loss to everyone else."

"So you won't tell anyone?"

"No, I won't." He stepped closer. "So, I was thinking. How about you and I take a trip into Boston next Saturday. What do you say?"

Her gray eyes widened, her lips trembled, and so did her hands. "I . . . no, I can't."

He took two steps back. "Addie?"

She turned around and grabbed her purse out of a cabinet. "I need to leave, Jaime. I have an appointment."

"Okay. Let me walk you to your car."

"No. Please, just go."

He backed out of the storage room. "I'm sorry. I didn't mean to scare you Addie."

"You didn't."

She was as bad at lying as she was with fashion.

Kendall pulled into her parking space and stared at the elevator. God, she didn't want to go back to the apartment and rip apart her old life and be forced to take a long walk down her not so happy memory lane alone. All she could

think about was how much of her life she'd wasted on
David. She didn't know if that was an improvement over
crying about Jack . . . shit, Jax. His name was Jax—maybe
someday she would remember that. Maybe someday she
wouldn't feel physical pain when she thought of him.
Maybe someday she'd stop loving the lying jerk.

She wished she had the money to pay people to pack
the place up so she wouldn't have to face her old life and
see what a sham it had been. Unfortunately, she couldn't
afford to waste a cent. No, she'd need all her savings just
to get into a new apartment. As it was, Erin had volunteered the moving services of her fiancé, Cam, and his
brothers, Adam and Butch, for the price of beer and
homemade pizza. She wasn't sure how the men felt about
being volunteered, but she had enough on her plate to
worry and cry over, without taking on more.

Someone pulled into David's space, and when Kendall recognized her best friend's car, she smiled for the
first time since the night before. She jumped out and
threw her arms around her friend. "Erin, what are you
doing here?"

"I knew you had a lot to face and I didn't think you
should have to do it alone, especially without wine and
chocolate." Erin reached into the backseat and pulled
out a big bottle of Shiraz and a one-pound box of Go-
diva Dark Chocolate Truffles.

"Oh, my God, I love you. You know that, right?"

"Of course." Erin threw a bag over her shoulder.
"We're having a sleepover, too. After we finish the wine,
I'll be in no shape to drive, and I thought you might not
want to stay here alone."

"And Cameron's okay with that?"

Erin smiled, "Oh, don't worry about him. He wasn't

happy about it, but I promised I'd pay him back. He'll
have the whole night to figure out an interesting way to
collect. I can't wait to hear what he comes up with." She
waggled her eyebrows.

Kendall could only imagine what Jack would do if he
had carte blanche in the bedroom or anywhere else, for
that matter. But Jax wasn't Jack. Tears stung the back of
her eyes. She blinked them back while she opened up the
hatch and grabbed her bags. "I guess I can't avoid it any
longer. At least we have all the necessary provisions to
get over disastrous love affairs and heal a broken heart,
right?" They headed to the elevator.

Erin pressed the call button. "Disastrous love affairs,
as in plural?"

"Jack turned out to be someone else."

"Is he married?"

"No"

"Engaged?"

"Not that I know of, but it's worse. He's Jackson Sullivan—my dad's boss, the man who owns half the town
of Harmony and a bunch of banks in Chicago."

"He's single and rich? I would think that would be an
improvement over married or engaged."

"Erin, he made me think he was some kind of carpenter who was working in lieu of paying full rent."

"You didn't recognize him?"

"I haven't seen him since I was twelve. He looked like
a construction worker—he wasn't walking around in a
three-piece suit. It's not like I've been cyberstalking him
all these years." She stepped into the elevator and hit 4.
"What is it with me and men who are out for total world
financial domination?"

"It sounds as if one of them was at least successful.

Frankly, I never thought David had the brains—I mean, he knew which asses to kiss. That was easy enough to see at all those damn events you dragged me to, but I've always wondered if he had the goods to really get the job done."

"Not in his pants, that's for damn sure."

Erin broke into peals of laughter, leaned against the wall, and crossed her legs. "Oh, damn, Kendall. Stop. You're going to make me pee my pants."

They made it to her apartment without further incident, and as soon as Kendall unlocked the door, Erin ran for the bathroom. "Pour the wine and keep talking—I'll leave the door open. I have to hear more about this."

Kendall stepped in and shivered—the place exuded the transitional yuppie style that David had insisted upon and had all the warmth of the arctic circle. She'd gotten so used to the feel of the cabin, she was shocked by the difference between the two places.

Kendall checked the thermostat and stepped into the kitchen. Even the granite countertops and stainless-steel appliances threw off a chill. "Sounds like a heck of an idea—pouring the wine, that is. I'm not sure about the talking part." What she wouldn't give to be in the kitchen at the cabin. She missed the comfort of the old, chipped yellow starburst Formica counter and antique white stove and the hum of the ancient refrigerator with the old-fashioned ice trays. Kendall opened the bottle with David's absurdly expensive, four-hundred-dollar Code38 Stealth corkscrew. He ordered it just as soon as he read about it in the *New York Times* and then hosted a wine tasting to show it off. He seemed to be the only one who was impressed with the titanium tool. At least it worked well. Lord knew she'd opened enough bottles with it for the tasting after David realized the corkscrew wasn't receiving the admiration he'd spent a small fortune to achieve. She was surprised he'd forgotten to pack it.

Kendall poured two big glasses and cut the cellophane wrapper off the chocolate. She took a sip of Shiraz and a bite of an Aztec Spice truffle and groaned at the mingling of the sweet, spicy taste with the wine—at one time she would have said it was better than sex. Now she knew just how lacking it was. Still, for a combination of chocolate and wine, it was almost perfection. Almost, but not quite. When she thought of perfection, she saw Jack— her Jack. She took another swig of wine to anesthetize her heart. She'd always known he was too good to be true. Too beautiful, too loving, too perfect to be real.

"Where did you just go?" Erin walked in when she was daydreaming, joined her on the couch, and grabbed her wine. "You had a smile on your face, and I don't think I've ever seen you quite so radiant."

"It's the wine and chocolate." Kendall got up to grab a throw that David always insisted she keep hidden away. He'd say, "You wouldn't want to ruin the lines of the furniture or, God forbid, make the place look cluttered." Or lived in. Living here was like living in a model home. There was nothing personal, no knickknacks or goofy photos, no notes on the refrigerator door held up by the tacky magnets she collected on vacation. No pictures that Janie, Erin's soon-to-be-adopted daughter, drew for her and decorated with glitter that left sparkles around, no matter how often you cleaned.

"Honey, I've plied you with wine and chocolate before and I've never seen that look. Spill."

"It doesn't matter. It wasn't real."

"What wasn't real?"

"Jack and everything I thought we had together." Her face tightened and she blinked back the tears, her eyes felt gritty and hot, and her heart felt as if it was in a vise that grew tighter and tighter with each beat.

"Kendall, I want all the details. Start at the beginning and don't leave anything out."

Kendall got up and turned on the gas fireplace, and Erin stretched out, pulled a throw over them both, and got comfy—or as comfy as you could on these über-firm cushions. Kendall missed the smell of burning wood, the crackle of a real fire, the life it contained.

She started and got lost in the story. She was surprised when Erin kicked her. "You did not call him the Grand Pooh-Bah to his face!"

She smiled thinking of it. No wonder he'd looked shocked. "I did. I just didn't know I was doing it."

"And you told him your ex was a Jackson Sullivan wannabe?"

Kendall shrugged.

"What else did you say about him?"

Kendal cringed. "When he said he was working in lieu of paying full rent, I was incensed. I may have called him Harmony's own Scrooge McDuck and told him he was too cheap to pay for labor."

"And you wonder why he didn't introduce himself?" Erin nudged Kendall with her foot and almost spilled Kendall's wine. "And it's not as if he really lied. I mean, technically, *Jack* is a derivative of *Jackson*."

"He knew I didn't know who he was, and he ran with it."

"You were pissed at David and took it out on this poor, nameless, faceless guy who just happened to be helping you out of a jam. You made him sound like the devil incarnate. Did you ever think that maybe he was just trying to save you embarrassment? I mean, could you imagine how you would have felt if he told you who he was?"

"I thought you were here to make me feel better, not to rub my mistakes in my face."

Erin refilled both their wineglasses. "Yeah, but sometimes a friend needs tough love and a good bullshit meter. You've been mine often enough. It's nice to be able to return the favor."

"I know I should say thank you, but I'm just not feelin' it."

"Don't worry—there's plenty of wine left. I'm sure after another glass or two, you'll change your tune. Go on with the story. I heard about both sex sightings. The rest of the story is a little spotty."

It took two more glasses of wine for Kendall to spit it all out.

"Damn, girl. In a week, Jax took you from the frigid depths of despair over David to sexual satisfaction and multiple, screaming orgasms. The man could get you off fully clothed, without ever touching you below the waist, and you're complaining about him withholding a little information?"

"It was his name."

"That's debatable and totally understandable too. You sounded like you hated him."

"He played me for a fool."

"And you paved the way for him. Sounds to me like he did all he could to resist your sexy self. Face it: you wanted a piece of that, and you teased him until he folded like a cheap suit at the Laundromat."

"I did. He was so different from David in every way. Erin, I'd been having bad sex for seven years and I didn't know any better. I had no idea what I was missing. David made me feel like there was something wrong with me."

"There is something seriously wrong with David. It's just not normal. I mean, look at you. You're better-looking than Liv Tyler. If I were a guy, I'd be all over you."

"Jack thinks David might be asexual. Not that anything is wrong with that—it's just wrong to blame any problems on your unwitting partner. I never thought about it before, but Jack might be onto something there."

"You talked to Jack about your sex life with David?"

"Well, yeah. There was so much I didn't know about sex. It was kind of embarrassing. And David was never interested in ... um, you know, other things."

Erin giggled. "Have more wine. I need to know what the hell David wasn't interested in."

Kendall finished off her glass. "Oral sex."

"For your benefit or his?"

"Both."

"You mean he never ... ?"

Kendall shook her head, and it felt like she was watching a slow-motion 3-D movie. She thought she'd better slow down on the wine consumption.

"Not even to try it?"

"No. David had a thing about saliva. I was curious ... and, well, Jack had never asked."

Erin almost choked on her wine. "Kendall, there are some things men don't ask for, and blow jobs are one of them. If a woman is willing to tame the one-eyed monster, they usually just give it a lick, and the guy's in heaven. I've never had to ask for permission, and I've never heard of a man who didn't love it—well, except for maybe John Wayne Bobbitt, but that would be understandable."

"How many men have you talked to about blow jobs?"

"Just a few. You know how it is. You go to a bar, you're talking to a strange guy you'll never see again, and the conversation turns to sex. You can ask anything and tell him anything—there's no pressure, as long as the man in question isn't buying you drinks."

Kendall's head lolled back onto the cushions and felt heavy. "No, I don't know how it is. I never went to bars unless I was with David. And even if I had, I wouldn't have talked to a strange man about sex. I could hardly talk to Jack about it, and I loved him."

"You loved him?"

"I do. . . . I mean, I did. I wish Jack were here. If he hadn't gotten the mother of all headaches, I'd be happily clueless. We'd have had more time. You know, it was no wonder he looked so relieved when I told him my parents weren't coming back until Thursday."

"You said they were back."

"They are. I thought they were coming in on Thursday, but they were supposed to arrive on Tuesday. Because of delays, they arrived early this morning—really early. I just keep thinking that if he hadn't gotten sick, we might have made it out before Dad came by the cabin."

"Your dad walked in on you?"

"I was clothed, thank God, which was unusual, since Jack introduced me to the adventures of cooking half-naked. It's fun, if you haven't tried it. Counters are cold, though."

"Back to your dad."

"I found Jack's prescription bottle for his pain pills with

his name on it." A tear leaked out, followed by another and another. Shit. "So I gave him his medicine, 'cause he looked really bad, and told him I knew who he was."

"What did he say?"

"The usual bullshit. He said he loved me and that he could explain. But I'd heard it all before, and I wasn't about to fall for it again."

Erin sat forward and grabbed Kendall's foot. "He said he loved you?"

She shrugged and wiped her face on the throw. "He didn't mean it."

"What if he did? Don't you think you owe it to yourself to find out? Here's a guy who is smart, talented, gorgeous, a gentleman, an amazing lover, rich, and he says he loves you—I'm not seeing the downside here. Kendall, what do you have to lose?"

"I don't know who he is. How do I know his name is all he lied about?"

Erin reached into her bag and got out her iPad. "That's easy. Let's Google him, shall we?" She typed in his name and hit Images—Erin was very visual. "Wow, the man was born to wear a tux. Look at him. I'm almost happily married, and I'm drooling."

There was a full page of pictures, most of which were taken at black-tie charity events in Chicago. It didn't look as if he was ever photographed with the same woman twice. What did he do, call 1-800-DIAL-A-D8? All the women he was photographed with were Kendall's basic nightmare—blond-haired, blue-eyed blow-up dolls. Kendall's exact opposite. Kendall might hold her own in formal wear, but she hated attending those functions. David would always dump her before the hors d'oeuvres were served, and she'd spend the rest of the night on her own, fending off drunken bankers.

"See? I'm not even his type."

"No, you're exactly his type. Look at these women—they're just dates. There's no connection. Look at the body language on his part—he looks as if he's posing for pictures before his turn in the electric chair."

Kendall rolled her eyes. "Right. I bet he slept with almost every one of them."

"Probably. A guy who looks like Jax would be expected to put out, but he doesn't care about them. Now let's look at his Wiki page." Erin fiddled around on her iPad while Kendall tried to ignore the voice in her head that sounded just like Jack's telling her she was the first woman he ever cared about.

"Wow, an Olympic-level swimmer. It says here his time would have beaten the winner of the Olympic Trials, and that a family tragedy prevented his attending. What happened?"

"His parents were killed in a car accident, and his sister was seriously injured. He mentioned the Olympics, but I thought he was talking figuratively."

"He started college when he was, like, sixteen or something, and graduated with an MBA in three and a half years after just losing his parents."

"He wanted to be able to take his sister in. I guess his family situation was nightmarish after his parents' death."

"Kendall, this guy's a freakin' genius. He was the youngest fund manager ever to hit Wall Street. He was written up in the *Wall Street Journal*."

"No wonder losing his ability to deal with numbers threw him for a loop."

"What?"

"Oh, my God. I didn't just say that out loud, did I?"

"I'm afraid so."

"He was in a skiing accident last month. Suffered a pretty serious brain injury and lost his ability to deal with numbers. It's coming back, though. I mean, I've seen real improvement over the past two weeks, but who knows if he'll ever be able to do what he did before?"

"Kendall, you need to talk to him. I understand why you ran—I do. Getting hurt so soon after dealing with what David put you through, well, that's a normal knee-jerk reaction. But this guy is the real deal, and except for his full name, it sounds as if he told you the truth. You have to at least give him the chance to explain. Can you imagine what's it's like to be him, to know what he used to be capable of and have that gift taken away?"

Yeah, she could imagine. Hadn't this whole thing with David made her question her own ability as a therapist? Jax's situation was so much worse. He didn't have to question it; he knew he'd lost it. The only question was how much of what he'd lost he might regain. Knowing who he was and what he did for a living, well, she could understand his wanting to keep the result of his injury to himself. He controlled billions of dollars of other people's money—their life savings. If word got out, he could lose millions. "You can't tell anyone about Jax's problem, Erin. Please. I just realized what it could mean to him and his company."

"Of course I won't say anything to anyone. Besides, I'm sure he has very capable people working for him. Are you going to talk to him?"

"Do I have much choice?"

CHAPTER SEVENTEEN

J ax Sullivan had billions of dollars under management, and felt like a recalcitrant twelve-year-old who had been driven home and sent to his room.

Unfortunately, he was too sick to do anything but suffer in silence. It turned out that when one tossed one's cookies soon after taking pain meds, the chances are pretty damn good those pain meds went out with the rest of the stomach contents. He wasn't sure that was the case. Since he couldn't pinpoint the amount of time between ingestion and expulsion, there was no way to really know. Which was why any sane person, even one in terrible pain who had just lost the love of his life, was stuck waiting for the phone alarm to tell him it was safe to remedicate.

After the first real dose, he slept, and now he waited for the third. It had been ten hours since Kendall left him. Ten hours was a really long time.

For the first time since his accident, the thought of being completely drugged out was a relief. For too short a time, he couldn't think about Kendall and wonder where she was, he couldn't recall the look on her face when she'd read his name off that damn prescription bottle, and he was able to erase the expression of sheer disbelief in her eyes when he told her he loved her.

He couldn't stand being in bed anymore, so he rolled off, doing his best to move his head as little as possible. Grace had pulled the blackout shades, so he wasn't sure if he'd crash again if he saw light. He grabbed his sunglasses and put them on before heading downstairs.

He hadn't eaten anything since the night before, and even that had been a light dinner. Kendall sitting across from him was even more appetizing than her food. They'd often returned to the meal after he effectively lured her back to bed—or, in some instances, a long stop in the hallway—but that hadn't been the case last night. No, last night had been special—even more special than usual.

Tears burned the back of his eyes—he barely remembered the feeling. He hadn't cried in more than a decade. Actually, he hadn't cried since before his parents' death. He wasn't sure if this was an improvement. Pain surrounded him; it was not only in his head, but also in his heart. It made it hard to breathe, it made it hard to think, it made it hard to put one foot in front of the other. He grabbed the banister on the stairs and sat. He needed to put it all aside and do something to get Kendall back. Crying wouldn't help matters.

"Jackson Finneus Sullivan, what are you doing out of bed?"

He blinked and focused and found Grace at the bottom of the steps, her silver hair catching the light from the overhead chandelier, her hands on the hips of her mom jeans. She wore a navy sweater that he knew would smell like Chanel No. 5 and a look that had made him cower ever since he could remember.

Damn, he was a grown man. He refused to cower.

"Grace, I love you, but I'm not a child and I refuse to be treated like one."

Now the similarities between Kendall and her mother became startlingly clear. He knew where Kendall got her eyebrow raise and her death glare—both of which were cutting into him. If he'd thought Kendall's was bad, Grace's was worse. "Jackson, the doctor said—"

"I know what the doctor said. I spoke to him. It was probably the drastic change in barometric pressure that triggered the headache. Stepping out into the blinding light didn't help matters, but that doesn't matter, Grace. I need to find Kendall. I need to talk to her. I love her. I can't lose her."

Grace took a deep breath and looked like she was about to blow. "You can't lose her?" Her voice got eerily calm. "I wasn't aware that you ever had her, Jax. Or should I call you Jack?"

He winced. Grace obviously knew all—well, all about his lie, anyway. As for what else she knew, he really didn't want to know.

Grace turned, and he thought she was going to leave him sitting there and not give him a chance to explain, but instead she opened the front door to reveal Jaime with his hand up to knock.

Jax took one look at Jaime and wondered if Jax looked half as horrified as Jaime obviously did to be back on Grace and Teddy's shit list.

Jaime shot visual daggers at him "Afternoon, ma'am. I just came by to check on Jax."

"Jaime Rouchard, I had a feeling I'd be seeing you today. You were always so good about facing up to your shenanigans, but I thought you were well past the age of teenage pranks."

"Yes, ma'am. I mean, no, ma'am." Jaime stumbled over his words like a toddler in his first pair of big-boy pants.

Jax shook his head and then regretted the action. The dynamic duo had gotten caught again, only this time they'd both have to bend down in order for Grace to box their ears—unless one or both of them were sitting on the steps. He grabbed the banister, concentrating on taking the stairs one step at a time, then hung on to the newel post in what he hoped was a nonchalant lean, before shaking Jaime's hand—he thought since he'd dragged Jaime into this clusterfuck, he owed him protection and did his best to maneuver between Grace and his best friend. Unfortunately, it meant now *he* was the one suffering the lethal burns of Grace's laser vision.

Jack refused to shuffle his feet under Grace's scrutiny—mostly. Grace was a scary woman. And now that he thought about it, Teddy had nothing on her when it came to radiating danger. When Teddy, the ex-Marine drill sergeant, was mad, you knew it. But Grace was different; she excelled in subterfuge. The woman could feed you cookies and then kill you.

"Have you eaten, dear?" She stepped around Jax, making a point to smile as she literally took Jaime by the arm and steered him toward the kitchen. "I've made a nice, savory stew with homemade sourdough bread for dinner. You'll be staying, won't you?"

Jaime let himself be led but turned his head in a pleading gesture, as if he knew he was headed to the gallows and Grace was the hangman.

Jax followed, and before he could come up with a good excuse to get them the hell out of there, Grace had both of them seated, plated, and damn near confessing all as soon as the aroma of lamb stew hit their olfactory

glands. Oh, she was good. Jax hadn't had lamb stew in
several years. But he remembered every bite of every
bowl he'd ever eaten and polishing off an entire loaf of
bread to sop up every last drop of the broth. His mouth
watered, and his empty stomach growled like a caged
tiger.

Teddy strolled in just as he'd raised his spoon, waiting
for Grace to give them the go-ahead to dig in.

Teddy pointed at Jaime. "You." Then he aimed his finger at Jax. "And you. The office. Now."

Grace and Teddy separately were formidable. Together
they were indomitable, and their timing impeccable.

Jaime gave Jax a we're-so-screwed look. They both returned their unused spoons to the table with a clank and
rose to their feet with all the enthusiasm of two tomcats
sharing the same leash.

They survived the walk, a trip both of them had traversed more times than they cared to remember, and
stood in their assigned places before Jax's father's old
mahogany desk—the same desk Teddy used to deal with
the estate accounts.

Jax and Jaime assumed the position—hands linked
behind their backs to hide all evidence of shaking, feet
shoulder width apart to prevent fidgeting, and eyes straight
ahead in military form, just as Teddy had taught them.
Unfortunately, they never seemed to control their reaction to the sound of the door closing.

Teddy walked past them with a back so straight, his
spine looked as if it were forged out of steel. He sat and
leaned back in the worn leather chair, looking like a
cross between John Wayne and Bill Cosby. There was no
way to know if he was going to pull out a six-shooter for
cleaning or perform Cosby-esque facial gymnastics; maybe

both. Whichever way it went, the silence seemed to last forever. Death-row inmates had shorter queues before their walk to the electric chair, and at least they got a last meal. The ticking grandfather clock ratcheted up the tension until it was difficult to breathe.

Jax's stomach clenched, and he was almost glad Teddy had insisted they have the talk before they ate. Getting raked over the coals was bad enough, but Jax was certain if he'd eaten, he'd be turning several shades of green instead of just growing paler by the moment.

By the time Teddy moved, Jax knew both he and Jaime looked so bad, they'd make albinos look tan. That Teddy left them standing long enough to sweat through their shirts; it could have been his trademark.

"What in the hell were you boys thinking?"

Jax swallowed audibly. "Kendall came up to the cabin for the same reason I did. We wanted to get away where no one in town would know we were in Harmony. If you and Grace knew either of us was having problems, you'd have been on the first plane home. Kendall wanted time to process everything, and I didn't want to worry anyone."

"I know about Kendall's job loss and what that sorry excuse for a fiancé did to her, but I'm still in the dark when it comes to why you felt the need to disappear, and not only keep your return a secret from everyone, but your identity a secret from Kendall."

"Kendall didn't tell you?"

"If she had, do you think I'd be wasting my time talking to you?"

"No, sir. I don't."

"Now, do you want to tell me what the hell is going on in that head of yours, son? I'm just about out of patience."

"No, sir. As far as I'm concerned, it has no bearing on the problem as I see it."

"And just what is that?"

"The problem is that I made a mistake and withheld information from Kendall, and it came back to bite me on the ass. For some reason, Kendall and everyone else in town seems to think I'm the devil incarnate. Kendall didn't recognize me. She told me all about Jax Sullivan before I got the opportunity to introduce myself. If I had, she would have hightailed it back to Addie's."

"And why would that have been a problem?"

"Because she would have told Addie I was there, and Addie would have felt obligated to inform you of my presence. There were two bedrooms, and I thought if Kendall stayed, we'd both get the peace and quiet we were looking for. I never expected to fall in love with her, sir. Believe me, a relationship was the last thing I was looking for."

"And yet here we are. I've never seen my daughter truly devastated before, and to find out that you not only abused our trust, but you also took advantage of her when she was already beaten down—" Teddy's gaze slammed into Jaime. "And you went along with this?"

Jax stepped forward. "He didn't find out until I was already in too deep to get out."

"Did you ever hear the saying 'If you dig yourself into a hole, the first thing you should do is stop digging'?"

"Yes, sir—from you. I asked Jaime to back up my story. I take full responsibility. I forced his hand. I put him in an untenable position—"

Jaime pushed Jax aside. "I did what I thought was right, and I'd do it again. You weren't there, Teddy. Kendall is the best thing that ever happened to Jax, and from

what I saw the other day, I think she felt the same way
about him. I saw them both happy for the first time since
we were kids. Jax may have gone about it the wrong way,
but he never intended to hurt her. As a matter of fact, Jax
played a big part in rebuilding some of the damage David
did. Kendall will see that when she calms down enough
to think clearly."

Teddy took his time staring at Jaime, who didn't so
much as twitch. "I heard Kendall paid you a visit before
she left."

Jaime's hands seemed to instinctively shield his pri-
vates, and he swallowed hard. "Yes, sir."

"No permanent damage, I hope."

"No, sir. I think Kendall has forgiven me. At least she
said we're even."

Jax shook his head and asked, "What did she do?"
Kendall was about five-foot-nine; Jaime was six-foot-two
and 220.

"Let's just say I took one for the team. I just hope it
doesn't affect my ability to reproduce."

Jax swallowed back a groan. Man, he knew Kendall
was pissed at him, but to be that pissed at Jaime . . .
"Sorry, man."

"Yeah, you don't know the half of it. After the swelling went down, I had to go face Addie. It wasn't pretty."

Jax met Teddy's gaze head-on. "I know I messed up in
more ways than I can count—"

Jaime faked a cough that sounded like "Literally."

Jax stopped feeling sorry Kendall had kicked Jaime in
the balls.

"I know I don't deserve your understanding or your
help, but you have to know how special Kendall is. How

could any man in his right mind not fall in love with her? Please tell me where she is."

Teddy scrubbed his face with his hands. "She went back to Boston this afternoon. She doesn't want to see you."

"But—"

"Jax, I know my little girl a lot better than you do. The best thing you can do right now is to give her space. When she's ready to deal with you, believe me, you'll know it. She gets that from her mama. If you push her, she'll go off, and the fallout will be irreparable. I'd help you out if I could, but I have Grace to contend with, and you know her: she's like a mama bear when it comes to protecting her kids—and, yes, that's including you and Racquel. After hearing what Kendall's been through in the last few weeks, Grace and I were torn. Right now it seems as if you're holding your own. Am I wrong?"

"No, sir."

"Kendall's devastated. I'll do what I can to help you out, but I have to go around Grace to do it, and that's like playing Russian roulette."

Jax wasn't happy about it. "I understand. Thanks."

Teddy looked at Jaime. "Go on out and tell Grace we'll join you in a few minutes."

Jaime shot him a you're-on-your-own look of relief and left the room, closing the door behind him.

"Tell me what the hell is going on with you, son. I know it's more than your headaches."

Jax sat on the chair behind him and rubbed his temples before looking back at Teddy. "This stays just between us? I don't want Grace and Rocki worrying about it until I know more. If that's a problem, tell me now."

Teddy paled. "You have my word."

If Jax thought it was difficult telling Jaime and Kendall, it was nothing compared to having to tell Teddy. Teddy didn't interrupt, didn't blink; he just turned and sat down as the ramifications sank in. After a few minutes of silence, he cleared his throat. "You have to get out of here. If you stick around much longer, Grace is going to figure it out."

"I know. That's why I didn't want to come down here in the first place."

Teddy seemed to center himself, although he still looked pale, and his eyes looked shiny, but he shook it off. "Okay, this is what we'll do. There's no way you're getting out of here before you eat dinner, so we'll just steer the conversation in safe directions. Then you go back to the cabin with Jaime to pack. I'll get you on the first flight out of Logan in the morning and make sure there's a car waiting for you at the airport to take you home. Be ready to head out by oh-four-hundred hours."

Jax cleared his throat. "Yeah, um, I can't tell time yet. But I'll have Jaime program it into my phone." Jax stood and took a deep breath.

Teddy came around the desk, grabbed him in a crushing hug, and held on. "You're going to be all right, son. I promise."

The last time Jax had heard those words was right before his uncles shipped him off to boarding school. Teddy had meant well, but he'd been wrong then, and he was wrong now. Jax couldn't see anything being all right ever again. So he pulled away from the closest person to a father he had. "Teddy, Kendall deserves to be loved by someone with all his faculties. I know that. And I tried to stay away from her. I really did. I might not deserve her, but I love her. I love her more than my own life. She needs to know I never lied to her about anything but my name. Not once."

"I'll tell her."

Loud, incessant banging woke Kendall. The sound seemed to hit every cold, hard surface in the apartment and ricocheted. It grew in volume and pulsed through her aching head until she wondered if her ears were bleeding. Whatever this was made Jack's hammering sound tame. "Oh, God. How much did I have to drink?"

Erin groaned from the other side of the sectional. "If you feel anything like I do, the answer to that question is, Way too much. Is that a gong?"

"No, I think it's someone knocking." Kendall rolled off the couch, and her stomach swirled like a Tilt-A-Whirl. She closed her eyes and swallowed back bile. "Coming." In her head it sounded like a scream, but it was probably closer to a whisper. She looked through the peephole, saw her father, and pushed back the weight of disappointment that crushed what was left of her heart. She hadn't even realized she'd been hoping Jack would come.

She opened the door to the big, strong bear of a man who had seemingly aged ten years in twenty-four hours. "Daddy?" He had dark circles under his eyes, and his shirt looked as if he'd slept in it. He was always the starched-and-pressed kind of man, yet today he looked as if he'd been thrown from a speeding car. "Daddy, what's wrong? Is it Jack? What happened?"

"He's gone . . ." She watched her father's lips move—he was talking, but she couldn't hear anything beyond the rushing of blood through her ears. She was going to be sick. She turned and ran to the bathroom, her hand over her mouth, her vision blurred with tears. She thought it was just one of his headaches.

He's gone.

Jack's gone.

Kendall barely made it to the toilet. She'd never vomited while sobbing before, and she couldn't breathe. She didn't even care.

"Kendall?" Her father crouched beside her; his strong hand rubbed her back.

A wet washcloth hit her forehead as she wretched.

She couldn't stop crying; she couldn't breathe. Oh, God, Jack. Inside her head she kept screaming No! No! No! This couldn't be happening, but it was. The cold of the tile floor seeped through the knees of her jeans. Her stomach roiled, and her skin felt cold and clammy.

"Here, let's wipe your face. Look, baby girl. I didn't mean to upset you, but Jax asked me to stop by and give you a letter on my way back from the airport."

She heard her father's voice, but nothing made sense. She tried to breathe normally. "The airport?" She let out a stuttered hiccup. "Wh-wh-what were you doing at the airport?"

"I told you—I dropped Jax off at the airport. He caught the first flight to Chicago this morning."

"Chicago? Jack didn't die? He left?" She sank back on her heels and looked through her tears at her father's pale face. "When you said Jack was gone—I thought you meant *gone*, like *dead*."

"Oh, God, no. I'm sorry. No, Jax is fine physically. It's just the rest of it that worries me."

"He left?" As she pulled her sweater around herself, she felt numb, cold, empty, and a strange humming filled her head. It was really over. Jack had gone. But instead of a Dear Kendall e-mail, he sent a Dear Kendall letter delivered by her father. She didn't think anything could beat David's exit, but Jack had managed to do it.

"Come on, let's get you up." Her dad lifted her off the floor, and she grabbed hold of the counter. Somehow her legs held her. She looked at her reflection in the mirror. She could pass as a cast member of some movie about the zombie apocalypse—blank, pale, vacant, alone.

Her dad filled a glass with water. "Here you go—rinse your mouth. You'll feel better. You just had a shock. Jax is okay. Everything is fine."

Everything was not fine. Jack had left without a word. He didn't even say good-bye. She'd been right: he didn't love her. It was just a line. She might have known better, but she still wished . . .

No matter how many deep breaths she took, no matter how many sobs she swallowed, no matter how hard she bit her lip or how many times her father told her that everything was going to be fine, she couldn't hold back the fall of silent tears.

Her father put an arm around her and murmured soothing words into her hair as he helped her to the kitchen.

Erin poured her a glass of water and tapped two Excedrin into her hand. "Do you want tea or coffee?"

When Kendall didn't answer, Erin squeezed her shoulder. "It's okay. I'll make both."

Kendall kept her eyes on the cool water glass she squeezed between both hands. Her tears dripped onto the front of her sweater, soaking in, making dark spots on the light gray material. "Did Jack tell you anything?" Her voice cracked and squeaked, so she pressed trembling lips together, trying to reel in her unraveling emotions, trying to get a grip on control.

Her father sat across from her and cleared his throat. When she met his gaze, he raised his brows and tilted his head toward Erin.

"Don't worry. Erin's a medical professional. She knows everything said here stays here."

He nodded an apology toward Erin, and his shoulders sank as if he'd sprung a slow leak. "Yes, Jax told me about his . . . um, problem."

Kendall barked a rough laugh through her tears. "His problem? That's an understatement. Losing the ability to comprehend and work with numbers would be a problem for any normal human being, but for Jackson Sullivan, it's a disaster of epic proportions with implications I can't even begin to fathom."

"Agreed. But he's not only worried about the news getting out to the financial community—he made me promise not to breathe a word of it to your mother and Racquel. He doesn't want to worry them unnecessarily. And while I don't agree with hiding things, I do see his point. There's nothing any of us can do but wait and pray that his brain heals."

Erin put her hand on Teddy's shoulder. "What can I get you—tea or coffee?"

"Just black coffee, please."

Erin handed him a mug, and he stared into it as if it held the answers to all of life's questions. Kendall wished it did; maybe then he could tell her why she'd fallen in love with two men who both seemed to be liars. Not only had they left her, but they made her feel like a fool for ever loving them. It wasn't even real. Everything she had with Jack . . . She'd fallen in love with a lie.

"Here you go, Kendall. Just how you like it." Erin placed a cup of coffee in front of her and pried her hands away from the glass she'd been focusing on.

"Kendall," Her dad waited until the silence got so loud, she was forced to look at him. She didn't want to hear this. She knew what was coming: the excuses. "Now that I know, I understand why Jax didn't tell you who he was. If this information were to get out, the financial ramifications could be disastrous, and that's before you take his personal loss into consideration. If Jax doesn't make a full recovery, I don't know what he's going to do. Jax's work has been his whole life."

Her father's words repeated in Kendall's head, *Jax's work has been his whole life* . . . his whole life. Kendall took a sip of coffee. Her eyes burned from crying, and her face felt swollen. "That's not true—Jack's whole life hasn't been work. He told me if his brain heals, he had a job. But now he knows the difference between a job and a life. He said when he was in Chicago, he had a job but no life." But, then, maybe that was a lie too.

Erin sat at the table beside her. "That's so sad. So why is he flying back to Chicago, where he has no life, when you're right here?" She tossed a few Excedrin in her mouth and chased them with water.

"I don't know." Kendall felt the tear flow increase to the point where her nose was running too, and she wiped it on her shoulder. She took a deep breath and let exhaustion overtake her. "Maybe he didn't want a life after all. I guess it's a good thing, then, that his brain is healing. I know it is." Tears kept falling, and she wiped her face. "His ability to understand numbers is returning. He might not notice it, but over the past two weeks, I've seen a marked improvement. I don't know if he'll ever be the same as he was before the accident, but I don't see why he can't re-learn the things that don't come back automatically. His intellect doesn't seem to have been affected."

Erin grabbed her iPad. "You know, after I met Janie and Cameron, I did a little research on the brain."

"Just a little research, huh?" Knowing Erin, she prob-ably knew enough about the human brain to pass the neurology board exams. "Dad, Erin's soon-to-be daugh-ter, Janie, survived a brain tumor. Erin met them when she was doing private-duty nursing."

"Oh, that's right. Grace told me you'd recently be-come engaged. Congratulations."

"Thanks." From her smile, Erin obviously had visions of Cam and Janie dancing through her head.

Kendall took a sip of coffee and cleared her throat. "You were saying something about research?"

"Oh, right. I read a study in the *Journal of Neurosci-ence* about researchers who studied epilepsy patients who had electrodes implanted into their brains to deter-mine the source of their seizures. During the study, they discovered a cluster of specialized brain cells that deal specifically with numbers."

Kendall didn't want to care. She didn't want to feel anything. She just wanted to go numb. But looking at her dad, knowing how torn up he was about Jack, how could she not? "Jack had no problem reading, which I thought was strange. Numbers and letters are both symbols, right? Why would his ability to read not be affected? It seems as if he only has problems with anything having to do with numbers."

"That's what the researchers wondered too, so they were able to study their patients' brains while showing them symbols, numbers, and letters, and the electrodes were able to pinpoint exactly where the brain activity was. When they showed them numbers, these specialized clusters lit up like Times Square. It turns out they're located in the region that extends into both sides of the head, near the ear canals." She pointed just behind the temple and slid her fingers back toward her ears.

"Jack said one side of his head and face took the brunt of the damage."

Erin sipped her coffee and nodded. "That makes sense. After all, that's where most of the pressure would be if he had a side impact." Erin looked over at Kendall's dad, who leaned against the kitchen counter. "The brain is like a sponge inside a ball. If you hit this side"—she pointed to the side of her head by her ear—"the brain will hit the skull here." She pointed to the opposite side. "And then slosh back and forth."

Kendall didn't want to think about the accident—or the sloshing back and forth. "The good news is, Jack's doing better. When the ceiling fell down—"

"What? What ceiling?"

"In the cabin. The roof had a bad leak, and the plaster ceiling in the small bedroom fell down. But don't worry: Jack is reroofing the place. He got it all dried in before the nor'easter hit."

Her dad looked pretty impressed. "He did?"

"Yeah, not too bad for a guy who couldn't count. You didn't expect him to just sit around, crying in his Wheaties and not do anything, did you?"

"I guess I hadn't thought about it, and when I was up at the cabin, I was too busy to notice."

"I helped him measure the furring strips. He would tell me how many of whatever it was he needed. He couldn't have done that a week ago. His sense of time has gotten better too. We played cards, and he had no problem recognizing the suits or the face cards, just the numbers. He's connecting them with the words. Once we got past his humongous ego, he did really well."

Her dad took an envelope out of his pocket and set it on the table in front of her. "He asked me to give this to you."

She stared at the envelope—her name printed with broad, slashing strokes that cut her to ribbons before she even opened it. She kept her hands tightly wrapped around the now-cool coffee cup to keep from reaching for it. If she opened it, it would be real, undeniable. There would be no question, no hope, no dreams. Everything would be final.

When her dad shifted in his seat and broke Kendall's stare, she realized she had no idea how long she'd been staring at that envelope. She tried to ignore it, but it was like a living, breathing thing, calling her. "Your mom told me what happened with David. I'd like to say I'm sorry, and I hate that he hurt you, but, baby girl, I never thought he was the right man for you."

"Yeah, thanks for the heads-up. It seems as if everyone knew he wasn't the one but me, and no one bothered to mention it."

Her dad took a sip of his coffee and smiled. "One day you'll see that the hardest part about being a parent is watching your children make their own mistakes. If I had said anything, you would have gotten your back up and done your best to prove me wrong. I was afraid you'd run to the nearest justice of the peace and marry the little bastard just to spite me." He smiled at Erin. "She gets that from her mother. My Gracie is one hardheaded woman."

Erin laughed. "I'm so not taking that bait. I know better—I've heard all the stories about you, Teddy Watkins." She rose, returned the creamer to the refrigerator, and stuck in her head. "Kendall, there's no food in here."

"What did you expect? I've been gone for two weeks, remember? I just stopped to pick up cream for coffee. I thought I'd do the big shopping today."

Her dad raised his eyebrows. "So, you're planning to stay in Boston?"

Kendall couldn't take her eyes off the envelope lying on the table. "Only long enough to give my landlord notice and pack my things. I want to move back to Harmony."

Her father let out what seemed like a relieved breath.

"I need to find a place to live and at least a part-time job, and I'm going to look into getting a SBA loan. I want to open my own practice, even if I have to start part-time. Even if I get a full-time job, I can still have office hours at night and on weekends until I build up my patient list."

"That's great, Kendall. I'm glad you're coming home. No offense to Boston, but I never felt like you belonged here."

Kendall touched the envelope with the tip of her fingernail. "Neither did I."

"Jax said you can stay at the cabin if you want while you're looking for a place of your own. If you're not interested, let me know, and I'll go and clear out the rest of the food and winterize it."

"He wants me to stay at the cabin?"

Her father nodded. "He mentioned that he probably wouldn't be back until spring."

She pictured Jack grabbing ahold of that tree branch

and swinging down from the roof. Her eyes filled again. "Yeah, he mentioned finishing the roof once the weather warmed up. I guess it's not good to put shingles on in the cold."

"No. No, it's not. I'd forgotten he could swing a hammer; it's been so long. He got into a fight with his uncles one summer, and they held his trust fund over his head, so he told them to stuff it and got a roofing job the next day. Jax always said he liked that job." Her dad stood, put his coffee cup in the sink, and then stepped in front of her. "Well, I'd better get going. I have a lot of work to catch up on. Addie's helped a lot while we were away, but there are some things I have to do myself. Besides, your mother is probably pacing the floor, waiting for a report. She wanted me to check to make sure you're okay. Do me a favor and give her a call to tell her when you'll be home."

"Mom didn't tell you to scare the crap out of me, did she, Daddy?"

"Um, no. And if she finds out I did, she's going to give me such a rash. Why don't we agree to keep that under our hats, and I won't tell her that her youngest daughter went out and bought three large boxes of condoms. Deal?"

"Oh, my God, Jack did not tell you that, did he?"

"Baby girl, he didn't need to. I saw the evidence myself. So, do we have a deal?"

She got up and hugged her father. "Yeah, we have a deal."

Erin made herself scarce while Kendall walked her dad to the door.

He grabbed the doorknob and then stopped and gave her a long, hard look. "Kendall, I've known Jax all his life, and I've seen him go through a lot of tough times—the loss of his parents, having his Olympic dreams dashed.

He sat by Racquel's bedside for days on end while she recovered from the accident, but I've never seen him look more lost and alone than he did yesterday." He took a deep breath. "If he wasn't sick as a dog, I would have kicked his ass, and, believe you me, I called him on the carpet. But he looked me square in the eye and told me that he loves you more than his own life. He said he told you, but you didn't believe him, and he wanted to make sure that you knew."

"Why are you telling me this?"

"Because that's the only thing he's ever asked me to do for him." Her dad shook his head. "He must know how stubborn you are and didn't trust that you'd read the letter."

"I'll read it." Eventually.

Erin stopped beside them at the door with her bag slung over her shoulder. "I'll ride down with you, Teddy. I need to get home." Kendall was pulled into another hug.

"Thanks for coming. I've missed you."

"Remember what we talked about, and call me if you want help packing or want to chat. Anytime."

"I will. Give Janie and Cam a kiss for me."

Kendall watched them leave, then closed and locked the door behind them, knowing that her father waited on the other side to hear the dead bolt thrown and the slide of the chain. She grabbed the envelope on her way back to the couch, holding it close to her chest, tugged the blanket up over her head, and cried.

CHAPTER
EIGHTEEN

———

Jaime stumbled into his house and found Addie asleep in his favorite chair by the fire. Addie was using one of his jackets as a blanket and had pulled it up under her pointed chin. She'd kicked off her shoes and tucked her feet under her. He sat on the ottoman and watched her sleep. The seemingly permanent worry line above her brows had disappeared in slumber, and her perfectly shaped mouth was curved up in a sexy little *Mona Lisa* smile—the kind that made him wonder what dirty thoughts were going through her mind, or if it was just wishful thinking on his part. "Probably wishful thinking fueled by lust and tequila. Not the best combination."

He and Jax swiped a bottle of tequila from the lake house—although technically it wasn't stealing, since Jax owned the property. Still, if Grace had gotten wind of it, she wouldn't have been too happy with either of them. Jaime had driven Jax around the lake to the cabin, and the two of them proceeded to put a pretty big dent in the bottle.

Jaime put a hand on her shoulder and gave it a shake. "Addison?"

Her smile got wider, but she didn't wake up. Shit. He

took his jacket off and threw it over the hook on the wall. What the hell was he supposed to do with her? If she slept like that for much longer, she'd have a crick in her neck.

He knew what he'd like to do with her: slip that ugly jumper off her, stuff it in the fire, and take off the rest of her clothes using only his teeth and mouth. Damn, he was getting hard just thinking about her.

He turned down the bed in the guest room and prepared himself for a long, painful night, and then spent the next five minutes trying to decide how to pick her up. He didn't think she'd appreciate the fireman's hold, which left him . . . what? The Rhett Butler carry. Damn, he hoped to hell she'd sleep through it. He wouldn't want her to think he was copping a feel.

"Addison, come on. Wake up." She slept like the dead. He shook out his arms, then took a deep breath before sliding one hand under her thighs and the other behind her back. He got a firm hold and did a dead lift. She was a lot lighter than she looked, and her head lolled against his biceps, so he lifted her a little higher until it rested against his shoulder. Then her breath hit his neck, and he nearly groaned.

Jaime carried her to the spare room, trying to tamp down all the Me, Tarzan feelings zinging through him. This was definitely not the time to start the whole chest-pounding thing. No, he just needed to lay her down, cover her up, and get the hell out of the room. And he did just that, stopping only to turn on the light in the bathroom, in case she woke up and didn't know where the hell she was. He closed the door behind him and released a breath. "Damn, Addison, what the hell are you doing here?"

He went to the kitchen and heated up a cup of coffee

in the microwave; if he brewed a pot, he was afraid the scent would wake his houseguest. He knew it was senseless to go to bed, because there was no way he'd ever get any sleep with Addie sleeping one room away. He took a sip of the reheated coffee and shook his head. Addison Lane could make him drink reheated coffee. He tugged his sweater over his head, then kicked off his Timberlands and booted up his computer. He might as well get some work done.

At six in the morning, he put on a fresh pot of coffee and poured her a cup. He tapped lightly on the door, and when he didn't hear anything, he stepped in. She'd kicked off her covers, hugged a pillow to her chest, and thrown her leg over it. Her dress had slid up enough to show off a nice length of creamy thigh but nothing else, which was a damn shame. "Rise and shine, Addison."

Her eyes shot open, and when she saw him, they widened farther. She sat straight up, hugging the pillow to her chest like a shield. "Jaime, what are you doing here?"

He just raised an eyebrow. "I think that's my question. You were the one in my living room, Sleeping Beauty." He handed her the coffee and watched her take a sip.

She closed her eyes and groaned. "God, that's good."

Addie definitely wasn't a morning person, and she looked a mess—her mane of hair was wild, like she'd been dragged through a hedge backward, her dress was twisted, and she had a pillowcase crease on her cheek.

"I just sat down for a minute to warm up. Hey, where were you, anyway?"

"Oh no. Where I was is none of your business." He stood because if he didn't, he'd be tempted to kiss that torqued look right off her pretty face. "I didn't know what time you needed to get up. It's a little after six.

There's a spare toothbrush in the medicine cabinet, towels on the counter, and shampoo and stuff in the tub. Use whatever you need. Breakfast will be ready in about ten minutes. Come on out whenever you're done and tell me what was so damn important that you felt the need to camp out in my living room. And you might want to remember that an unlocked door is not an invitation to enter." He left her sitting there with her mouth hanging open.

Jaime was not in a good mood. He slammed a cast-iron pan on the stove, turned on the heat, and tossed in the bacon, then grabbed a loaf of bread to make toast and took the eggs out of the refrigerator.

He had a nightmare day scheduled, so he took out the makings for a few sandwiches. He wouldn't have time or the energy, thanks to his sexy little houseguest, to go out and pick something up. "Addison, do you want me to make you a sandwich?"

"What?"

He turned around, and she was standing there in nothing but a towel wrapped around her, the corner stuffed between her breasts. Her hair was wet and drops of water slid down her chest.

"Did you say something?"

"Yeah . . . um . . . Do you want me to make you a sandwich?"

"Thanks, but you don't have to."

He stepped back, because his finger itched to pull out that corner and see what was hiding under the terry cloth. What was she thinking coming out of the room naked? "That's not what I asked. Do you want a damn sandwich or not?"

"Yes, please. If you don't mind."

"I wouldn't have asked if I minded."

"Jeez, Jaim. Did you wake up on the wrong side of the bed this morning or are you always like this?"

"I didn't get to bed." He mumbled.

"Why not?"

"Roast beef, turkey, or both?"

"Both."

"Mustard or mayo?"

"Both, please."

"Fine." He shook his head.

She stood there dripping and stared at him. "Thanks, Jaime."

"Just go get dressed before you freeze to death."

"Oh." She looked down like she just realized she was standing there wearing nothing but a towel. She might not have noticed, but he sure as hell did.

Five minutes later, she came out wearing the same clothes she'd slept in. Her hair was dried and tied in a ponytail hanging down her back.

"More coffee?"

"I'll get it."

"Suit yourself. You always do anyway."

She leaned up against the counter and watched him.

"How do you like your eggs?"

"Over easy."

"One, two, or three?"

"Two, please."

"So, what the hell was so all-fired important that you needed to come all the way here and wait for me?"

"I wanted to find out what you learned."

He raised an eyebrow. "And it wasn't something that could wait until morning?"

"I wanted to make sure you were okay too. I know

how close you and Teddy have been over the years. I thought if it didn't go well, you might need a friend."

"Uh-huh." The last thing he wanted from her was friendship. Damn, didn't she get that?

"Kendall left me a note telling me she was going to be in Boston, packing up the apartment. I know she met with Grace at my place before she took off, because Grace brought over a loaf of pumpkin bread."

"Yeah, well, Jax is getting ready to fly to Chicago. I think he has an eight o'clock flight. Teddy was pretty adamant that he leave Kendall alone until she cools off. Besides, he needs to get his shit together too."

"Kendall's going to think he left her. Just like David did."

"That's ridiculous. Jax told me he was going to write her a letter and explain everything. He has responsibilities in Chicago—he has to at least go back and decide what he's going to do. He's been away more than six weeks."

She shrugged. "Kendall is coming off a bad relationship. David was manipulative. What seems reasonable to us might not if you're looking at it from her vantage point. Desertion sucks, and twice in a few weeks would tend to put a woman on the defensive. Kendall might just see his explanation as nothing more than a Dear Jane letter."

"It's nothing of the kind. Or at least I don't think it is. Jax told Teddy that he loved her."

"He did?"

"Yeah. He's got it bad."

"And what about you?"

"What about me?"

"Are you doing okay?"

Hell, no. But it had nothing to do with Teddy and everything to do with her. He turned her eggs, threw a few pieces of buttered toast and bacon on her plate, and then plated the eggs. She stood way too close to him, and even with different soap and shampoo, there was something about her that made him want to nuzzle her neck and drink her in.

"Go sit down." He finished cooking his eggs and sat beside her at the breakfast bar. Shit, he should have just eaten standing up in the kitchen.

"You didn't answer the question. Was Teddy that upset with you?" She slid a piece of bacon between her lips and he couldn't look away. Everything she did seemed erotic. "Jaime, what's the matter with you?"

He spun her barstool around, put a hand on either armrest, and leaned in. "You come to my house uninvited and fall so soundly asleep in my chair that it would take an atomic bomb to wake you. I had to pick you up and put you to bed without so much as copping a feel. I've been awake all night, fighting a hard-on and trying not to think about you sleeping in the next room, and you're asking me what in the hell is the matter?"

Her gray eyes looked green in the light and seemed to darken. Her color came up and she licked her lips.

He almost groaned. "Addie, the last thing I want to be is your friend. So if that's all you want, I'm not interested. Eat your breakfast, take your lunch, and leave."

"And if it's not?"

"If it's not, you should probably eat your breakfast, take your lunch, and leave anyway, because I have a full day of work ahead of me, and so do you."

"Oh." The pulse in her throat beat like the wings of a

hummingbird, and he had an overwhelming urge to slide his tongue over that spot and suck on it.

"Are you going to wear a turtleneck today?"

"Maybe. Why?"

"Because I want to suck on your neck."

"You do?"

"I do. Bad. It might leave a mark. I want to do a whole lot more to you too, but I'm in a rush. I just need to taste you, okay?" As he slid a hand behind her head and drew her close, his nose rubbed against her and he smiled. "Breathe."

She let a breath out and sucked in another.

He kissed the corner of her mouth and slid the tip of his tongue across the seam to the other side. Her eyes were still wide open, either in shock or excitement. Then he went in for the kiss. Her lips were tense and her whole body vibrated. He wanted to soothe her, excite her, and then shock the hell out of her. He started out soft, sweet, and slow, and waited for her to relax. It wasn't happening. When he opened his eyes, hers were filled with terror. He pulled away slowly and stepped back. "Addie, you're okay."

As soon as he gave her space, she vaulted off the barstool. "I have to go." She wrapped her arms around herself, shaking, and stepped way back. Out of reach.

"Don't forget your lunch." He didn't make a move; he just held the bag out for her to take.

"Thanks for . . . Well, thanks for everything. I'm sorry . . ." She brushed her hair back with a shaking hand. "I really need to go."

He sat at the counter and did his best to shoot her a smile. "Make sure you call Kendall after school today and tell her to read Jax's letter, okay?"

"I will," she grabbed her coat and missed the armhole twice. "You know Kendall when she's hurt. Once she finds out he lied and then ran ..." She shook her head and punched her other arm through the sleeve before hugging herself again, the paper bag crunching in her hand. "There's no telling what she's going to do."

The food he'd eaten sat like lead in his stomach. Jaime nodded, like nothing out of the ordinary was going on, like she hadn't just about jumped out of her skin, like he hadn't just scared the shit out of her with a simple kiss. He felt sick. "You have a good day, Addison. I'm glad you came by." He grabbed both plates and put them in the sink. "Take your time getting your stuff together. I'm just going to get in the shower. I was supposed to be at the shop fifteen minutes ago. I'll see you later. Let me know what Kendall says, okay?" He didn't wait for a response; he just turned and headed to his room to give her time and space to calm down.

His first thought was to put his hand through a wall, but that was the old Jaime. The only thing that would get him was another cast, if he hit a stud like he had the last time he'd lost his temper. No, what he needed was about an hour in the basement—just him and his seventy-pound punching bag.

He didn't know what had happened to Addison, but someone had hurt her. Someone had hurt her bad, and if he ever found out who the hell was responsible for the look of sheer terror in his Addie's eyes, he'd kill the bastard with his bare hands.

———

Jax stepped out of the limo, and the doorman did a double take before recognition crossed his face. Since he'd never seen Jax wearing anything but a three-piece suit, he supposed worn Levi's, a wool sweater, and hiking boots were a little out of character.

"Hi, Tom. How's it going?"

"Just fine, Mr. Sullivan. Do you want me to have your bags sent up?"

"No, thanks. I've got them. Do you have the time?"

Tom gave him a weird look, but looked at the clock above the elevators and smiled. "Twelve-oh-five, sir."

It was an hour later in Boston, and Jax wondered what Kendall was doing. Had she read his letter? Did she decide to stay at the cabin? Was she okay? It had been almost thirty hours since he'd seen her, and it felt like a lifetime.

Tom called the elevator for him, and Jax stepped in and inserted his key. He was doing better with numbers, but he was beat, and right now he was thankful he lived in the penthouse. A few moments later, the elevator opened into the entry.

Jax had spent the night at the cabin alone in his bed but didn't sleep. He just lay there surrounded by Kendall's scent, thinking about her and remembering the way she smiled when she'd catch him watching her, what she looked like before her first cup of coffee, how she'd tilt her head when she questioned his sanity, and the spark in her eye when she lost her temper. He missed her so much, his body ached with it.

He tossed his bag on the black-and-white marble entry, noticing that his hiking boots looked strange against the shiny surface. He didn't think he'd ever really noticed the floor before. He supposed he was used to just thinking that his dress shoes would be fine, but his hiking boots were a different story. They tended to drag a lot of crap in on their treads. Then again, the cleaning crew came in twice a week whether he needed it or not, so what the hell? He might as well give them something to do.

Jax headed straight to the wet bar—he hadn't taken any painkillers stronger than Motrin or Tylenol all day, so he poured himself a scotch. He stood beside the floor-to-ceiling windows and stared across the frozen lake. The cold radiated through the thermal panes. Even at midday it was flat and gray, just like his life and his apartment. There was no color, no warmth, no life. He tried to remember if he'd ever had anyone over to his apartment. His assistant had dropped off a contract for his signature once when he was down with pneumonia. She brought him a pot of homemade chicken soup and some orange juice, and even picked up a prescription for him. It was the nicest thing anyone had done for him since he'd started working at Sullivan Industries. Rocki also visited once for a weekend a few years ago.

He'd lived here almost five years and he'd had only two people into his home—unless you counted the cleaning service.

Jax might not have a life yet, but he wanted one, and he wanted it to include Kendall. All he had to do was figure out how to make that happen.

He headed to his room, stripped down, and took his drink into the shower with him. Today he was going to do his best to sleep, and first thing tomorrow morning he would start fighting for his life—fighting for Kendall. He just needed a little help, and he knew just who to ask.

He picked up the house phone and pressed the button for his office.

"Good afternoon. Jackson Sullivan's office. This is Anne Pivens. May I help you?"

He stood there wearing a towel, listening to his assistant's greeting, and tamped down his nervousness. "Yes, hi, Anne. It's Jax."

Silence.

"Jackson Sullivan."

"Mr. Sullivan, hello. How are you?"

"I'm good, thanks. And you?"

"I'm fine. What can I do for you, sir?"

"Mrs. Pivens, I need a favor. I was wondering if you would be able to meet with me tomorrow at my office here in the penthouse, and bring a copy of our confidentiality agreement with you."

"Our agreement, sir? As in, the agreement I signed, or the boilerplate Sullivan Industries confidentiality agreement?"

"Yours."

"Is there a problem, sir?"

"No, no problem. I just need to go through it before we talk."

"I'll bring two copies, then. What time would be good for you?"

"Nine o'clock, but call me at eight, and, um, if you wouldn't mind, could you order something for breakfast to be delivered?"

"Certainly. Will that be all?"

"Yes, thank you. I'll see you tomorrow." He hit the End button, tossed the phone on his bedside table, flipped the switch to lower the black-out blinds, and slid between the fresh sheets of his bed. He closed his eyes and tried to pretend he was home, lying beside Kendall. It didn't work.

Kendall slept and dreamed about Jack. She rolled over, reaching for him, only to wake up hot and bothered and alone. She opened her eyes and they landed on the envelope lying on the ugly coffee table, silently mocking her.

She went to the kitchen, made another pot of coffee, and stared into the living room. She'd always hated the furniture. David had seen the room in some yuppie magazine and wanted to re-create it.

Why was she moving furniture she hated? Then it occurred to her that she didn't have to keep it. She took a picture and thought she'd see if the consignment shop would be interested in taking it, because she wasn't. No, she was going to get rid of everything in the apartment she didn't love. She was going to purge David from her life.

Kendall looked at her list as she set out for the day. She stopped at the bank to make sure David's name was off all her accounts, then stopped to pick up boxes and moving supplies on the way to her favorite consignment shop. The owner loved the furniture and even offered to pick it up, which totally worked for Kendall.

By the time she finished her take-out Chinese dinner, the ugly furniture was history and she had a stack of book boxes already filled and labeled.

Kendall heard her phone ring and had to feel around the dining room table to find it. Addie's face flashed on the screen, and just seeing it made Kendall smile. "Hey, Addie. How are you?"

Kendall did her best to ignore Jack's letter sitting on top of the TV as she and Addie chatted. She thought that if she just kept busy she wouldn't have time to obsess about Jack. So far, she'd been wrong.

"I've been worried. How are you?"

"I'm okay. Keeping busy—the more I do, the less time I have to mope, so that's good."

"Jaime told me Jax went back to Chicago."

"Yeah, he left. He's gone. It's over. He even had Dad to deliver his Dear Kendall letter."

"What did it say?"

Kendall picked up a framed picture of her and David. She took the picture out of the frame and tossed it in a pile before wrapping the frame. "I don't know. I haven't opened it yet."

"Kendall, what are you waiting for?"

Courage, the pain to subside a little, maybe another bottle of wine? "Is it so hard to believe that I'm just not chomping at the bit to have my heart stomped on again? I'll read it. Eventually. Just not now. I've hit my pain quota for the day—maybe the month."

"Oh, Kendall. I'm sorry."

The tears started again. "Addie, he left without so much as a good-bye."

"See, I knew you'd take it that way."

"You knew he was leaving and you didn't tell me?"

"I found out this morning. Jaime said he had an eight o'clock flight, so he would have already been at the airport when I found out. It's not as if I had the flight number."

"What were you and Jaime doing before eight o'clock this morning?"

"We had breakfast—that's all."

Oh, really? That definitely wasn't all there was to it.

Addie cleared her throat. "Kendall, let's look at this logically—just the facts, no emotion. You walked out on Jax first. You wouldn't let him explain."

"He lied to me. I didn't even know who he was. It's

like our whole relationship, everything about it, was a lie. I was hurt." But *hurt* didn't do the pain justice. Her whole body ached like she had the flu. It was all she could do to keep moving and not curl up in a ball and cry.

"From what Jaime said, Jax was really sick. He couldn't even drive. Besides, he had to go home eventually. He has a company to run."

"He has a huge company, and I thought he was a handyman. I'm such a fool." She brushed away a tear. "Look, Addie, I just can't go there now." No, she was going home. She took a stack of books off the shelf and piled them in a box.

"Do you want me to come down tomorrow? I can help you pack, and that way you're not alone when you read it."

"No." The last thing she needed were more witnesses to her meltdown. The last time Jack was with her, and she knew how well that worked out. "Addie, I know you want to help, and I love you for it. But this is something I'm going to do alone. I'm going through everything, getting rid of what I don't like, and packing the rest. I just want to move on. The sooner I get out of here, the better."

"Do you want to come and stay with me until you find a place? I have plenty of room."

"Thanks for the offer, Addie, but I think I'd rather be alone and figure out what I'm going to do with my life. I might go back to the cabin until I find a job and a place to live."

"Oh, okay. Let me know if you need help, groceries, whatever. Oh, and Kendall. Read Jax's letter. You're not going to be able to move forward until you do."

"I will—I just don't know when. I'll let you know when I hit town."

CHAPTER
NINETEEN

Jax waited for the elevator door to open, nervousness licking his insides and tension crawling up his neck, promising another killer headache. He rubbed the back of his neck and thought about Kendall. She gave the best back rubs in the world.

The elevator doors slid open, and Anne Pivens, in her usual work attire—long wool coat, skirt, silk blouse, jacket, and sensible heels—appeared. She had her pocketbook thrown over one shoulder and her briefcase over the other, and she pushed a silver cart in front of her.

She stopped in front of him and blinked. He supposed he should have at least put a pair of dress slacks on, but something about seeing his suits and dress pants hanging in his closet in order of color made his head ache. He'd thrown on a pair of jeans and a cashmere sweater instead. It was a good thing he decided to put a pair of loafers on rather than just going barefoot or wearing his boots. Her eyes widened. "Am I early?"

"No, I'm sure you're right on time." She'd never been anything but punctual in all the time he'd known her. He waved her toward the dining room. "Come on in. And thank you for meeting me here. May I take your coat?"

She dropped her briefcase, set her purse on the center table under the crystal chandelier, and then shrugged out of her coat and handed it to him.

"I thought we'd eat in the dining room and then head to the office. Is that okay with you?" He hung up her coat, and when he turned around, she already had her purse and briefcase in hand and was pushing the cart toward the dining room.

She hadn't answered him. She just set the table with stilted efficiency. He never remembered seeing her anxious, but, then, he might not have noticed. He had a feeling he'd missed a lot. Anne Pivens was an amazing assistant. She kept him on schedule, had whatever he needed at her fingertips or in that brilliant mind of hers, screened his calls, guarded his privacy, and handled everything he'd ever thrown at her with the utmost professionalism.

She poured coffee into china cups, doctored hers, and set his black coffee beside his plate.

He held the chair for her, and she looked shocked, then pleased, as she sat. "Do you have that confidentiality agreement?"

"Yes." She flipped open her briefcase, pulled a folder from it, and handed it to him.

"Thanks. Go on and dig in. I just want to look this over quickly before we get started."

She took a sip of coffee and watched him as he read the contract. The food sat untouched in the middle of the table, hidden by the silver warming covers. She rolled her napkin in her lap, spread it out, then rolled it again.

The confidentiality agreement seemed to be airtight — as airtight as it could be. When it came down to it, all it would take was one word to the right person to send an entire division of the company into a downward spiral.

Jax was heavily invested personally, as was typical for a fund manager. His having skin in the game built client confidence, but it also put him in a really vulnerable position. He was the figurehead, and how much confidence would an impaired funds manager inspire? If word got out, it could ruin him and the company.

Ho'd been working with Anne Pivens for almost ten years, and he'd never seen her falter, he'd never heard a bad word about her, and he'd never seen her gossip. She was security conscious—even when she left for the day, her workspace was pristine, not a paper out of place, and she shredded every piece of paper except tissues. Every night, all the files they'd worked on were locked up tight. There were only two keys: his and hers. Anne Pivens was meticulous, and in all the time they'd worked together, he'd never seen her leave anything to chance.

Jax tossed the contract back on the folder and mulled it over. When it came down to it, he either trusted Anne implicitly or not; it was a judgment call. He had to go with his gut, because there were no guarantees. No matter what the confidentiality agreement said, corporate espionage was alive and well—there was always someone out there with enough bribe money to make talking worth her while. Still, Jax trusted her.

"Okay, come on. Let's eat." He reached across and removed the warming covers. Eggs Benedict, hash browns, and fruit salad. He dug in—he hadn't eaten since he grabbed something at the airport yesterday morning. When he looked up, Anne sat there as still as a statue. "Something wrong?"

"Yes, there is. Mr. Sullivan, you left on a vacation in early December, and a week later I receive a call from legal, informing me that you were taking a three-month leave of absence. I worked for two months without a word from you, only to receive a cryptic phone call yesterday, requesting my presence and a copy of my confidentiality agreement at a breakfast meeting in your home. I would like to know what's going on. Am I in some kind of trouble? Has our security been breached? Has something happened?"

"Yes, something happened, but it has nothing to do with you. I'm sorry if I upset you. I need to talk to you about something very sensitive, and I needed to see where we stand legally, for your protection as well as my own. I don't want to put you in a compromising position."

"And?"

"And I think you'll be fine—these agreements are for your protection as well as the corporation's. As for me? I have to ask you to keep everything said today in the strictest confidence. I don't want anything written down, no mention of this in the office or anywhere but here. Is that understood?"

"Of course, sir."

"Look, Mrs. Pivens, what I'm going to tell you is personal. We've been working together for almost ten years; I would hope we know each other well enough to be on a first-name basis. So can we drop the *sir* and *Mrs.*? Just call me Jax or Jackson. Heck, I'll even answer to Jack."

"All right. And as for me, Anne is fine, but forgive me if I forget. I'll do my best, but old habits and all that."

He scrubbed his hand over his face. "Tell me about it. Now would you please eat?"

"One question."

He took a bite of his potatoes. "Sure."

"You don't have a terminal illness, do you?" Her voice cracked.

He looked up, startled, and saw she was actually blinking back tears. "No, I'm fine."

She let out a relieved breath and sank back in her chair. "Oh, thank God. I just couldn't imagine. . . . I've always been so careful about security. I know I didn't leak anything, but with corporate espionage and computer security breaches . . . well, you never really know. But if it wasn't that, the only other thing I could come up with was a Steve Jobs scenario."

"I'm sorry. I didn't know how to discuss this, and I really did need to look at this." He tapped the confidentiality agreement. "I was in a skiing accident. I'm told I caught an edge and went headfirst into a tree, but I don't remember anything that happened that day. I was in a drug-induced coma for a few days. They had to drill into my skull to relieve pressure from the swelling. I woke up in the ICU."

"But you're okay."

"For the most part I am, but have been some aftereffects. I don't know if it's permanent. I'm supposed to have another MRI in the next few weeks and see if how it's healing."

"Aftereffects?"

"Yeah, that's what I have to talk to you about. Right now, I'm incapable of doing my job. I need to reevaluate our succession plan—we might have to make some changes. I've been thinking a lot about it, and I'm not comfortable with the way it stands now."

"What kind of changes?"

"I have lost all ability to deal with numbers. Counting, telling the time—hell, I have a pocket full of money and

I don't know how much I have." His face split into a grin. For the first time, it was actually kind of funny. "Nothing else seems to be affected. Right after the accident, I had a hard time coming up with the right word, the order of things, but that's gone away. I have no trouble reading and understanding the words. I'm told I'm making progress with numbers. I have a better handle on the passage of time, and I'm able to recognize numbers and put a name to them. I don't know if it's something that came back to me or if it was relearned."

"And who is privy to this information?"

"Teddy Watkins; his daughter, Kendall; my best friend, Jaime Rouchard; and now you."

"I know Jaime and Teddy, but Kendall is new to me. Is she trustworthy?"

"Yes."

"And how are you?"

"I just told you."

"Mr. — I mean Jackson — it must have been quite a shock. You went from being a veritable mathematical genius to not even recognizing a number. You spent the past ten years of your life living, breathing, and sleeping the markets. You're an analytical guru. You've done nothing but keep your finger on the pulse of the world's economic trends, and you know most financial news before the *Wall Street Journal* and Reuters get wind of it. I can't imagine how someone deals with that kind of loss."

"They go and hide out in a cabin in the woods and reroof the place."

She blinked a few times, then laughed. A robust, hearty laugh.

He shook his head. "I'm serious. That's what I did."

She smiled and cut into her eggs Benedict. "How did you measure?"

"I drew a lot of lines and made a lot of cuts. It kept me busy. It kept me mostly sane. And then someone came crashing into my life and showed me everything I missed when I was living, eating, breathing, and sleeping work."

"And that would be Kendall?"

"Yes."

She looked around the apartment. "Is she here with you?"

He shook his head. "No, last I heard, she was in Boston. When we reconnected, she didn't recognize me. We hadn't seen each other since my parents' funeral. Because of my situation, I didn't tell her who I was. I said I was renting the place, since I didn't know if I could trust her, and she had no problem talking to a total stranger and letting him know she didn't have the highest opinion of Jax Sullivan."

Anne let out another bark of laughter and then covered her mouth, clearly shocked at her outburst. "I'm sorry, but that's just . . . well, hysterical, really. Talking to you about you. What did she say?"

"She called me the Grand Pooh-Bah of Harmony and accused me of being Harmony's answer to Scrooge Mc-Duck. I found out her ex left a bad taste in her mouth when it came to anyone in the financial industry. She said he was a Jackson Sullivan wannabe."

"Ouch."

"Yeah, exactly. I spent Christmas with my sister, and trying to pretend that I was the same old Jax was exhausting. It was really nice not to have to pretend and watch everything I said. I figured as long as she didn't know who I was, telling her about the accident wasn't a big deal."

"And I take it she found out who you were?"

"The day before yesterday. I tried to explain, but she wouldn't listen, and she left me."

"You didn't go after her?"

"No, I haven't been cleared to drive—not that I had a car. And her father wasn't too happy when he found out about us."

"That's right—Kendall is Teddy's daughter."

"Yeah, talk about an awkward situation. In order to keep my condition under wraps, I had to leave. I wrote Kendall a letter and explained everything. Teddy said he'd give it to her."

"Even after he found out you lied to his daughter?"

"Once I explained why, he understood. He wasn't happy with me, and, believe me, I haven't been called on the carpet like that since the day he found out I took my parents' car out for a joyride when I was thirteen."

"The two of you have a complicated and unusual relationship. You're his boss, and he's like a father to you. It looks like you survived it."

"Yes, I think Teddy and I will be fine. As for Kendall and me, I haven't a clue. She's just getting out of a long relationship, and she needs to figure out what she wants. I need to do the same. I don't want to be the rebound guy, and I don't want to wonder if we're together because we found each other right when both our worlds imploded. We both need time to deal with the fallout and then see what each of us wants."

Anne tilted her head as if in contemplation. "You love her."

"Yeah, I do."

"Does she love you?"

"I don't know. She was really angry and hurt and, well, you can imagine. I don't know if it's something she can get past. I hope so, but at this point, I don't know if she'll even read the letter I sent. She has a wicked nasty temper, so for all I know, she's ripped it up or tossed it in the fire."

"Sounds like she's a keeper."

"I think she is, but why do you?"

Anne sat back and smiled. "She didn't just fall at your feet when she found out who you were. It sounds as if she was more upset that you lied than she was impressed with your bank balance."

"She doesn't have the highest opinion of wealthy people. It's probably not an asset as far as Kendall's concerned."

"And that tells me she knows what's important in life. Money is nice, but it doesn't buy happiness. You're living proof. I don't think I've ever seen you truly happy, and, no, I don't mean a flash of happiness—I mean the content-with-your-life kind of happiness." She finished off her breakfast and set her plate aside. "So, other than revamping the succession plan, what do you need from me?"

He rose. "Let's go in the office and I'll show you."

He walked in and held up the math primers Kendall had bought. "I got started on these last night. I thought if you wouldn't mind finding me a collection of math textbooks, I could go through them. I don't want to question if I'm missing something."

"So you're going to go through every math book between first grade and graduate statistics and applied business calc?"

"If that's what it takes, that's exactly what I'll do."

Anne sat down at his desk and brought up a Web site for an Internet bookstore. "I'll order them today and have them overnighted. I'll print out the succession plan so you can look that over while I'm on the Great Math Book Hunt, and then we'll talk about that." She looked at her watch. "I can stay here for another couple of hours; then I need to go to the office."

"Okay. Would you mind working from here half days?"

"No, that would be fine. I can have the phones transferred. I'll just push the managers' meetings to two o'clock, and start BCCing you the reports, so you can get back up to speed."

Jax sat in the chair facing his desk while she blew through a task list that was mind-boggling, sifted through e-mails, answered questions, and ordered him enough textbooks to get him through high school calculus. Before he got through the third-grade primer, she was packing up her computer.

"Anne, thank you. I can't tell you how much your help means to me."

"You're welcome. I'll be back at eight tomorrow morning. Do you need anything before I go?"

"Yeah," He rubbed his neck and shook his head. "I was wondering if you could program an alarm for six. I want to start swimming again, and that should give me enough time to get in my swim and be back before you get here."

"Sure." She stuck out her hand. "Anything else?"

"No, I think that's it. If I concentrate, I can dial phone numbers for takeout, and I'm figuring out how to count money, thanks to these." He pointed at the pictures of change. "Before you go, let me give you a key to get in, just in case you get here before I return. My sense of time isn't the best yet."

Anne followed him to the kitchen and leaned against the counter while he searched for the spare keys. "I'll tell the doormen to let you in anytime."

"Thanks. Oh, and the restaurant will be by to take the remains of breakfast before five. Just send it down in the elevator. I put everything on the expense account."

"That's fine." He helped her into her coat and called the elevator.

"Jackson?"

"Yes?"

"I hope you don't take this the wrong way." She pulled him into a hug. "I'm so glad you're okay. I was so worried about you."

He'd known her ten years, and they might have shared a handshake before. He smiled and hugged her back. "You have no idea how nice that is to hear. It's good to be back."

She brushed his beard with her hand. "Is this going to stay?"

"I don't know. It's kind of nice not shaving every day."

"It'll have to go before the first board meeting. But I like it. Breakfast tomorrow?"

"That would be great."

"Okay, but don't expect a repeat of today's service, especially now that I've got the goods on you. I'll stop and pick up breakfast sandwiches or bagels, and you might think about hitting the grocery store. We're going to need coffee—a lot of it."

Kendall pushed her way through the door of the cabin, juggling a full box of groceries that felt like it weighed almost as much as she did. "Yeah, I might have overdone the whole shopping thing." She made it to the kitchen, dumped them on the counter, and headed back to the Jeep.

Her whole body ached from packing and moving. Now, thanks to Erin, Cameron, Butch, and Adam, everything she owned was either in the back of her Jeep or in a storage unit in town.

Next she pulled her suitcases out of the trunk and dragged them through the cabin. When she stepped into the room, she half expected to see Jack.

It felt as if he were still there, as if nothing had changed. She took the letter out of her pocket and set it on the bedside table, then sat on the bed and hugged his pillow to her chest. It still smelled like him.

She'd thought the cabin would feel different, empty, cold, *something*, but it didn't. She closed her eyes to hold back the tears and cursed. She didn't have time to sit and cry—not yet. No, she needed to get the car unloaded and her clothes unpacked. In her messenger bag, she had an SBA loan application to fill out and two newspapers' worth of want ads to get through; she needed to find a job.

Kendall put Jack's pillow back and smoothed out the wrinkles. She had to keep moving. If she kept going until she dropped, she might just be able to sleep. She was putting the groceries away when someone knocked on the door.

Jaime stood on the porch, several steps back from the door, when she opened it. "Are you still mad?"

"No."

"Oh, good." He pulled the flowers he held from behind his back. "Then these just changed from an I'm Sorry as Hell bouquet to a welcome-home bouquet. Can I come in?"

"Only if you help me unload the Jeep."

"I'm on it." Jaime smiled, handed her the flowers, gave her a kiss on the cheek, and then jumped off the porch.

Kendall put away groceries, arranged the flowers in an old milk pitcher she found, and unpacked a box of kitchen equipment that the cabin had been missing. "Jaime, do you want to stay for dinner?"

He carried in her TV. "Sure. Are you going to get a satellite dish?"

"No, I won't be here that long. I just thought I'd hook up my DVD player so I can at least watch movies."

He set the TV on the coffee table. "Where do you want it?"

"I was going to see if there was a table somewhere to set it on temporarily."

"Why? You've got the bracket taped right onto the back. I can hang it for you."

"Thanks, but I don't want to go and mess up the walls."

"Don't be ridiculous. Jax won't care. He just wants you to be comfortable. So, where do you want it?"

"I don't know. On the wall across from the couch, maybe?"

"Is the toolbox still in the mudroom?"

"Unless Juck took it with him."

"I doubt it. He didn't take much."

"Have you heard from him?"

Jaime shook his head. "You?"

"No, but, then, I didn't expect to. How's Salisbury steak with mashed potatoes and gravy sound to you?"

"Like heaven."

"Good. I think it's a comfort food kind of night."
While she started dinner, Jaime found the toolbox, hung
the TV, and hooked up her DVD player.

Everywhere she looked, she could see Jack. Every
time the door opened, she found herself expecting him
to walk through. She missed their conversations, she
missed the way he always touched her, she missed how
he used any excuse to kiss her—he'd kiss her hello when
he walked into any room she occupied and kissed her
good-bye even when he was just going out to get firewood.

She missed sex.

A lot.

She had dreamed about making love to Jack, and
woke up all twitchy and frustrated. She'd never had hot
sex dreams before she met him. Just thinking about him
had her girl parts perking up. Damn, she felt like one of
Pavlov's dogs. She stuck her hands in the bowl to mix the
meat and let out a frustrated growl.

"What'd I do now?" Jaime stuck his head in the doorway, and she noticed he left his body in the hall, well out
of reach.

"Nothing, I was just thinking of Jack."

"I guess the letter didn't help, huh?"

She continued mixing the meat. Did everyone know
about that damn letter?

"You did read the letter, didn't you?"

She ignored him and turned the heat on under her
skillet.

"Kendall?"

"What?" She grabbed a handful of meat and shaped
it into a patty.

"You haven't read the letter yet?"

She shook her head.

Jaime turned off the stove. "How come?"

Because it was safer to be mad than hurt. She had a feeling whatever Jack had to say in that letter would hurt even more than what David had said to her face. Jack knew her. He really knew her, and still he left. David . . . well, David didn't seem to care about who she was, just what he wanted her to be. His leaving hadn't hurt nearly as much. Which, when she thought about it, was pretty incredible. How could she fall so deeply in love in with Jack in just two weeks? How was that possible? A big, fat tear slid down her cheek. Damn, she really didn't want to start crying.

Jaime pulled her into a hug.

"Don't. My hands are all greasy."

"I don't care." He rubbed her back. "Don't you think not knowing is worse?"

"But once that genie's out of the bottle, I can't put him back."

"Look, after you read it, if you want me to, I'll go to Chicago and beat the crap out of him—I'll just, you know, avoid his head."

Kendall felt her face crack into a smile. "You'd do that for me? Even after I kicked you in the balls?"

"Yeah, why not? For a man, getting kicked in the balls is like giving birth is for a woman. The pain goes away, but you never forget it. I figure now I can hold my own at baby showers."

That had her laughing. Picturing Jaime at a baby shower, regaling everyone with his experience of getting nailed in the nuts, put it over the top.

"Go wash your hands and read the letter while I finish

making dinner. Then, if you want, I'll even buy ice cream and we can watch a movie."

"A chick flick?"

He groaned. "Okay. I hope Jax's letter does the trick, because I don't think I can take a double feature."

She went to the sink and washed her hands. She took her time drying them and looked around the kitchen. "Just make the patties, brown them on both sides, and then pour the sauce over them." She pointed to the four-cup measuring cup she used to mix her special sauce. "Then add the mushrooms, and stick the whole thing in the oven. It's already preheated. The potatoes should be done in about fifteen minutes. The masher is in the drawer; butter and half-and-half are in the fridge."

"I got this. Go ahead. No more stalling." He gave her a nudge toward the bedroom. "I'll call you when dinner's ready. And no faking it either. I want a full report, young lady."

Kendall didn't see how she could get out of reading Jack's letter and still have her pride, so she dragged her feet down the short hallway, took a deep breath, and stepped into the bedroom, closing the door behind her.

Her gaze zeroed in on the envelope. Goose bumps sprang up on her arms, and she shivered. She grabbed the throw from the foot of the bed and wrapped it around her shoulders, hugging it tight to her chest, and swallowed hard, wishing she'd brought a bottle of wine. With a resolute sigh, she picked up the envelope and ran her finger over her name. Her hands shook, her heart raced, her skin prickled, and her throat tightened.

She bit her lip and blinked back tears while she slid her finger under the flap and unfolded the letter.

*Thank you, sweetheart. I know if you're read-
ing this, it's taken you awhile to decide to open it.
I'm picturing you biting your lip, your brow fur-
rowed, thinking about what an ass I am. I wanted
to talk to you face-to-face and tell you I was leaving and explain my reasoning, but I'd have had to
do it in front of your father, and as much as I love
and respect Teddy, there are some things that are
best left just between you and me.*

*I want you to understand why I felt I had to
leave Harmony and go back to Chicago. Kendall,
when I left Chicago, I was just going to ski for a
week. That was in December. Like anyone in my
position, I had a succession plan in place, but now,
since the accident, since meeting you, I'm questioning my decision in that respect. I'm questioning myself.*

*I need to return because leaving without a back-
ward glance smacks of running away. I might be a
lot of things, but I'm no coward, and I'm not a
quitter. I'm leaving Harmony because I can't stay,
not because I'm running. And, yes, there is a difference.*

*You're still pissed as hell—I know. Don't go
shaking your head at me. I didn't run away from
you, remember? You're the one who took off.*

*Yeah, I know you had a good reason. I really
am sorry about that, but the day we met, when I
heard you talk about me, I honestly didn't know
who that guy Jax was. I can see you rolling your
eyes, but it's true. I'd been pretending I was the
same guy who hit that tree, but I wasn't. When you*

crashed into my life, I didn't know who I was anymore. All I knew was that it was a relief not to have to pretend to be Jax. With you, I could just be. With you, I was Jack.

Sweetheart, if you know one thing, know this: nothing about our time together was a lie. Nothing.

I asked you once if you were happy where you were—with me—and you couldn't answer. You needed more time. We both knew it.

You asked if I had a life to get back to, and I told you I had a job but no life. Now I wonder if I had a life, but I didn't know how to live it. It's a subtle difference, but I need to try living the life I have. I need to try it on for size and see if it fits, if I fit.

We both need time, sweetheart, so I'm giving you the time you need to figure out what you want your life to look like and decide if you really want me in it—all of me, even the part that's still, and always will be, Jax Sullivan, the Grand Pooh-Bah of Harmony.

I'll be back this spring to finish everything I started at the cabin. I hope you'll decide to be a part of that.

Whatever you decide to do, please know I love you, Kendall, my gold-medal girl. I always will.

Jack

Kendall read Jack's letter three times. She wanted to hate him for leaving, but she couldn't. Hadn't she said the very same things?

Jack needed to figure out who he was. He needed to try to combine the Jack she knew and loved with Jackson Finneus Sullivan III and see how this new person fit into his old life he'd yet to start living. She needed to put her plan in motion and live the life she'd imagined when she hiked on the ridge, and she needed to do it on her own. Sometimes you have to walk alone just to prove to yourself that you can, and Jack was giving her time to do that.

She'd never planned to fall in love—not for a while anyway. She didn't know how it happened, but in two weeks, Jack carved a place in her heart. And when he left—no matter how valid his reasons—he took that piece of her heart with him. She was on her own for the first time in twelve years, but that didn't mean she was going to sit around, pining for the likes of Jack or anyone. Okay, she'd do her best not to.

She was going to take this time and focus on her work, start her practice, and surround herself with people she cared about. She would make her own decisions, step out of David's shadow and into the sun, and forge her own path, and pray Jack found his way back home. Back to her.

When Jaime knocked, and she wiped the tears from her face and watched the door swing all the way open.

"Dinner's ready. Are you doing okay?"

She nodded. "Yeah, I am." She got up and looked around the room, their room, where she could still feel his presence so strongly. It probably would always be the case here. "Everything between Jack and me happened so fast. He said in the letter that we both need to figure out our lives separately before we can see if we fit together, and I know he's right. I said the same thing myself. But no matter how valid the reason, leaving someone you love sucks."

"So, does that mean I need to buy a plane ticket to Chicago or not?"

She laughed through her tears, slipped the letter back into the envelope, and tucked it into her pocket. "No, but can I have a rain check? A girl never knows when she'll need a henchman."

CHAPTER
TWENTY

Jack looked up from his computer and smiled his thanks when Anne dropped a sandwich on his desk, while his fingers continued flying, pounding out the new succession plan.

"First day of spring and it's snowing. Again. Welcome to Chicago. Tomorrow you're running for lunch." She walked out, heading back to the office.

A half hour later Jax stopped, stretched, and rubbed his whiskered chin—he might have to wear a suit and tie when he came to the office, but he couldn't bring himself to shave, if only for the shock value. He kept his beard short and neatly trimmed, and just long enough for it to stay soft.

He read over the document and knew he'd get pushback from his uncles, but not enough to change his mind. It was the right decision for the company, and that was best for all of them—even his uncles. Jax had Rocki's proxy, and together they owned two-thirds of the company.

"Anne," he hollered, "would you come in here?" He picked up the folder containing the succession plan and grabbed his sandwich.

The intercom beeped. "Would you please use the intercom?"

"I'm not at my desk. Besides, what's wrong with just hollering?"

She rolled her eyes on her way through the door and took a seat on the leather couch while he stuffed half the sandwich into his mouth. "I get enough of that at home. I have three teenagers, remember?"

He couldn't help but smile.

"Don't give me that look. You know, when I brought you home to meet Mike and the kids, I thought you'd be a good influence on them, but instead I think they've been a bad influence on you. I still can't believe you took the boys out and stood in line for hours to get that new Xbox game when it went on sale at midnight. I think they've created a monster."

"It was fun, and I won a *Call of Duty* T-shirt."

"You're trying to recapture your misspent youth, aren't you?"

He'd wondered about that too. He really had had a great time hanging with Anne and Mike's kids. "When I was their age, I was so busy swimming and trying to get through school, I didn't have time for anything else. I didn't play a video game until Scotty dragged me down to the cave."

"Yeah, I remember. I was the one who had to drag you both out." She sat down. "Now, what do you want?"

"Two things, actually. One is business, so you need to look this over, think it over, and then we can meet and discuss it." He handed her the unlabeled folder.

A what-are-you-up-to? look crossed her face. "Do you want me to look at this now?"

"No, it's something you'll probably want to discuss

with Mike before we meet." He could tell she was itching to see what it was. "I talked to Rocki the other day. She and Slater are planning to bring Nicki up to the lake house for a couple weeks over the Fourth of July. I'll be there, and I was wondering if you, Mike, and the boys would like to come out. I think the kids will have a great time, and there's plenty of room."

"Are you just inviting Mike and me so that you and the boys can have that *Call of Duty* tourney you've been talking about?"

His lips twitched. Why hadn't he thought of that? He'd have to get an Xbox for the house and a bigger TV. Oh yeah, that would be awesome. "No, of course not. I just thought it would be fun for all of us."

She wasn't buying it.

"Sullivan Industries always sponsors the fireworks and the picnic downtown. I haven't gone in years, but I loved it when I was a kid. There's a lot to do—we can go sailing, waterskiing, biking, tubing, hiking, or we can just sit on the porch overlooking the lake and drink."

"Are you sure you want us up there? Wouldn't we cramp your style?"

He sat back and laughed. "I don't have a style—at least I don't think I do." He looked out the window, and as often happened, his thoughts drifted to Kendall, and he wondered what she was doing. He knew she'd opened her practice and was working at the hospital too, but that was the only thing he'd been able to find out. Every time he asked Jaime how she was, he'd tell him that if he wanted to know, he should get his ass out there and find out.

"Don't you think it's about time you find out?"

He almost choked on his sandwich. He didn't know if

he'd missed something or if Anne had read his mind. He wouldn't put it past her. "Find out what?"

"Jackson, how long have you been back in Chicago?"

"Almost three months." Eighty-one days, which was eleven weeks and four days, or—he checked his watch—1,950 hours, give or take fifteen minutes. "Why?"

"You've accomplished what you came here to do. I think you might actually be better than you were before your . . . um, vacation. Now you're more in tune with the people on your team. You not only have great instincts, but over the years you've hired exceptionally qualified people with great instincts of their own. You've learned the art of listening, and they feel more comfortable coming to you. Since your vacation, you've become more approachable."

"Maybe it's the beard." Jax watched Anne—he'd gotten to know her a lot better in the past eighty days. He'd watched her work people and knew she was using her power on him. It was a bit disconcerting. He'd seen her do the same thing with her son, Charlie.

"Jackson," she patted his hand. "You know I love working with you, don't you?"

Oh, shit. She wasn't going to do something like quit on him, was she? "I hoped you did. Why do I feel like there's a *but* coming?"

"Because you're pretty perceptive. Jackson, when you returned from vacation, you had some lofty goals, and you've accomplished all of them. It was an amazing thing to watch. You've attacked your problem with a diligence and a sense of determination I've never seen anyone possess. You've caught up to, and in some ways even surpassed, the level you'd achieved before your vacation. But the one thing I've noticed more than anything else is that no matter how hard you try, no matter how much you accomplish, you're just not happy."

"Anne—"

She held up her hand. "Now, just let me finish before you start arguing with me."

She had that same tone of voice she used with her kids; the only thing she was missing were the words *young man*.

"Jackson, you remind me of Charlie. He was asked to the Sadie Hawkins dance. It was in November, I think. So he got out his nice khakis and his best shirt, and spent an hour showering and doing his hair. Seriously, it takes him more time to primp than any girl I've ever seen. He goes to put on his clothes, and we find out that he'd had quite the growth spurt since the last time he'd worn them and couldn't even button his pants. And the shoes—well, the boy wears a size fourteen shoe now. I had all of an hour and a half to buy him shoes, shirt, and pants."

He must have looked confused.

"Jackson, Charlie outgrew his clothes, and you've outgrown this." She held up her hands to encompass his office. "Maybe the job would be enough if you had something other than this company and the few friends you've made, but, let's face it: as much as we love you, my family members are not really your contemporaries—although I do wonder sometimes when you spend time with Scotty, Charlie, and Sam. You need to go back to New England. You need to find out if Kendall is as lost without you as you are without her. I know you think about her all the time. You get this secret smile on your face and you look so happy, I hate to drag you out of it."

"Anne—"

"So, I'll get you a seat on the first flight to Boston tomorrow, shall I?"

"But I have meetings scheduled."

"They're nothing I can't handle. I got pretty good at doing your job when you were on vacation, remember?"

"Yes, I do remember." He knew she could handle everything here; besides, he would be only a phone call away. He was more worried about himself.

"You have unfinished business, Jackson, and I remember you saying you needed to return in the spring and finish the project you started. You still need to shingle the cabin, don't you?"

"Yes, but—"

"Guess what. Spring has sprung. You've answered all the questions you returned with except one. And you're not going to know the answer unless you go back to Harmony."

———

Kendall packed up her briefcase, bit into an apple, and held it in her mouth while she stepped out of her office and locked the door. She crunched her way to the elevator, pushed the Down button, and stared at a picture of Jack—one of the big hospital donors. Evidently, his donation to the hospital was why she had a job; it allowed the small rural hospital to expand patient services. She wondered if he had any clue at the time how much money the Sullivan Trust donated to the facility that saved his life. Probably not.

She smiled at his picture, blew him a kiss, and headed home to Harmony. She had a lunch date with her mother and Addie at twelve thirty; patients at two, three, and five; and then a hot date with a glass of wine, leftovers, and a bubble bath.

She'd been cooking for one for almost three months

and still hadn't gotten the hang of the single-supper routine. Finally she gave up trying to cook for one and started inviting Jaime over about once a week to help clear out the leftovers. He ate almost as much as Jack did, and, over the months, Jaime had become an even better friend than he'd been before.

Jaime had helped her move into her little clapboard house on Main Street. She turned the first floor into a nice little office and waiting room, and she lived upstairs in a two-bedroom apartment. It felt like home—she loved her nine-hundred-square-foot slice of heaven and everything in it. The only things she kept from her old place were the bookcases and the hall table, which she used in her office.

Jaime was always willing to lend her his truck whenever she found a piece of furniture she just couldn't live without, so she was having a great time combing through antique stores and consignment shops. Kendall woke up every morning in a room filled with a sunshine-yellow antique dresser, vanity, and tallboy that Jaime and she lugged up the steps, and she slept on a bed whose headboard and footboard were fashioned from an intricate leaf-and-bird-covered antique wrought-iron gate she'd found in a falling-down barn.

She also loved spending time with her parents. She and her mom took an upholstery class together and used her secondhand down-filled classic sofa as their first project. She covered it in an apple green fabric that popped against the beige walls. It was the perfect napping couch, with rolled arms that were just the right height to rest a pillow on. She found an old, metal-wheeled wooden warehouse dolly the perfect size and height for a coffee table and refinished a beautiful farm table that stood in her dining area.

Kendall ran through her apartment into the bedroom and kicked off her heels. She tossed her business suit on the back of a chair and slid into a pair of slacks and sweater set with a pair of boots she bought on sale the last time she was in Boston. She finger-combed her hair and she ran across the street to Maizie's Tea Room, worried she'd be late for her lunch date.

Maizie's was a sweet old federalist clapboard with a wraparound porch perfect for summer dining, and fireplaces in almost every room for cozy winter meals. Today was a gorgeous early-spring day—another month, and the daffodils would be in bloom. She stepped inside and waved to the owner, who pointed in the direction of the back dining room.

Red velvet wallpaper covered three walls, and where it should have been gaudy, with the twelve-foot ceilings and ornate marble fireplace, it worked. She kissed her mother's cheek before she slid into the chair between Grace and Addie. "Sorry I'm late."

Both of them stopped talking and stared at her.

"What?"

Grace patted Addie's hand. "Nothing, dear. How are you doing? I haven't seen you in almost a week."

"I'm fine. Business is picking up now that the weather's turning nice, so I'm running from the hospital to the office and having evening appointments too. I have three today. It's good—exhausting but good."

Addie seemed to let out a relieved breath, which was weird—almost as weird as her going out to lunch on a weekday.

Kendall raised an eyebrow toward Addie. "How did you get out of school for lunch today?"

"It's a half day. There's no kindergarten, so I got out early."

Grace gave Kendall her signature stare. The one that made you wonder if she had superhuman psychic powers. "You look tired, dear."

Kendall squelched the squirm and scanned the menu for specials; she needed major protein. "I am tired. Just working a lot, but that's good. The practice is doing well. I'm doing well. Mostly. Life would be perfect if David would stop calling me to chat late at night—" And if Jack would start. She'd even Googled him. The projections for the first-quarter reports for his company were supposed to be good. Other than that, she was at a loss. There weren't even any Jack sightings. She combed the *Chicago Sun-Times* and had yet to see him at a charity function. There were no mentions of him in the society pages, and not even a word from her mother or Jaime—not that she'd had the nerve to ask.

Her mother and Addie stared at her again. Then Addie leaned forward. "Why?"

"Why what?"

"Why is David calling you?"

She waved away the question as if it were an annoying gnat. "Apparently the job in San Francisco didn't work out. He's back in Boston, in our old apartment, no less, and he wants his furniture back."

She wasn't going to tell her best friend and her mother that David wanted her back too.

Addie sipped her water and grinned. "Did you tell him you sold it?"

"The furniture? I sure did. I even gave him the address of the consignment shop. If he wants it, he's going to have to buy it back." She couldn't tamp down the smile. That would be just fine with her, since she'd get sixty percent of the take. And since the money left in her savings account was a whole lot less than half of what she remembered it should be, she didn't have a problem with it. After all, he'd said the furniture was hers.

Kendall looked over her menu. "Do you want to order? I'm starved. All I had today was an apple." She wasn't used to dealing with both her mother and Addie at the same time. If waterboarding were a sport, they'd tag team it. Now that she was sitting across from them, she wondered if *let's do lunch* was code for *time to spill*.

Kendall caught Addie's glance before she could hide her angst. Kendall set her menu down. Addie seemed off—almost uncomfortable.

Grace took Addie's hand and gave it a quick squeeze, and then raised a subtle brow at Kendall. "I'm going to the ladies' room. Go ahead and order for me when the waitress comes by. I'll have the Cobb salad, with blue cheese dressing on the side."

Kendall watched her mother disappear and then looked back at Addie. "Well, that was subtle—not. Sorry."

Addie looked mortified and even more pallid than usual. Khaki wasn't Addie's best color on a good day. Today was not a good day.

"Okay, Addie, what's wrong? What did I do?"

Addie had gone from fanning her napkin to origami— bad origami.

"Listen, whatever it is, you'd better tell me before my mom gets back, or I won't be responsible for the fallout."

Addie's cheeks faded to a sallow cream. She was probably remembering when Kendall's mother sat them both down and told them the facts of life. She could tell by the twitch of Addie's eye that, yeah, she'd gone there.

"Is Jaime your new rebound guy?" Addie asked it so softly, Kendall barely heard her.

"Did you just ask if Jaime was my rebound guy? Seriously?" Kendall wasn't ready for that one. "Jaime? Why would Jaime be my rebound guy? He's my mover, my painter, and my human garbage can—that boy cleans out my refrigerator at least once a week. Jaime Rouchard is a lot of things, but definitely not my rebound guy. I use him—with his permission, of course."

"But I saw him leaving your apartment really late Saturday night."

"That's because we watched a double feature—*Some Like It Hot* and *When Harry Met Sally* . . . I made popcorn."

"So, you two are an item?"

"What are you talking about?"

"If Jaime Rouchard is at your house on a Saturday night, watching chick flicks, it's got to be love."

Kendall felt the blood drain from her face. She wasn't sure if it was low blood sugar or shock. Where was the waitress? Where was her mother?

Addie slowly choked the origami swan. It looked painful.

Kendall put her hand on the mangled napkin. "Addie, Jaime and I are just friends. We are not an item. We have never been an item. We will never be an item. I consider him a BFF with benefits."

"You're using him?"

"Hell, yeah. Who else is going to loan me his truck whenever I need it and haul my furniture up a flight of stairs? I pay him back with food. A lot of food. It's a win-win."

"You mean you're *not* sleeping with him?"

"Eew, no!" Kendall shivered—and not in a good way. "At least not together. He slept on my couch once. It did not end well. He fell off and twisted his back. We were supposed to paint my office. It cost me a whole weekend and an entire bottle of Midol."

Addie stared at her with the look of the damned.

"It's a muscle relaxer. Duh." Then Kendall felt her cheeks tighten. Oh my God. Had she misinterpreted Jaime's friendship? She sat back. No. Jaime thought of her as an annoying little sister. "Oh, wait a minute!" Kendall drummed her fingers against her lips. It was all coming together now. "You're the one he keeps grumbling about. I should have known."

Addie flinched. "What?"

"He said something about angels, green apple shampoo, and tempera paint.... Oh, my God! You stayed over at his place. On a school day, no less."

Addie's eyes widened and she started to sweat.

"Addie, you little hussy, you. You totally did!" Then Kendall thought about it some more. "What did you do? Break his heart? Why else would he make me watch *You've Got Mail*? Twice. And, believe me, that's not my favorite movie."

Addison groaned and slumped in her chair. The swan was decapitated.

It definitely added up. "Jaime eats more ice cream lately than even I do. If you keep this up, Ben and Jerry's is going to have to open a new plant. Jaime's got it bad." Kendall sat back and couldn't keep the grin off her face. "Hey, I just thought of something: Jaime's not over at my place to help me out at all. He's there to hide. He doesn't want to go out, and he doesn't want to stay home alone. And all this time I thought I was using him, but, no, he was the one using me."

Addie looked like she was going to be sick. She took a slug of water, and it sloshed over her shaking hand.

"You do know what this means, don't you?"

Addie shook her head. "Oh no."

"It means it's time for another makeover. Once Jaime sees you, he'll go even crazier than he already is."

Grace strolled up to the table. "I'm back. Have you ordered?"

Addie held up a shaking hand. "Can we get some service please?"

———

Jaime sat in the cab of his truck in the cell-phone lot at Logan International Airport, grumbling. It was ten in the morning and he'd already driven 111 miles. Jax's plane was late. Kendall had left one of her damn hair clips on his truck's seat, and he sat on it. That woman was a real pain in his ass—literally. The thing looked like it could be used as a torture device, and he wondered if she had it out for his junk. She'd almost maimed him—twice—and to top it off, he hadn't caught a glimpse of Addison in weeks. He was going through Addie withdrawal, and he was living on a diet of Kendall's leftovers, ice cream, tequila, and beer. When Kendall finally finished painting and decorating her place and using him as her reach-it, haul-it, and paint-it boy and giving him a hell of a workout, he might actually have to go on a diet.

His phone dinged, announcing a text. It was about time. He started the engine, headed for arrivals, and pulled up beside Jax. He looked good—Jaime couldn't help but resent it at least a little bit. The dude looked like a freakin' movie star. Jaime scanned the sidewalk and counted six women and two guys checking Jax out. Personally, Jaime could do without the male appreciation, but it would be nice to have the one woman he wanted not hide from him or fear him.

Jax tossed his bag in the back and jumped in.

"Took you long enough."

"What crawled up your ass this morning?"

Jaime grabbed Kendall's hair doohickey and tossed it in Jax's lap. "That. And, let me tell you, it hurt. I swear that woman is trying to turn me into a freakin' eunuch."

"Sounds like a personal problem."

"It's a Kendall problem."

"My Kendall?"

"I don't know if she's yours, man. All I know is some dude's been calling her all hours of the day and night."

"And how do you know that?"

He shrugged. "I crashed on her couch after a double feature and one too many Chunky Monkey mudslides." He held up his hand. "Don't even ask. It's a hangover disguised as a milk shake. That girl's dangerous when she starts inventing cocktails. Anyway, the phone rang at, like, two in the freakin' morning. I thought it was you she was talking to, but when I asked, she said she'd hadn't heard a word from you."

"Who in the hell was it?"

"No clue, and it's not as if I can ask her. I mean, we're friends, but she doesn't talk to me like she does Addie or Erin."

"Erin?"

"Her best friend in Boston. Erin's engaged to a firefighter—

he and his two brothers moved Kendall's stuff to Harmony. I guess it could be one of them."

"So, she's dating?"

Jaime shrugged. "Did you think she was sitting around waiting for you to get your head screwed on straight?"

From the look on Jax's face, that was exactly what he'd thought.

"And I suppose you've been living like a monk."

Man, if Jax had laser vision, Jaime would be vaporized. "Wow, three months without sex? That's gotta be some kind of personal record for you."

"What aren't you telling me?"

"Nothin', man. Like I said, she doesn't tell me shit like that. I don't have the right equipment to be a best girlfriend. The only things I have going for me in her eyes are a full-size pickup truck, my ability to haul all the furniture she buys up to her apartment, and the fact that I can eat leftovers like nobody's business. She has a thing about wasting food. It's been great. I haven't had to cook a dinner in ages. She even sends stuff home with me. It makes up for the back problems.

"So where are you going—the lake house or the cabin? Have you told Grace and Teddy you're on your way? Have you given Kendall a heads-up?"

"Shit. I should have thought this out a little more. I mean, Anne just gave me one of her lectures about her son Charlie outgrowing his clothes, and the next thing I know, I'm standing at O'Hare, waiting to board a plane to Boston. Can you call Addie and ask her if Kendall's seeing someone else?"

"What do you think this is—middle school? Sure, I'll pass her a note in study hall. Besides, I haven't seen her in weeks. I think she's hiding from me, and when she's not hiding, we just snipe at each other. And after you've been gone so long without even a word, I doubt Addison is going to be any happier to see you than she is me."

"What happened?"

"It's a long story."

"We've got an hour and a half drive. Besides, hearing about your problems helps me not think about mine."

CHAPTER
TWENTY-ONE

J ax conned Jaime into stopping to pick up the shingles and flashing he'd ordered at the Home Depot in
Concord. He knew he'd have to show himself soon, but
having to hump cases of shingles up to the roof would give
him the time he needed to figure out how to handle it.

Jaime backed up the truck close to the cabin. "Are you
going to open the place up, or are you going to stay at the
lake house?"

He stared at the cabin door. "I'll probably stay at the
lake house. I don't know how long I'm going to be here,
and I don't want make more work for Teddy." He got out
of the truck and was almost afraid to go inside. He didn't
want to see the place without Kendall there. If he didn't go
in, he could still imagine her there. When he thought of her,
she was always there in the cabin.

Jaime rounded the truck and stepped onto the porch.
"Are you cleared to drive?"

"Yeah, but I haven't. I left my car here at the lake
house."

"Just take the truck, and I'll have one of my guys pick
it up tomorrow. There are cables in the box if your car

needs a jump. It's been sitting for five months. If I'd known, I would have pulled the battery out for you."

Jax shrugged. "I hadn't even thought about it. Listen, thanks for the lift and the information. I appreciate it."

"When are you planning to see Kendall?"

"I'm just not sure. I need to figure out how to approach her."

"You'd better figure it out soon. Oh, and just so you know, if you hurt her, you'll answer to me. I've already offered to fly out to Chicago and beat the shit out of you. She took a rain check. At least if I have to beat you up, I won't have to fly to get there."

If he hurt her, he'd deserve a beating. "Glad I could save you the trip. I don't want to hurt Kendall. I love her—probably more now than I did when I left. I just don't know how to say it so she'll hear me. Hell, I don't know if she wants anything to do with me."

Jaime crossed his arms and leaned on the porch rail. "Keep it simple, stupid. You brainiacs overthink everything. The less you say, the less chance you have of sticking your foot in your mouth and pissing her off."

"Probably not bad advice." He should have thought to ask Anne what to do. She seemed to know everything. "Jaim, how many women have you told that you love them?"

"None."

"Then what do you know?"

"I'm no expert, but I've been hanging with Kendall for the last three months. I'm the guy who strong-armed her into reading your letter, and I've been watching a lot of chick flicks and I've taken notes. I know Kendall better than most, and my advice stands. She just needs to see the real you. The guy I grew up with is the man she fell in love with."

"She loves me?"

"I think she did. Whether or not she still does is the question. Three months is a long time to be ignored."

"I wasn't ignoring her—I was giving her space."

"Without asking her if she needed space or finding out exactly how much space she needed. The problem as I see it is that you have no fucking clue when, in Kendall's mind, being given space might have turned into being forgotten."

"Shit. That never occurred to me."

"Yeah, I figure if you haven't already crossed that line, you're heading that way at lightning speed." Jaime turned and headed toward his cabin. "Oh, and I'm not going to come out and tell Kendall you're here, but I won't lie to her either. If she asks, I'll tell her. But for your sake, I'll do my best to avoid her. Still, you'd better hurry the hell up and decide what you're going to do."

"I'm going to hump the shingles up to the roof, go back to the house, and shower, and then I'll go see Kendall."

"Okay. She has appointments until six tonight. She lives above her office, right across from Maizie's, and, as far as I know, she doesn't have plans tonight. She said something about a hot date with a bottle of wine and a bubble bath."

Jax laughed. "Yeah, and you think she doesn't talk to you like she would Addie. You're in danger of having your Man Card pulled."

Kendall walked her client out and held her two-month-old baby while she set the car seat on the chair and stuffed the burp rag, bottle, and pacifier in the baby bag.

Sandra Buxton had three children under the age of seven, suffered from postpartum depression, and had a husband who was emotionally and physically unavailable to her—not a good combination. At least the medication her psychiatrist prescribed was having a positive effect. "Do you need help out to the car?"

Sandra laughed, "No, but thanks for the offer. One kid at a time is a piece of cake. It's when I have all three that things gets crazy."

Little Stryker was so sweet, and Kendall cuddled him close, drinking in that baby scent she loved. She tried to ignore her biological clock and kissed his peach-fuzz-covered head before setting him in the seat and strapping him in. "There you go, little man. You be good for your mama." She tucked the blanket around him. "I'll see you next Tuesday. If you need anything, just give me a call."

"Thanks for letting me bring Stryker. My mom can't handle all three by herself."

"It's not a problem, really. Feel free to bring him anytime. It gives me a chance to get a baby fix." She opened the door to the world's smallest lobby, then held the outer door and watched until Sandra got the car seat settled and her car started.

Kendall went through her evening routine, gathering her notes, shutting down and packing up her laptop, and turning off the lights, while she did the math in her head. She was twenty-six, so if she met the right guy right this moment, she probably wouldn't marry for a few years; then it would be smart to wait for a few more years to have some good couple time before even trying to have a baby. She'd probably be in her early thirties by then. Suddenly the ticking clock's volume increased. She'd always wanted at least three kids. She stepped back into the waiting room. "Well, best-laid plans and all that, Kendall."

"You're talking to yourself now?"

Kendall jumped and spun around, "David?" Her hand went to her throat, and her heart seemed to stutter before flatlining. He stood between her and the door. For the first time since starting her practice, she realized how vulnerable she was. She should have locked up before she went into her office to shut down. But this was David. He might be a narcissistic asshole, but he'd never done anything to make her fear him. "God, you scared me. What are you doing here?"

"I came to see what you left me for."

"Left you?" Was he delusional? "Look, I just set the alarm. I have to lock up the place, or the service will call the police. I have less than a minute before the alarm goes off. Why don't we run over to the diner, if you want to talk?" She walked past him and held the door.

David took a long look around and then stepped out behind her. Standing way too close for her peace of mind.

"I'm expected at my parents' house for a late dinner. If you had called, I would have told you I really don't have time to talk tonight." The hair on the back of her neck stood on end. She locked the door, stepped outside, and locked the outer door too, holding her briefcase between them, and headed down the street to the diner.

David took her arm, and she shot him a don't-touch-me look he didn't seem to notice.

Kendall didn't say anything. She didn't know why, but

something seemed off with David. Maybe it was the way he looked. He'd always been so starched and perfectly groomed—a metrosexual to the nth degree. Even Erin, who always saw the best in people, referred to him as a stuck-up pretty boy. David was always so fastidious; he kept an electric razor in his car for touch-ups between appointments because he hated razor stubble. Yet it didn't seem as if he'd shaved today, and his hair looked like it was a few weeks overdue for a cut.

Kendall let out a sigh of relief when she pushed through the door to Old Town Diner. She waved at Candy. "Two coffees and the check, please?" Kendall sat in a booth by the window and cringed when David sat beside her. Sure, they used to sit like that when they were kids, but that was a long, long time ago. "David, if you want to have a conversation, it would be better if we faced each other."

He put his arm around her like the past three and a half months had never happened. Not that he would have stepped foot into a diner back then. No, diners were too lowbrow for the likes of him.

"David, excuse me. I need to wash my hands and freshen up. I was holding a baby and, well, I think his diaper might have leaked."

That got David moving. Any mention of bodily fluids was enough to gross him out. She grabbed her briefcase and hightailed it into the ladies' room. Shit, shit, shit. How was she going to get rid of him? She could call her father, but the last thing she wanted to hear was another lecture about how he and her mother had always known David wasn't the man for her. So no Dad. That left the only other man she could count on. She grabbed her phone and texted Jaime.

David showed up at my office. Told him I had to go
to my parents for dinner, but something's not right.
I'm at Old Town Diner & need a henchman. Are you
around?

He responded immediately:

On my way. DO NOT LEAVE THE DINER.

Okay, thx.

Kendall let out a breath, washed her hands, and
tucked her phone into her pocket. If Jaime was home, it
would take him fifteen minutes to get there. She could
deal with David for fifteen minutes—hell, she'd dealt
with him for twelve years. Fifteen minutes should be a
piece of cake.

———

Jax drove into town and parked in front of Maizie's Tea
Room. The light in Kendall's office was on, and he watched
her through the window, holding a baby, kissing its head.
The look of longing on her face as she set it gently into
a car seat made him wonder what their kids would look
like.

He'd never thought of having a family, but he could
see building a family with Kendall. Giving Grace and
Teddy grandkids to spoil, and Rocki's new daughter,
Nicki, a bunch of cousins. He could imagine them all together at the lake house, and envisioned it filled with
love and laughter and Legos.

Kendall walked her client out and waited under the

light while the woman settled the baby in the car and took off. Kendall wore a blue sweater and pants that made her legs look even longer than they normally did. He couldn't help but stare, since she looked even more beautiful than he'd remembered. And he'd remembered a lot.

He still hadn't come up with a plan as to what to say to her, but he supposed it was dependent on her reaction to seeing him. When she went back inside, he knew he couldn't stall any longer. He got out of the car and was just about to cross the street when he saw a man opening the door to her office and walking in. Shit. Maybe Jaime was wrong; maybe Kendall had a date with more than a bottle of wine and a bubble bath.

Maybe she was seeing someone and keeping it to herself. The guy rocked back on his heels and did a full turn, taking in the small waiting room as if he'd never been there before.

When Kendall stepped back into the waiting room, there was no hug, no kiss, and the way her hand flew up to her neck looked as if she'd been startled. Jax bit back a curse and leaned against his car, trying to ignore the urge to grab the guy and toss him out on his ass. Instead he watched the woman he loved with another man, feeling way too much like a stalker.

Kendall stepped out and held the door for the guy to follow before she locked the office without turning off the lights. Leaving the lights on was a pet peeve of hers. She was downright miserly when it came to wasting electricity. It was odd for her to leave all the lights on in the office like she'd be returning, yet carry her briefcase. And why would she bring her briefcase and not her purse?

Why would she bring her briefcase on a date? She held it between them awkwardly, like a shield.

His adrenaline kicked up, the muscles of his neck and back tightened, his legs stiffened, and no matter how many times he told himself it was his imagination, that he was only seeing what he wanted to see—Kendall wasn't interested in another man—he didn't believe it. He'd admit he was jealous as hell. Seeing her with someone else made him crazy, but that didn't change the fact that she looked nervous. It was in the set of her shoulders, the tilt of her head; her whole posture was off. If it was a first date, he'd bet his '69 Ferrari there wouldn't be another. Then she took off toward downtown at a pretty good clip. If she was on a date, why wasn't she wearing a coat or even a jacket? It had gotten up to fifty degrees that afternoon, but the temps were dropping with the sun, and they had only another hour and a half or so of daylight. It would be dark by seven thirty. Even he had grabbed his leather jacket before leaving the lake house.

The guy wore a jacket, and you'd think he'd offer it to her. Any decent man would see she was cold. Instead he took her arm. Jax swallowed back a growl. It was one thing for him to stand beside Kendall, but another thing for some dude to touch her. Damn. He found himself following behind, both of them oblivious to his presence. He couldn't see Kendall's eyes, but he knew that tilt of her head. She was giving the guy her death glare—it looked as if she didn't like him touching her any more than Jax did. Still, she didn't pull away.

She waited for traffic to pass and jaywalked, making a beeline for the Old Town Diner. He let out a breath he didn't realize he'd been holding. So the guy was not only an inconsiderate bastard, but he was also cheap. Who would take a woman like Kendall on a first date to a freakin' diner, even if they did have the best bacon cheeseburgers known to man?

He stood across the street in the shadow of the law office and watched Kendall sit in a booth by the window, affording him a great view. Instead of the guy sitting across from her, he sat beside her. She didn't look happy. The next thing he knew, Kendall was holding up her hands and the guy got up, letting her pass. She carried her briefcase with her. Maybe she was leaving?

He waited, but she turned toward the bathrooms. Damn. He leaned back against the cool brick and tried to talk himself into leaving. He told himself if he saw even a hint of a smile on her face when she returned, he'd go.

His phone vibrated, and he checked the caller ID. Jaime. "Hey. What's up?"

"Are you in town?"

"Yeah, why?"

"Kendall texted me and asked me to meet her at the diner. Her ex showed up at her office, unannounced and unwelcome."

So that was David. "I thought David was in San Francisco."

"Apparently not."

"Kendall said something was off with him. She told him she was supposed to go to her parents for a late dinner, so she has an out. Still, I told her to stay there. I'm at the house. It'll take me fifteen minutes to get there. I thought if you were closer—"

"No problem. I'm not far. I'll head over there now and surprise her."

Kendall stepped out of the bathroom, looking a little

more relaxed, and sat opposite David. Good girl. Jax let out a relieved breath, happy to know he hadn't gone completely around the insanity bend. He hadn't imagined her discomfort, and now he was going to put a stop to it.

———

Kendall was happy to see Candy at their table, pouring coffee and chatting with David. They'd all gone to school together. Candy married Hal Reichert right out of high school, and they already had four kids. Candy joked about working the dinner shift to get out of having to put the kids to bed. Still, she looked happy. She and Hal were always seen walking around town with their brood and still holding hands, which was amazing after four kids and eight years.

Kendall missed being able to reach over and hold Jack's hand. She missed everything about him—the way he smiled, how quick he was to wrap his arms around her. She missed his kisses—all of them: the sweet, quick ones; the long, deep ones; the nibbly ones; and the I-have-to-have-you-now ones—yeah, especially those. She missed the way his beard felt against her cheeks, her thighs, her stomach. God, she missed everything about him.

She slid onto the bench opposite David, took a close look at him, and wondered who he really was. She'd thought she'd known him better than anyone else, but now it was as if she were looking at a stranger. What if she felt the same way about Jack when, or if, he returned? She brushed her thigh and felt his letter in her pocket. She carried it with her wherever she went. She'd read it so many times, she had it memorized. She heard his voice in her head. Like she was having a conversation with him. "David, I don't have a lot of time, so talk to me. Why did you come here?"

"I went back to our place and you were gone. Why did you leave me?"

"David, you moved to San Francisco. You left, took your name off the lease, and divided our bank account. Did you expect me to stay in an apartment I couldn't afford? Or did you forget that I lost my job? You were gone. I'm sorry things didn't work out for you in San Francisco. I really am. But I've moved on."

She almost felt bad for him — almost, but not quite.

"You call this moving on? What do you have — a part-time job at a rinky-dink hospital and a handful of psychos? Don't be ridiculous."

Kendall took a deep breath and refused to take the bait. "Why, exactly, are you here?"

David's mouth hung open; then he closed it, his lips pressed together like the seal of a pressure cooker rattling the steam gage. "I've decided to take you back."

"Why? I'm a modern-day Betty Crocker with a Carl Jung fetish, remember? I thought you needed someone who could hold her own at cocktail parties and do more than point out the personality disorders of your clients. I thought you needed an equal — or as close as you could find."

"I do. That's why I've decided to take you back. You already know what my needs are. You know how I like my clothes hung, what type of food I prefer. You're reasonably proficient with choosing the correct wine, and you're an adequate hostess."

"Well, thanks all the same, but I wouldn't want you to lower your standards."

He reached over and grabbed her arm. "You need me, Kendall. You are nothing without me."

She was just about to kick him in the balls when a big body stood way too close to the table to be polite. Her gaze was level with his fly and headed north over a flat stomach covered in royal blue cashmere, up past his chest to a corded neck, and then his face. The eyes that bore into hers were ice blue. *Jack.* And he was wearing his pissed-as-shit look. "Hey, sweetheart." He shot her that stronger-than-a-defibrillator smile, then stared down David with a get-your-paws-off-my-woman silent threat.

David reacted as if he'd been burned and placed both hands under the table.

Jack slid in beside her and wrapped his arm around her shoulder, pulling her into his chest. "Sorry I'm late."

God, he felt good. All the tension she'd held seemed to slide right off her.

He leaned in and kissed her—not a little peck either. The kiss was between a damn-you're-hot and an I-need-you-now kiss.

She felt her cheeks flame and her nipples perk up.

He brought his mouth to her ear and whispered just loud enough for David to hear. "I thought we were supposed to meet at your place before heading to Grace and Teddy's."

"Um . . . I'm sorry about that. I had an unexpected visitor."

His brow went up. "I can see that. Are you going to introduce me?"

"Jack, this is David. David, Jack. David recently moved back to Boston from San Francisco. He just dropped by to say hi." She slid her hand over Jack's thigh to make sure he was real. To make sure she wasn't dreaming this time.

His hand covered hers and then squeezed. It was just like she remembered: big, warm, and callused. Jack.

David puffed up like the Stay Puft Marshmallow Man and glared at Jack. "Who the hell are you?"

She pulled her gaze away from Jack and looked across the table at David. His normal modus operandi was subtle cynicism, veiled cuts, and snide retorts meant to sound smart and witty. This David was new—abrupt, direct, and openly rude, with a dash of desperation.

Jack ignored the question and turned his body into hers. "I'm sorry it took me so long to get here. I finished that big job and then spent all afternoon humping shingles onto the roof of the cabin."

"A roofer?" David leaned in, all of his attention targeted on Kendall. His reddening cheekbones accentuated fine white lines bracketing his lips. "You're fucking a roofer?"

Kendall couldn't believe David went there.

She checked Jack's reaction, expecting the exact opposite of the ear-to-ear grin she found. Not only was he grinning, but he looked thoroughly amused.

He might be enjoying this, but she certainly was not. "Well, you know what they say about the rebound guy, David. Women go for the exact opposite of what they had."

"That's quite step down—even for you. You must have gone diving in the shallow end of the gene pool to find this guy."

Kendall tilted her head into the crook of Jack's neck and felt lips brush her hair.

Jack leaned back in the booth.

"It's an honest living, I like it, and I don't have to wear a tie." Jack looked over at her. "Sweetheart, are you ready to go?" He checked his Rolex. "Your parents are expecting us."

He stood and helped her out of the booth. The door banged open and in strode Jaime, looking as if he were ready to brawl. "Jack, Kendall. What'd I miss?"

Kendall shook her head. "Nothing. We were just leaving."

Jaime saw David and clapped a heavy hand on his shoulder. "David. David Slane. How are you doin'?" He slid into the booth, flashed an I-got-this grin at Jack, then waved them off. "Have a good time, kids."

Jack pulled out his billfold, peeled off a Benjamin, and tossed it on the table. "Candy can keep the change."

Kendall gave David a good-bye nod and then led Jack out of the diner before David found his tongue.

CHAPTER
TWENTY-TWO

ax was led out of the diner by a very determined
Kendall. She'd grabbed his hand and was halfway
down the block and still hadn't dropped it. He wasn't
sure, but he thought that was a good sign. He hoped to
God it was, because it had just occurred to him that he
had no idea how to do what he needed to do. All he
knew was that Kendall held his hand and he never
wanted to let her go.

Kendall turned to cross the street.

"Where are we going?"

"My office. I need to finish closing up."

He knew it—hell, he knew her. Leaving the lights on
was driving her nuts.

"Do my parents know you're here?"

"If they don't already, they will soon. This is Harmony.
There were plenty of people in the diner, and I'm sure
every cell phone in the place was in use. They probably
have pictures of me kissing you and of David's reaction—
it might be on YouTube by now."

Kendall stopped in front of her office, still holding his
hand. The light coming through the window lit her face
as she bit her lip and watched an old lady in a Caddy do

what might eventually be a twelve-point turn. "Are you driving again?"

"Yes, I've been cleared for everything. But I left my car here after the accident, so today was my first opportunity."

"What kind of car do you drive?"

"Aston Martin DB9. Why?"

"Where is it?"

"Across the street." He raised his thumb to point over his shoulder.

"Do you like it?"

"Yeah, I do. Why?"

She smiled at him and then looked away again. Her eyes got big, and then she blew out what looked like a relieved breath. "I thought old Mrs. Montgomery might take out your fender, but she made it without a crunch. Of course, she backed up traffic on Main Street."

He turned and, sure enough, there were stopped cars. He just didn't know if it was for old Mrs. Montgomery or to stare at them.

"In Boston, people would have been honking and cursing the whole time. But not here. That's why I love living in Harmony." She stopped and smiled up at him before turning to unlock the door. "When did you arrive?"

"This morning. I called Jaime to beg a ride, and we stopped at the Home Depot in Concord to pick up the roofing supplies I needed."

"You did?"

"I told you I was humpin' shingles up to the roof all afternoon—I had to unload Jaime's truck. Then I ran to the lake house, grabbed a shower, jumped in my car, and came to see you. Jaime said you had patients until six."

"Really? What else did Jaime say?"

"Just that he's your paint-it, haul-it, and reach-it boy. That you pay him back in leftovers, and you're dangerous when you're mixing milk shakes and liquor—he mentioned the Chunky Monkey mudslide incident."

"He didn't have to drink four of them. The man's a pig."

She unlocked the door and he held it open for her. "It's small, but I just needed a waiting room, an office, and a restroom."

He followed her through the waiting room, and she flipped on the lights in her office. It was a warm, professional-looking space with a comfortable couch, pillows, two chairs, an end table, bookshelves, and a desk. Artwork and her diplomas decorated the walls.

He pulled her closer. "This is great. I'm so proud of you."

"Thanks. I am too." She blushed but smiled. "I'm still contracting with insurance companies—that takes time, but it's getting there."

"It's one thing to talk about starting a business. It's another to actually do it. To make a plan and follow through. Are you happy?"

"Here in Harmony? Yes, I like my job at the rinky-dink hospital and working with my psychos, as David put it. I love my apartment. Tonight I was headed upstairs when I found David in the waiting room. I knew he was back in Boston, but I had no idea he'd show up here."

"I thought you looked surprised—and not in a good way."

"You saw us?"

"From across the street. I watched you help your last patient with the baby and was about to cross the street when David walked in. I'd been standing there like a dumb-ass, trying to figure out what to say to you. But when I saw David, I didn't know who he was or what to think."

"I didn't know what to think either. It was so strange. David's never been aggressive. He's never grabbed me like that. He's changed, and not for the better."

"I had a feeling something was wrong, but I thought it might just be wishful thinking on my part. But then Jaime called and told me you texted him about David showing up. I was relieved. I didn't think you'd be interested in reconciling with him, so I hung back. I thought you'd want to handle him on your own."

"I did."

"When he touched you, though, all bets were off—the man's lucky his hand is still attached."

"If you had waited a few moments longer, I would have handled it myself. Still, I'm glad you showed up when you did. I think David got the message—and so did the entire town. I doubt he'll be back."

She took his hand and turned off the lights as they walked through. "Come on up. I'll show you my apartment."

He followed her back into the entry and up the steps, off to the right. He stood behind her while she unlocked the door. The entire time his fingers itched to touch her. He wrapped his arms around her waist and kissed her neck while she fiddled with the lock. "I missed you every day—all eighty-two of them." He brushed her hair aside and kissed that place where her neck met her shoulder, right by the beauty mark. "I dreamed about you every night."

Her stomach muscles tensed under his hand, and when the door swung open, he lifted her up and carried her in, her bottom tight against his fly. He kicked the door closed behind them. "I've loved you every second I've been away—all seven million of them. But I still managed to do what I had to do to get back here."

Kendall turned in his arms and grinned at him. "Me too. I missed you so much. I knew we needed that time apart—I just didn't think we needed as much time as you gave us. I was really beginning to wonder if you were ever coming home."

"I'm sorry, sweetheart, but it took me a while to set everything up to allow my assistant, Anne, to run things from Chicago. Anne has told me often enough that she'd had a lot of practice doing my job when I took a leave of absence, so this should be a cakewalk for her. I can handle most of my work from here. It took some doing, but we've finalized plans to have Anne run the Chicago office. I might need to go back a few times a month. That would be manageable, right?"

"Manageable?" Kendall's eyes widened. "You're moving home to Harmony?"

"If you want me to. Kendall, if the past three months have taught me anything, it's that I know, without a shadow of a doubt, that no matter how I live my life, I don't want to live it without you."

"That's good. That's really, really good."

"I'm back to being a human calculator."

She wrapped her arms around his neck and stood on her toes. "I can deal with that."

"I'm great at my job—maybe better than before, but it doesn't mean anything without you. Nothing means anything without you."

"I know the feeling."

"Anne and I have gotten really close in the past three

months, and she can't wait to meet you. As a matter of fact, Anne, her husband, Mike, and their three boys are coming out for Fourth of July. Rocki and her family will be here too." He thought the Fourth of July would be a great time to get married. Everyone could come up to celebrate; they'd have the whole family together, and he'd never forget their anniversary.

"Okay . . . You want me to meet your assistant?" Kendall looked confused, as she had that are-you-nuts? tilt to her head and a furrow between her brows. Shit. He was doing this all wrong.

"Whataya say? Do you wanna spend the rest of your life hanging out with me?" Marriage was hanging out together for the rest of your life. . . . He really needed to sell that idea.

She kissed him and nudged him backward. "I bought a really big couch with you in mind."

"We can make love every chance we get." Okay, what else? Think, Jax. Think.

She walked him back until he ran into the very couch she mentioned.

"It's green." Wow, that was brilliant.

"Uh-huh. Sit."

He did, and she climbed on his lap, straddling him so they were face-to-face. He pulled her tight against him and groaned—she fit him even better than he remembered, and he'd remembered everything. "I thought we could keep checking off items on your sexual bucket list." He'd really be enjoying this if he wasn't scared spitless and his heart wasn't doing its damnedest to break out of his chest.

"Jack?"

"We can sleep together every night."

"Jack?"

"Wake up together every morning."

"Jack."

"Oh, and do you think you could manage to never look at another man the way you look at me?"

Her eyebrow rose at that and she pulled back a little. "Do you think you could manage to never look at another woman the way you look at me?"

"Sweetheart, I never have. You're the only woman I've ever loved. And Harmony is the only home I've ever known. All I could think of when I was in Chicago was coming home to you. That's all I wanted. That's all I can ever imagine wanting. Would—"

"Jack." She placed her fingers over his lips.

Really? She was interrupting him now?

"I don't think my parents are going to be happy about us hanging out together for the rest of our lives. Besides, I have plans, goals, lists, and timetables to keep."

"Huh?" He asked through her fingers. His grip on her waist tightened. Was she letting him down easy? He broke out in a cold sweat. He tried to breathe but couldn't manage it. The sound of the ocean filled his ears. He couldn't lose her. He just couldn't.

"I want to get married and have a few kids. So, will you marry me, Jack?"

Marriage? She wanted to marry him? He pulled her hand away from his mouth and kissed her, crushing her against him as relief vied with euphoria. He pulled away, rested his forehead against hers, and closed his eyes. Thank you, God. "Kendall, I was leading up to that."

"You were rambling. Besides, it's one thing to make a plan and another to actually follow through."

He picked her up and flipped her on her back, then

reached into his jacket pocket. "I would have gotten to it eventually." He opened the velvet box he'd been carrying around for almost three months. "Kendall, will you marry me? I love you. I'll love you forever. And I don't want to live another day without you. These last nineteen hundred, eighty-two-and-a-half hours have been torture."

She gave him one of her sexy smiles. "If I say yes, does that mean we can christen the couch?"

"Sweetheart, you can count on it."

She kissed him. "And so can you."

Continue reading for a preview of the first book
in Robin Kaye's Bad Boys of Red Hook series,

BACK TO YOU

Available now from Signet Eclipse.

"I think you killed him."

Ten-year-old Nicoletta said it with such immutable calmness, Breanna Collins wondered if this wasn't the first time a strange man had entered Nicki's room at three in the morning and been taken down by a woman wielding a cast-iron frying pan.

Bree's heart traded punches with her sternum, winding her more than a ten-mile run uphill. She sure as hell hoped Nicki's assessment of the intruder was right. Better a dead burglar than a live one.

The dim glow of a streetlight outlined the shadowy figure lying facedown on the carpeted floor between Bree and Nicki. Dropping the skillet, Bree skirted the body before grabbing Nicki's arm, pulling her off the bed, and shoving her toward the door.

The man groaned, and, like something out of a horror flick, a viselike grip closed around Bree's ankle. She landed hard, kicking and screaming. She reached for the frying pan, only to be flipped like a tortilla on a hot griddle and covered with one extralarge serving of man.

"Get off me!"

He held her hands on either side of her head as his breath washed her ear. "I'm not going to hurt you."

"Yeah? Well, I'm going to hurt you."

"You already have."

Light flooded the room, causing temporary blindness. When Bree's vision cleared and she saw he wasn't an intruder, she wanted to crawl under the pink princess canopy bed and hide. Instead, she dove right into the turbulent ocean blue eyes of an enraged Storm Decker — the past occupant of Nicki's room. Storm Decker — a man Bree had known since before she started wearing sexy underwear. Storm Decker — a man who epitomized the reason women bought the uncomfortable lacy stuff in the first place.

"Breezy, a frying pan? That was the best you could do?"

Bree hated that nickname — maybe because Storm was the only one who dared to use it. It didn't help matters that the sound of it rolling off his tongue had always been enough to make her breath catch. She struggled, trying to slide from beneath him, but succeeded only in pressing her body against his. His heat scorched Bree through her Mr. Bubble boxers and matching tank top. She couldn't believe Storm would be a witness to the remnants of insanity caused by a wild shopping spree at the Walmart in Secaucus. Women built like her shouldn't wear tank tops — not even to bed.

Storm didn't move a muscle, keeping her pinned beneath him. He didn't behave like a gentleman should and get off her, help her up, and make sure she was all right — not that she was surprised. Storm Decker was a bad boy, and he had the rap sheet to prove it.

He had the nerve to shoot her his guaranteed-good-time grin, the one that made any woman in the vicinity want to remove the sexy underwear she'd purchased with him in mind. "If I were out to hurt you, you'd be in a real tight spot right about now."

"No, she wouldn't."

Storm's attention snapped to Nicki standing in the doorway, holding the phone in one hand and the frying pan in the other.

"You'd be out cold again, and the cops would be on their way. Now, do you want to get off her, or am I gonna have to use this?" She waved the frying pan and did her best to look menacing.

Nicki was too cute to manage that, but Bree gave her points for trying.

Storm turned back to Bree, their noses almost touching. "Who's the kid?"

"Storm, this is Nicki. Nicki, meet Storm Decker, Pete's son." She tried not to think about Storm's proximity and concentrated on the pained and confused look on his face. He wasn't the only one confused. "What are you doing here?"

Storm rolled off her. She thought she'd be able to breathe better without two hundred pounds of man crushing her, but she was wrong. No, the breathlessness was still there. Crap. She was twenty-eight and a far cry from that seventeen-year-old caught in Storm Decker's wake.

"Logan couldn't get away from the vineyard—something about harvest season. He got ahold of me and told me Pop was sick. Since Logan was unable to make it, I was elected. I've been traveling for"—Storm glanced at his watch—"twenty-three hours, and this is the welcome I get? No wonder I haven't been home in years—"

"Eleven years." Bree sat and hugged her knees to her chest.

"So you did miss me."

"Yeah, like a rash."

"I might not have seen you, but I've been home a few times. The last time was five or six years ago. You were probably away at school."

Bree rose and brushed herself off, just to have something to do with her hands. "You must have left quite an impression. Funny, no one mentioned it to me." She took the phone and the pan from Nicki. "It's late, sweetie. Go back to bed."

"Aw, Bree."

Dropping a kiss on Nicki's forehead, Bree cut her off. "I'll see you in the morning."

Storm rose to his feet. He'd looked a lot smaller when he was out cold. He picked up his duffel bag with a grunt, one hand held against his head over what must have been one hell of a lump.

Bree waited for Nicki to climb into bed and curl around a big teddy bear before pulling up the light cotton blanket and brushing a hand over her hair. "I'll be in the next room if you need me."

"Okay."

Bree followed Storm out, doused the light, and closed the door behind her. Without looking at him, she headed straight to the kitchen, grabbed a bag of frozen peas, and tossed it at him. "Are you okay? Do I need to take you to the emergency room to have your head examined?"

He sat on a barstool and winced when he placed the bag against his head. "I'm fine."

She looked him over—his pupils were equally dialated. "Any nausea?"

"Why, Breezy, if I didn't know any better, I'd think you cared." The side of his mouth quirked up.

"I don't. I just don't want to be charged with murder. Now answer the question."

"No, I'm fine." His phone rang, sounding like a foghorn. Pulling it off his hip, he checked the caller. "I'm sorry. I have to take this."

"Fine." Bree started out of the kitchen, but he wrapped his fingers around her wrist and held on. The tingle shot straight to her breasts. She didn't dare look down.

"Storm Decker." He listened for a moment, and a smile spread across his face as her cheeks ignited. His black hair was cut short, much shorter than she remembered. It only served to accentuate the chiseled features of his face, while his strong square jaw covered with dark stubble added to his dangerous look. Blue eyes watched her and changed color with his mood. When he'd been on top of her, it had been like looking into an angry sea, and now his eyes were the color of a summer sky—deep blue and full of promise. When he smiled, his perfect teeth gleamed white against his tan skin. His voice was as soothing and buttery as a bottle of Macallan's fifty-five-year-old single malt scotch. At $17,500 a bottle, she'd bet a case of it that the person on the other end of the line was female.

"Hi, Sandy."

Bingo. Bree twisted her wrist and pulled away, breaking his grip.

"How are things at home? Any problems today?" Storm's gaze lingered on Bree's chest before moving to his pricey watch. She wondered if they sold cheap knockoffs on the street corners in Auckland. She doubted it. It looked more expensive than the run-of-the-mill Rolex. They probably charged extra for the dive watch to withstand the pressure of the ocean's depths or the corner office. Then again, maybe his watch had been a prize for winning the Sydney to Hobart Yacht Race. So okay, she'd Googled him and found a picture of Storm and his team holding the Rolex Cup. It was just her luck the photo hadn't done him justice.

"Tell Laurel I'll be back in plenty of time to go to the yacht club dinner. This should only take a week, two tops."

Bree did a quick boob check while she wiped the already clean kitchen counter and tried to look as if she wasn't listening to every word of his conversation. Unfortunately, the girls were standing at attention. Still, it didn't keep her from wanting to smack him upside the head with the damn frying pan again on general principles. A one- or two-week visit was no help. She had called Logan because she needed someone responsible to stay for the next couple of months at least. It sounded as if Storm's plan was to blow in, stay just long enough to assuage his guilty conscience, then leave for the next eleven years or until Pete's funeral, whichever came first. It was disappointing, but not unexpected. He probably had Peter Pan tattooed on his incredible ass.

Storm snapped his phone shut. "I guess I should thank you for the great homecoming. Now, do you want to tell me just what the hell is going on and who that kid is in my old bedroom?"

"Who are you to walk in here and start demanding answers? You ignored Pete for years, and now . . ." Storm was . . . God, he was *here*. Her energy level bottomed out, and she leaned against the counter for support. "Why couldn't Logan have come? And if he had to send someone, why couldn't he have called Slater?" After all, Slater was safe. "Slater's in Seattle. And last I checked, Seattle is a hell of a lot closer to Brooklyn than New Zealand, if you're still in New Zealand." With the Storm Chaser, one never knew.

"I get that you're not happy I'm here. Deal with it, Breezy, because like it or not, I'm all you've got."

"Lucky me. When it comes to helping someone other than yourself, you were always as useless as an inflatable dartboard."

Storm's head snapped back, and his chin followed, as if Oscar De La Hoya had hit him with a right cross. "People change."

She'd won this round. She'd pinned him against the ropes with the two-ton weight of her gaze, willing him to explain his disappearance years ago, but his eyes told no tales. "Pete collapsed at the Crow's Nest. Heart attack. They did bypass surgery, and he's not handling it well." She threw the sponge into the sink and wiped her hands on a towel. "I have a hard enough time managing the restaurant and Nicki single-handedly. I can't take care of Pete too. I need help. I'm surprised Logan called you, but I'm even more surprised you came."

"Why wouldn't I have come? Just because I moved away doesn't mean I'm not close to Pop."

"Oh yeah, I heard you friended him on Facebook. I'm sure that means so much to him." Bree took a deep breath and released it slowly. "He's at Methodist Hospital, and with any luck, he'll be out in a few days. He needs to heal, and I don't know how much he'll be able to do once he's back on his feet."

Storm stood and in two steps was around the breakfast bar. "Breezy? Is Nicki yours?"

"Mine?" She stepped back. "Why would you think that?"

"Why wouldn't I?"

Bree ran her hand through her hair and tucked it behind her ear. "No. Nicki is Pete's."

"Pop's? Since when?"

"It's been a few months now." If Pete hadn't told him about Nicki, it wasn't her place to do it. "Look, I'm tired. I'm going back to bed. Help yourself to whatever you want. There's beer and leftover pizza in the fridge. The guest towels are in the linen closet. I'm in Logan's old room. You can stay in Pete's room tonight—the sheets are clean. Good night, Storm." She brushed by him on her way out of the small kitchen.

"Good night, Breezy."

Bree felt his eyes on her the whole way back to her room. She closed the door and thought about locking it—not sure whether it would be to keep him out or keep her in. Climbing into bed, she fought the searing memory of the last time she'd seen Storm Decker. He'd been running out that same door and leaving her behind.